'As a detective, I very often deal with the bizarre. Sometimes involving murder. Always involving mystery. Deep down though, I'm a Pragmatist, bent on finding practical solutions to claims of perculiar activity.
Even when I fail, I think I come pretty damn close . .
.

. . . I'll let you be the judge.'

Cameron Josey

Book 5

MISSING SOPHIE

James Davis

James William Davis

Missing Sophie©
Written by James William Davis

Published by James William Davis
divisible@yahoo.com.au

Copyright 2025, James William Davis
International Standard Book Number
ISBN 978-1-7641958-0-5
©

National Library of Australia Cataloguing-in Publication entry
Author: Davis, James W.

Title: Missing Sophie/ James William Davis.
Draft: 025B. 2025 Book 5 'Missing Sophie'.pdf
Cover: 002 9781764195805 Perfect Finish final art
8-8-25.psd
ISBN: 978-1-7641958-0-5
©

Cover Design and Layout by James William Davis.

James William Davis, *(Jim)*, first branched into writing during his time in the film and television industry. Story telling became a driving force in his working life, albeit with word or picture.

Word: that essential step prior to all other forms of expression.

List of Books
by
Jim Davis

THE IMMORTALITY CONNECTION

MIND SET

ZEROZONE

HOLIDAY HORROR

GHOST WRITER

OVERKILL

FIND ME

MISSING SOPHIE

The mysterious disappearance of Sophie Bryant catapults her family and friends into a world of suspicion and innuendo.

Detective Cameron Josey's investigation into what really happened to the five year old girl is rife with lies and misinformation.

What starts out as a simple search for the truth becomes a cesspit of life threatening incidents – and a conclusion that not even he sees coming.

James William Davis

CHAPTER ONE
The Perfect Getaway

The Bryant family decided to take an Uber to Sydney Airport to avoid the hassle of parking.

As you do, their driver made an attempt to start a conversation with the small family but quickly sensed talking wasn't their thing.

Mitchell Bryant rode in the front seat while Beverly sat with her five year old daughter Sophie in the back.

Little Sophie's calm voice came as a welcome break in the ongoing spell of silence. "Where are we going, Daddy?"

Daddy's lack of response turned the Uber driver's head to check if the guy was awake. His pillion seat passenger was totally off with the fairies.

"Mitchell," his wife prompted, "Sophie asked you a question."

Her husband dragged himself from his trance. "Sorry, *Sophie* – we're going on a holiday."

The little girl looked up at her mum with an enquiring smile and asked, "Aren't we already on a holiday?"

To which she received warm confirmation, "Yes we are: Daddy means we are going somewhere new."

Sophie didn't get to see the despair that appeared the moment her mother strategically turned her face away.

The puzzled driver couldn't resist the occasional glance in the mirror at his cute little backseat passenger, barely high enough in the mounted children's chair to be seen.

With mum distractedly staring out at surrounding traffic, it wasn't hard to imagine something of a heavy nature was gripping this small family. He pushed it from his mind with a view to carrying his passengers the rest of the way in silence, but being well aware of their having stayed at the airport hotel, he couldn't resist asking, "Where're you folks coming from?" He had glanced to the man at his side for a response but got the answer from Mum in the back seat.

"We're from the UK – originally."

"I picked up on that," he tittered. "Where *abouts*?"

"Wellingborough."

"I can't say I know it."

"Not surprising, it's a small town."

Her answer had no warmth in it, and since she hadn't turned from the window or embellished the information with any sort of effort, it was more than enough body language for the driver to abandon his attempt to start a conversation.

At the terminal, Dad's mind was still elsewhere as he got handed their luggage from the boot, giving no more than a bland nod to the driver.

Back behind the wheel, the curious Uber-driver kept watch on the family as they receded to the terminal entrance. Perplexed by the off-putting experience, he shook his head absently and pushed the cab away from the curb, and his thoughts well away from the troubled and detached demeanour of the kid's Parents.

Bryant, apart from his cloudy expression appeared a well-presented gent, his neatly pressed slacks and light sports coat over a snow-white T-shirt showed no sign of travel fatigue. His defined jaw delivered to his face a sense of specialty, and a full head of hair gave him the presence of a sustainable youth, which managed to put him anywhere between thirty and forty.

At a few inches shorter, his wife Beverly comfortably matched his height in heels, but presently clad in sneakers she sat just above his shoulders. She was really quite a pretty woman and looked to be around the same age as her husband. Her sex-appeal wasn't in the least bit flaunted, yet her fresh easy flowing skirt that clung as she walked made her unavoidably noticed as they took their place in the queue.

Sophie had come along in the third year of their marriage, now a cuddly five year old baby doll with neatly pig tailed blond hair, presumably manicured carefully by her mum.

Fascinated by all the hustle and bustle, Sophie didn't say a word until arriving at the check-in, suddenly indignant at seeing her little red and yellow backpack disappearing onto the conveyor belt, along with her parents large travel bags. "Why are they taking my bag?"

The Qantas girl picked up on the distant distraction in

the father, who seemed quite happy in allowing Mum to deal with the perfectly tangible question. "They're just carrying them for us, sweetheart."

The pleasant staffer handed Mitchell their tickets. "Enjoy your flight, Mr Bryant," she offered while vying for an amiable response. Having failed dismally she lifted from her seat enough to look across the top of the tall desk for a proper look at the little girl, "And you too, Sophie."

The sudden appearance of the young woman brought about an expression of sheer surprise from Sophie, but the confusion that followed was squarely directed at Mum. "How does she know my name?" she whispered from her lowly position.

Still hunched over the counter, the girl gave her one of her warmest smiles. "We put your name on your ticket so that we know who owns the bag; just like *you* do on your school bag. I'll bet you're old enough to go to school are you?"

Sophie glanced up at her mother uncertainly.

"It's all right, cherry-pie you can answer."

The little girl raised her moon-sized eyes to the pleasant face peering down from above, cutely smiling and yet shyly dumbstruck.

"Well, *my* name is Tracie. You have a wonderful holiday, Sophie; I might see you when you come back."

The delight on Sophie's face was permanently etched.

"Enjoy," the parents were offered as Tracie sank back in her seat.

Looking back at her new friend as they drew away from the counter Sophie was pleased to receive a wave and a smile, which she returned with a smile of her own and the sweetest little wave; the other hand firmly clasped by her mother.

Upon reaching security, Beverly lifted Sophie into her arms while placing a small handbag and keys on the conveyer belt. Her daughter watched in fascination as the items disappeared momentarily, travelling through an opening to come into view again at the other side. While moving clear of the collection area with her daughter still in her arms, Sophie had another question, which she delivered tucked close to her mother's ear; her hand cupped so that no one else could listen.

Beverly was still smirking when her husband walked up after collecting his scanned hand luggage. "What's got you tickled?" he asked with limited interest.

She looked into Sophie's sweet face with a forced smile. "Tell Daddy what you said."

She frowned at her mother.

Beverly turned to her husband and then a glance at his emerging business case on the conveyer belt. "She wants to know why their giving us our bags back."

For a moment it seemed Mitchell might not respond to the light-hearted statement, but then thankfully graced her with a mild grin. His wife couldn't hide her relief, thankful that he might be loosening up at last.

They made their way into the lounge and sat at a small table for coffee. Sophie thought she was just-it when her very own baby-chino arrived.

"Are you calling *now?*" Beverly enquired of her husband when he stood from the table with phone in hand.

"I am," he responded distractedly, more focused on getting on with it than wasting time explaining.

Sophie's eyes fixed on her father as he walked away. "Mummy, where's Daddy going?"

"He's making a phone call, sweetie."

By the time her husband reached the broad window overlooking the tarmac, it was apparent to Beverly that he had made his connection.

Sophie was beckoning to be picked up and nursed. With her wish granted, the impressionable little girl gave her mum an earnest cuddle, squeezing as hard as she might. "I love you, Mummy."

The sweet sentiment brought a glistening tear. "I love you too, cherry-pie." Mum's attempt at hiding her face aroused feelings of uncertainty in her daughter.

Mitchell noticed the heartfelt embrace upon return from his somewhat speedy call. He noticed the raw emotion that was being hidden from Sophie's view, his wife's cautious intent to hide the tearful sign of alarm.

The sight of her husband's equalled emotion fetched even more tears, and gave her an instant instinct to reach for a table napkin to pat her eyes.

"Mummy, you can let me go now," her little voice beckoned in response to the tight hug she was getting.

Realising she had been holding her daughter far too firmly, Beverly hastily granted her wish, placing her gently onto her feet while turning away so as not to divulge she was crying.

Dad responded quickly to attract his daughter's attention. "How about we walk over to the window and have a look at the aeroplanes."

Sophie answered by happily taking hold of his hand to lead the way. He looked over his shoulder and saw his wife tearfully miming a *thank you.*

Sophie slept through almost the whole of the five hour trip to Perth, that Australian city at the bottom edge if the west coast, only checking the sky-high views from her window seat during take-off and landing.

Off the plane with bags in tow they headed straight to the Hertz counter and organised a smart looking deep blue BMW.

From the time they picked up their bags till the time they drove away from the airport, they were being observed from a safe distance by a well-dressed man in his late forties. He watched them leave in the BMW and then walked away, making no attempt to follow as though his job was done.

They made it onto the Kwinana Freeway and travelled down as far as the Bussell Highway before stopping for lunch at a Subway. The Caravan Park was only about another half hours' drive, but it was after two in the afternoon and the chances of getting lunch there was doubtful.

The small family trio never failed to turn heads. One filter-less old lady in the company of her husband eagerly approached the family's table as if drawn there by a magnet. "Oh my, aren't you a pretty girl."

Sophie continued licking the confectionary that was dripping onto her tiny fingers.

"How old is she?" the lady asked.

"She just celebrated her fifth birthday a few days ago."

The young mum's English accent was noticed. "Oh, that's lovely, are you on holiday from the UK?"

Mitchell gave his wife an awkward glance, which she

ignored with equal discomfort. "Yes, - um, we're on our way to Margaret River."

"Yes, what a beautiful spot."

The old lady's husband appeared anything but certain they weren't interrupting. "Pet, we should order."

She glanced at him and got the message. "We will let you finish your lunch," she promised. Then she smiled at Sophie, "I hope you have a wonderful time young lady; bye bye."

Beverly cleared Sophie's treat from her mouth so as to wipe her face, allowing her to answer. "Say goodbye," she encouraged.

Sophie panned her big eyes uncertainly between Mum and the strange old couple.

The jovial lady gave a small satisfied laugh as she moved off with her husband. The old gent caught Dad's eye with a sort of apology for the intrusion.

Mitchell shook his head; subtly disguising he was disappointed with his wife for being so willing to engage with strangers. He felt they had a very good reason not to.

Beverly knew why she'd put his nose out of joint but again pretended there was nothing in it.

Throughout the rest of the journey Sophie was sound asleep in the kid's bucket-seat and barely stirred when they pulled up outside the office of the caravan park, just in time for afternoon coffee.

"Let her sleep," Mitchell suggested looking over at his daughter on the back seat.

"I'll wait here," Beverley opted to say.

"Maybe you should meet the owner."

She thought about his reasoning and took his point. "Right, you go ahead I'll just be a second."

His lack of response as he turned off the engine and stepped out of the car was his way of showing he agreed with her acceptance.

The office was as you'd expect, an unattended counter with an internal door that presumably lead to the proprietor's private living quarters. Promotional posters advertising activities and services plastered on each and every wall.

"Good afternoon and welcome," a pleasant female voice invited.

Mitchell turned from the posters to respond to the lady who had arrived through the doorway behind the counter. "Hello, I'm Mitchell Bryant."

Of equally pleasant appearance she came across as genuinely pleased by the visitor's arrival. Her matter-of-fact delivery was toned in friendliness and warmth. "Yes, we have been expecting you. How was your trip from Sydney?"

The usual niceties followed while signing in. Business turned to pleasure when Beverly came in with Sophie.

"Well hello, who do we have here?" Her comment clearly directed at Sophie, still half asleep from having been woken.

Beverly proudly swivelled around with her daughter on her hip to provide their host with a clearer inspection. "This is Sophie."

"And I'm Josephine," she informed the parents, "But most people call me Jo."

Sophie managed a tired smile at her, which was more than enough.

"You're going to have a wonderful time here, Sophie," her mother promised before turning to the owner. "Jo, I'm Bev."

"Very nice to meet you folks, I hope you'll enjoy your stay."

"We will," Mitchell told her as he took the keys she was handing him.

"Let me know if you need anything. The office closes at nine, but if there's anything urgent you can call me on my mobile."

"Many thanks," Mitchell offered.

"A pleasure," She attested while catching Sophie's eye again, "Bye, Sophie."

Beverley assisted her daughter's arm in performing a wave. "Say bye, Jo."

She imitated her mother's sing-song tone on cue. *"Bye-Jo."*

"She's just so gorgeous," Josephine offered ahead of extending her arm in the direction of their cabin. "Go all the way down to the beach front, turn right and it's the fifth one along."

The couple's happy go lucky persona, which was in contrast to that presented on their journey from Sydney, vanished as soon as they stepped outside the office. It was quite noticeable but the park owner placed little importance upon it.

"I'll walk with her." Bev suggested to her husband as he was getting in the car.

Receiving no response yet again she set off ahead to follow Josephine's directions on foot.

As Bev placed Sophie down to walk by herself, she heard Mitch's car start up and begin to roll forward on the gravel behind them, prompting her to face her daughter around in order to watch him pass, "Wave to Daddy," she urged.

Daddy leaving was yet another puzzle for Sophie so Bev thought she'd better explain. "He's going ahead to our cabin, sweetie."

"Why didn't we go with him?" she sang sadly.

"It's because you and I are having a nice walk to see the beach."

The beach turned out to be of little interest, Sophie was more concerned about where daddy had gone, so Beverly wasted no time heading in that direction. Approaching cabin 26, she noted that it couldn't have been placed any closer to the water if they'd tried, the timber foundations were literally in the sand.

Mitch was lifting the bags in when they arrived, most were already sitting on the timber porch. As he walked in ahead of his girls, a small parcel the size of a shoe box was the only thing in his hands.

"What's Daddy carrying, Mummy?"

"I don't know, sweetheart," she pretended, "Maybe it is a surprise."

Sophie did a little excited skip and began pulling on her mother's arm to hurry her up. "Can we see it?"

"We'll have to ask Daddy nicely."

Mitch had the box on the table when they walked in. He was tapping on the parcel playfully, as though he was waiting for the obvious question from her.

"Can I see the surprise, Daddy?"

"That depends." Mitchell was clearly trying hard to please.

She screwed up her cute nose questioningly.

Beverley couldn't have been more delighted with Mitch's change of mood, this is what Sophie needed; kids are so sensitive to something being wrong. "I think he means if you're good."

"I *am* good," she responded with a hung lip.

"I can see that. So, shall we open it up?"

She skipped on the spot and clapped. "*Yeah!*" she bellowed on top of her voice.

Mitch set about removing the plain paper wrapping and scrunched it up before handing it to her. "Can you put this in the bin for me?"

She swivelled her head looking for the bin.

"It's over there, sweetheart," Bev revealed pointing.

Sophie snatched the crumpled paper from her father, ran to the bin and lobbed it without waiting to see if she hit the mark, returning excitedly to see the surprise.

"Are you ready?"

She clapped and gave a resounding, "*Yes!*"

Mitchell's arms were buried inside the box; lifting its contents painfully-slow. When it appeared above the rim, Sophie's usual screwed up nose told a story. Her deep frown clearly portrayed her confusion. She asked, "What is it?"

He unfolded the inner wrapping. "This young lady – is something that can fly."

"How does it fly?"

"You know what – how about I show you, how would that be?"

She shrugged as though an answer wasn't needed.

With the drone firmly held he jammed in the battery pack. "I'll have to show you outside, let's go?" He moved toward the door without further explanation.

Bev's smile never vacated, but the sentiment failed to reach her eyes. Taking Sophie's hand, together they followed Mitchell out onto the sand.

By the time the drone lifted off, a group of children and their parents had gathered around to see the spectacle.

Sophie screamed with delight and followed its every move; it went high; it went left; it went right; and then it came down right in front of her and hovered. She seemed a bit uncertain about this, so Mitch showed her a replay on the console's tiny screen.

Her eyes lit up at the sight of herself with Daddy and Mummy. With tongue shyly planted in her cheek, she turned from the fascinating picture to her mother, who quickly averted her daughter's attention back onto the drone. "Watch, sweetie, it's about to take off again, look."

The growing audience applauded when it lifted from the beach with a whirring sound and a parting blast of sand directed at the spectators.

One of the fathers, a man in his mid-sixties, opted to say, "You've got a real handle on that thing – how long you been doing it?"

"About a week."

"You're a fast learner."

"It's not that hard," he was saying while keeping the crowd amused, taking the drone out across the water, hovering above swimmers. This was a very different Daddy Bryant to the one that arrived in Margaret River stressed to the *hilt*.

A voice from the crowd turned heads. "I hope you've got a licence to fly that, Mitch."

The preoccupied pilot turned to face the owner of the park. "Sorry, Jo, I probably should have asked."

A few boos went up from the kids.

Josephine was grinning. "All right you lot settle down, there's no problem." She locked eyes with Mitchel. "Just be careful – it's my responsibility if someone gets hurt."

"Understood," Mitch promised.

She walked away to a chorus of kids putting in their bit.

"She might have a point," Beverley diplomatically warned her husband.

"What do you think, *Soph*; should we do as Mummy says and put it away?"

Sophie placed her hands on her hips and demanded, "No."

The audience erupted in approval and cheeky laughter from the kids, bringing a rare smile to Mitchell's face as well.

In the spirit of holidaying, Mitch took over preparing the dinner, a fresh flathead that he picked up from the local fishmonger. Sophie divided her time between watching her mother prepare the salads, and her father scaling the fish for cooking on their own personal BBQ that sat out on the balcony facing the beach.

Following the meal it was expected that their daughter would become weary enough to go to bed. However she lasted till nearly ten o'clock, finally falling asleep with her head resting on Mum's lap. For an hour they stayed on the sofa overlooking the beach, abstractedly studying the surf gently whispering in across the sand, and the peaceful angel face of their daughter.

They finally carried her to bed, into her own special room, and took turns kissing her goodnight.

Little Sophie Bryant never saw, or felt, the tears that fell while they watched her sleep.

CHAPTER TWO
Missing

Josephine Jackson awoke to horrendous yelling. Bleary eyed she checked the time on the little clock at her bedside – it was 3am.

"What is it this time?" she mumbled staggering out of her single bed.

A moment later Josephine ventured out from her little cottage onto the main street of the park dressed in her *trackies*. The scene before her was nothing short of surreal. If anyone in the park was still sleeping it wouldn't have been many, most people were in their PJs.

Nearly every man woman and child had some sort of torch, which they were panning and tilting into every dark corner – and yelling on top of their voices.

She quickly made her way through the panicking array, toward the bobbing lights that extended onto the beach at the far end of the road.

"What's happening?" she called out to people nearby.

One woman responded with, "I have no idea; I've just this minute come out."

Josephine continued on to where most of the activity seemed to be centred. Most of the people around her sounded as confused about the yelling as herself.

Where the roadway met the sand she stopped, trying to make sense of what was driving the pandemonium up and down the beach. She spotted the park's caretaker in among the throng of holiday makers. "Teddy!"

The caretaker turned to the sound of her shrill voice.

"What's going on?"

"A little girl's missing," he shouted above the rest of the yelling

Jo's heart skipped a beat, "Who?"

"She is staying with the couple who came in yesterday afternoon."

That's when Josephine heard the name they were calling; *Sophie.* "Oh-god no," she breathed in shock.

Teddy started the short climb off the sand toward where Josephine was standing.

"Where are her parents?" she asked as he reached her.

"There down amongst this somewhere. They're pretty upset as you can imagine."

"Did *they* raise the alarm?"

"Yeah, I was out checking what was making one of the dogs bark. That's when I heard the father yelling out her name. I could hear the panic in his voice. I ran as fast as I could down to his cabin and when I got there the two of them were already armed with lights, yelling her name and searching all around."

"Has anyone called the police?"

"It's difficult to say; maybe. I'm afraid I came out without my phone, but I think it's time someone did."

"All right you stay on it here; I'll make the call. Get your phone first; I may need to call you."

Teddy understood this was big trouble for his boss. "Right'o, let's just hope she's wandered off, maybe she's a sleep walker."

Josephine wasn't a young woman and she carried a little weight, but she could jog pretty well when she needed to. That's what she did all the way back to her cottage and the phone. "This is, Josephine Jackson, at the holiday park, on Rivermouth road," she announced to the lady-cop on panting breaths.

"You're talking with Officer Jill Paterson," The helpful voice returned, "Tell me exactly what's happened."

"We have a missing child, only five years old."

"How long has the child been missing?"

Josephine felt a little guilty for some reason in saying, "Not a long time really, since about 3am – her and her parents only just arrived in the afternoon. She's a pretty little girl, you know.

We're all worried sick. The whole camp is out looking for her."

"Okay, we'll get a car over there with some lights. I'll get you to stay put so our guys can find you when they arrive. Are the parents with you?"

"No, but I can get them here."

"We've got a car close to your location, so sit tight."

Josephine exhaled with fleeting relief. "Thanks, I'll be waiting." She hung up and dialled Vince about getting the parents to the office.

Following the calls the owner went outside and paced up and down the small porch that adorned the front of the park office, anxiously waiting for the police, and the daunting arrival of the Bryants.

Jo had owned and operated the park for the past ten years and in that time had had only one other really major problem. There'd been scores of small issues to deal with over the years, but the big one had been finding a dead body in one of the cabins; that was as about as big as it gets. She had to admit though, a missing five year old girl comes pretty close, and it's not over yet – the question now was; how would it end. The thought of not finding little Sophie alive ran through her veins like ice.

On the beach, among the concerned searchers, Teddy located Mitchell and Beverly and filled them in about what was happening with the police.

He felt bad tearing them away from their desperate search; their distraught tears weren't helping in the task.

"We will all keep looking," he assured them as they left hand in hand to comply with the police instruction.

When they arrived at the office the Police Patrol Car was pulling in. A Male and female officer alighted and stepped up to the porch to speak with the owner.

"Are you Josephine Jackson?" the male officer asked officiously.

"I am," she answered with a quiver in her voice.

"Are the parents here with you?"

She pointed at Mitch and Bev as they melted out of the dark toward them. "They're just here now."

The police faced the worried parents. "We're here to help in any way we can, all right," the lady cop said with her eyes fixed first on the mother and then the father. "I'm Officer Smith and this is Officer Jenkins. Can we have your names?"

Mitchell gestured to his wife and his voice shook. "Bev - Mitch."

The Male copper launched a little too quickly into investigation mode. "Can you start with what you know, about your daughter's disappearance?"

In better light the female cop's sudden embarrassment might have been noticed, apologising reflexively to avoid putting her partner on notice. "We have to ask, okay – just in case you may have suspicions of your own." Clearly the distressed parents were incapable of responding to Jenkins, getting answers right away was going to take a little diplomacy, which she had already applied in dealing with her partner's brashness.

Josephine focused on Jenkins with no such concerns – she really didn't appreciate his tone. "We understand you guys have your jobs to do, but please, these people are beside themselves with worry. Can we just get ourselves back to searching for the little girl?"

"She's right," Mitchell told Jenkins with borrowed strength, "Frankly I'd rather continue searching."

In better light the female cop's sudden embarrassment might have been noticed.

Then with no immediate aim, Beverley countered her husband's well put argument. "There are fifty people out looking with far clearer minds than us. Let's answer their questions and get it over and done with."

A police utility loaded with location lights pulled in and parked adjacent. Dressed in navy blue overalls the driver alighted and stood with his hand still on the wheel as though ready to drive off, speaking to the male cop across the roof of the car. "Where do you want us, Sir?"

Sergeant Jenkins gestured to the officer to hold. "Give us a minute." He turned to the father to explain. "We have lights to assist in the search, forget our questions for now. Can you give us her name so we can put it over on the PA."

Beverly wiped away tears as she answered, "Her name is Sophie."

"Have you any idea where she might have gone?"

"We think she's probably wandered down onto

the beach," Mitchell divulged.

"Their cabin is right at the edge of the sand," Jo volunteered. "You can get to it by driving down to the end of this road."

"Right," Jenkins noted ahead of turning to the truck driver and pointing toward the beach. "Straight ahead, constable"

The two officers commanding the lighting vehicle were driving away as directed, while Jenkins, with somewhat adjusted attitude, gestured toward the beach where they were headed. "Let's see if we can help find little Sophie," he summoned on the foot.

"I'll be joining you?" the camp owner advised warily following, not really sure whether or not the bombastic Sergeant may have other ideas about her involvement.

"We'd prefer it," smith offered with a touch of much needed warmth, "another pair of eyes."

"We'll stay with you guys," Jenkins propounded to the parents with authority. "While we search we can talk."

"That's fine," Mitchell agreed flatly.

By the time they made it to the bottom of the road, the officers had the on-board generator running powerful search lights across the beach in both directions.

They followed Mitchell onto the sand as he took up the lead, heading in the opposite direction to the cabin. Jenkins picked up the pace to come in beside Mitchell, while Smith hung back with Bev.

"How much of the beach have you covered

already?" Jenkins asked.

"I've covered south of the cabin; I'd like to check out the other way."

"Is there any chance Sophie could have wandered out of the park?"

Josephine heard the question and advised, "Unlikely, there was no sign of her on any of the cameras."

"How many do you have?"

"We have one on each street and boundary."

"And the beach?"

"The beach closes at dark. My caretaker Bence patrols the sand in front of the cabins to make sure no one goes swimming after hours."

Mitchell was pleased they were asking the owner all the questions for now; it was giving him time to clear his head. That was about to change—

"When did you become aware Sophie was missing?" Jenkins asked Mrs Bryant with sudden bluntness.

"A bit before three, when we woke."

"Did something wake you?"

"The call of nature."

"And?"

Bev balked at his tone. "Seeing as how I was up, I checked in on Sophie – my heart sank when I saw her bed was empty. I got Mitch up straight away."

"Just the facts if you wouldn't mind, we're not really asking how you felt."

Jenkins focused in on her husband. "When you saw that your daughter was missing, what'd *you* do?"

Mitchel was cementing the notion this guy was about to equal a bunch of trouble; *he's already treating us like suspects*. "I went outside and started calling out her name, we both did. Before we knew it we'd woken the entire camp."

Jenkins looked out across the pitch dark sea as though he might be considering a search out there, but that wasn't what was on his mind. "She had her own room?" he finally asked as though puzzled as to why.

"She told us she is a big girl now and wanted to have a room of her own; we didn't argue – in hindsight we wish we had."

"I understand."

This wasn't believed by Mitchell for a minute.

Smith dropped back and slipped in beside the owner, the seemingly deliberate manoeuvre not unnoticed by Beverly.

"Josephine," Smith hedged, "do you mind if I ask you a question?"

"I've been expecting you to."

Smith smiled and kept her voice low. "You'd know better than anyone what sort of mood the parents were in when they arrived."

"How do you mean?"

"I mean, were they happy – sad?"

"Well, you know, I thought Mitchell seemed a bit out of sorts, but most people arrive here all up-tight – especially those from the cities. They did seem a lot happier during the afternoon. Mitchell, he spent a lot of time with the little girl, flying a drone over the beach, much to her delight – and the rest of the campers to be honest; it was quite an event."

"Are the Bryants regulars to the park?"

"No, this is the first time I've had them."

"How long ago did they book in?"

"A month."

"So it wasn't a spur of the moment thing?"

"I would say not. Why is that important?"

The female cop just smiled.

"I've got something!" someone called out.

The yell came from up ahead at the top of the beach where the sand meets the long grasses and the rampant surfside succulents.

Mitchell broke into a run, smartly joined by the police. Bev held back, perhaps afraid of what she might see. What she did see at twenty paces was shocking enough.

The man who made the find was holding up a little red Jacket with a light yellow collar.

"Oh no, it's Sophie's" Beverly told Josephine who had remained steadfast at her side.

The camp owner wrapped an arm around her guest in support; she remembered seeing the jacket when they first arrived.

"Is this your little girl's?" the man holding the jacket asked the father as he drew close. "It doesn't look like it's been here long."

"Yes," Mitchell confirmed sullenly, "its Sophie's,"

For the cops, this changed everything; the finding of clothing belonging to a missing person usually indicates abduction, in this case seemingly easing the suspicion the Bryants were involved.

"I'll be perfectly honest with you, Mr Bryant," Jenkins admitted, "This is not a good sign for us."

"I hear you." Mitchel agreed looking back at his distressed wife.

"Go see to her." He told the husband.

Beverly was trembling in Josephine's arms when Mitch got to her.

Officer Smith was ushering them all back toward the road when her partner called to her. "Smith, I need you with me!"

"Will you folks excuse me," the cop asked.

Beverley didn't say anything, she had no words.

"Go ahead; I'll take them up to the office," Josephine offered.

"Good, thank you."

Bev stopped walking and turned to watch Officer Smith head back to where Sophie's jacket had been found. "Will they keep looking?"

"The police will do a thorough search," Josephine guessed, "now they've found the jacket . . . Come on, let's get you two out of the night air."

While the Bryants headed back toward the office with a cool sea breeze at their backs, their thoughts lingered on what the police would make of Sophie's discarded red jacket.

After an hour, the search activity had died down. Information about the jacket was gradually filtering through to the campers. Mum's and Dads kept their kids close, fearful for their safety.

Mrs Bryant had succumbed to a needed lie down on Beverley's bed, albeit sleepless. If Jo tried to talk to her she just cried.

Bev and her husband appeared to be giving up hope, and that the realisation their little girl was really missing was perhaps sinking in.

The police continued to search the beach, the park and the neighbourhood - even though the security camera had shown the girl had not gone out through the front gate. Officers poured over the footage until the sun rose, they then made use of the daylight to look for clues within the park itself. No one was told why one officer stood watch at the water's edge on the beach, but he had been instructed to look for any grizzly arrivals that might happen to wash up. By 10am, there was nothing.

The search for clues weren't restricted to the park grounds, firstly all campers were ordered not to leave the park and not to lock their cabins as the police would be going through them. They didn't say why, but it was easily guessed that they would be making sure the little girl wasn't being held captive by one of the holiday makers. All these painstaking procedures came up empty.

Then it all changed yet again.

There was a knock on Josephine's door. She opened up and found Jenkins standing there with a serious look on his face.

Jo thought the worst. "Oh-god no – don't tell me."

"It's not the girl. Is Mr Bryant inside?"

"Yes he's with his wife."

"I need to talk with him – just him."

"Yes all right. I'll get him for you."

The cop nodded his approval.

The moment Jo walked into the bedroom they both knew something was wrong.

"What is it?" Mitchell asked.

"Officer Jenkins wants to talk to you."

Bev started to get to her feet.

"It's not Sophie," Joe hastened to halt her. "He insisted that it's just your husband he wants to talk to."

The Bryants exchanged a concerned glance before Mitchell abided without choice, making his way into the office with deep forboding.

"Have you got your car keys with you, Mr Bryant?" Jenkins asked as their detainee approached him at the front door.

"I have; why?"

"I'd like you to take a look at something. I need you to follow me."

It sounded ominous and not a request. But whatever the hell it was, at least he knew it wasn't Sophie.

He followed the cop down the roadway that led back toward the beach without a word spoken. They turned and slogged in their shoes along the sand until they reached the Bryant's cabin.

Jenkins didn't lead him inside as expected, but rather to the back of the hire car parked outside.

"Can you please explain what's happening here, Sergeant, before I have a goddamn coronary."

He pointed at the ground, just below the rear fender. "One of the officers found this blood."

Sure enough, what looked like dried blood was caked on the blades of the grass.

"What are you saying?"

"Nothing yet, but I'll need you to open the boot."

Mitchell pulled the key from his pocket and pressed the beeper – the boot clipped open, which Jenkins gingerly helped the rest of the way. The sigh he let out was genuine relief. He stuck his head inside and without touching anything inspected the rubber mat.

"It's in here too," he told Bryant.

Mitchell peered in and saw that he was right.

"Do you have any idea how this blood got into the trunk of your car?"

He stood straight and met the cop's eyes. "Honestly, I haven't a clue."

"This complicates things for you, Bryant."

Using Mitch's last name seemed to be the cop's way of making the situation sound even more ominous – he was obviously familiar with this kind of stress in people suspected of wrong doing and appeared to be getting some emotional buzz out of it.

"Complicates – How?"

"You look like a smart man to me – understand that when you're hit with the questions that are deemed to follow, don't play dumb. That's just a piece of friendly advice, okay?"

Mitchell shrugged resignedly. "I guess I'd better keep that in mind."

The copper smirked in response to the suspect's subtle sarcasm. "Good man, now I have to ask that you not leave the confines of the park until further investigation is carried out."

"Am I being arrested?"

"No, but it won't look good if you ignore the order."

Mitch glanced around as though wishing he was somewhere else. "What happens now then?"

"We'll be taking the car, and you'll be staying in one of the cabins – not this one. It'll be taped up so I suggest you don't try and go back inside."

"What about our stuff?"

"It's already been moved to your new cabin."

"Wow, if you don't mind me saying, you're sounding like we're suspects."

His grin was loaded with affirmation. "If you haven't done anything wrong you've got nothing to worry about."

"Yeah, right."

Jenkins showed no sympathy for the holiday maker, even though if this guy *was* innocent of wrong doing, the worry of going to gaol would conceivably be surpassed by the loss of his little girl. He closed the boot and kept the keys. "All right, let's get you and your wife into your new accommodation," he said leading the way. We will keep you informed if we find anything."

Mitch thought the cop had made it sound like they were looking for a lost dog.

Sullen personas stifled conversation as Mitchell

and his wife opted to sit on the deck of their new cabin. They sat for twenty minutes without saying a word. Thankfully the cabin was a few feet above road level and with a couple of well-placed beach towels draped over the rail, people out for walks couldn't see them, and vice versa, but the low mutterings of passers-by could be heard drifting past.

Above the rail they saw the tow truck pass, turn right at the bottom of the street and return twenty minutes later with their absconded Beamer. It was a sight that sealed the deal – they were captives.

They were feeling like criminals. Earlier, the police had asked them; *who puts a five year old staying in a strange place, in a room of her own?*

Who leaves the front door unlocked?

They had explained that it *was* locked, but that they'd left the key in the lock on the inside.

Did you think that was safe the police then asked, suggesting the little girl possibly let herself out?

Again they had to explain Sophie had been told never to leave the cabin without them, and to call out or knock on the wall of the adjoining room if she needed anything.

Of course this raised an obvious question; *why would Sophie leave the cabin if she had been told not to?* They had no answer . . .

"I didn't see this coming," Mitch said to his wife breaking his train of thought.

"What do you think will happen to us?" she asked rhetorically.

"It frightens me to think."

His wife considered his comment and it brought tears.

Mitchell turned to her and felt responsible for her stress. He placed his hand over hers. "We'll get through this," he told her.

She couldn't face him, or speak. With no words of his own he cupped her head and gently coaxed her to lean against him. They stayed like that for some time, privately mulling over the possibilities.

"What's your take on the blood?" Mitch finally said exposing his thoughts.

Her lips tightened in consideration. "If it wasn't for the blood on the grass, I'd be tempted to think it was in the car when we picked it up."

Josephine Jackson's voice interrupted, calling from the blind side of the towels. "Are you there Mr and Mrs Bryant?"

They gave each other an unsettled glance as Bev took the initiative to stand and allow being seen across the rail. "Oh, hello – is everything all right?"

"That's probably my question, but I'm not here to pry – I'm here to ask you to join me for dinner."

They hadn't even considered eating. "We're not really that hungry, Josephine to be honest." She looked around at what she could see of the park and the flashing blue lights that were reflecting off the cabins. "Actually I'm not sure we should."

"I hear you, but I've already cleared it with the head honcho and I'm not taking no for an answer."

Bev didn't appear particularly enthusiastic and was about to refuse until Mitchell stood.

"Jo," he nodded, "We'd be happy to, apparently the police don't consider that we still need to eat."

"I was thinking that might be the case. Come over when you're ready, I'm just whipping up a light salad."

"Sounds good, we'll see you soon."

"I'll leave the door to the office open, just come in and call out."

"Will do."

Mitchell and Beverly followed her instruction and made themselves heard after entering the office.

The owner appeared and invited them into her little abode. It was clear from the outset that she lived alone, the room they came into was as neat as a pin, and they could see her single bed via an open door on one of the walls. Their judgement of the dwelling from the outside made it an easy guess that there wasn't much more to be seen.

She gestured for them to sit at the small table that was positioned in front of a window that faced out onto the entrance to the park.

"It's nice of you to take the trouble to come over; it gets a bit lonely here on my own."

The Bryants hadn't yet decided if that might be the real reason for the invitation, rather than concern over them missing out on dinner.

"Please, sit." She was leaning across the table lifting the lid on a salad bowl as she'd said it, "Eat by all means, but don't if you can't."

"It looks very nice," Bev said peering at the

contents.

"Help yourself, take as little or as much as you like."

Beverly opted to serve for her husband and herself because she suspected he might not take anything.

Jo was filling their glasses with water as she said, "I can almost hear what you're thinking but you're wrong, what happened to little Sophie is none of my business. I will say this though, I've been saying a little prayer for her – I mean, I don't know if you folks are religious; sorry, you don't need to say – like I said, none of my business."

Mitchell nibbled on the salad Bev had put on his plate and then looked up at their host, "Feel free to talk about it, Jo; we don't mind. Maybe it will help."

She pointed at the air as if to highlight her upcoming point. "You know; I've always said *that*." She thought for a moment. "I guess if I had to ask anything, it'd be have you had any thoughts as to what could have happened to Sophie."

Mitchell had no intention of mentioning the blood, any talk on the matter would turn to rumour.

Thirty seconds of no response to the loosely disguised question was enough for their host to abandon all further attempts to interrogate.

"I want you to know if you need any help from me, like when the police start asking questions – I'll be only too happy to give them a character reference. I've seldom had the pleasure of meeting such a happier little family at the park."

"That's very kind of you, Josephine," Beverly offered. "But I really don't think we are under any sort of suspicion."

"No, I'm sorry – of course not ..."

They couldn't be sure if she believed that to be true. Mitchell and Beverly assured her they found no offence and that seemed to satisfy her. They mostly felt that she was a nice lady – harmless; and possibly very helpful in the future if the police needed a good character reference. It was still uncertain just how heavy handed the police might become, especially when it came to the mysterious blood on the grass and inside the boot of the car.

CHAPTER THREE
The Inspector

Top dog at the Police station was Morris – at least he was this day – he'd come down from Head Quarters in Perth; that was protocol for a small cop-shop like the one in Margaret River, a timber building consisting of an open office area and a male and female bathroom.

Mitchell and Beverly Bryant sat waiting at a desk in one corner of the open area with their backs to the rest of the room, and the low murmuring voices of the two investigative coppers they had encountered back at the park. The Bryants guessed the hushed conversation was probably about them.

The voice belonging to Inspector Morris rose a little higher. "All right we'll talk later," he told the two cops.

The nervous suspects heard his footsteps trace

across the floor, turning in unison to face him as he rounded the desk to take up the empty chair opposite.

His weight pushed air from his leather seat as he sat, his eyes fixed on a sheet of paper in his hand prior to patiently making eye contact. "This shouldn't take long folks; it's all a bit mandatory, I've got the police report in front of me; self-explanatory really." He flicked his eyes onto the report in his hand then placed it flat on the desk before returning to their gaze. "Have you read your copies?"

Mitchell glanced at his wife and back, "Yes we have."

Morris gave them both a comfortable smile. "Good."

With matching impressions of their interviewer, they felt he was a man of understanding, a man who had probably sat opposite countless couples dealing with the deep stress of being questioned, not to mention a missing child in their case.

In appearance Morris was a kind giant. Middle age brought with it a wealth of experience in putting people at ease, which wasn't always possible, yet he felt these two were holding it together really well; once again, out of experience he read nothing into this observation.

His smiling eyes reflected enough of the seriousness in his mouth; he didn't want people thinking he was insensitive to their plight or for that matter a pushover.

"Do you have any questions about the constable's

written account of what happened?" he asked.

Beverly released a calming breath ahead of saying, "No, we think it is accurate."

He looked at her husband and got a subtle sense he might have a question. "Mr Bryant?"

"All good, Inspector; we've got no complaints."

With eyes once again held on the report, he asked, "The blood's got everyone confounded."

"Us too we have to say," Mitchell admitted truthfully.

Their enquirer lifted his eyes from the report. "I mean, on the ground is-one-thing, but inside the boot is a real puzzle. Somehow we have to get to the bottom of what that means."

Beverly opened her mouth and took a deep breath as if to say something, but paused.

"Do you have a question, Mrs Bryant?"

'Sorry, yes I was just wondering if the blood inside the car was the same as the blood outside."

"It's a superb question, one we've also been asking."

"I assume the blood is being tested," Mitchell delved.

"Yes, we're checking both samples and waiting for the results." He could see the mystery of the blood was as worrying as their missing daughter. But, if they had something to hide they were doing a great job of not showing it. "I see in the report that this is your first time to this particular holiday camp."

"It's our first time in Margaret River," Beverley advised, "Not our first time in Australia."

"Was there any particular reason; that you chose to

come here – to Margaret River?"

She frowned at the thought of how she and her husband made the choice. "A brochure – it was a damned brochure; you know, it looked nice – what can I say."

The inspector looked past them to one of his officers trying to gain his attention. "Excuse me, folks," he apologised, "Yes, constable?"

Beverly was able to turn and see him – he was holding a sheet of paper. "Sorry to interrupt," he offered to the Bryants as he stepped forward to hand the page to the inspector across the desk.

"Thank you, Merve."

Merve left without speaking, avoiding eye contact with the visitors. For Mitchell and Beverly it was a worrying demeanour.

"Hmmm." Morris's abstruse reaction to what he was reading was even more worrying.

"What is it, Inspector?"

When he lifted his eyes to the husband, they were laden with notice. "It's the blood results, Mr Bryant."

Mitchell and Beverly stared at him, afraid to speak.

"Both samples are Sophie's."

Their continued stares were obligatory.

"Is there any chance you can explain this?"

Mitchell made some sort of void sound while Beverly enunciated, "No."

Morris raised an eyebrow, "To be honest I thought the blood would be yours, Mr Mitchell."

A quizzical expression led him into responding with, "Why would you think that?"

"Only that I thought you might have cut yourself inside the boot then dripped onto the grass – that would make sense, don't you think?"

The inspector's quite reasonable explanation didn't exactly calm him. "I take your point," he rolled his hands, inspecting the lack of any sort of injury; not even a tiny scratch, "nothing; as you can see."

"Which means we're no closer to understanding how the blood got there, or why it turns out to be Sophie's."

"Inspector," Beverly enquired, "May I ask how you determine the blood is our daughter's?"

"DNA," her husband offered.

"Close, but not quite – we got Sophie's records from a hospital in Sydney. She was admitted last year for tonsils, correct?"

They looked at each other and back to Morris.

"Oh, right," Beverly remembered.

"So, what does this information mean for us?" Mitchell asked pensively.

"It means nothing's changed. I'm afraid you'll be required to stay in Margaret River a while longer."

"We have no intention of going anywhere until our daughter is found," Beverly promised him with an edge of annoyance.

Morris knew his comment had been insensitive, which was unusual for him. "I'm sorry, a lot of what coppers say can sound a little lacking in tact; please accept my apology."

Mitchell put his hand on his wife's shoulder. "It's all right, Inspector, we're both a little under the weather at the moment."

Tears spilled onto Beverly's cheeks and she quickly rescued them with the back of her hand.

Morris could see they'd had enough. "I want you guys to know we're doing everything we can to find what's happened to little Sophie. I can't make promises other than to say we are on the case; extra people have come down from Perth to help. As is expected you might see quite a few volunteers in and around the town; we welcome them."

Beverly got a hold of herself enough to say, "We do too Inspector, we're very grateful for any help that comes our way."

He appeared hesitant. "There's something else I need to tell you; it's not something you should worry yourselves about unduly." He hesitated again. "We're setting you up at a hotel, at our expense. Protocol prevents us from allowing you to return to your cabin. In fact, it's probably the last place you'd want to be at the moment, it's swarming with curious reporters the last I heard; do you understand why we have to do it this way?"

Mitchell took the reins. "We understand."

Their kind hearted interrogator stood from the desk and offered his hand to Mrs Bryant in order of social practice. "If we're to be seeing a lot of each other you both need to drop the inspector stuff, the name's Fin."

She shook his hand somewhat surprised by the old fashioned sounding name.

"Short for Finnie," he advised as he presented his hand in turn to Mitchell.

"That works both ways, Fin – Mitch and Bev."

He showed some pearly whites. "Mitch and Bev it is."

Inspector Morris stood outside the station watching the Bryants leave in the patrol car that had been ordained to take them to their hotel, their new abode for the foreseeable future.

Looking like he'd been caught out, Sergeant Jenkins stopped whatever he'd been saying to Smith as the inspector came back in from seeing the suspects off.

"Would you care to repeat that, Sergeant Jenkins?"

Jenkins wore the face of innocence. "Sorry, Sir?"

"Repeat what you were just saying about the Bryants."

"You heard that?"

His expression confirmed it. "It's a gift – thankfully not one our visitors share, *hopefully*."

"I'm not following."

"Let me catch you badmouthing again and I'll see you follow the Bryants right out the door."

Officer Smith was feeling uncomfortable, enough to move away and find something else to do.

"Frankly, Jenkins, I think it's exceptionally poor form, especially in front of your young offsider."

Jenkins wasn't enjoying the reprimand, but figured cops need to air their feelings in regard to suspects. "It's just an opinion . . . Sir?"

"In future you'd do well to keep your opinions to yourself." He began walking away but stopped and turned back to the Sergeant. "Do you and Smith feel like joining me for a beer? I'm as dry as Sunday."

The offer seemed to squelch Sergeant Jenkins' less

than amiable mood, and it was time to shut shop anyway; that's what often happens in towns with two cop shops; the other station was a couple miles away and was open twenty-four-seven.

Smith returned from her self-inflicted exile carrying a going home bag; strolling past the two men as if she had no time to chat.

"Where's the fire?" her sergeant asked playfully.

She kept walking toward the door. "You two can stay here flapping your jaws, but last one to the pub pays."

Inspector Morris swept his arm invitingly. "After you, Sergeant Jenkins."

Officer Scott, the driver of the Bryant's patrol car, swept into the underground car-park and put the vehicle where he'd been instructed to; apparently he'd be staying. His other instruction from the inspector was to monitor the detainees whilst avoiding getting in their faces; his only job was to report any problems that might occur.

The Bryants were allowed the freedom of the hotel, insofar as leaving their room for meals or any other needs. They could also step outside the hotel so long as they were in the company of Scott, who'd been assigned from the main police station.

The inspector made it very clear that they were not to be tempted to walk the town in search of their daughter; among other considerations it was in no way certain that they weren't in danger themselves.

They took dinner in the restaurant and returned to their room around 8pm, after which Scott took up his post downstairs in the lobby in order to stakeout the lifts – he was officially on night duty and required not to cheat by taking a nap.

In the quiet comfort of their hotel room the Bryants opted to climb into bed. They didn't sleep; they just nestled into each other and talked in hushed whispers – whispers of confusion, and hope.

At that very moment hope was about to become the very last thing they would be awarded, plans were already in place to look further into their involvement in the disappearance of their daughter Sophie.

CHAPTER FOUR
More Blood

By 9am the following morning, as the Bryants sat in the hotel restaurant having their breakfast, the police investigation had moved back to Josephine Jackson's holiday park, back to cabin 26; empty now except for the two forensic officers officiously conducting their measured search for hints of what happened to five year old Sophie Bryant.

Officer Carter stood atop a step ladder inspecting dust that had gathered on the blades of a ceiling fan, a seemingly absurd place to be looking. His partner officer Barretti was interested in dust too. She lifted everything from bed lamps to vases to see evidence of anything that had been moved – small heavy objects were her main focus, heavy objects that could be used as a weapon during a fit of rage perhaps.

"Got anything?" she asked as Carter came down from the ceiling fan.

"Not a mark."

She knew that to mean no rope or implement had been attached to it whereby something could be hung; like a small child – a grim idea, but they'd unearthed grimmer things in their time. Whilst repulsive, it couldn't remain outside their consideration.

Carter moved to hidden areas, such as draws. He found nothing in the kitchenette and nothing in the open living area. He checked Sophie's bedroom, neither of them could fathom why a couple would book a cabin with two bedrooms when it was only them and their five year old staying there.

Sophie's room was clean, and he knew that wasn't because the cleaners had been through, the cabin had been placed off limits since the Bryants had vacated it—

"I've got something, Bruce,"

Barretti's voice had come from the parents' room. When Carter walked in he found her standing atop the step ladder, holding a large fishing knife gently held in her gloved hand

"The boys must have missed this," she assumed.

"Sloppy," he added to the observation.

She ran her eyes over it for any signs of blood. "It looks clean but might not be, this one needs to go with us."

Similarly gloved he reached up to relieve her of the knife. "I think we're done here, let's get this back to the lab."

They pulled up outside the park owner's office, where Josephine sat waiting; perhaps deliberately so as to pick up any Intel she might be permitted, she didn't really hold much hope.

"We're leaving now," Barretti said dangling the cabin keys out the window from the driver's seat.

Jo was already on her feet stepping down from the timber porch. "Anything I should know?" She felt foolish the moment she asked, enforced by the noncommittal grins she was getting from the two officers with as much as to say, *we can't talk about that.*

"Okay, I hope everything goes all right for those two lovely people."

Having come down from Perth, these forensic officers hadn't had any personal contact with the suspects, but they personalised their expressions anyway so as not to offend. Carter looked across from the passenger seat to thank the owner for her help and they drove out the gate, leaving Josephine to wonder what fate awaited Mr and Mrs Bryant, and indeed little Sophie.

Already looking like life was anything but rosy for Mitch and Bev, it was about to get a whole lot worse; beginning with the approach of Officer Scott as they were leaving the lobby following breakfast, his order to stay out of their faces seemingly reneged upon.

"Please forgive me you two," he apologised, "I'm under orders."

Foreboding swept across their faces, making him feel worse, "I've been asked to drive you back to the station to see Inspector Morris right away."

Clearly as confused as his wife, Mitch asked, "What about?"

"I'm sorry, I haven't been told." He then hastened to add, "I wouldn't worry too much, this is how it goes when dealing with police – dotting the '*I*'s and crossing the '*T*'s. It can all be a bit of a pain."

Mitch wanted to say, *tell me about it*, but said, "Can you give us a few minutes in our room?"

"Yes, of course; I'll wait here for you." The polite copper couldn't help feeling sorry for them as they walked away hand in hand toward the lift; to him they even appeared to lack the strength to speak to each other.

They entered the police station again hand in hand. Sergeant Jenkins having not learnt a thing from his superior officer's reprimand watched them from his desk in the corner.

The Bryant's thought his demeanour appeared anything but welcoming, he could easily have been thinking *what a bullshit show of solidarity* – it was hard for them to tell, but it was a very uncomfortable feeling.

It brought satisfying relief to meet the un-accusing eyes of Inspector Morris as he approached, welcoming them with his usual charm.

"Officer Scott informs me that he interrupted breakfast, come have a seat." Leading the way, he rounded his chair and gestured for them to take up their seats opposite.

"There's been a development of sorts," he told them without a smidgin of delay or meaning. "We'll need your help with it"

Mitch jumped in to ease the tension. "Please tell us what this is about, Inspector; my wife-and-I are worried sick."

"We've found something at your cabin that needs to be explained."

They looked at each other and at that moment Mitch saw something in Bev's face that rang alarm bells; he stifled the urge to ask what it was, it was time to let Morris do the talking. Their focus shifted back to him as he reached into a desk draw. Pulling out an object wrapped in a plastic bag he placed it on top of the desk. The semi opaque bag made it impossible to see what was inside, but the shape of it presented an immediate clue for Bev. Her recognition was picked up by her husband, ringing the alarm bells even louder.

Morris smoothed out the folds in the plastic, pulled apart the zip lock and slid the fishing knife out for them to see. "Is this yours?" he asked casting his eyes from one to the other, ending on Mitchell.

"Yes, that's my fishing knife, we left it at the cabin with the rest of our stuff; are you saying you've only just found it?"

"Yes and I'm afraid this one is on us. It had been placed on a high shelf above the clothing rack; did you have any particular reason for placing it up there?"

"Yes, to keep it away from our little five-year-old,

she has a habit of opening up cupboards."

Morris was secretly pleased he'd said she *has* a habit and not she *had* a habit.

"Is there a problem with the knife?" Mitchell asked.

"I'm afraid so, it has Sophie's blood on it."

Mitch's mouth dropped open. "*What?*"

"You seem as surprised as we are."

"*Surprised* is an understatement."

"I'm not," Beverley's sudden announcement was as sharp as a knife in itself, raising surprised expressions. "And I can tell you how it got there."

Mitch's booming alarm bells clanged to a halt in realising he hadn't misread the expression on Bev's face earlier, "Bev, what is it?"

"I need to tell you something," she proclaimed with fear in her voice.

He looked at her with trepidation. "Am I going to like this?"

"No, you're going to really hate it."

He saw that she was tearing up. "Bev, we need to be open with each other – and the police, just tell us."

She swallowed a lump in her throat. "I know how Sophie's blood got into the car – and onto the grass and the knife."

"And you know this *how?*"

"Because she came to me crying, just after you'd been out flying the drone; holding her sweet little finger in the air with blood dripping from it. She'd cut herself on the fishing knife."

Mitch immediately painted a mental picture, a

possible explanation as to how Sophie could have gotten hold of the knife, recalling that he'd left the boot of the car open. He had opened it wanting to get Sophie's present out of sight before the girls came down to the cabin, and then after going inside with the luggage forgotten to return and close it. But he was still confounded about his wife's actions, "I don't understand, Bev; why wouldn't you have said something?"

She glanced at the inspector, who had been sitting silently letting them talk it through. "I was afraid it would get us into trouble."

"I don't mean to the *police*," Mitch complained, "I mean why didn't you tell *me*?" The words had barely left his lips when he realised answering him in front of the police could lead to the sort of trouble Bev was afraid of, meaning the fits of temper that had plagued him in recent times. The reason behind his moments of rage needed to remain a secret between husband and wife – at least for now, because right now it would really give police something to latch onto.

The thing about small offices is that desks are close and voices carry. If Jenkins thoughts had been written on his forehead they wouldn't have been any clearer, Morris hated that he was thinking the same thing as Margaret River's suspicious Sergeant.

The slight hint of rage in Mitchell's voice hadn't gone unnoticed; not by Jenkins and not by the inspector; it was enlightening to say the least. "Your husband asks a good question, Bev; what reason did you have for not telling him - about your daughter cutting her finger?"

Her answer wasn't immediate, and when a cop asks a question every second of hesitation counts; she finally told him. "Sophie didn't want me to tell because I'd warned her some of Daddy's things are dangerous. I promised her we would keep it our little secret." She glanced at her husband. "I guess you didn't notice the Band-Aid."

Morris returned the knife to the bag and put it back into the draw. "I won't lie to you; this isn't looking good for you guys. Especially since the bloodied knife was put on a high cupboard after the alleged accident in the boot of the car."

A chill ran through Mitchel as he recognised his mistake in not mentioning the knife in the boot as soon as it came to mind, now it was going to look like a cover-up. Without choice he divulged the truth to Morris, rightly blaming himself for Sophie being able to injure herself.

Beverly immediately came to her husband's defence. "If anyone is in trouble it should be me."

"It doesn't work like that, both of you are going to be asked some really tough questions from here on out. Initially, all investigators see are the facts. And the facts are, we have a missing girl, and we have her blood on your knife, and in your car. Unless Sophie is found, the spotlight falls onto what police know, not what they don't."

Morris couldn't have felt sadder for the couple sitting in front of him, especially since their explanation of how Sophie's blood got onto the knife wasn't all that hard to believe, but because there was no chance of questioning Sophie, proving anything beyond doubt would be a sticking point.

Mitchell released a nervous breath, "What happens to us now?"

To prevent his voice from projecting beyond the backrests of the two chairs opposite his desk, Morris lowered his voice to a murmur. "We wait."

Mitch twigged to why the Inspector was keeping his voice down and followed suit. "For what?"

"We wait for further developments in finding your daughter . . ." He'd abandoned the rest of his sentence and the reason was only vaguely understood by the suspects.

"And if she's not found?"

"There will be a hearing to determine if a trial is on the cards."

"What determines that?"

"The prosecution has to show reasonable evidence that you have harmed your daughter."

"Reasonable evidence, what does that look like?"

Morris appeared unwilling to answer but then said, "We're getting ahead of ourselves, I think you're best to accept there is still hope of finding Sophie, and that so far there is no one that I know of who is thinking of pressing charges. For my money I'm still praying Sophie is safe, and that she will be returned to you."

Morris's phrasing hit an emotional nerve in Beverly, forcing her to cover her face and weep openly.

"I'm very sorry it has turned out like this," Morris empathised.

While comforting his wife, Mitchell asked Morris, "What's to be done with us; as in right now?"

He stood and rounded the desk to explain. "Let's get you back to the hotel for now; we'll sort out what happens in a few days' time. For now I'll get Scott to take you back to your accommodation. My suggestion is to lay low and wait to hear from me. I'm heading up the search and I'll be calling you every day with an update on anything we find; all right?"

Mitch helped his wife to her feet. "Yes, thank you."

Noticing Constable Smith enter the station Fin told her, "Let constable Scott know Mr and Mrs Bryant are ready to return to their hotel."

"Yes, Sir," she said pivoting at the door to carry out the order.

Morris walked with them to the door, giving Jenkins an occasional glance to make sure he kept his eyes down to his desk, the man was better at throwing daggers than a circus performer.

CHAPTER FIVE
Vanessa Bryant

On her flight to Perth, Vanessa's mind ran over what she knew about the trouble her brother was in. *Things like this happen to other people.*

So far all the information she'd been given had come to her over the phone, directly from Mitchell himself. She had no reason to doubt that every word of what he was telling her was anything but an absolute accurate account; nothing at all resembling the vague assertions contained in a report she had seen on the news back in Sydney.

She was at her desk when she first saw the breaking news, *'A five year old girl goes missing while in the care of her parents'*

She wasn't aware she was shaking her head until it attracted the attention of the well-dressed man sitting next to her. "Are you okay?" the aged man asked.

Embarrassed and slightly wary, she brought her mind back and looked at him, but a response failed her.

"Sorry, I'm being nosey."

She grinned, "A little maybe."

His wise and elderly eyes agreed. "Any excuse to-make conversation I always say."

She couldn't argue with that. After a glance out at the clouds below from her window seat she turned and faced him. "Are you visiting family?"

"Sort of." With a half hour left on their flight he seemed in no hurry to continue, yet the grin in his eyes showed he would. "I'm returning to Perth to reunite with my wife," he finally mused without any hint of embellishment.

A million meanings swept through her mind and she asked hesitantly, "Has your wife been in lockdown?"

He released a rich manly chuckle that relaxed her.

"Oh, no," he explained wearing a frown, "nothing like that, I mean this was much bigger than a few measly weeks of *Covid-lockdown*; fifty years in fact."

Vanessa's jaw dropped in appropriate response to what was intended to impress. "*Moses*, dare I ask why so long?"

He lent in a little. "We're remarrying," he told her with the proudest of grins.

"Wow, that's something, thank you for sharing."
He looks such a nice man, she thought; *or is that just the friendly brown eyes and the grandpa like greying hair.*

"Are you married?" He noted her cautious eyes on him while considering her answer. "I can see you're happy to talk to me provided I don't ask questions."

This embarrassed her enough to say, "Yes I am, I'm married to a great guy. We have no kids as yet. How about you – any kids."

His eyebrows lifted in a complete giveaway. "There not kids by any stretch of the imagination, as you can probably guess they are all over fifty – two boys and a girl."

She turned her head away as if to take in the sky-high view. In reality she was fighting back tears and hardly seeing the passing clouds that slowly drifted by beneath the plane.

From his vantage point, and the pregnant pause, he could only wonder whether or not she intended responding. He began to sense something he'd said had upset her, something that he may have inadvertently sparked.

She sniffed, confirming he may be right.

"I'm sorry; did I just touch a nerve?"

She knew that ever since learning that her little niece was missing there would come a point when she would break down, but she didn't expect it would be in the presence of a complete stranger. Unable to look him in the eye, she kept her face to the window.

"Excuse me, are you feeling unwell?" she heard the stewardess ask leaning across from the isle.

Wiping her eyes she forced herself to turn and respond. "I'm all right; I just had a little moment."

The old guy looked decidedly uncomfortable,

which needed fixing. "This is not your fault," she promised him, "I'm being a complete idiot."

The stewardess tried to read the expression on the face of her companion but got little.

"Could I have some water please," Vanessa requested.

"Right away, I'll bring some tissues."

"Thank you."

After she left to get the water Vanessa gently rested her hand on his coat sleeve. "Please forgive me for this."

"Please don't apologise, I usually sense someone is upset before I open my big mouth."

Vanessa gave him the most forgiving smile, "I think I'll close my eyes for a spell, do you mind."

"I'd be a rat if I did – please, you go right ahead."

She sighed with relief and lent her chair back. "Thank you," she breathed, and then shut out the world. At least that's how it looked like to him.

In reality her brain was allowing the flooding return of distressing thoughts; thoughts that the kindly old gentleman had momentarily relieved her of – although in the end his kindness was enough to license her the gift of sleep—'

She awoke to the sharp jolt of touchdown, and her travel companion appearing as fresh as a daisy. She peered at him blurry eyed.

"Welcome back," he said kindly.

She checked her watch.

"You were out for a good twenty minutes."

On the whole she felt refreshed; it seemed easier

now to respond to the man in a manner he deserved. "How damn blessed are we to have sleep."

"Amen to that."

They sat in silence as the big jet engines reversed, thrusting them forward against their seatbelts.

They didn't speak again until they came together at the baggage carousel, and that wasn't until she saw him walking past her with his bag. She drew his attention, "Congratulations and all the best on your *rerun*."

"A little age and wisdom works wonders," he laughed.

"I hope everything works out well for you;" She hesitated on the mistake of not getting his name—

He beamed, "The name's Bill."

"*Bill*, it's very nice to have met you – *Vanessa*."

"Right back at you, Vanessa, all the best, love." He slid away into the crowd of travellers.

Vanessa pushed her hire car toward Margaret River, pretty much following the path of her brother to reach the location of his forced confinement. The thought of he and Beverly being held up in that hotel brought back echoes of the *infamous-covid* lockdowns.

She had all the clearances to visit them in their room, the checklist beginning with talking to the manager at the front desk. He had been advised in advance of her visit.

"Take the lift to the fifth floor, room 56," he advised. "We can mind your bag here if you would like."

"Yes, that would be good, thank you."

As she made her way in the lift, the thought of what lay ahead was making her feel nervous about what state Mitch and Bev might be in. The sight of the officer outside their room cemented the notion that they were anything but free. The guy locked on her from the moment she stepped into the hallway, eventually walking right up to present her ID.

"I'm with Mitchell Bryant," she announced.

They were suddenly interrupted by the Bryant's door sharply opening.

Mitchell had emerged looking reasonably settled; it was a relief to see him masked with a brave face. "I hope you're not giving my little sister a hard time, Officer Scott."

The cop blushed.

Wow, Vanessa thought, *this looks very cordial, making jokes with the cops no less;* it served to put her at ease as well. "Hello," she simply said to her brother ahead of a kiss, which didn't even come close to all the rehearsals she'd carried out inside her head.

Her tiny and shapely figure was undeniably having an effect on the sentry, so Mitch thought it best to keep things moving. "Come in Sis."

She gave the officer the warm smile she thought appropriate and sank into the room past her brother.

"Take it easy, Jeff," Mitchell offered the guy distractedly nodding as he shut the door.

Beverly and Vanessa came together in the middle of the room and entered into a long hug, raising untethered emotions, and tears.

Mitch let them vet their feelings while he prepared some drinks. By the time he returned to the table next to the large window where the girls had taken up their positions, they had settled down considerably. "How was your flight, *Van*," he asked despondently.

"I slept through half of it."

He placed her drink within reach and she immediately brought the welcome refreshment to her lips, pausing to say, "Thanks, I need this."

They all did, and over the next hour in which they brought each other up to speed as to what was known and unknown, they consumed quite a bit of booze, more than was usual for them.

With inhibitions firmly suppressed, and with Vanessa having built the courage to ask about what happened the day of Sophie's disappearance, she began to delve into the hard questions.

What started as a brother and sister talk turned into somewhat of a professional interview, which didn't really faze Mitchell, he was well aware of where her approach was coming from. As a social worker, helping people was her thing; it's what she did for a living. Mitch got the feeling though that she was leading up to something other than simple support.

Most of what she knew already had been learnt from listening to media, but that Intel was just the usual bunch of cold facts one expects. He knew that what she craved was to hear the story directly from him.

Vanessa sensed her brother was quite happy to abide, although when asked what *they* thought might have happened on the night Sophie disappeared, the two of them came up empty, and a little uncomfortable talking about it. She decided to focus on the police. "What do you think Morris really believes? He seems all right from what you've told me."

"In a way he's hard to read, he projects empathy, you know, given we're stressing about our daughter. He seems loath to accuse us of anything. But he also seems to be giving us warnings."

"Like about the blood on the knife?"

He glanced to his wife who was clearly rattled, given the mistake she'd made. "That, and the fact we didn't disclose it at the first meeting."

"What other warnings has he given you?"

"He thinks this could end up going to court."

The worry in her eyes matched that of her brother and sister-in-law. "That won't occur without a hearing, but I don't believe you'll end up going to court. How seriously are they treating the search?"

"How do you mean?"

"For instance, does Morris feel they'll find her?"

They both set eyes on Beverley then and saw she had tears threatening to spill.

"I'm sorry, Bev," Van apologised.

"Frankly, Vanessa, I'd prefer you didn't ask questions like that." Her voice had trembled.

Mitch's sister caught his eye to see if he felt the same way. He was hard to read.

"It's probably best we tone it down, *Sis*. I know you mean to help. You're doing that by just being here."

Vanessa still wanted to ask if her brother and sister-in-law believed her niece was abducted, or worse, but it was difficult to address that question now; she did have a solid purpose for asking. She decided to get on with her main reason for meeting with them, to tackle her proposal head on. "I have a suggestion, I'm not sure if you'll like it."

Beverly looked woeful, weakening Vanessa's resolve to continue, but she was determined to try. "There's this woman I know, she works with us at *Blokes . . .*"

They knew *B.L.O.K.E.S* was the outfit that Vanessa worked for, an outfit that specialised in looking after men who have fallen on hard times.

"She's a woman who sometimes works with the police to investigate the whereabouts of missing persons. She's amazing. I know of three cases where she has led police to areas to be searched, with positive results."

"Are you talking about a clairvoyant?" Mitchell asked sounding unsold on the idea.

Beverly seemed frightened by the suggestion. "What exactly does *positive* mean?"

Vanessa recognised her mistake and quickly had to find another way to push her point. "It means you'll have an answer. At the moment you don't have that."

Mitchell was shaking his head. "That sort of stuff does sound farfetched to us, Sis."

Vanessa lent forward in her seat and placed a hand on her sister-in-law's knee. "Bev, I promise you, this woman is real – and she gets real results."

It appeared to Vanessa that Mitch might be caught between two schools of thought - find out Sophie is alive and feel a whole lot happier than they are now - or learn she's not and lose all hope.

When he spoke, it felt like it was entirely something else that was on his mind.

"I'm sorry Van, like I said we know you only want to help us."

Vanessa sat back in her chair, resigned to their decision. "Please promise me one thing," she pleaded, "don't mention Jillian Edison's name to Morris; I'm guessing he will have heard of her. And don't make any reference to it coming from me, family are supposed not to have any contact with these sorts of people."

Mitchell took a quick look at his wife before saying, "Fair enough, Van - just know that in the end it will be our decision."

"Mitch, Of course," she caught Bev's eye, "My heart goes out to you guys."

Beverly moved to sit beside her, "We know that, Van; we know how much you love little Sophie."

The two women cried in each other's arms and Mitchell could do little other than watch and worry about what the future might reveal – with or without the clairvoyant.

Beverley nearly always wore a skirt when leaving the hotel, but this day she opted for black slacks to hide the ankle bracelet that had been fitted, Mitch wore one as well, avoiding the wearing of shorts. They didn't mind at all, it allowed them to drive themselves to where ever they pleased to go within the city. They rented a modest two seater Hyundai for the purpose, having no further need of Officer Scott or his police vehicle.

In spite of a week of anguish over the fact Sophie still had not been found – and that the police had no leads – they decided any mention of Jillian Edison to Inspector Morris was not an option. They didn't need to in the end because he was the one to bring up her name.

Mitch thought to ask if any of this was coming from Vanessa, but became wary of his sister's warning not to make any connection between her and the clairvoyant. Knowing Van as he did though, it would not have surprised him if she'd taken it on herself to meet with the inspector the moment she'd arrived in Margaret River, *that's the sort of person she is* he thought.

"Jillian Edison is someone the police have used on many an occasion. I've only worked with her once myself." He noticed a slight unsettling in the couple, "Is there a problem?"

Mitch looked at his wife and they held on each other as though somehow mindreading, resulting with him then saying to Morris, "Did this woman help find who you were looking for?"

His whole expression signposted some doubt, "It was an odd case I have to say – the question of did she help; the answer would have to be, yes-and-no."

"Meaning?"

"When we went to the location we found evidence everywhere that the person we were looking for had been there, -but had moved on."

"Alive?" Beverly questioned.

Morris twigged to her concern. "Yes, absolutely, we eventually located him and arrested him."

It hadn't occurred to them that the example was about a *wanted* person, not just a *missing* person.

Mitch again glanced at his wife, "We'll be honest; Bev and I aren't sold on the idea of bringing this woman in." He then made sure the inspector understood their reasoning; to be told Sophie may no longer be alive, and without really knowing, it would be more than they could endure.

He *did* completely understand and yet was forced to quantify; he let out an unsteady breath. "Unfortunately, I have to tell you that this is out of your hands; and mine, Jillian Edison has been assigned to the case by the District Head Quarters in Perth already."

"I would have thought a thing like this would be our choice," Beverly complained.

"Only if you make the request before we do, even then *you* can't choose a clairvoyant yourselves, and the police need to be familiar with whoever it is – there's no need to go into whys-and wherefores."

Mitchell sat completely back in resignation. "So that's it then, we're forced to go along with this."

"That's out of your hands too; involvement of—" *he baulked on what he was about to say . . .*

Mitchell closed the sentence for him, "*Suspects*, is that what we are?"

"I'm very sorry; it's just the way the police operate on these sorts of cases." The Inspector had no real reason to feel ill at ease, after all he was just doing his job, but in fact it was getting harder by the minute for him, and not the first time he'd found himself sitting opposite distressed subjects like them, who at the present time were being considered both victim and perpetrator. "Let's hold our breaths and see what Jillian Edison comes up with."

"When is this supposed to be happening?" Beverly asked on an unsteady breath.

He looked at his watch, partly answering the question. "She's coming down from the city, *today* actually."

Bev bent across the arm of her chair and picked up her small shoulder bag and studied the inspector for a moment to see if he had anything more to say. "Are we finished here?" she asked offhandedly.

"Yes, thank you both for coming in." He looked at his watch again. "Actually Edison could arrive at any minute, which means I need you two out of here, like I say; you're not allowed to have any contact with this woman." He was on his feet and rounding the desk to engage in a hand shake. "Sorry to put you through all this." He didn't expect positive participation from Beverly and got none.

At the door he bid them goodbye and returned to his desk, where he spent the next fifteen minutes thinking about the case and where it might lead.

Like most suburbs in country towns, Margaret River presented no real parking problems and the Bryants had been able to leave their car right across the road from the police station. Mitchell was at the driver's door about to get in when he noticed that Beverly's attention was drawn to something. She was standing with her door open and staring across the road, hesitating.

He followed her gaze. Apart from the police station that they had just come from, there was nothing other than a stocky middle aged woman alighting from a cab adjacent to the cop shop entrance. Hearing the pillion door close and his wife's footsteps rounding the front of their car, he swivelled round to see what she was up to. "Bev?"

"It's her," she was saying as she reached the curb and stepped onto the road.

An almighty squeal of tyres heralded the arrival of a moving vehicle, breaking heavily with wheels locked in a desperate attempt to avoid the sudden appearance of Beverly in its path.

Shocked to the core, she now stood motionless just inches from the tip of the stationary vehicle's bonnet. A blue cloud of rubber and singed tar floated ahead like a deadly ghost laden with an arid smell, a chilling reminder of what almost just happened.

Peering wide eyed at the driver, who was equally as shocked over the incident as she, her only adrenalin driven emotion was profound relief; thankful that he had managed to stop so quickly. She felt guilty, and yet remained distracted by the woman across the street, the woman who had arrived in the cab, now staring at her in disbelief.

"Jesus, Bev," she heard her husband saying as he entered onto the road to reach her side, "What the hell were you thinking?"

Even as he was sending a visual apology to the stunned driver, Beverly was somehow empowering herself to snap from her frozen state to begin making her way toward the stunned lady on the pavement. He gave the driver one last apologetic gesture before following his unsettled wife.

"Are you all right?" the lady asked as Bev mounted the pavement and approached her.

Beverly was clearly *not* all right, but somehow she managed to gather herself, albeit still shaken.

"I'm Mrs Bryant."

The woman's frown smoothed in realisation without clearing the confusion, and concern. If her original plan had been to enter the cop shop she was now changing her mind, turning her back on Beverly to move along the path until reaching the edge of the building, where she stopped and faced her enquirer, away from any of the windows.

Beverly was breathing like a marathon runner. "Are you . . . *Jillian Edison* . . .?"

The supposed clairvoyant glanced at the entrance to the police station and noted no one had yet poked their head out, which was odd given the recent loud screech of tyres. She led Beverly by the arm away from a direct line of sight of the doorway, just in case someone did come out.

"Bev, what are we doing here?" Mitch was saying as he followed suit, sharing in the embarrassment.

"It's all right Mr Bryant, your wife has something on her mind," And then to Bev. "Yes, I am Jillian Edison."

Mitch didn't know what to say, yet in hindsight it wouldn't have been that hard for Bev to work out who this person was, given the Inspector had glanced at his watch twice, concerned they might run into the woman.

Edison had the same concern. "You do know I'm not supposed to be seen with you people."

"Yes we know that," Beverly admitted, "but humour me - just tell me one thing – is what you do *real*?"

Edison glanced again toward the station to make sure none of the police were watching. Screeching tyres should have been enough to bring them out. She placed an empathetic hand on Beverly's shaking arm. "You're in shock, Mrs Bryant." She looked at Mitchell and raised her brow. "No surprise."

A light toot from a car horn drew their attention to the dazed driver, who appeared uncertain about driving off. "Is she okay?" he enquired across the light noise of cars slowly passing him on the wrong side.

"She's okay, sir!" Mitch called back with a wave and thumbs up – "Sorry, and thank you!" he added.

The man drove slowly away, glad that the ordeal was over, for him at least.

Beverly ignored the departing driver, not out of contempt, rather from having to deal with the situation she and her husband were in, not to mention she could have been lying on the road right now, dead or dying. "Forgive me, I . . ."

"There's nothing to forgive, Beverly. I understand you have doubts, not to mention immense stress."

The shaky yet agreeable nod she received allowed Jillian to shift focus to Mitchell. "Your sister told me how you guys feel about using me, and that's fine, I fully understand."

Mitchel put forward an obvious point. "Won't having talked to my sister already land-you-in-trouble?"

"If I do get caught out; I'll just be put off the case. That may not mean a lot to you right now, but I promise you I have a very good record of finding people . . . I tell you what; I can keep a secret as much as anyone if the shoe fits – I can call you if you'd like, once I know something – the police don't have to know." She could see they were wondering how much the police had told her. "I don't mean to appear insensitive, but I know you're on the suspect list."

Beverly's whole persona locked tight, even if she'd wanted to respond she couldn't have.

"Take your wife home, Mr Bryant; on top of everything else she's just had one hell of a shock."

Mitchell was already firmly holding Beverly to steady her on her feet. "Will do, and thank you for being candid with us."

She smiled with a cautious glance to the windows of the police station. "Perhaps save the thanks till we know we're in the clear."

The question of being seen by police was realised a few minutes later when Edison was sat down opposite Inspector Morris at his desk. She was saying to him, "Judging by the look on your face I expect you saw me talking with the suspects?"

"What suspects?"

"Can I take that to mean I'm not off the case?"

"You can." He noticed her confusion. I've spoken with Mitch's sister and I know she recommended you. I gather you know Mrs Bryant in particular isn't really keen on Clairvoyants."

"Trust me, that's not what I picked up from her just now."

"Really," The Inspector couldn't fathom the sudden change of mind and simply put it down to stress. "Good to hear."

Jillian didn't hesitate in moving on. "Excellent, may I see the jacket?"

He reached into the draw and brought the red and yellow cotton garment to the top of the desk.

She looked behind to take in young Constable Smith working away diligently at her desk, the only other person in the room. "Would you have somewhere private we can do this?"

"There's a courtyard out back. I take it you don't need a darkened room with candles and the like."

She grinned amiably, "Humour – I like it."

They sat at a wooden table under a Jacaranda tree in relative privacy. She was happy to have the inspector sitting opposite; having people around was never a distraction so long as they were respectful of her gift. She didn't need to close her eyes or go off into a deep trance; in fact looking around at her surrounds seemed to be conducive to the *messages* that came in.

"They're not really messages," she'd tell people,

just as she was telling Finnie Morris right now, "They're more like feelings that come to me."

Morris made no attempt to respond or ask questions, he knew that although she didn't need dark candle lit rooms she did need to concentrate. He watched her run her hands across the light cotton of the red and yellow jacket that belonged to little Sophie, secretly hoping that she would be able to give the Bryants a positive answer, one that would move their status from suspects to relieved parents.

Of course finding Sophie alive had no guarantee she would stay that way. But, if with Jillian's help she could be located there was a very big chance she may be returned to Mitchell and Beverly alive and well.

"Someone did come to the cabin," she absently said aloud.

Wow that was quick, he thought, knowing Edison was referring to the cabin at the park.

"She's not afraid – she's on the beach – not far from the cabin – I'm not quite picking up why she is so unafraid – she's, - sleeping, sound asleep – it's as if she is floating, and . . ."

Morris had no intention of interrupting her, he knew it was considered unhelpful, but her lengthy silence and puzzled expression forced him to speak. "Jill, what are you seeing?"

She let out a breath she'd been holding, "That's just it," they locked eye to eye, "I'm not seeing anything, only that the little girl is unafraid."

"Does this mean what I think it does?" he asked hopefully.

"It means I'm not getting her."

"You're talking in riddles."

"Because that's what it is. Not being afraid doesn't prove she's alive."

Morris scoffed, "Are you saying she *could* be dead?"

She pushed the jacket across the table to him. "Don't lose this, I may need it again."

"Wait," he protested openly when she stood from the table as though she was done. "Is that it?"

"It is for now."

He pushed from his chair and followed her back into the station. "What am I supposed to tell the parents?"

Officer Smith glanced up as they came back in from the yard and noticed Morris subtly shaking his head about something, unseen by his visitor as he took up the rear. Smith followed them with her eyes until they'd returned to his desk, at which point she focused back on her work to avoid revealing her curiosity.

Morris positioned himself next to his chair as Jillian collected a small business case that she'd left on her seat, clearly she *was* done.

"Can you give me *anything,*" he protested with a hint of desperation – "at all?"

"Yes, you can tell them what I said, that their daughter isn't afraid . . . I'm sorry, Fin, I'll need more time on this one." She held up Sophie's jacket. "May I keep this?"

His incredulous frown was all he could offer, *that* and, "Yes of course."

She refrained from commenting until they reached the door. "We needn't be telling the parents their daughter is dead, even if we knew she was – but judging by the state those two are in I don't believe it's at their hands. It's just that right now, I can't tell you what's happened to Sophie." She took a couple of steps out onto the pavement and turned to face him again. "I'll let you know if anything else comes to me."

He knew she'd arrived in a cab, but wondered why she hadn't asked him to call another. He watched her walk away from the station and at the first corner turn toward the beach. *It is a warm day*, he thought, *she's on her way for a dip.*

Inspector Morris extracted all the drama and intrigue from his voice when he rang the parents with the news a few minutes later, "Jillian Edison believes Sophie is alive," was all he said. He heard them reacting with delight and positivity – as expected – but they had very little to say.

Morris was somewhat confused by Jillian Edison's complete mood change toward the end of the reading; having been unable to sense Sophie coming through. He'd felt uncomfortable pushing her on it, she had seemed reluctant to continue.

Was she telling him what she thought he wanted to hear?

An hour after Morris's call to the Bryants, Edison showed up at the hotel with Mitchell's sister in tow. The two of them had met at the beach a short hop from the police station, and spent the hour nutting out how to fill in Mitch and Beverly on what Jillian had picked up on.

The meeting was to take place in the hotel room in order to avoid attracting attention from the watchdog Constable Jeff Scott.

The clairvoyant was visiting unofficially and quite outside of police protocols, not even Morris was privy to this particular gathering.

At the beach earlier, Edison had been given a key to let herself in while the captives were in the bar under the watchful eye of their sentry, and then to wait.

Vanessa had also been given heads up by Edison about her meeting with the inspector, and the way she had deliberately hedged around the question of Sophie's wellbeing in order to protect the two suspects. In her usual style Vanessa asked Edison the hard questions right in front of her brother and sister in-law.

The answers she got were cryptic even so, "I often have people come-through who are very much alive, like Sophie, but this has never happened quite the same way before"

Beverly panicked, "What do you mean?"

"Little Sophie's connection completely altered; one minute she was happy and unafraid, then she changed and became frightened."

"Frightened of what?"

Edison hesitated, "Has Sophie ever had any bad dreams?"

Beverly eyed Mitchell in a weird way, which was noticed.

"Is there something you haven't told us?" Van

asked bluntly.

Their silence prompted Edison to say, "If I'm to help you guys, I have to be told everything, no matter how painful it is for you – can you agree to do that?"

Vanessa was just as anxious to hear their answer, "Mitch, Jillian is sticking her neck out for you guys, the least you can do is talk to her openly; she's on your side."

"I know that, Sis; it's just that we don't know what we can and can't say without running into strife with the police."

Edison set them straight, "Do I look like the police? Think about it, I wouldn't even be here risking my good name with the law if your sister wasn't a very good friend of mine, so believe me when I say, what's said in this room, stays in this room. As you know I haven't fully disclosed what I saw to Inspector Morris."

Beverly sighed, "You mentioned bad dreams, what did you see to ask us that?"

"Your daughter was hiding in terror – Afraid that someone was trying to hurt her – sometimes horrific experiences formulate in bad dreams. Children often have difficulty differentiating between the dream and the reality."

If Beverly and Mitchell needed any more proof that Jillian Edison was the real deal, this was it.

"You're spot on," Mitchell told her. "She has been having bad dreams for a few months; it's a large part of the reason we brought her on this holiday."

Edison had a comfortable smile on her face,

pleased her reading made sense to them, yet needing no sanction. If what she revealed hadn't impressed them she would have been disappointed, suspicious even. "All right, let's leave it like that for now. I'm pretty happy with the way it's going, so I'm going to pursue this further. Please don't let it slip that I am talking to you direct. Even with Morris's blessing, Mum's the word; otherwise, well, I think you know I'll be forced out of the picture."

'We understand," Mitchell told her.

She glanced at his wife questioningly. "Beverly?"

"Of course."

"Good, I'll get out of your hair."

Mitch countered with, "Which means we'll get out of *your* hair and ferry Scott back to the bar so you can leave."

After their goodbyes, sitting in the bar with no sign of Officer Scott, who had been relieved of his job to keep watch on them, they summed up their experience with the Clairvoyant

"Well," Vanessa quizzed her sister-in-law, "What'd you think?"

She turned to her husband and ran her answer by *him*, "I think she seems harmless enough, sweet."

Mitchell was gently nodding, "I have no problems at this point, Van."

Vanessa wondered what it would take to get these two excited; she had nothing to add.

CHAPTER SIX
One hundred and Eighty Degrees

Two weeks later Inspector Morris was called away to work on a murder case up north in Townsville. For Mitchell and Beverly Bryant, everything was about to change; and not for the better.

Mitchell took the call that came in at the hotel just after they'd had breakfast and returned to their room. "Hello,"

The voice that answered sounded officious. "This is Sergeant Jenkins, Mr Bryant; just a quick call to let you know I'll be stepping in for Inspector Morris while he's out of town. From now on any questions you have about your case must be directed to me; I understand you have the station's number."

"Yes, I do, Sergeant; Can I ask when Inspector Morris will be back?"

"I'm not privy to that information; do you have any other questions right now?"

Beverly could see that the call was putting her husband on edge.

"No, no other questions right now."

"Good."

Mitchell pulled the handset from his ear as he heard the line disconnect. "That was Jenkins."

"You look worried, what did he want?"

"Maybe it's me, but he didn't sound too friendly – what else is new?" a little sarcasm added.

If they'd been privy to a conversation the Sergeant just had twenty minutes earlier the answer would have been abundantly clear . . .

. . . "I'm telling you, Ivor, this guy is as guilty as sin," Jenkins was saying to the person on the other end of the line.

"You can tell me all you like," the sceptical voice responded in his ear, "but what makes you so sure?"

"Just hear me out, once you hear what I have to say I think you'll agree."

"This might not be your call, Dave; you need to be careful what you say."

"It's between me and you at this point, what Morris doesn't know won't hurt him."

"He'll know soon enough."

"Not unless you tell him, do I have your word you'll keep this to yourself until you've made up your own mind."

Following a slight pause he heard Ivor say, "Fair enough."

'Okay, now, firstly let's look at the jacket they found on the beach. If she was wearing that when he harmed her there would have been traces of blood on it – right?"

"I don't see your point."

"It means he put the garment there to convince the police that the little girl was abducted. He knew that the lack of blood would allow police to at least consider no harm has come to her."

"That's pretty thin, Dave; why didn't he clean up the blood from the boot of the car if he was trying to hide something – I mean, you're the one who found it, how did he seem at the time?"

"Suspicious, nervous, surprised he'd been caught out."

"That's your word against his."

"I'll accept that, but what about the blood on the knife – if it happened the way he says why hide it?"

"Again, it's conjecture that he was hiding it, other than from his daughter."

"All right, let's get back to the jacket, who would put a five year old to bed in a frilly little jacket instead of pyjamas? – did you know there were no PJs found amongst their luggage?"

"No, but couldn't that explain why they put her to bed in her street clothes."

'Or, they did put her to bed in her pyjamas and got rid of them because they were covered in blood."

"Do you know if Inspector Morris asked that question?"

"Morris is soft, I'm telling you. There's no doubt he's being blinded by empathy, that's the way this guy is, I've worked with him before."

"Well, yes, I've heard he leans toward innocent until proven guilty, but that's not such a bad thing."

"Ordinarily I'd agree."

"Then you'd better have more than you've just given me before I can lift a finger."

"Well here it is, Listen up. You're aware Jillian Edison is on the case?"

"Yes, has she come up with anything yet?"

"Yes-and-no."

"You'll need to expand on that."

"Try this for expansion; she's been talking to the parents."

"You're kidding."

"I kid you not."

"How do you know this?"

"The same way Morris does, we saw her – right outside the station. He doesn't know I know."

"So you're saying he's allowing this."

"I am, and there's more – Edison is a close friend of Bryant's sister, Vanessa Walters, well known for her social work."

Ivor Stamford went quiet for a short moment, clearly digesting what he'd just been told. "I don't feel real comfortable getting Jillian into the shit."

"Now that you know, it puts you in the shit too if you don't act."

"I'll have to give it some thought."

"Let me help you, if I'm wrong and this guy is innocent of wrong doing, it'll come out at a hearing. As far as your understandable alliance with Edison, if she ends up in trouble over what's said at the hearing, it won't fall on you; because as the aligned Police Prosecutor you won't be required to give evidence."

"A small concession if you ask me, and I'll be honest I wish you had something else to act on."

"If it helps, there's the question of why rent out a separate room for the little girl if not for the sole purpose of covering up for not hearing an intruder. I'm telling you the whole thing is a cover-up; the kid wasn't abducted, even if Jillian Edison says she saw it in her reading."

"That's what you meant when you said *yes and no*."

"You got it. Think about it, Ivor; call for a hearing, what've you got to lose?"

"A friend maybe, but hey; I hear you, okay?"

"Okay, I'll leave it with you."

"Thanks, I guess; bye."

Sergeant Dave Jenkins hung up the phone and snidely whispered, "No, thank *you*."

Constable Mary Smith waltzed in from the back of the station and saw Jenkins wearing a smirk. "What's got you so pleased with yourself?"

"Maybe I just picked up a *hot date*."

She hated his sleazy jokes, they always smacked of innuendo; she would have rolled her eyes but he would have loved that so she said convincingly, "In your wet dreams Dave."

He didn't laugh and she decided to ignore him for the rest of the day.

CHAPTER SEVEN
The Link to Josey

In less than a fortnight, and with still no sign of Sophie, Mitchell Bryant was summoned to appear at a hearing that was to take place in Sydney, his home town for the last two years.

When Inspector Morris got wind of it he placed a call to Mitchell to get his take on how the case had come to swing against him. Mitchell pulled no punches when telling him the Margaret River sergeant had it in for him. Being too much of a professional cop, Morris wouldn't allow himself to be drawn into encouraging this kind of thinking. What he did say was for Mitchel and his wife to see it for what it was, pointing out that a hearing wasn't a trial and that most likely a trial wouldn't eventuate. "Do you have a family lawyer?"

"No, we've never needed one."

"What about your wills?"

"We did our wills with the same solicitor we used for buying our house. As far as I know he doesn't go to court."

"Just so you know, a hearing isn't held in a court – it's a fairly informal affair with no jury, just a judge and the two barristers. Actually it's remiss of me to be saying that, it can become more complicated than you expect sometimes."

"Why am I not surprised?"

"If I put you onto a guy I know, would you talk to him?" Morris heard Mitchell's uncomfortable sigh, and yet clear resignation that the situation had to be faced.

"I think that would take a bit of a load off, thank you. Where do we need to go to see him?"

"He's in Sydney, which will work for you because that's where the hearing is; have they told you?"

"They have, apparently we're not wanted in Margaret River anyway."

"Who've you been talking to, in Sydney?"

"A guy called Ivor Stamford, do you know him?"

"I do. He'll be the one putting up a case against you, the police prosecutor assigned to your case. The man you need to see in Sydney is Basil Rathbone; he's a retired Judge. He specialises in legal advice for novices, a beautiful old gent who I promise will help you feel at ease."

"We think you've done quite a bit yourself in that regard and we can't thank you enough"

"My pleasure – give me a call after you've spoken to him. Unfortunately I'll be stuck up here for some time, but I'd like you to keep in touch if you would."

'We will, and thank you again."

Mitchell past on all of what was said to his wife and they both found solace in knowing someone was on their side.

It felt wrong to be leaving Margaret River, the place where little Sophie had gone missing. Constable Fellows had delivered them to Perth Airport and they were to be picked up in Sydney by an officer of the court, intimidating in itself. The flight back to Sydney without Sophie felt empty. They hardly spoke, either on the plane or in the cab that took them to their hotel in the nightlife capitol of Australia, Kings Cross. They continued to guard their thoughts, pleased at least to be able to bask in each other's company, especially since their chaperone had no interest in making any sort of connection with them.

Mitchell followed up on Inspector Morris's suggestion and rang Basil Rathbone at 9am the following morning. The old gent as Morris had called him sounded the right age to be retired, yet turned out to be nothing short of sharp.

When they entered his office and saw him sitting behind his old timber desk, that may well have carried him through his entire career as a Judge, he looked exactly as he had sounded on the phone.

The first thing he did was stand in the presence of a lady. "Mrs Bryant, Mr Bryant, it's very nice to meet you both; please, have a seat and relax."

He waited for them to sit then followed suit. He sifted through a few papers on his desk and put them out of sight in a drawer as if to present a sense of tidiness. He was saying as he did so, "I was most saddened to hear of your Sophie's disappearance, it's a shocking tragedy is it not." There were fading undertones of Irish in his accent.

"Yes it is Mr Rathbone and we want to thank you for seeing us today."

"You are to call me Basil, and I you, Beverly and Mitchell if I may."

Mitchell cleared his throat, "Beverly and Mitchell it is."

Genuinely pleased with this arrangement he got straight to the point. "Now, Mitchell, I hear this is to be your first hearing and that you would like me to enlighten you about what you're in for." His smiling eyes met Mitchell's from above the rim of his reading glasses. "The first thing to understand is that you won't be on trial, and certainly not while in *this* room." He'd encompassed his office with a lovingly sweep of his arm.

The judge had that old school charm about him, a man in his mid-eighties with a subtle hunchback from years in the chair and a quiet calmness that comes with years of gained wisdom. "Right, well let's get down to the nitty gritty as they say. Firstly, there is a document that they call 'A statement of Facts'. This encompasses what the prosecution believes to be the facts. Now, please remember that no one knows the facts better than you, and if you see or hear anything that wavers from the *facts as you know them to be*, you must inform your defence lawyer."

The Bryants spent another hour with Judge Rathbone, coming away with information overload. They were left clinging to Inspector Morris's promise that it wouldn't go to court. As it turned out, he was on the money. The hearing lasted less than an hour, ending with the Bryants being set free, on the proviso they surrender their passports until such time as all efforts to find the girl alive or otherwise had been exhausted. On the whole, it was to be assumed the small girl had indeed been abducted, as claimed by the parents.

The judge, being forced to consider the absence of a body, and the lack of any real evidence, was left little choice other than to deem the Police prosecutor had no case.

Following the proceedings; before they even made it to their car, Mitchell placed a call to Morris to give him the good news and to thank him for his support. He also rang Judge Rathbone; the old gent couldn't have been more delighted for them, and offered to help if they ever needed it again. The elation over their success was short lived, their minds returning instantly to their missing daughter.

The night of the acquittal at the hotel in Sydney, attempts to discuss their next move with Mitchell's sister Vanessa, were upset by endless calls from members of the press vying for interviews. It was clear Mitch and Beverly wouldn't be staying in Sydney, seeing as they had no ankle restraints while on the excursion; they'd more or less decided they couldn't wait to return to Margaret River anyway; especially after being told by police that they had evidence their daughter was thought to be being held in the area.

Mitchell had had about as much as he could take with the calls on his cell phone and was ready to divert them to message bank.

Beverley was already doing that, but a familiar female voice leaving a message changed her mind—

"Hello are you there Bev, This is Molly Pyrmont. My apologies for calling, I know you must—"

Beverly opened the line to accept the call. "Molly its Bev, it's so great to hear your voice. How are you?"

"I think I should be the one asking that question."

Beverly accepted her point with a light titter. "To be honest the press have been driving us around the bend."

"I can well imagine. And poor little Sophie; you must be worried sick."

"We're at our wits end. We've decided to head back to W.A. as soon as possible – we need to know the police are doing their best."

"Bev, this might be from a little left field, but that's the reason I'm calling."

There was a pause on the line . . . "Really, I'm not following?"

"Do you recall my telling you about my father, the private detective?"

Mitchel watched on without knowing who his wife was talking to or what was being said, but it wasn't hard to see Bev was feeling a little awkward.

She noted his unease and masked the phone with her hand, "It's Molly Pyrmont,"

All she got was a frown that asked *why's she calling?*

Gathering her composure she said into the phone, "Molly – yes I remember you saying."

None the wiser, Vanessa had no idea who the caller was. Mitch's gesture dismissed her need for concern.

Molly was saying to Bev on the phone, "Would you consider meeting with him, he's very good at finding people and he may be able to help. I know the police are looking, but Dad goes that extra mile. I promise you this is not his daughter talking – he really is very good at what he does."

"Well, I'm not saying no, but I'll need to talk to Mitch about it."

"Of course, but if you do decide to let him help you, I've already spoken to him about it and he's ready to make a start." Molly was left waiting for a response—

"Molly," Bev began after the pause, "we hadn't even thought about hiring a private investigator – this is all pretty sudden. Mitch and I will have a chat and call you; how's that?"

"Perfect, Bev."

"It's great to hear from you, how long has it been?"

"It must be a decade at least."

"Whatever you decide I'd like to see you before you leave for W.A. if you've got time."

"I'll call you tomorrow and work something out."

"Done, I'm looking forward to seeing you again."

"Likewise, it'll be great, see you then, bye."

Bev ended the call and faced her husband. *"That's a call I wasn't expecting, she's suggesting we hire her father to try and find Sophie."*

"Maybe that's not a bad idea," Vanessa piped up.

"Sis," Mitch said holding the reins, "we'll talk about it."

"How do you know Molly?" she asked her sister-in law.

"We were at university together quite a few years back."

"You know, I was going to suggest you get a private detective – I mean, if you know the guy's daughter, why not bring him in. It's worth finding out if the police are really focused on finding Sophie, especially now that Morris isn't on-board – this bloke who's taken over treats you like suspects."

This conversation bent back and forth before Mitchell had to politely suggest she leave him and his wife to think about it. Vanessa conceded there was no point in arguing about it and she left them in peace, and in the hope they would see the merit in seeking outside help.

CHAPTER EIGHT
Josey

By 10am the next day, Vanessa had called her brother and found out it had been decided not to meet with the private detective.

Believing they should take up their friend's offer of help, she took matters into her own hands, broaching the matter cautiously; aware her action may get back to Beverly via the detective's daughter Molly. Vanessa went ahead and phoned Cameron Josey with a view to coming to his office for a chat, insisting she didn't want to say what it was about over the phone, or any mention of her name once given to him. "It may facilitate my *hiring you* being found out; it's kind of a secret at this point."

At his office that same afternoon she opened with, "I need this to be confidential, can you agree to that."

"Confidentiality is part of my job description," he

told her with maximum amounts of charm and sincerity.

I wasn't expecting him to be quite so good looking she thought. "You might be able to figure out who I am when I say it involves Mitchell and Beverley Bryant."

This, Josey wasn't expecting but she was right, he knew exactly who she was.

"You're Mitchell's sister, right?"

"You got it; *Vanessa*. Molly as you might also know is a friend of my sister-in-law, Mitch's wife."

"I have to confess Molly didn't know your name, but she does know *of* you. I was having breakfast with Molly and my wife Rebecca when Molly decided to call Beverley. We'd been watching the TV reports about the case and we had been going over it together."

With the-who's-who out of the way it didn't take long for Josey and Vanessa to understand each other, and once past her explanation for her evasiveness they got down to business.

The Clairvoyant Jillian Edison got an early mention, and an unreadable *non-response* from Josey, he wasn't about to admit to his seriously sceptic-streak for fear of bursting Vanessa's bubble of hope. He figured and trusted Sophie might possibly be alive regardless of fads of Clairvoyance.

Maxine Priest, Josey's partner and all round assistant sat in on the meeting to take down notes; there were plenty of them - as it was soon learnt. So many in fact that Max opted to switch over to recording the interview to be transcribed later.

Vanessa was taken aback by Max's punk appearance at first, yet her likable personality quickly filtered to the fore.

The meeting and the recording lasted an hour; that hour was then repeated privately via Josey's phone during his flight to Perth the following day. He played it again while driving to Margaret River.

Each time he played the transcript, the people and events that had turned this case into one of great interest to him became more and more familiar. There was Mitchell Bryant's sister, Vanessa Bryant, now his client and one of Mitchell's best allies, professing total trust in her brother.

Jillian Edison, what could be said about her? Presumably they would eventually have to meet and he'd be forced to listen to her clairvoyant feelings about the wellbeing of the little girl, he hoped she was right in believing the toddler is alive.

Josey was looking forward to talking with the park owner Josephine Jackson, another ally, and Bence the caretaker who was known to have said he saw nothing unusual around the time of Sophie's disappearance.

Mitchell and Beverley's hearing was now over a fortnight ago, before Josey came on the scene. That didn't stop him knowing all about it first hand from Mitchell's sister Vanessa. What he learnt was that it was all based on circumstantial evidence and was thrown out.

What was on trial was not only the Bryant's innocence or guilt, but the breaking of protocol between the accused and the clairvoyant . . .

. . . Jillian Edison was on the stand explaining her involvement with the Bryants, and how it came about due to an untimely road altercation in which Beverly Bryant came close to being killed.

Armed with the facts, the defence lawyer seemed to have a handle on clarifying the situation to the court. "Mrs Edison, would you please tell the court what happened after Mrs Bryant came close to being run down outside the Margaret River police station."

"Yes, Mrs Bryant was heavily distressed when she approached me, requesting to know who I was. In those few moments that we spent together, I did not deny who I was because I believed she already *knew who I was.* I did not collaborate with her in any way, other than to advise her that it is not permitted for her to talk to me. This was the first time I had ever met Mrs Bryant and the last."

"Objection your honour," Stanford protested. "We only have her word on this."

"If it please the court your honour, I believe the rest of Mrs Edison's testimony will satisfy the honourable Ivor Stanford's concern."

Judge Schmidt waved his hand. "Continue."

"Thank you your honour. Mrs Edison, can you please tell us about the frame of mind Mrs Bryant was in when she ran across the road to confront you, and what roll the police had in what took place."

"Well, as I said, Mrs Bryant had just been involved in a near fatal accident, which was right outside the police station. She was not at all well and her only concern was that she did not believe in my gift, made clear by what she asked me."

"And what did she ask you?"

"She asked if what I do is real."

"And what did you tell her?"

"I didn't tell her anything, I told her husband to take her home and look after her. He understood that I could not talk to them about the case."

"What about the police?"

"As you can imagine, the police were drawn to the commotion outside when they heard the screech of brakes, and consequently they all witnessed me talking with the Bryants.

"Having been seen by police in the company of Mrs Bryant, I was then asked to answer to Inspector Morris about it."

"So the question of secrecy has clearly never been an issue. Tell the court what Inspector Morris had to say about it."

"He understood as well as Mr Bryant did, I was cornered by Mrs Bryant, because she had just been in to see the inspector and was subsequently told about the use of a clairvoyant, and why talking with me was not permitted. All of this was witnessed by the other two officers in the open office of the police station, who also witness the aftermath of the accident right outside. I fail to see what's so secret about it."

"We're not interested in the defence witness's opinion Your Honour."

The judge frowned at him. "You might not be, but I am." He addressed the clairvoyant, "Thank you Mrs Edison, you may step down . . ."

. . . And, the so called facts about the meeting between the clairvoyant Jillian Edison and the Bryants were deemed to be a fabrication by Sergeant David Jenkins. Yet the mere mention of the suspicions was already a sticking point for Josey. He needed to prove what was true and not true for himself.

The means, by which the blood got on the fishing knife in the car and on the grass, was originally deemed to be believable by police, and therefore the damning opinions of Margaret River's Sergeant Dave Jenkins, although disregarded as fanciful, still had to be looked at closely; *perhaps even why Jenkins would feel the need to push the point.*

All of this was practically immaterial to Josey's task right now, the criminal charges were all but dealt with, and albeit excluding the suspected half-truths; his focus had to remain on locating Sophie, a little girl who mysteriously vanished in the middle of the night.

Josey couldn't dispel wondering, *why would the Bryant's choose to refuse help from a private detective?* It was a question the police wouldn't currently be dealing with; because apparently they had not been told a private investigator had been eventually hired, or more importantly, that the Bryants were originally not so sold on the idea.

CHAPTER NINE
The vanishing point

Josey figured the answer to the riddle of Sophie's disappearance may in fact reside from where Sophie went missing, so he decided he'd make a start at the Margaret River Holiday Park, heading straight from the airport to Josephine Jackson's camp site to book in.

Noting the park was open to anyone who chose to wander in was a common alarm bell, but it was too soon to rule out options other than casual visitors. He strolled past the office and down to where he'd reach the beach. To the right was where he knew to find cabin 26, and to the left the sand loving succulents where the jacket was found. He went to the right.

The cabin was at the edge of the sand, just as it had been explained to him. Imagining someone sneaking inside in the middle of the night wasn't any sort of a stretch, except that he'd been told it was locked from the inside.

Apparently there was no indication of a break-in, which presented only two possibilities, Sophie had let herself out, or someone was let in. If it was the latter, that person might have encouraged Sophie to come to the door and unlock it. Josey began to wonder if this question had been raised at the hearing and if so what was the conclusion?

With the hearing over and done with, the cabin was no longer a potential crime scene. Josey tried the door; it was locked and through the open blinds he could see it was empty. Perhaps the owner was keeping it that way because of the adverse publicity, something that was of no concern to Josey. He strolled back to the office to acquaint himself with Josephine Jackson. He liked her right off; it wasn't hard to figure why the Bryant's considered her an ally, her welcoming personality was void of deception.

He announced his name and a request for short term accommodation; minus mentioning he was a private investigator, for now. She dragged her eyes away from him to run a finger down the list of bookings. "We've got five cabins and two vans available."

"Great, I probably only need a couple of nights."

"No problem."

"I'll take a cabin if I may; I've had a look around and wouldn't mind the one right on the sand, cabin 26."

Her expression changed, her smile wavering.

Josey knew exactly why. "I have a confession, I am aware of what happened here."

She became wary. "You're not a reporter are you?"

He showed her his identification. "Perish the thought, no."

"Are you working for the police?"

"Would it matter if I was?"

"Maybe."

"I've been hired by Mitchell Bryant's sister."

Josephine looked past him to the window affording a view of the street, as though she was recalling the morning the police pulled up right outside. "I hope like hell you're here to find that little girl."

"I am."

"You do know the cops have gone through the Bryant's cabin with a fine toot comb – trying to accuse them of doing something foul to their sweet daughter."

"So I hear – what was *your* impression of Mitchell and Beverly?"

"They weren't criminals I can promise you that—"

The bell on the door to the office announced someone entering.

Josephine caught their eye and said, "I won't be a moment."

Josey glanced and noted the patient smiles of a middle aged man and his wife. When he came back on the owner she had keys to cabin 26 ready in her hand for Josey to take, "I'll come down and see you once you've settled in if that's all right."

It definitely was; Josephine Jackson was really

keen to talk. He nodded politely at the potential customers as he slid past them to the door.

Retracing his steps back to cabin 26 he let himself in. While he waited for Josephine to arrive, he brought to mind what had been described to him about the interior layout. The key points of interest were the high shelf where the knife had been found; the fan where officer smith presumed to check for signs of disturbance, and finally Sophie's room. He thought about the two ways in which Sophie might have left the cabin. The window that faced the beach was a definite contender for a way of attracting Sophie's attention from the outside.

Was it left unlocked perhaps?

Did she exit the room that way?

Were footsteps found in the sand? Perhaps just one set if she was being carried.

Josey stepped outside and went around to the space provided to park a car. The grass beside cabin 26 had grown longer than that beside other nearby cabins, almost as if the ground keeper had missed it. Josey was on his knees when Josephine arrived.

"Looking for the blood?" she asked knowingly. "If you're lucky you might find some, I was instructed not to cut the grass."

He ended his inspection and looked up with a grin. "Indeed I have," he assured her while withdrawing one of his plastic sample bags from his shirt pocket.

She watched as he housed a blade of grass to return it to another pocket. "Will that help you, Mr Josey?"

"Please, call me Cam – and yes, unless someone

else has been bleeding here lately this gives me Sophie's blood type and DNA." He got to his feet. "Would you be able to show me where the jacket was found?"

"Why not."

He followed her lead back onto the sand as she headed north along the beach. "Was your caretaker out and about on the night?"

"That's Bence, he finishes his shift around three a.m. From that the police assumed she was taken between then and first light – around six."

Josey had been noticing the placement of lighting poles. "Do the beach lights stay on all night?"

"These go off at eight, but the street stays on until eleven p.m. We're here," she added pointing at the vegetation on a high bank above the beach. "This is where they found the jacket."

Josey zeroed in on what markings he could see. There wasn't much in the way of footsteps due to the lack of visible sand. What was clear though, the plant-life had been trodden down by someone, left untouched by the fact the mound was above the tide line.

The row of neatly trodden down grass had been deliberately avoided by investigating police, their steps carefully placed so as not to disturb evidence.

One thing was certain; the prints that interested them were singular and made by someone wearing shoes, indicating Sophie was being carried. Josey compared the length of the shoe with that of his hand and wrist - *a male adult*.

Josephine walked precisely in Josey's steps as he

tracked the direction of the shoes. The inspection took them to a concrete pavement that lined the edge of a road on the perimeter of the park, *from where she could easily have been taken in a car.*

He considered that the Jacket had been discarded, not dropped. And, it wouldn't have been worn to bed on such a warm night, as had already been stated. *Were the rest of her clothes left at the cabin?* It was a question he would have to ask police when given the chance.

On the way back along the beach Josey took the time to confirm what Josephine knew, or thought she knew - about the small family.

"They were Catholics," she told him as though it bore weight on what had happened.

"They told you that?"

She corrected him with a head shake. "They attended Sunday Mass the morning after the abduction; I saw them leave. A lot of staunch believers go to mass while on holiday. Quite often we get them heading off early in the morning without breakfast, then order up big when they get back. The Bryants had said earlier that they didn't feel hungry, which I'd say is the reason they didn't even eat when they returned. All the others booked breakfast the night before. The poor souls were feeling wretched."

"I've heard the police were a little rough on them, it's a wonder they were allowed to go off to church on their own."

Her expression conveyed distaste. "One of the coppers went with them."

"Going to church doesn't make you a saint I guess."

She smiled at his comment. "There's good and bad in all walks I've always said. As for me I'm not all that religious but I do say a prayer now and again; I'll say one for you in the hope you find that little girl alive and well. Anything else is too dreadful to consider."

"Amen." He thanked Josephine for the help and promised to keep her in the loop, hoping that knowing might help to set her mind at ease. In the meantime he requested she not mention him to police.

Leaving the park via the front gate in his white hired Ford, Josey casually noticed an old black Mazda sedan parked near the entrance - with a driver nebulously visible behind the wheel. Paying no special heed to the driver doing an about-face, turning to follow, Josey carried on into town, aware he may have a tail. He put it from his mind when the vehicle eventually turned off into another street.

He spent the morning walking around the well-attended pavements, impressed by the number of Sophie Posters that had been put on display. People he engaged with in casual conversation indicated the little girl was on the forefront of their minds; television and newspapers were abounded with *reports and articles* also. There was only one person that he came across that knew nothing of the missing girl, a guy who reasonably explained he was a tourist, a fresh arrival.

He dropped into a library to glance over

newspapers. The reports were fairly general and not much help. It was time to lift the ban on his presence, deciding to try his luck at the cop shop where the Bryant's were first questioned. Making no secret of the fact he was a Private Eye was all about gaging their reaction, he knew they'd be tight lipped. Sergeant Dave Jenkins – the copper he'd been told bore no love loss for the Bryants – stood out like a sore thumb, especially when Josey enquired about Inspector Morris's return from Townsville. The question was intended to rattle him; *it did*.

What's it to you, had been his sharp response.

From then on Josey decided on drawing even more attention, this was one of those times when advertising was to his advantage. Stirring the stones at the bottom of the pond brought them close enough to the surface to be useful.

He dropped into a pub, ordered a schooner and sat drinking it at the bar so that he could scan the pond so to speak. By the time he'd finished his beer he'd slyly chatted up several people with a view to getting around to Sophie Bryant, proving once again that Sophie's demise was on the tip of everyone's tongue.

Josey wasn't expecting any of these conversations to bear fruit, it was a ploy to be noticed by one particular pebble that he'd first realised was showing interest in him. He thought back, the casual glance he'd given the black Mazda as he left Josephine's park became a significant observation, along with the driver's black cap. That cap was now sitting on the head of a man sitting at a table nearby, and his Mazda already noted was now in the pub's car park out back. The guy sat on his own, just three metres from Josey and a few of the people he had befriended, concernedly and loudly engaging on the top topic. Josey made sure the lone drinker heard him tell his newfound friends that he is a P.I. investigating the abduction. He picked his moment to catch the guy's eye; making him decidedly nervous, enough to get up and leave.

Josey followed with deliberate intent in order to incite further discomfort.

The stalker easily recognised that he was now the one being followed, which was Josey's whole point.

The anxious man didn't return to the black sedan in the hotel car park, which was kind of a waste of a tangible evasion; the vehicle was hired, making it a real means of getting away scot-free. His choosing to walk was playing right into Josey's hands. In a couple of blocks he would confront him and see how that played out; trusting the stalker was connected to the Sophie Bryant case.

The plan fell off the rails when the man abruptly turned into a busy shopping centre and broke into a solid run. Josey could only see his black cap bobbing amongst startled shoppers – startled all the more by Josey's arrival in the running man's wake.

The runner's next tactic was to enter onto the escalator to the floor above, only to take the opposing escalator back down. Josey's pursuit was less tidy given he was dealing with some of the patrons having being thrown off their feet by the pushy predecessor. The delays allowed the man to increase his chances of a getaway. Josey saw him exit the back of the shop that led onto a laneway, heading toward the pub again, presumably to his black sedan.

This guy was too good to lose, which might be the outcome if he continued to follow on foot. Appearing to abandon the chase, Josey headed for the front exit that led out to the main road, a route that would take him back to the entrance to the pub and on through to the back car park.

Someone yelled out from behind the bar when he saw the dangerous manoeuvre. Keeping up the pace, Josey arrived at the exit to the car park as running man was powering his old Mazda away in a cloud of smoke, jittering in a rare display attributed to both car and driver.

Although no hell raiser, Josey was confident he could keep up with a driver no younger than his mid-sixties. The need for speed never arose. As soon as the stalker felt he was free, due to not having seen Josey exiting the hotel, he began to slow his vehicle. Josey relaxed in the knowledge, following in a relaxed manner so as not to be detected doing so. With ease, he kept the stalker in sight while himself hidden among other traffic.

A mile later the black Sedan pulled into the curb outside a convenience store. The driver got out and went inside the shop without locking the car.

He returned carrying a plastic bag lightly laden with his purchases, but it was enough time for Josey to change tack, brazenly switching to the mystery man's unlocked vehicle.

Hidden from view; splayed out on the floor in front of the back seat, Josey relied on listening. He heard the man climb in behind the wheel and throw the bag on the passenger's seat before driving off.

It felt to Josey like they'd travelled maybe a couple of miles before pulling into the curb again. This time the security inept driver locked the car.

Lifting his head to take in the surroundings, Josey saw that the street was lined with standalone houses on each side, interrupted only by a small church that was set back fifty feet from its fence line.

The guy crossed the road ending up on the pavement in front of the building, but evidently it wasn't the stalker's intended destination. He continued on and passed several houses before Josey considered he might be abandoning his hire car.

Easily able to unlatch the doors and exit the vehicle, Josey alighted and broke into a light trot in the man's direction. His footsteps were heard, and on turning to see Josey, the man made the unexpected decision to run back to the steps of the church, where upon he strode three steps at a time to the top and through the entrance.

Funerals and weddings were usually the reason for Josey to enter a place of religion, deliberately following a stalker was something new. He had to admit though, the silence, stone walls and stained glass windows seemed to offer a feeling of peace for the splattering of folks that were quietly meditating in the pews.

He paused at the entrance as though waiting for

permission to sink deeper inside, but in fact there was no sign of the standout black cap, not unusual in a place of worship where hats are not permitted for men.

Josey walked the side aisle scanning the fervent faces, assuming the stalker would freak out and expose his position once he realised the game was up. By the time he reached the altar rail he'd become the centre of attention. None of his audience stirred. A few people began craning their necks cautiously.

A voice interrupted his search. "Are you looking for someone?"

Josey turned to a young man who had apparently appeared from one of the doors on either side of the altar; a deacon possibly. He had to think carefully about his upcoming lie. "Sorry, it's not that important; a man who just came in here left me his name but didn't give me his number."

The deacon faced the scant congregation and spoke with customary authority, gesturing toward Josey. "If any of you folks are familiar with this gentleman, please raise your hand."

A light murmur arose as the patrons discussed the odd arrival in their church, but no one responded.

"Is it possible you've made a mistake?" the young man enquired diplomatically.

Josey glanced toward the two exit doors positioned each side of the Alter. He could only make a guess as to whether or not they connected to a common area; if they did, the deacon could be covering for the stalker – but *why would he?* Josey figured it was more likely that the guy in the black cap did in fact use the church as a means of escape.

"I'm sorry," the deacon apologised, "we are about to serve mass."

Josey knew better than to stand and argue. "Of course, maybe I only thought he came in here; sorry."

"I hope you find the man you're looking for," he said to their intruder with a polite motion to go out the way he came in.

Josey abided, hesitating for a moment in front of three doors that graced the side wall. He knew they were confessionals and thought about checking to see if the man might have hidden in there – so he did; all three were empty.

Unimpressed by Josey's continued snooping, the deacon agitatedly began heading in Josey's direction. "I'll have to ask you to leave," he said in a raised voice as he drew closer.

Empty handed, Josey continued his retreat along the side aisle, people panning their eyes in fascination, but some more brazen looks of scorn followed him as he made his way to the back of the church. A couple of giggling kids craned their necks, openly appreciative of the added entertainment. It crossed Josey's mind that the very fit looking deacon might get heavy handed, effectively supplying the kids with fisticuffs within the sanctuary of the church.

Josey knew he had been completely outsmarted the moment he stepped out onto the stone staircase at the entrance to the church – the hired sedan was gone, along with the unidentified stalker.

CHAPTER TEN
Sighting

Josey called it a day and booked himself into a hotel as close as possible to the heart of town. By the time he'd called home to fill everyone in, including his family and his client Mitchell Bryant's sister, followed by a shower, it was time for a little pick-me-up from the minibar before dinner. It made sense to snap on the TV. It was either do that, or study a blank wall.

He did better; he fell asleep on top of the bedcovers.

The sound of Sophie's name woke him. Through cloudy eyes he sat up on the bed to see her little face filling the television screen; it was the posed picture out of the family album; it was enough to make anyone with a heart weep. The voice over that had spoken Sophie's name was that of a forty year old woman, who then came onto the screen explaining what she saw, talking to someone off screen about the circumstances of having seen the girl in Margaret River, sitting in a car by herself.

The interviewer was pushing, "You weren't able to get a picture of her?" he asked with a bit of an edge to his voice.

She just said *no* and waited for another question, then said, "It was dark and the car had tinted windows – Taking a picture seems a bit creepy if you don't mind me saying, but I didn't have my phone with me anyway. I mean, it was after eleven, I'd just stepped out to get something from the bottle shop. I was thinking that someone as young as her should have been asleep in bed, and certainly not alone in a car in the middle of the night. If not for the poster taped to the pole next to the car, I probably wouldn't have taken much notice of her."

Josey had moved from the bed to a chair that he had pulled closer to the television.

"You didn't see who the driver was, the interviewer continued without missing a beat.

"I wanted to wait and see, but my husband needed to leave."

"Where was the car parked?"

"At the back of Woolworth's."

"Was there anything noticeable about the car?"

"I wouldn't know one car from the other," she told him as though he should realise that. "It was dark – a dark colour."

"From what you saw, do you believe young Sophie is alive?"

She looked at the screen as though she was looking

at the parents. "I'll say this much, if it wasn't Sophie, she was a dead set lookalike judging by the younger picture shown on the TV. If you are watching Mum and Dad, I hope for your sake that it is your little girl."

The reporter eased up on attitude, ending with an amiable grin. "All right, thank you for talking to us."

While the TV program moved on, Josey was already on the phone making a call to the station. After a bit of sweet-talking he managed to gain a meeting with one of the executives.

The following morning he sat in the office of Joshua Bedford, deputy manager of news. Josey had gotten past introductions without being thrown out and was now promoting his need to assist the family in finding Sophie. "Your report is good news for the Bryants; I can't tell you how excited they are. I understand your hesitation putting me in touch with Sonya Westfield, but if I were to find the little five year old you wouldn't be disappointed would you?"

"No, of course not; but can I ask if you have a solid lead; other than the one we just gave you?"

"I have more than one."

He hedged. "And if you did manage to find her, do you think you would have a story to tell us?"

"I do."

Bedford grinned like he was on the verge of a scoop. "Would you consider coming on air - tonight?"

"Right now that wouldn't be a smart move."

He let out an accepting sigh. "Maybe, but if you want Westfield's contact details I need assurances you will give us your story."

"I can do better than assurance; give me Westfield's contact details and you've got yourself an exclusive."

The guy gave a slimy grin and Josey extended his arm across the desk with an open palm. Bedford accepted the gentleman's seal with a damp hand shake.

Josey didn't want to freak Sonya Westfield out by just showing up on her door step, so he rang first with the same story he gave Bedford at the TV station. She was hesitant sure, but just the thought of being instrumental in finding the missing girl brought her on-board, but there was a couple of conditions, not hers, rather her husbands.

"My husband is a lawyer," she told Josey up front, "He would like to be at the meeting, but he's away for another week. He said he'd be happy to talk to you on the phone about the sensitivity of what I have to show you. Will you agree to talk with him?"

A little elation drifted through Josey's arteries. "Yes of course."

Josey rang the lawyer husband and got the go-ahead after agreeing to abide by the rules of engagement. He was at Sonya's house by 10a.m. Over coffee and cake they discussed what she'd seen. Not just that, but with a myriad of photos on her phone she'd handed to Josey for him to cast his eye over. He began to understand the sensitivity in question; plainly she'd been untruthful about not taking pictures. The multiple photos she had of the girl sitting in the back of the car clearly showed she was around five years old, if this wasn't Sophie; the girl in the photo was an identical twin.

"As he apparently has told you, my husband advises we make no mention I have these. You'll understand I'm sure that this might not be the Bryant girl, in spite of how much it looks like it is. But if it is the case this girl in the car is someone else, someone whose parents would probably react badly if their little girl were suddenly to appear on television, I could find myself in a lot of trouble – just for even taking the pictures."

Josey remembered her saying to the reporter that it would have felt creepy taking photos of a little girl who was ostensibly unknown to her, which would have influenced her even further in deciding not to admit to *having taken the pictures*. She was being a bit too hard on herself Josey thought, but most likely right in her decision to keep the photos a secret. Ordinarily pictures like this would give any case a huge leap forward, yet the best results for the Bryants would be to know their daughter is alive, and even though they didn't have any really recent pictures, the latest being when she was two, he believed their point of reference after just one look at the girl in the car, would allow them to recognise it was Sophie – the quality of the photos was not unclear. There was no point in hiding from Sonya Westfield, his intention to show the pictures to the parents; he'd already sensed Sonya was disappointed about not being able to let the parents see them. Her disappointment disappeared once she knew that they would see the photos with strict condition they did no show or talk about them.

There was one disappointment for Josey though with the pictures, the car the girl was in was not the old black Mazda, the car in Sonya's pictures was a Kia and burgundy, seemingly differentiating the driver of the Mazda from the driver of the vehicle in Sonya's photos. And yet it didn't mean one single driver couldn't have hired one vehicle and own another, or perhaps even hired two.

"You said this happened at ten PM, I'm assuming it was the day after the abduction was reported."

"It was."

"I'm supposing you haven't allowed the police to see the photos?"

"We haven't. Do you think we should?"

"I think I see your point, about getting into the bad books for photographing a very young child that you don't know. The thing is, even if the law turned a blind eye, you'd probably get tied up in red tape over it."

"That's what my husband said. He told me you agreed not to show my photos; will this harm your chances of finding her?"

"Actually I don't need the pictures; just seeing them makes me believe Sophie is still alive, and that's one hell-of-a plus for me, and for Sophie's parents."

Josey explored the carpet at his feet for a moment while he constructed his next question. "Did this little girl seem scared, or relaxed do you think?"

She gestured to the phone. "What's your opinion?"

He took her point. "I'd say she looks a little sad, but not frightened . . . Did she see *you* at all – maybe turn and face your way?"

"She did look my way actually, but didn't react; she seemed very tired I'd say."

He couldn't help but agree; he told her so and thanked her for her help, promising to get back to her if the pictures ended up giving him a lead. He made no mention of his interest in the colour and make of the car in the picture, or her own mention of the girl *seeming very tired*.

Josey left the home of Sonya Westfield with two locations to visit, the Woolworths car park and a revisit to Josephine Jackson's Camp site.

CHAPTER ELEVEN
Investigating the Camp

The thing about sightings is that they tend to increase exponentially the more the reports show up on TV. More than once, Sophie showed up in two places at the same time. Witnesses had her in cars, trucks, buses and even a tiny scooter. One young fellow swears he saw her riding down the main road of Margaret River on an E-Bike. The reporter had to remind the guy that she's only five years old. In spite of all these wonderfully promising revelations of Sophie's safety, Josey had to remind himself that someone didn't want him involving himself in the search for her. It meant that taking too high a profile could actually endanger the person he was trying to protect.

Presently he could not fathom any other reason for the stalker's obsession with following him, and unless there was a completely innocent explanation for doing so, the guy had to be considered dangerous.

Alert to the possibility his stalker might resort to violence he started wearing his gun wherever he went.

When Jackson the camp owner rang to inform Josey she had some important information, he tended to take it a little more seriously than the hearsay sightings.

On his arrival at the camp, Josephine told him there were two things he might like to follow up on. The first was a camper she'd discovered having lied about his identity.

She remembered him being a pleasant man of around 40 years and slightly over dressed for a camper. "The name he gave was *Reg Chappell*. He was on his own, which I felt was odd right from the start. We mostly get couples and young families."

"Is that the reason you checked him out?"

"Not directly, I was feeling really helpless not being able to do something that might help the Bryants, so I started sniffing around into everyone's details."

Josephine had spent hours doing this and found that Chappell was the only camper whose address and other details didn't check out on closer inspection; having paid with cash was the first thing that was out of the norm, and from what she saw, he had plenty of it.

The question of, *could this lone camper also be the stalker, although considered,* didn't ring true with Josey because two entirely different personas presented themselves. The abductor appeared to present no recognisable threat, whereas the stalker behaved in a decidedly unhinged manner.

Josephine's second piece of information was to come from a man who was a permanent camper, having lived at the park for many years and highly respected and trusted. Jo suggested her caretaker Bence Kovács take Josey to the man's cabin to speak with him.

"I cannot say how much our friend will be able to help you," Bence admitted to Josey as they walked, "but I do believe the information that he has is truthful. Worth your while I think."

"Every witness is worthwhile, Bence," Josey assured him.

By the time they'd reached the beach, Josey had learnt that Bence was an asylum seeker, having left his home country after the death of his wife and only child. Here was a man familiar with death and sadness, both well hidden behind the constant smile.

The caretaker was a stocky man in his fifties with bushy eyebrows and plump lips that seemed to smile at hidden thoughts, or perhaps this was just his resting expression. His eyes were dark yet encouraged a sparkle from available light. His voice was rich and honest, laced with a mild foreign accent, presumably diluted by having lived the last two thirds of his life in Australia.

"I figure your job here must allow you to notice things that others might dismiss," Josey prompted.

He chuckled lightly, "That might be so, but I'm afraid I will not be much help to you on this, I was sleeping very soundly, like most people."

"Maybe you can tell me about the events after you awoke. Did you speak with police??"

"Oh yes, they asked me all the usual things you would imagine . . . of course I had nothing to tell them."

Josey looked along the beach to the left. "Do you mind if we take a walk up to where the jacket was found, before we go see the witness."

"Sure."

When they got to the sandy knoll Josey led the way until they reached the roadway that edged up against the sand. "During the night, would you happen to recall seeing any cars parked here?"

Bence wasn't expecting the question and had to think about it. "Yes," he eventually brought to mind.

Josey pulled a photo from his pocket, the burgundy Kia that Sonya Westfield had seen Sophie sitting in at the shopping centre.

"I saw that on TV," he revealed without hesitation.

And that was that – another dead end.

He wasn't done. While tailing his stalker, Josey had snapped a shot of the black sedan, and the H.C. plates.

"What about this black sedan?"

He shook his head. "Sorry."

"Don't apologise, let's go see the witness."

Bence led the way to the southern end of the beach, which happened to be heading onto the same area as where the Bryant's stayed.

Josey thought back to his visit to the rental company where the mystery stalker hired the Black

Mazda. The plates and the car had been rendered useless and of course the hirer had left them with a fictitious identity.

Sounds familiar, Josey thought.

He hadn't mentioned to Josephine his suspicions there may be a connection between the stalker, the abductor and the man sighted with Sophie being one and the same person, all of which would have been confirmed if there was a picture of even one of them; there seemed little point given the campsite cameras failed to produce clear pictures at night, helped by the lighting favouring the ocean to detect swimmers ignoring rules.

"Did you have many regulars staying at the camp on the night?"

"If you include lengthy stayers there's plenty. Jock is one of them; in fact he is a permanent."

"And you can't recall anyone that stood out for any reason on the night?"

"No – it was a very *normal* night. Perhaps it is fair to say Mr Bryant attracted attention *himself* actually."

This was *news* to Josey. "How so?"

"In the afternoon around four o'clock; he was, how do you say - flying one of those *toy things,* down on the beach, it was a present for his daughter I was told. It must have brought every single kid, and their parents, to watch I think - it attracted a big crowd."

This hit an unexpected nerve with Josey, not one that was particularly conducive to the task at hand or worth mentioning.

When they arrived at Jock's cabin it was yet

another revelation, as it was suggestively close to cabin 26 where the Bryant's had stayed.

Bence knocked on the door and lowered his voice to say, "A word of warning, he is a bit of a character."

A wiry fellow in his sixties came out and grinned knowingly at the caretaker before setting eyes on his companion. "Who's this with you?"

Josey noted the man's gaze was slightly offline and quickly realised he was seriously blind. Intrigued as to how he could be the witness, with an enquiring glance to Bence Josey revealed to the guy, "I'm investigating the Sophie Bryant case,"

"Another copper," he moaned in frustration, "you mob found that little girl yet?"

"I'm not with the police."

"Yeah I know; I'm pulling your leg, Detective. Jo told me you were coming and that you're here to help, unlike the bloody coppers who have her *dead already.*"

Awkward – Josey needed to muster some tact. "I'd like to ask you some questions if that's okay."

Jock let out a breathy chuckle while rolling into, "*You* wouldn't be here if it *wasn't*. But *before you start*, there's no point asking me what I *saw*."

Josey glossed over the man's limitation of being blind. "And yet, I believe you have information *right*?"

Josey's amiable tone made the guy laugh heartily this time. "You are right, Detective; and since you're taking me seriously, I can tell you that I *have*, and it's nothing as useless as the so-called sightings you've been hearing about on your TV. Jo probably mentioned I clamped up on the cops; their attitudes pissed me off. He didn't laugh this time. "Anyway, I know you PIs like details so let's get started with the time; 3a.m it was." He was holding out his wrist displaying his brail watch and tapping the surface. "I was awake, I don't sleep much; mostly I get my shuteye in the day. I was out on the porch. I'd be surprised if the codger didn't see me – he'd have to be *bloody-blind* not to." This deserved a *light laugh* Jock decided.

His habit of laughing at himself prompted Josey to offer Bence a polite grin ahead of asking Jock, "Did the guy say anything?"

"Not exactly, the little girl spoke and he shushed her up real quick."

"What'd she say?"

"It sounded like she maybe wanted to know where they were going – not exactly certain about that, she spoke real soft like."

"How could you tell it was a man she was with?"

"Do I need to mention I've got real sharp hearing? He paused for a reaction then carried on in its absence. "The weight of his walk, in the sand like; it were a man; *trust me*."

Josey harboured more trust than the guy could possibly realise. "How do you think Sophie sounded?"

"I know what you're asking," he revealed amiably, to be honest; I reckon she sounded fairly relaxed."

"So you think the man meant her no harm?"

"Hard to say, she might have been a bit confused, you know, like she hadn't been made to understand what was happening."

"And there was no one else with them?"

"Not that I *heard*, unless the guy was carrying more than one kid."

Josey couldn't dispel the feeling Bence should have spoken to police; his reasoning for not doing so didn't quite wash – he was about to let that go but decided to say, "I'm glad you trusted talking with me, your information may just help save Sophie's life."

The guy stared in Josey's general direction as if sizing him up, "Is that it?" he asked after a bit.

Josey thought, *this guy could be playing with me*, and decided to test him on it. "Any other sensory gifts you haven't told us about, Jock?" he asked with a smirk that infiltrated his tone.

Jock really liked Josey for this one and let out an unrestrained laugh. On regaining his composure he teased with, "I have an excellent sense of smell since you ask."

Josey dropped the flippancy, smells ranked high in his list of favourite things. "I'm listening."

"Musk."

"You smelt musk?"

He nodded like he was enjoying the sensation. "Make no mistake, Detective - this bloke reeked of it, like the Cologne could be some sort 'a compensator."

Jock couldn't see Josey smiling but easily guessed he might be. "I thought you'd like that, Detective;

I've heard you PIs like t' follow your noses."

"You thought right – and if you don't mind me saying, I suspect you might be pretty good at it yourself."

"I can tell you this much, I can sniff out a phoney, and you're anything but, buddy. All jokes aside, I really hope you can return that little girl to her family."

Josey appreciated the candid wishes. "Good man, Jock – you've already contributed big time my friend. I thank you for your help."

Bence jumped in. "All right – we'll get out of your hair, Jock."

"Probably best, I got no intention of inviting you in. Bye." He turned, went inside and closed the door.

Josey shared a bemused glance with Bence.

"I did warn you, Detective."

"You did; there's one thing though," he added as they stepped down from the porch, "he made a good point there when he said the guy should have been able to see him."

"No, it is very likely he would not have, Jock does not know that his porch light has been out for the last couple of days; I've been meaning to fix it; not that he needs it. He didn't say if he was sitting when he heard Sophie being taken, but if he had been, he would have been in deep shadow without the overhead light."

Driving away from the park, Josey had to marvel on what he had been handed by Jock, not just the fact Sophie left with a man, but a man who liked to smell of musk. That musk smell had reached Josey's nostrils recently, indicating the man on the beach was indeed the same man that drove the black Mazda; the Mazda had smacked strongly of musk when Josey spent time hiding in the back of it.

Josey mentally branded this unidentified entity, *'The Musk Man'*.

CHAPTER TWELVE
Search for Musk-Man

Josey continued chatting with business people in and around Margaret River. He thought of going back to the hire company but decided it wasn't worth it, there was nothing left of any worth there. The pictures that had been obtained when Musk Man walked into the fields of the security cameras were all extremely fuzzy, and the vehicle had been thoroughly cleaned inside and out – more than once, to the point where the smell of musk was completely gone.

Thanks to Jock's unofficial witness report, Josey now had information that the police did not, and as is often the case, the dilemma of withholding evidence loomed as a temporary burden.

If not for concrete evidence that at least one copper in town had it in for the Bryants, withholding evidence would probably have ended up being off the cards. As things were, he would be carrying the load until more was known.

Using the photo from the Bryant family album, when she was four, Josey struck real-gold at the local bottle-shop in Margaret River. The guy behind the counter was beside himself with enthusiasm, he'd been talking about the Sophie Bryant case ever since it hit the airways. Apparently he had seen the five year old the morning after the abduction – again, with a man.

If Sonya Westfield had stayed long enough after taking her photos, she may have seen the driver and been able to verify his appearance.

But Josey got a promising description from bottle shop owner, including that the guy had a well-trimmed grey beard, aged around forty and well spoken. This could have been describing the Mazda driver that had taken Josey on a wild-goose chase to the local church.

When asked, the informant assured Josey the girl was relaxed and seemingly happy - like she might have known the guy she was with. He might have even been her father because *she called him that*, which to Josey seemed a strange term for a modern day young child to use, as opposed to Dad or Daddy. This made little sense because clearly she already had a father. If Bryant was with Sophie at the bottle shop it was another case of being in two places at the same time, a scenario already cancelled by the fact Bryant and his wife were being constantly watched by police.

He again considered that this man—the man who

the bottle shop owner had seen with Sophie, a man neatly dressed, who might even in fact be the musk-smelling abductor—could also be Josey's stalker. He needed to return to the bottle shop and check if the owner recalls the particularly strong aroma.

Presuming that Sophie had been with both abductor and stalker – and if they were indeed one and the same person – had a very big plus attached to it; it was solid evidence that the girl was still alive, vindicating the clairvoyant.

Sophie's reasonably relaxed persona raised an obvious question, who among the Bryant's known male associates would be familiar enough that the little girl would feel safe going with him, and without her parents. Why would she even go with someone, in the middle of the night, if she *didn't* know who this mystery person was? The broader concern was even more baffling; if Sophie *did* know the man, this might equate to her parents also knowing him – which could mean, the Bryants knew she was to be taken all along, *but to where - and why?*

Feeling a little tired he decided to call it a day; he had to be at the airport early in the morning to pick up his daughter Molly, she would be arriving with her mother Rebecca, along with their unlikely companion Vanessa Walters, Josey's acquired client and sister of Mitchell Bryant. Molly and Mitchell's sister Vanessa hadn't known each other prior to Molly making contact with the Bryants. The subsequent hiring of Josey to find Sophie now gave the women a lot in common.

Molly and Rebecca's arrival in Margaret River was primarily to provide moral support for their man and to make sure he behaved himself. Vanessa's motivation was more convoluted; being financially invested in the detective's task—as well as her deep concern for her Niece's safety—produced a great deal of stress.

The girls set up camp at Josephine's caravan park in a cabin next door to Josey and Rebecca, the park only being a kilometre away from the Bryant's hotel.

The following morning Molly met up with her mother and father for breakfast at their cabin, having been invited along with Vanessa.

Josey was surprised to see his daughter didn't have Vanessa in tow. "Where's my client this morning, not coming to breakfast?"

"She's gone off to church apparently; she does know you invited her."

Josey absently wondered if Vanessa might possibly be attending the Catholic Church where his stalker took him; it was reasonably close to the park, as were the Bryants, who were also catholic. He found it odd that religion had entered his life twice in the last few weeks – *well sort of.*

Josey felt there remained more to this case than he presently knew.

He made no mention of the stalker because he wasn't ready to share it with his family. Given their scrape with death on his last case, he completely understood why they would still be worried.

Following breakfast Molly flattened out on the irresistible gold strip of sand that ran directly past the front door to her cabin. Close to nodding off in the warmth of the sun, her mind drowsily imagined the fear the Bryants daughter must have felt at the moment she was being taken away on this very sand in the middle of the night. She wasn't sure why she opened her eyes at the moment she did, but what she saw was alarming.

A man was walking slowly past her parent's cabin, showing a little too much interest, walking slow as if to peer in beyond the gloom of the wide open doorway.

From beneath the shade of her wide brimmed hat she watched as he stopped, standing directly in line with the doorway. Her father's work caused a higher sense of danger in her than most people experience, and yet able to reason that the guy might just be studying the cabin because he liked the design or something. He didn't particularly look out of place, wearing swimmers with a colourful towel draped over his shoulder.

That said, she decided to put him to the test without giving rise to undue interest in him. She casually rose to her feet, picked up her belongings and took the few steps that brought her to within a few feet of the cabin, where the guy still stood fixated on the bungalow rather than the beach.

This changed when he caught her out the corner of his eye. At first he didn't know what to make of the way she was looking at him, and why she was just standing there as if waiting for a response. He opened his mouth, appearing as though he might be about to speak to her but quickly changed his mind, turning away to pace along the beach.

She knew better than to follow, keeping her eyes on him until he went from view, having turned into one of the avenues, presumably to then continue between rows of cabins that she knew headed toward the park toilets.

Josey and Rebecca were preparing a light lunch when she came in from the beach looking a little rattled.

Beck glanced up and noticed the look on her face. "Sweetheart, is something wrong?"

Josey turned from what he was doing, driven by the alarm in his wife's voice. "Molly, what is it, pet?"

She shook her head as if to clarify what she saw. "It might be nothing but there was this guy outside paying a bit too much attention to the cabin, like he was trying to see inside."

Josey was already heading out to check.

"He's gone now, Dad."

Josey made it onto the sand followed by his anxious daughter. "What did he look like?' he asked looking up and down the beach.

"He was in swimmers with a bright green and yellow towel."

Beck was sliding in beside her daughter, aware of the edge in her husband's voice. "Cam, is there something we need to know?'

He kept his eyes on the stretch of sand. "Which way did he go, Moll?"

Molly stepped down from the deck and pointed. "He went a hundred yards up there and made a right back toward the toilets."

Josey's instinct was to pace along the beach and try finding someone who matched Molly's description, but then quickly quelled the idea to avoid stressing his family any more than they already were. The risk of regurgitating bad memories was too great, their close encounter with death still haunted him. He knew their fear for him was the reason his girls wanted to be by his side in Margaret River, making damn sure he wasn't placing himself in danger.

He also knew from bitter experience that keeping things from them was usually a disaster, especially now because it was Molly who had encouraged him to take the case, *a missing person's investigation might be an easy way of you easing back in to the job* she'd said.

He decided it was time to dispel this belief by bringing them up to speed. "I need to explain what's happening."

They had moved off the beach and were seated at the little table inside the cabin. He went over the whole thing; the clairvoyant, the sightings and the ambiguity embedded in Mitchell's story, but as Josey expected the clincher that prompted Rebecca to insist they all leave Margaret River was the stalker.

She did her best to convince Josey to return to Sydney with her and Molly, knowing full well that he would block the idea, even in spite of the trauma they had all been through.

He presented a good argument. "I don't believe I'm in any particular danger in continuing with this, and I'm confident I have a better chance of finding the little girl than the police do. It would be unfair to the Bryants if I just up and walk away now."

"And what about this guy Molly just saw snooping around?" Rebecca asked nervously.

"There's little doubt he's involved, in the sense he may be the one who took her, but as I said I think we'll find he's known to the parents. At this stage I'll admit I can't be certain what to believe, although I'm confident Sophie is alive and in no danger."

Rebecca had great trust in her husband's abilities to avoid danger yet his job had a way of turning that on its head. She also trusted that he was harbouring hunches that one would need a crowbar to extract from his mind. "I'm not about to stand in the way of saving Sophie, I know she has no better chance than you."

He kissed her fervently. "Thank you, sweetheart, I will not be taking any risks, I promise."

He wasn't a *hundred percent* sure she believed him.

For the rest of the afternoon, with the girls deciding to plant themselves on the beach, Josey spent some quiet time focusing on where the case was up to. His belief was that the church had something to do with it. He did have a hunch as to what it was, and even though there was no reason for him to read anything into his client attending a Sunday-service at the same church in which his stalker had evaded capture, he dutifully requested that if Vanessa were to revisit, she should watch out for the grey bearded man with the strong musk aroma on his person.

She attended mass every day for the next few weeks but the man never showed up at any of the services, or was ever seen hanging around the church grounds.

Having his client conduct the recognisance was a long shot anyway; there was no real evidence the man had anything to do with the church, except for the hunch Josey had developed the bottle shop owner attested to hearing Sophie call the suspect abductor *'Father'*.

Could she have been talking to a *priest*?

The evidence that he was undeniably the person who took Sophie on the night of her disappearance had never left Josey's mind.

Could Musk-man be playing three rolls in this; the one who took Sophie, Josey's stalker, and a *man of the cloth* from the local Catholic Church?

These questions alone assured Josey that finding Musk-man would solve the case and find Sophie alive and well.

He thought to assure the clairvoyant that she was on the money in respect of the girl's wellbeing, but chose to keep her out of it in case it got back to the unfriendly copper at the station, Dave Jenkins.

In the interest of keeping those closest to him in the loop, Josey had Vanessa join him on a visit to the Bryants in order to fill them in on what had been learnt, with strict instructions not to pass the information onto anyone, including the clairvoyant.

The parents were very relieved to hear the detective's positive attitude to finding Sophie alive, their apparent sincerity managing to ease Josey's mind regarding a suspicion they might be involved in her disappearance somehow, at least beyond some sort of misconceived plan that would most likely turn out to be completely innocuous.

Beliefs aside, all the discoveries were contributing nothing to illuminate what was truthfully the driving force behind the Sophie Bryant disappearance.

CHAPTER THIRTEEN
The Arrest

The latest sighting wasn't the first over the past few days and it wouldn't be the last. Just like Elvis, people were seeing Sophie in so many places at the same time that she couldn't possibly have been in all of them, and it was more likely that she hadn't been present in any.

For television viewers, the fact that Sophie was by all appearances taken from her parents and not meant to be found, equated to her not openly walking the streets, or catching a bus or train; the suggestion should have been enough to quell the fanciful stories. For Josey, based on his hunch, the far-fetched stories were nothing short of ludicrous, and her not being able to be found made perfect sense.

As for the stories, one woman reported on TV that she had witnessed a teenaged boy with Sophie.

They'd left Margaret River on a particular bus known to take passengers to Perth, which was ostensibly not worth investigating because in that same hour, another eye witness swore Sophie had been taken onto a plane bound for the Gold Coast in Queensland, an entirely different state thousands of kilometres away.

Josey being Josey, on a gut feeling he covertly snapped pictures of the two witnesses from the TV screen as they incredulously told their stories as though they were gospel, just as he had done with the bottle shop council worker.

Double checking footage from a street camera at the Margaret River and Perth bus terminals, there was indeed a teen and a girl similar to Sophie, but after asking the Bryants if they'd seen the report, they said the girl on television didn't come close to looking like their daughter. It was unlikely some sort of drastic facelift had been applied to such a young person, not to mention there was no time to achieve such a thing, or find a plastic surgeon mad enough to touch such a hot potato.

The airport security cameras didn't pick up a lookalike at all; convincing Josey this claim was also bogus.

Of course he couldn't watch all the TV channels at the same time and obviously ran the risk of missing some of the reports; this was the one downside of not working with police.

He tackled this deficiency by dropping in to see Joshua Bedford, the news manager at the local TV station. It wasn't known what to expect in the way of help until Bedford took him into a room where half a dozen people were studying individual monitors, *many eyes making light work.*

"We watch all the competition," the manager explained, "just in case like you we miss something. The fact is you only have to watch one channel because any decent broadcaster won't miss a thing."

Josey left the station satisfied there were no eye witness accounts that he hadn't seen. He felt there would be nothing more to be learnt this day – *he couldn't have been more wrong.*

What was about to happen would change everything - potentially even his hunch.

The moment he walked into his cabin back at the camp he found his girls sitting to the edge of their chairs glued to the Television. The subject of their fixation was yet another eye witness that had come forward, this time with much more damning evidence.

Rebecca pointed at the screen with a mandatory expression. "You need to see this."

She was dead right – as if on cue, Mitchell Bryant's close up picture came up as Josey focused in.

A man's voiceover was saying, "Police today arrested Mitchell Bryant, the father of the missing five year old. Bryant, who still maintains his daughter was abducted from their holiday cabin in Margaret River, while he and his wife slept, refused to add further comment on the charge. A witness that now claims to have seen Sophie, at a shopping mall in Perth this afternoon, and in the presence of her father; captured the following evidence . . ."

The so called evidence fills the screen, a video clip taken on the witnesses' cell phone. Even to Josey the man and young girl in the clip did have a striking resemblance to the father and daughter, except that it is a distant shot with little to no detail. Apart from this observation, their heights, ages and hair-colouring are a remarkable match. The alarming footage is damning even though not true, and more so given the girl looked stressed, the man appeared to be losing patience and provided her with a physical reprimand. It was only a light slap on the rump admittedly, yet no doubt shocking in the minds of viewers.

. . . "Mitchell Bryant has been placed in custody and bail has been set tonight at five hundred thousand dollars."

Rebecca flicked off the sound at the conclusion of the report and turned to her husband. "What do you make of it?"

This was a question perhaps a little early to answer, the surprising news had caught him off-guard. "They've got it wrong obviously. Firstly the less than convincing footage does nothing to alter the fact Mitch and his wife were together. If they weren't we'd have known about it, and so would the police."

Molly hated seeing her father seemingly out of step. "Can you fix this, Dad?"

"I can only imagine Vanessa's watching this right now—" Josey's trilling phone broke into his answer; recognising the caller he announced to the girls,

"Speak of the devil," and into the phone, "Vanessa, We were just talking about you." He put her on speaker for the girls to hear.

Her voice was crisp and worried. "This's total bullshit. I haven't left their side since I last saw you."

In spite of knowing the report was a farce, Vanessa still felt fearful for her brother. "These arseholes need to know that guy had a different walk to Mitchell."

"We know Mitch wasn't there, Val – so do the police; I wouldn't worry about this."

"But he's been arrested, why would they arrest him if they know the story is bullshit?"

"I'm guessing the arrest has nothing to do with the supposed sighting."

"Than *what*?" She sounded close to tears.

"*That*'s what we need to find out."

She realised the detective didn't need convincing, the impossibility of the accusation spoke for itself. She got on with her original reason for calling. "We need to speak with Mitchell, will that be possible?"

"Until we know who's arranged the arrest probably not. But listen, this is a storm in a teacup." He heard her sigh in frustration and changed focus. "How's Bev handling it?"

"Not good, she's been in tears. I'll be staying with her til we get to the bottom of this."

"Good, I'll make some calls now and see what can be done."

"Thank you, Cam; call me if you find out anything?"

"Of course, if there's no joy tonight I'll pick it up in the morning, once I find out where he's being held I'll try and get some help from Inspector Morris."

She released another nervous breath. "Good luck then, let him know how upset Beverley is won't you."

"He'll understand. Don't let this get under your skin," he told her. If you don't hear from me tonight try and get some sleep, we can follow this up in the morning."

Having failed to reach Morris or make any headway with police, Josey sat up with his family discussing this latest setback. It was comforting to know his girls still believed Mitchell Bryant was innocent.

While Vanessa and Beverley were on their way to the police station with Josey the next morning, Vanessa couldn't let go of the obvious reason Mitchell could not have been seen with Sophie after her disappearance. It wasn't that she didn't understand; it was because she didn't trust the police. She insisted on reaching beyond the obvious, just in case the police had something on Mitchell that even Detective Josey wasn't aware of.

He let her air her thoughts on Mitchell's walk, and the clothes being worn by the other girl, because it was good evidence and a great backup.

Van turned to Beverley, who had been sitting quietly listening. "You told me about the clothes isn't that right Bev."

Beverley gave her answer to the detective. "It's true, Cam; I agree with Van, I think it's worth mentioning."

Josey had no objection to mentioning this evidence. "Agreed," he admitted, "but I don't believe it will be necessary, because although the differing clothes is excellent evidence, I figure getting Mitchell out of the lockup should be a given even without it." Josey and the ladies were on the same page, he saw no reason for police arresting him either, and with Mitch already in an ankle bracelet, refusing expunction of the massively ridiculous bond was complete overkill. Considering the sighting was a nonissue, he agreed with Vanessa that there must be some other reason for the arrest.

But, be that as it may – inexplicably the Custody Sergeant appeared to have ideas of his own.

He gave off a parrot-fashion explanation for police adhering to Mitchell's arrest, and their suspicion that foul play concerning his little girl was at play; Mitchell was to remain in Custody until further investigation was carried out – the Bond of five hundred thousand dollars would also remain, "At least for another twenty four hours," he concluded.

Vanessa went into a wild rave, verbally attacking the Custody Sergeant. She couldn't accept that the police were turning a blind eye to the facts.

It was water on a duck's back. Their arguments failed to wash with the Custody Sergeant, who managed to keep annoyingly coolheaded.

Josey stepped in to quell the impossible situation. "We understand you're just doing your job, sergeant; clearly we need to talk with someone who knows more."

After calming Vanessa, Josey made a request to see Mitchell, which was accepted. He knew the sergeant couldn't have refused anyway.

Mitchell was sitting in a small cell furnished with a table and chair, and a toilet and sink attached to a windowless wall.

It was something akin to grief that drove Vanessa to make an extraordinary offer; she could not stand the sight of her brother behind bars for a crime he would never perceive of committing. She also needed her brother to be with his wife, and not in a goddamn cell. With tears threatening Vanessa promised Mitchel and Beverley she would find the bond money. "It's just a loan to these arseholes, brother. I'll get it back as soon as they realise you're innocent."

When she told Mitch about his wife's observation on the clothing, and Josey's belief Sophie is still alive she was silently concerned that his reaction was bland. She of course realised being alive didn't necessarily mean Sophie was not in any danger.

Van pushed like hell to have Mitch accept her help with the money, but he flatly refused to accept her offer, claiming he had his own means of finding the funds. He confirmed the sergeant's claim that the bond was being reconsidered, so it was a wait and see. His appreciation of his sister's offer was however very genuine. Ultimately, his adamant insistence to take care of the bond convinced her to give in to his wishes. At least the outcome would be the same; he would be given freedom to return to his wife while they waited for whatever happened next.

Overnight, talk of immediate freedom was snatched away; abolishment of bail had somehow once again been refused.

Following the failed attempt to free Mitchell, Josey had endless meetings with his client and her sister-in-law, which included a long conversation with Inspector Morris on the phone. The crux was, Morris promised to see what he could do to get Mitchell home with his wife, and to look into who instigated the decision to go ahead with the arrest.

Josey had great trust in the inspector; he had become aware the copper had good friends in high places. "If anyone can get your man home it's this guy," he told Bev in confidence after the call.

His cell trilled in his jacket pocket, he checked and saw it was Josephine Jackson. "Excuse me girls," he apologised for the interruption.

The Park owner came on saying, "How are those poor people going? What in hell is going on in those coppers minds, Detective?"

Josey scoffed, "Not a lot, Joe."

"Well, I've got something that might help pull their heads *in*."

The girls saw the positive expression that appeared on Josey's face, brought there by whatever had been said to him.

Josephine was waiting outside her office on the small verandah when Josey arrived. He parked near the foot of the stairs and got out wearing an expectant grin.

She came down the couple of stairs as she spoke, "I don't know how I missed this."

The grin on Josey's face broadened into a gleam. "Talk to me."

"It's one of the campers, a man called Reg Chappell, if that really is his name." She ushered him forward with a light touch to the arm. "Let's walk, Detective: I think you'll be interested in where he stayed."

Josey obligingly matched her considerable pace, clearly heading toward where the road met the beach. "Joe, can you tell me before I burst."

"I can tell you he paid cash upfront – the day before the Bryants arrived. Then, he up and left the day after Sophie's disappearance, even though he'd paid for a whole week. He didn't even hand in the key, or try for a refund."

"Can you describe what he looked like?"

"He was middle aged, a prominent grey beard, and way-way overdressed for a run of the mill camper." Josey's gained interest lifted to his face.

"Does this mean something to you?"

"Indeed it does, you've just described the man who took her."

"Oh my God, *oh my God* I knew it."

Josephine seemed far more upset by this disclosure than he expected, raising concern and a smidgin of curiosity in Josey. "What is it, Joe?"

"I'm so sorry, I should have noticed." She quickened her pace and led the way to the end of the road in silence.

At the beach they made a turn to the right, Josey already beginning to sense what it was that had Josephine quite so stressed; he was right. She'd pulled up exactly where he'd expected, nervously gesturing to the cabin closest, the one right next-door to that of the Bryants.

Her voice faulted, "He was in there, the night little Sophie disappeared."

This was no small discovery. The camp owner had inadvertently confirmed the identity of the abductor, and the name *Reg Chappel* – the man who'd been right next door to his target on the night that was heard by Jock leaving with Sophie, and the man seen with Sophie at the bottle shop who she referred to as *father*.

Josey could no longer dismiss the notion the Bryants may be implicated in the sudden disappearance of their own daughter. But what it also did was strengthen a revamped hunch he had, and the belief the clairvoyant was right, that Sophie *is alive and happy*, possibly still in the presence of her abductor, the *Musk-man,* who we now know to be *Reg Chappel*. Even the question of *why* was beginning to gel.

He considered Josephine with admiration. "This is real progress Jo; well done."

She countered with. "If you think *this* is progress, there's more." She turned away toward the surf. The beach was void of people bar one, a fellow standing at the water's edge with his back turned.

"That man down there, he needs to talk to you. He says he'd rather it be you than the cops."

Josey stepped past her onto the sand, pausing to turn and ask, "Are you not coming?"

Her response was gloomy. "I'm not sure you'll like what he has to say."

As truly ominous as this sounded, Josey knew not to badger her on what she'd been told. He trod across the expanse to reach the waiting man; the squeak of his shoes in the sand approaching from behind failed to arouse his attention.

The lapping water at the man's feet prevented rounding him to meet his gaze so he stood behind to announce himself. "You wanted to talk to me?"

He turned then, a man with a chubby face that didn't match his slim physique. He wore no smile. "I don't want to get anyone into trouble, that's why I'm not talking to the coppers."

Josey's expression offered no judgement. "What you say to me is just between us."

"Yeah well, if it isn't, I'll deny I ever met you."

"Understood."

The man began to amble along the edge of the gently lapping water, encouraging Josey to keep pace. "I consider myself a fair judge of character. I was out on the beach the afternoon those people arrived. If that guy was capable of murdering his beautiful young daughter I didn't see it; I still don't. Those people had nothing but love in their hearts. To think that man could do what their saying, it is absolutely not possible in my mind – no way." He fell silent, head bent watching the passing sand ahead of his bare feet. "I can't stop whatever it is you do with the information I give you, but

Josephine tells me you are a fair minded person." He faced Josey for the first time. "Like I said, I'm a good judge of character, and I agree, you look okay to me."

Josey lifted a respectful grin and waited for the man to continue.

He did so after returning to studying the passing sand beneath his feet. "Don't ask me what time it was, I didn't bother to check. Obviously there was no one around but us. He didn't see me; it was a particularly dark night. I saw *him* though. It was the girl's father. I caught a glimpse when he first came out of his cabin and stood looking around, as if he was making sure no one was watching. He was holding something but I couldn't make out what it was. After a bit, he set out along the beach. I kept close to the cabins and followed at a safe distance. That's when he stopped."

The story teller stopped as he said it, Josey with him. They were standing on a small sand dune covered in seagrass.

"This is where he dropped what he was carrying."

Josey was aware the man was referring to Sophie's top. "The red and yellow jacket"

"Yes, but I didn't know that until I came to look, after he'd gone back to his cabin."

"Did you see his wife through all this?"

"If she did come out, I didn't see her."

The informant Bradley Sharp hadn't volunteered his name, but Josey got it from Josephine before he left the camp. Bradley's proclamation to have seen

Mitchell deliberately place the red & yellow jacket on the sand dune, forced Josey to consider the only possibility that he was prepared to accept; that Mitchell Bryant was implicit in little Sophie's disappearance, anything else seemed untenable.

Had this witness held off making his claim for the reason he said? Josey understood that people who prefer not to come forward at first will often open up if their information coincides with that of other witnesses. In Bradley's case, he may have been influenced due to hearing that Jock, the blind informant, had been only too eager to talk with the private detective.

Driving away from the holiday camp gave Josey time to digest what he had learnt from Josephine Jackson and the new eye witness Bradley Sharp. The problem now was who to tell it to. In not so many words Bradley had made it abundantly clear he didn't trust the police to be fair minded given such incriminating evidence. Josey felt the same way, especially if Constable Dave Jenkins were to sink his teeth into it. The cops could wait; his first port of call was to go see the Bryants—

An incoming call trilled from the car speakers, sharply intruding his thoughts.

"Cam," he answered calmly.

At first he heard only silence on the line . . .

Then, a man's gruff voice broke in, "Listen carefully, Detective Josey," he demanded in a slow considered intonation. "You've got two choices . . . The first, go home to Sydney, and take your lovely family with you;

The second; if you don't . . . I promise they'll both be travelling back in pine boxes."

Josey's calm persona flew out the window; threats to his family so soon after last year's horror cut into him like a machete.

"I know you think you're doing the right thing, but you're not . . . You need to back off . . . Proceed and you will have more than the death of your family to contend with . . . You, will end up with Sophie Bryant's blood on your hands as well."

Torn between the terrifying threat, and yet another clue that the five year old is still alive, made it sound like a dangerous double-edged sword, except that once again, this was playing into Josey's hunch. This didn't stop him from taking the warning seriously, not when it came to the safety of his girls, or indeed Sophie – never again would he place his family in harm's way, even though the harm was only potential.

Josey's lack of response convinced the caller to sever the callous communication – *job done*.

Again, whoever had been watching him, and clearly continuing to do so, was undoubtedly a person capable of extreme violence. He reaffirmed his earlier promised to himself to go nowhere without wearing his gun. Again though, it wasn't himself he was most concerned about, knowing full well his girls did not carry weapons, a ruling of his own making, it was imperative he take steps to keep them out of harm's way.

CHAPTER FOURTEEN
The Attack

Obliged to inform the police, Josey abandoned his planned visit to the Bryants and headed straight over to the police station, dreading having to contend with Constable Dave Jenkins' less than amiable attitude.

There was an upside; if he could manage to get Jenkins to listen to the content of the threat then it may help convince the objectionable cop that Sophie is still alive. Either way he had no intention of holding his breath waiting for such a momentous outcome. His visit to the cop shop was to be purely the first step in getting his family to pull up stumps and return to Sydney.

Coming up ahead was a crossroad that had giveaway signs left and right of the main thoroughfare that he was on. Subconsciously he scanned the corner for unforseen dangers. There was just one car being held to wait in the street on the right, close enough now to believe the driver would wait to allow Josey to pass before entering the intersection.

He didn't.

At the last moment he shot out much faster than a collision could reasonably be avoided.

The brazen vehicle was on line to T-bone him at the driver's window. Instinct drove Josey to accelerate, yet the move failed to avoid an impact at the rear of the car, an action that created a spin that took his vehicle a hundred or so yards down the road before lifting into a dizzyingly airborne rollover.

Inside the cabin the experience was surreal; spinning this-and-that-way till no longer bearing the truth of his predicament; his muddled perceptions topsy-turvy as if within the power of a hurricane; coherent ideas failed to emerge from the churn.

This was no accident his own voice whispered as he began to dream—

From out of the disordered reality came coherent fixations, threats of eminent harm gave no time to comply, no time to save himself – not even a chance to back off or change the outcome, perhaps the lack of time to respond was—

. . . *Consciousness* returned with no notion of lost time, the gap filled by a memory of the incomplete fantasy—

Sight, *sound,* and time's connection to events, offered no concept of the reason for the dust and smoke that swirled randomly to escape the inexplicable tangled cocoon that now enveloped *him,* with his having no chance of following.

Again, coherency drifted away unnoticed . . .

People on the sidewalk saw the driver that caused the collision alight from his damaged vehicle, supporting a slight limp, and yet appearing to show concern for the other driver, still pinned in the overturned wreck a hundred yards away.

A young man entered onto the road and positioned himself alongside the limping driver to keep pace. "Are you all right, mate"

When ignored, the concerned Samaritan persisted in following, receiving a less than friendly response for his trouble. "Get lost, kid."

Caught off-guard by the hostile comment he abided, offering no further interest in helping.

Josey sensed an inexplicable prodding against his shoulder, refocussing him on the mangled mess and the wafting scent of smoke.

At the gaping hole that once was the driver's window; he saw the face of the man who unbeknown to him had limped all the way from the other car. At first he had no inkling this was the person who had crashed into him, yet his memory of the altercation was solidifying.

"Is the driver okay?" a second man enquired from somewhere.

Annoyance lifted onto the face of the first man to arrive, along with a trickle of blood that began running down from his hairline, provoking Josey to realise this was the driver of the car that hit him.

"Is he okay?" the other man tried again.

The offending driver half glanced in the direction of the repeated interruption with a warning. "Keep back will you – make yourself useful; call an ambulance."

Josey heard the guy agree to the blunt order but couldn't help wondering why the instruction sounded so deeply irritated.

Is he blaming me for what happened?

"Lie still; I'm a doctor," the maddened man barked.

The blood that had now made its way the length of the so-called doctor's face, had begun profusely dripping from his chin, convincing Josey this was indeed the guy who had driven into him.

Josey's own voice melted to the surface of his mind like oil, a red flag birthed in a dream; *this was no accident it reminded him.*

He began to realise this man had just tried *to kill him*, and that he was not the caller who had just threatened him over the phone; the timing of it didn't make any sense, nor did the threat itself.

Why would the caller make a threat that had an escape clause with no given time to take advantage of it?

There were two different people involved he decided conclusively, with *completely different agendas.*

Yes, any idea this guy was a real doctor had already evaporated, and yes, he was taking a *hypodermic* from the inside pocket of his coat, but his demeanour was strongly suggesting that whatever was in this advancing syringe, was not something Josey wanted infiltrating his arteries.

He attempted to put up a defence by drawing away, discovering with alarm that the sandwiched wreck was restricting his ability to make any sort of move to do so.

Meanwhile the hypodermic needle continued its drift toward him; a miniature missile and probably just as deadly, the needlepoint advancing toward the shoulder of Josey's jacket, a completely inadequate barrier—

"Can you step back please, Sir."

The hypodermic sped away from Josey's sight in an attempt to reach the pocket from which it came, yet was quickly accompanied by the sound of it falling to the roadway, left among the carnage in the hope it wouldn't be noticed.

With *doctor death's* plans vetoed, the culprit and the victim engaged in an impromptu mutual mind game, trying to read the mind of the other with little time left to do so—

Driven to leave, the indelible face reluctantly cleared the window, replaced by that of the friendlier face of a paramedic. "He's with us!" he called to his approaching backup team. The sense of his comment was clear, *the injured man is alive!*

As dazed as Josey was, the memory of the hypodermic man's face persisted well after he'd moved from sight; something was vaguely familiar about him.

He looks like someone . . . like—

It hit him like a barrow of bricks, and it landed smack on in the middle of his mounting hunch –

each brick aligning so perfectly that elation overrode the fact he was presently trapped in a mangled car.

It was suddenly obvious that this perpetrator was not only at complete odds with protecting Sophie, but was an imminent danger to everyone connected to the case.

This encounter had sorted out the confusion over who made the threat on the phone. Josey not only knew it wasn't the man who crashed into him, he had worked out why each man had appeared to have a different agenda, in fact their agendas were the same; *to stop him finding Sophie* – but for *entirely different reasons*.

Now that Josey had both their identities, he knew exactly where to tread next; there was just one problem, he first had to get out of this present situation alive.

The arrival of the helpful ambulance officer was a thankful distraction from the bizarre attack, a welcome sense of safety. And yet, real danger hung even heavier over his vulnerable family; this in fact was an impending storm, and for the moment, there was nothing he could do about it.

He tried voicing his concern to the paramedic that was reaching in through the window, but was frustratingly unable to clearly verbalise. "S,s,stop', *the*, man," he forced on a breath . . . "t, th, *other*, *d' dr*—"

The ambo figured from the way the victim was trying to turn in the direction of the fellow who'd just left in a hurry, pacing as he was toward the offending vehicle, it might be about him. He was forced to release the thought when he heard his team moving in.

"He's delirious and bleeding big time," he explained as he moved out of the way, "You'll need to be quick on this . . ."

Josey's comprehension of the man's words began to diminish; along with the solidity of his confinement, further and further into the distance, entering into a blinding veil of swirling black fog; relentlessly stifling Josey's confused and troubled mind—

Inside this dank place, he sees an equivocal shape approaching; reflecting light in spite of the gloom that surrounds, passing then to descend back into the void.

This nothing-place offers no sense of himself; he sees only what lies immediately in front of him, faint shapes that seem to be attempting solidity yet failing to evolve into anything other than smoky avatars of; people?—

A flash of fire-hot orange heralds the explosion of a gun, held by a ghostly shooter, yet the gun is as solid as if real.

Out of the mist that had devoured the bullets, victims emerge smothered in blood, bright red and as real as the gun, and indeed the vanished bullets—

His girls, Molly, and Rebecca, stand before him, forlorn and terrified, ready to relinquish everything.

Their dead; waiting the pull of gravity to take them down—

Josey tried screaming but could make no sound until impossible effort was applied, his desperate cry for help grudgingly released, breaking the barrier—

"He's back!" the paramedic shouted with a mixture of alarm and relief in his voice.

Josey looked pathetic, gasping for the breath he hadn't taken in quite some time.

"You're doing real good, mate – you'll be fine. Stay with me okay, no more sleeping."

Josey felt the warmth of his own blood veil his eyes and saw everything turn a hazy crimson. He gave the paramedic a decent start by grabbing at the medico's wrist to gain his attention.

"Just relax now okay, we're about to get you out." As startled as the paramedic was by the victim's perceived panic, he became drawn to why his injured patient was staring profusely at the wreckage splattered all over the roadway, prompting him to ask, "What's got your attention there, buddy?"

It took a measure of effort for Josey to point at the reason. *The hypodermic lay completely camouflaged.*

The paramedic followed the victim's eye line to the wreckage that was strewn everywhere. He couldn't fathom why Josey was being so earnest. Concluding the victim was suffering shock and possible hallucinations he got on with his job. "Come on old-mate, let's get you *out 'a* there."

The Jaws of Life replaced the attending officer at the window as he stepped aside to give the machine's operator room to move. The mighty mechanical claw gripped the door and wrenched it from its hinges, creating a wide open space for the paramedics to reach in and do their life saving work.

For Josey, the remainder of his rescue would be forgotten, *but not the hypodermic – and not the bogus doctor with the familiar face.*

CHAPTER FIFTEEN
A change of course

The local police patrol car blatantly drove into the ambulance bay and self-righteously parked in one of the vacant spots, two officers alighting to enter the hospital via the corridor usually reserved for delivery of patients.

At the nurse's station on the third floor, the guy on duty responded to the approach of the two uniformed coppers, who for no apparent reason wore seriously glum faces.

Heading up the duo, Sergeant Dave Jenkins began displaying his badge while he was barely ten feet from the desk. "Police," he announced as though their uniforms weren't a big enough clue. "Where can I find the patient Cameron Josey?"

The nurse knew all about the cops coming. "Straight down the end of the corridor, last door on the left."

A thank you would be nice the nurse thought as they strode off. "No trouble," she slurred out of earshot.

At the last door on the left, the officers barged in as though they owned the room as much as they did the parking bay, immediately annoyed that Detective Josey already had three visitors standing around his bedside.

The group turned toward the intrusion questioningly, their attention drawn to the one who seemed in charge; again with his badge out like a rite of passage, "We need to talk to this man. We'll have to ask you people to leave."

"And you *are*?" Vanessa insisted without making a move from where she stood.

He didn't appreciate being spoken to like that, but reluctantly managed to implement an apology. "The name's Jenkins, sorry - *my bad*."

Josey knew Sergeant Jenkins, and that he wasn't in the least bit sorry for his abruptness. He wanted to say *this is my family, shithead*, but said "My family were just leaving."

Vanessa looked at Josey slyly with, "If you say so."

He smiled knowingly dismissing the blatant snub directed squarely toward the cop; to his wife Rebecca he gave a *wink*.

Beck got up from the chair she'd been sitting on in order to muster a peaceful exit from the room, spoiling her amiable attitude with, "*People*, let's leave."

Vanessa was last to abide, eyeing Dave Jenkins as she went. Thanks to Intel from her brother, Jenkins' attitude toward Mitchell and Beverley had been established.

With the visitors vacated and the door closed the bombastic cop ploughed ahead. "We've been told you may have recognised the man from the other car, is that correct?"

"You've been misinformed I'm afraid, where are you getting this from?"

"Not that I deed to disclose anything to you but since you ask, from the paramedic at the scene."
Josey feigned putting on his thinking cap . . . "I'm told I was delirious, I hardly think I'd even have recognised my mother if she was there."

Jenkins looked at his constable as if to gain support for having to deal with the detective's wise-arse comment; he got nothing.

Josey knew that the sergeant's polite young offsider was the one responsible for babysitting the Bryants at their hotel, and that Mitch and Beverley had only good things to say about officer Fellows, which explained his reluctance to bolster Jenkins ego.

Jenkins came back onto Josey looking set to get something off his mind; it was already clear that this copper believed him to be working with the Bryants – to somehow cover up their crime. "I don't know what game you're playing at, but you need to know you're wasting your time trying to save these people, they're flat-out guilty."

Josey smiled disarmingly. "And from that

deduction what do you make of the guy who seems to want *me* dead?"

Jenkins baulked, trying to emulate Josey's nonchalant mood, instead it just caused the corner of his mouth to quiver. "Maybe you've been given a taste of just how dangerous these people are."

Josey released a breathy chuckle. "You don't seriously believe they're behind this. Sergeant, you're deluding yourself – the thing is, I can't figure out why."

"Let's see if you're so smug when this gets to court."

Jenkins hated it when the detective saluted cheekily and began fluffing out his pillow as if to put his head down and rest.

"We're not done here, Detective," Jenkins promised.

"Oh, I'm sorry, was there something else?

"Cute, try this; having them pay you for supposedly finding their girl is a complete farce, you and I both know she's already dead."

Officer Jeff Fellows glanced at his superior cautiously, believing him to have crossed the line.

Clearly unfazed by what people think of his take on the case Jenkins persisted. "I've run this by some friends of mine in high places and they agree the evidence will convict the Bryants of killing their own child. Are you going to tell me you haven't noticed how cold Mitchell Bryant is, he and his wife haven't shed a single tear."

"Neither did Lindy Chamberlain if you'll recall."

Jenkins scoffed, "That was different; the

Queensland coppers had no real evidence to get a conviction."

"And yet they did."

The poignant statement rattled him. "Look I'm not going to stand here arguing with you about this. I just want to say one thing; when the Bryants are found guilty, and they will be, I'll be coming after *you*."

"Fair enough, sergeant, I'll consider myself warned."

Aware the private detective wasn't taking his warning seriously, Jenkins maintained his glum face and sharply pivoted away without so much as a *Get well soon.* Jeff Fellows took time to glance back and give the detective an apologetic parting shrug, the amiable rookie slipping from view through the door that his boss had irritably pushed open to make his disgruntled exit.

He momentarily re-appeared ushering Josey's visitors back inside the room, getting all smiles from the family with a noticeably extra gleam from Molly.

Fixing on her father with an equally noticeable blush, the young cop unnecessarily informed him, "I'm on guard duty in the hall if you need me," then closed the door to provide the privacy they deserved, not to mention quickly hide the glow he felt had lifted to his cheeks.

On reaching her husband's bedside, Rebecca noticed a gleaming slather of sweat had layered his forehead, a new addition since the visit from the brash copper who had abruptly asked them to leave the room. She used her hand to disperse the perspiration. "You're looking peeved. What did that guy want with you?"

"Let's just say he's got an issue with the Bryants."
She frowned questioningly.

"They're guilty as sin in his mind. He claims to know Sophie isn't alive and that it was them that murdered her."

No one in the room believed that was even possible.

Vanessa voiced the sentiment, "Why would this guy be so sure of himself?"

It was a question Josey was also asking, was it possible that the creep might know something yet to be revealed. "I've shown him all my evidence in their defence, but he refuses to buy it." He picked up on Molly's concerned expression. "Pumpkin, are you all right?"

"I don't feel like you're safe in here, Dad? That young copper out there doesn't exactly look like a front row forward."

Her worried mother was nodding agreement. "She's right, Cam."

Vanessa joined the covenant with a promise. "Just so you know; I'm getting some help in here." She held her palm up to quell all possible objections from the detective. "No arguments please."

"Good luck with the hospital allowing it, not to mention police."

"I can be persuasive when I want – *and I want*." She received no further response from him.

Josey had no grievance with the plan because his

girls were undoubtedly right to be worried. Somewhere out there was a killer; he didn't dare mention that he knew why.

As they were leaving the hospital room Rebecca's sister-in-law dithered in the hallway. "Sorry, I just remembered I need to talk to Josey for a moment; can I meet you downstairs in the lobby?"

Although puzzled, Rebecca reasoned it was probably something quite innocuous between her husband and his client. "Sure," she agreed with no obvious reason not to. "But hey, I want you to know I'm helping pay for security."

"No you're not. Sorry, it's just that I'm responsible for hiring your husband, and that means I'm responsible for his safety. With respect, I don't think you should mention *your* offer in front of him, not while he's laid up in hospital at least, he'll probably insist you're right. I'm not trying to be rude I really think he shouldn't have to worry about it."

Rebecca wasn't certain her concerns were valid but figured any further discussion about it could wait. She touched her arm saying, "I understand."

After Vanessa left to return to the hospital room Molly whispered gently to her mother, "I think we should ignore what Vanessa said, we've got more interest in protecting Dad than anybody."

"She could have a point though, sweetie, the less Dad has to worry about the better – he may reject her paying exclusively anyway."

Molly accepted her mother's logic and they set out for the lobby.

Back inside Josey's room, sensing he had company

he opened his eyes to find Vanessa standing just inside the doorway appearing troubled. "That was quick, is there something wrong?"

Vanessa gently closed the door and made her way to his bedside. "There is, I couldn't say anything in front of your family, I didn't want to worry them until I'd spoken to you."

Her blunt message put him on edge, "Something's happened."

She was nodding. "Yes." A glance over her shoulder made sure they were alone, permitting her to continue. "Driving over to the hospital, we were followed."

Glancing at the closed door that led out to the corridor, alarmed and suddenly alert he lifted his weight onto an elbow. "Are my wife and daughter still here, have you told them this?"

"No, they're waiting downstairs for me."

He began discarding his covers, monitors and oxygen mask tearing away as he started out from the bed.

"Don't even think about it," Vanessa demanded while blocking his Ill-conceived pathway to injury, "you're not going anywhere – at least not on your feet."

He was about to ignore her mandate when the door flung open and a desperate nurse paced in to see what the patient was doing, sent running by the tell tail alarm from where she had sat surrounded by monitors. "Hey! Back in bed, you," she scalded on seeing how stupid he was being. She needn't have concerned herself trying to persuade him further, even as she spoke he was already doubling up in crippling pain. With deft strength she caught him, avoiding a potentially damaging fall to the tiled floor.

Crippling pains in places he didn't know he had, were taking over control of his entire body. The agony was a far more convincing argument than the upset nurse could have mustered; rendering him truly thankful she was so quick to move to his aid.

Settled in at the hospital café downstairs, his girls had no idea of the drama going on with their man back in the hospital room. Molly couldn't stop wondering why her mother's offer of help was so adamantly rejected by her father's client. "What do you think she wanted to talk about with Dad?"

Rebecca had already being thinking on that question while sipping her coffee. "I'm not sure but I intend to find out."

"You know, I think Vanessa looked worried when we arrived at the hospital, did you notice that?"

Rebecca quickly finished the remains in her cup and got to her feet. "I did, come on I need to know what's going on."

With the nurse gone and now settled back in bed, he got straight onto his phone without mentioning to Vanessa who he was calling, leaving her wondering about the urgency. While waiting for whoever it was to answer he appeared inordinately stressed, switching to mild relief when he finally got connected.

"*Hey-Cam,* long time no hear," a cheery voice sang in his ear, "How you doing—?"

Although relieved Josey was in no state of mind to match moods. "Pat Listen, I need your help."

His friend's demeanour sank in response to the anxiety being clearly exhibited, responding with due respect. "Of Course, mate. What's happened?"

"It's my family, they're in danger."

"Jesus, where are they?"

"They're here; we're *all* here, in Margaret River."

"I see why you rang *me*, what can I do?"

"I need to hide them."

"Hide them – *from who?*"

He had to swallow his answer, stifled by the door to his room suddenly swinging open and his girls striding in with looks of despair and want; "Josey, you there," Pat's voice sparkled in his ear?

With eyes pulling away from his storming family he refocused, "It's a bit of a long story, I . . ."

"I've got time, why are you hesitating?"

"I'm putting you on speaker . . . *hold on.*"

The girls had reached his bedside just as Pat's voice emitted from Josey's cell, which he now had placed on his lap. After Vanessa was released from the strange look she was getting from Josey's wife she sat right back in her chair, indicating acceptance of whatever was bugging Josey's wife, which no doubt was about to be revealed.

Now with her glaring gaze turned to her husband, Rebecca asked, "What's going on, Cam?"

Her voice being recognised by the caller brought a concerned retort from Pat. "Bec, what's this I hear about you guys being in danger?"

"Patrick, hello," her voice smiled, yet with

troubled eyes never leaving her husband. "It seems I know as much as you do."

Patrick went stone silent, expecting to learn the extent of severity.

"They've just walked in," Josey clarified to his friend, "I'm laid up at the hospital."

"Mate, you had better start explaining yourself by the sounds of it."

Rebecca scoffed. "Yes, *mate*; I'd like to hear this too."

Vanessa and Josey exchanged looks of being *caught unawares* by his family.

He had a lot going on in his mind, and not just the obvious threat from the emerging assailant. Those shocking events of a year ago still persisted with relentless assertion. Memories of how close his family had come to death now moulded all of his decisions when it came to their safety – and more so now.

As awkward as Josey felt in asking for such unusual favouritism, his friend felt absolutely no discomfort in accepting 'the request for sanctuary', *unconditionally.*

In order to safeguard Josey's family, Patrick Bentley's property, sitting as it did in complete isolation fifty kilometres outside of Margaret River, was indeed an unexpected and fortuitous choice.

It was no accident that the detective knew of Bentley, Patrick was a private investigator himself. The two men had worked together when Cam was still a cop. It was Pat who egged him to go private following a shootout with a felon that resulted in the death of Freddie, Cam's then partner. The loss of Josey's partner lay so heavily on Pat that he too decided to get out of the force.

In light of the imminent danger they were in, Josey warned everyone, including Mrs Bryant later, that it would not be safe to revisit the hospital. The worry over Josey's safety promoted the question, how safe would *he actually* be in the hospital.

He explained that he needed to stay put so as not to attract attention being relocated, he couldn't dispel the possibility he was being watched on the outside. He reminded them that the entire hospital staff had been informed of the danger, plus extra coppers were place up and down the corridor outside his room. No one was feeling relaxed about it until he exposed the complete plan ahead, a plan that would protect them all.

During his remaining stay, Josey had time to pour over recent events. When it came to *hypodermic man*, due to the shortness of time between the call and the crash, less than a minute, *doctor death* couldn't have been the same man that threatened him on the phone. The call was no more than an idle threat – nothing more than a scare tactic. It was meant to sound more sinister than it was, and it still fitted in well with his hunch, albeit with a necessary update, meaning there were now *three* contributors invested in stopping his investigation. He knew who they were and he knew what was driving them.

There was still one vital step before he could get the plan rolling.

The Bryants being in more danger than anybody, he called Inspector Morris requesting the apprehension of Mitchell Bryant be relocated to somewhere safer, along with the others. Morris worked his magic, getting the authorities to accept that this change of venue was not being considered a release without bail, but rather a suspect's protection order, in which he would continue wearing his ankle bracelet, along with—and in the constant company of—his wife at the new designated safe-house.

That *safe-house* being, Patrick Bentley's *Silo*—

CHAPTER SIXTEEN
Silo

The assault against Detective Josey was by now convincing enough evidence to beef up security around the suspects and their associates. Now with the ruling that Mitchell and his wife were not allowed to leave Margaret River quashed, the sticking point for the second part of Josey's request for help from Morris was able to proceed. Morris knew of Patrick Bentley back when he was still a cop, before the eventual recluse had decided to leave the force. This went a long way in helping him see merit in Josey's idea.

One phone call from Morris had gotten the authorities on-board. The Bryant's then received the official sanction to move to the safe-house that same afternoon.

With things looking up for those in the Bryant camp, disruptive news appeared state wide that

Mitchell's court case was about to be fast tracked. But in fact it hadn't even been deemed that there would be a court case. This news was obviously coming from those officials who have a legally given right to an opinion on the matter, but they were considered by those opposing a trial to be talking out of school.

Assurances from Inspector Morris and Detective Josey that there was nothing to be concerned about in making the move, didn't allow the Bryants to relax about it.

The sanctioned departure to the hideaway property occurred less than five hours later. Josey and Morris took all care not to alert anyone outside of their circle about the slightly unorthodox exodus, resulting in the decision not to use a police vehicle, settling on a van that X-cop Patrick Bentley owned, equipped as it was with substantially dark windows.

Under the cover of night, the van was driven into the hospital's underground car park; where upon Bentley's precious payload was picked up in complete secrecy, now including the extra passengers, the Bryants and Mitchell's sister Vanessa.

The only people in the police force privy to this arrangement remained that of Inspector Morris, along with the men and women he trusted implicitly, and even they hadn't been told of the location.

Upon their arrival at the safe house, the shawl of night and the tinted windows defused what they were able to see from the van. They passed through an open timber gate that offered no more than a symbolic barrier, free to continue along the smooth earthen track that snaked between two rows of bloodwood gums, purposely planted perhaps many decades ago.

Rebecca had the clearest view of what lay ahead through the clear glass of the windscreen. "Is this it?" she asked bemused by what she saw.

"Yep," Patrick confirmed with pride. "It was a wheat silo in its *hay day*." A few chuckles prompted Pat to cover with, "You know what I mean."

Rebecca looked over her shoulder to those settled in the back seat. "Wait till you see this," she announced.

"Put your windows down for a clearer look," Patrick added.

Molly was on the best side of the vehicle and with the window down could see the massive Silo had been painted from top to bottom with brilliant art, its curved walls decorated with Larger than life Australian birds frozen in flight. "Wow," was her solitary retort.

This was the word on everyone's mind as they pulled in close to the tower. "We're here, folks; welcome to my humble abode." He turned off the engine, opened his door and stepped out onto the expanse of grass where he'd parked.

Mitchell was first to follow. He'd been on the opposite side to the colourful Silo and had to round the vehicle to appreciate how high the structure towered above everything else in the immediate surrounds. He reached the nose of the car and stood to take in the full height of the edifice. In trying to imagine what it might look like inside, he picked up a slight hint from the four layers of windows that circled its cylindrical shape at the top, the largest windows placed highest, perhaps providing the best view.

He whistled in sheer appreciation of the art, along with Patrick's dream of converting an old silo into a place to live, a place that could only be described as a unique country style high-rise apartment.

Their host led them toward a closed doorway that cut into a massive impression of a nesting magpie. He turned to gain their reactions, "This is my home, and yours too until you're able to leave."

Patrick Bentley wasn't understating it, no one knew when leaving would be safe.

The hapless guests followed the property owner in through the small door beneath the nesting black and white magpie, passing between its flared downward facing wings. They gasped at what they then saw inside. The hollow Silo was essentially empty, all signs of grain gone. Nestled against the wall they had just passed through was a small glass-walled elevator. Tracks and pullies traced a diminishing line that carries the lift to the distant ceiling. They were yet to learn that the ceiling in fact was the floor of whatever had been built beyond, access made possible via a recess that matched the circular shape of the elevator car. The whole thing miraculously clung to the concrete wall by means made invisible by its builder.

The visitors disconcerting ride toward the top saw the base of the Silo giddily fall away, as surely as the first level somewhat ominously approached from above.

The elevator melted into the underside of the slab, its glass wall revealing the inside of a claustrophobic shaft that seemingly slid by for an inordinate length of time, providing the belief the concrete might be of immense thickness. Visible only by the grace of light from the interior of the lift, the oppressive wall finally slid away to gently settle level with the floor on which they stood, the car now at rest in line with an opaque ingress. The inner and outer doors slid open in unison, the welcome opening revealing a well-lit circular room sparsely furnished. On stepping into this space they first noticed a uniquely curved table that swept beneath a bank of windows, with a dozen chairs positioned on either side. Unique in itself, the room also sported such things as a double day bed, a small coffee table surrounded by cushioned layback chairs. Beyond was an ornate floor to ceiling bookcase, with unimaginable genres bound in hard covers fashioned either side of a recessed mini bar that encircled a kitchenette. Other items of comfort partially went from view, hidden behind a cylindrical wall set in the middle of a circular room, appearing to have at least one door with a curve to match.

They learnt that this door entered a shaft housing a second elevator; the core of the silo, a conduit that linked to three floors below, effectively allowing access to three lockable self-contained rooms.

The first floor could be thought of as the lowest

level, consisting of three triangular rooms the shape of a slice of pie. Two rooms took up half the entire area and the third a whole half. The second and third floors were identical. Each level had a door leading into the lift and a spiral staircase from which every other floor could be reached.

"You will all be allocated shared or private rooms at your discretion," their host informed them sounding like the proud owner of a holiday resort.

He informed them that the top floor where they were, is intended as a general meeting place and dining area, and the only room able to be reached via the elevator that went to the base of the silo; preventing access from uninvited guests.

This strange house was where Patrick had lived as a recluse since leaving the police force. For his present guests if nothing else it felt safe. During his time in the force Patrick had made some unsavoury enemies who he felt might be worth keeping at arm's length, hence the fortress-like silo. Safety aside, one could only imagine what this un-married man got up to in a man cave like this, he wasn't exactly ineligible.

A week later Josey was released from hospital and secretly picked up in Patrick's dark-windowed van.

Shortly following his arrival at Bentley's property, once over the absolute amazement at the grandness and security attributes of the silo, he approached his friend to ask if two others could be accommodated. When it was explained to him who these people were and their importance to the case, he agreed without hesitation.

Josey got straight down to arranging for Maxine Priest and Carl Norris to come from Sydney to join them, which they did, arriving the next day.

With the arrival of the new boarders, Bentley set himself up on the day bed in the meeting area so that every one of the visitors could be comfortably housed.

Having his partners Maxine and Carl at the location would provide him with the backup he would soon need. There was plenty for Max to keep busy, one of the needs was communication; calls to the Sydney office were already off-limits and other methods would be required. For Carl there was an entirely different plan, he was soon to learn he would be asked to cover Josey's back in the best way he knew how.

Josey had held off mentioning the details of this to his family prior to the arrival of his agency partners, but the time had come; especially since part of his intention was to return to Margaret River in order to continue with his field work, which involved identifying and locating the man who had attempted to kill him, preferably without drawing attention. So far his family were only aware of the known facts about the crash and nothing of the man's effort to inject him with something. Josey had kept this information from the police as well.

He also avoided divulging his hunch about the guy's motive and his identity; any mention would only have raised further alarm, enough to encourage his girls to insist he drop the case. With what happened a year ago they had that power.

As always, Carl was the perfect man to help move his plan forward in a manner that was safe, and Josey did feel reasonably at ease about letting his family know what the plan was. And he knew that they trusted Carl as much as he did. If it hadn't been for Carl's talent as a disguise artist, primarily his ability to become anyone he wanted – *male or female*, they might all have met their final demise a year ago.

Even with the assurances offered, Rebecca wasn't comfortable with her husband returning to Margaret River, with or without backup from Carl. She had to concede though, having him with her husband was somewhat of a plus. It was impossible for her to sweep aside how Carl had saved all their lives on Josey's last horror case. He had a knack for turning up in the right place at the right time.

None of this prevented her from letting her risk-taker husband know how nervous she felt.

It was again up to Carl to remind her of his brilliance; applying a little of his magic with a demonstration.

He and Josey had spent three hours locked in one of the rooms in preparation.

The man and woman who finally emerged from the off-limits room were no longer Carl and Josey. If Patrick hadn't been told what to expect, he might have believed two intruders had climbed the walls of the silo via the well hidden emergency escape ladder, a climb not for the fainthearted.

Now transformed into a slim and slightly aged ethnic farmer with a scruffy grey beard and prosthetic nose, Josey would not have been recognised by his mother. The wardrobe for these disguises had been brought from Sydney by Carl. Patrick actually did wonder why he had been so heavily laden upon arrival, and just how long he intended staying.

Aware the woman was in fact Carl; Patrick initially found himself in a state of disbelief, followed up by some discomfort over the way she was looking at him. He'd gained this expression from women many times, but never before from a cross dresser.

Seeing them decked out like this brought about unrestrained laughter, essentially they had become a black bearded farmer and his somewhat attractive wife. It was settling sight, relaxing everyone about the two of them returning to Margaret River.

With sudden unease they noticed not every audience member was enjoying the performance.

Josey broke away from the performance and went to his wife's aid, she hadn't been laughing as he had expected – instead she was crying. "Sweetheart, what's the matter?" He held her close when he realised she couldn't even answer, she was so distressed. "Hey, come on now – you don't have to worry."

She shoved him away. "You fucking say that as if it's easy for us—"

Molly understood her mother was including her in the worry stakes, and although having a level of agreement with her mother, she knew her father well enough to know he would never take his family's concerns in any way lightly. She joined her parents and wrapped her arms around them both. "Mum – *Dad will be alright.*"

Laden with guilt, Josey couldn't bear to see them like this. "Sweetheart, listen to me – Just say the word and I'll call it off. Please believe I do understand how hard this is for you and Molly."

Tuned into this drama, the reactions of those in the room were varied. Carl appeared embarrassed, perhaps for offering his support to his boss. Vanessa might have been feeling dejected; after all, the detective had made such incredible headway, it would be a disaster for her brother if he were to pull out now. Beverley Bryant seemed confused; beyond this she was completely unreadable. Patrick was decidedly uncomfortable; he of course didn't know all the gory details of what went down last year when the family found themselves in a lot of trouble; not just them, Carl the disguise artist too.

Beverley Bryant sharply expressed *her* feelings. "I would like to end this too."

Annoyed by the disgruntled expression Beverley was wearing, Vanessa let fly, "I'm not surprised you'd say that, Bev. You've been against this from the start. I've been wondering why that is."

"All right stop all of you!" Mitchell's reverberating voice permeated the room with such volume; it left no choice other than to tune in to his command, he was *Beyond* angry.

Stunned and guilt ridden expressions circled the room, presenting Josey with a dilemma. With what he knew about the Bryants, he could either face disclosure now or tiptoe around it until he knew more. The choice was hard because if he disclosed the information now, which was ostensibly still a hunch, it may disrupt his whole plan to get to the absolute truth.

In spite of her own questionable attitude, Beverley wasn't letting her sister-in-law's acid remark slide. "So you're implying Mitchell and I have done something to our daughter?"

"Not my brother, but if the shoe fits—"

Mitchell went quiet, receding in defeat.

"*HEY!*" This time it was Josey drawing the attention, taking it on himself to sever the argument.

What they saw wasn't anger, it was *disappointment*.

"This has gone too far," he told them in a moderate tone, his hard decision made. "I'm opting out of the case so you can all calm the hell down."

"No, you're not," his wife decreed, still teary and shaken by what she felt she had started, now sounding quite immovable on her unexpected change of mind.

Josey saw the determination in his wife, and knew that whatever was on her mind, had better be listened to.

"I'm the first to admit – we have all forgotten about little Sophie." She glanced to Beverley. "I for one do not believe that you or your husband Mitchell could do anything to harm that helpless sweet child – and neither does my husband."

Beverley welled and tears flowed, mouthing *thank you* without any sound passing her lips.

Rebecca swept her eyes onto her daughter and then to her husband. "Molly and I know you don't mean to frighten us; we know your heart is always in the right place. You need to finish what you started. It's the right thing to do – for little Sophie."

Vanessa swallowed her feelings and moved to console her sister-in-law. "I'm sorry; I shouldn't have spoken to you like that."

"And what about what you *believe, Vanessa*?"

"*I believe*, like Rebecca says, we all need to focus on the safety of your daughter."

"And, *your brother*," Josey's wife avowed in support of Mitchell, "who I know you love dearly."

It was Josey's client Vanessa who welled this time, struck by Rebecca's understanding and Beverley's forgiveness.

What Josey took away from what just happened, apart from Beverley Bryant having nothing whatsoever to do with harming her daughter, was that Bev and Mitch her husband were definitely hiding a secret . . .

He thought, *it fits my hunch – disturbingly so – far too close for comfort.*

There wasn't a single person among them that was unaware of the potential danger that always subsisted during any prying investigation; it remained distinctly understood that people who wished not to be found or apprehended can become menacing if cornered.

During the mandatory isolation in the silo, what was happening in the media was on constant watch on level four, there was always at least one person in front of the generous screen. This Intel kept everyone abreast with what the press considered was happening with the case, who it seems were most at odds with what the police were saying about Mitchell Bryant's move to a safe house, annoyed at not being told where that was; they very much were missing the point of a safe-house.

The media-story that most prevailed was the opposed abolishment of bail, to a suspect that was largely perceived by public opinion to be guilty. It wasn't clear what they thought he was guilty of; it was just that on camera he appeared to be cold; in the minds of many he just had to be involved, *what other explanation could there be?*

The most unexpected and unwanted story dominating multimedia was that of a private detective being hired to help the Bryants get off the charge.

In contrast the traffic incident, in which the detective had been involved, made the story even more poignant, in that it brought Josey's identity into the scrutiny of the public eye. This one incident was responsible for bringing the detective into the limelight, and thereby placing him in danger. There was however a distinct upside to this.

The perpetrator's action against the Bryant's Private Detective – deemed to be a premeditated attack – had unintentionally given those people in Mitchel Bryant's corner and in some cases those undecided, an actual boost.

Still, this opinionated yet positive swing, having

only managed to change public opinion minutely, meant that those at the silo were prepared for what happened next.

Unknown faces, grouped together in offices within the gaggle of lawyers advising the direct members of the prosecution, somehow launched an opinion-swinging campaign that began with a release to the media, stating the court case would be going ahead and was being fast-tracked, expected to begin in one week's time.

Josey got straight onto the phone to Inspector Morris to find out if there was any truth in it – he got the answer he didn't want. Morris empathised but had no knowledge of how or why the decision was made. The court case had indeed been set for a week from this day.

Disappointment ranked high at the safe-house. They were feeling guilty over having earlier been part of a premature celebration, the unveiling of the disguises now seemingly void of use.

Plans to return to Margaret River were immediately abandoned.

"I realise this puts your plans in a bit of a ruin," the inspector mused, "and to make things worse you'll probably be called to give evidence. In fact if you decline it will be a huge loss to Mitchell's defence; catch twenty two."

"Not really."

"Not really," the cop repeated sceptically.

"If I'm right, the prosecution will find a way to block me."

Morris held his silence for a moment before

saying. "You may have a point, as a detective investigating the case you are neither a witness nor a defender; is that your point?"

"It is."

"You make this sound like staying out of it will help, what's on your mind?"

Josey was very familiar with windows of opportunity closing, but also with new ones opening. He had found this winning window on many other occasions, and in this case it was already in play, and ready to let in fresh air. "There's more than one way to influence which way this goes."

"Should I be nervous about this?"

"It depends on your take. I'll admit I've been keeping a few things to myself, no surprise there, *right*."

The inspector scoffed lightly.

"There is more evidence of Bryant's innocence than one can shake a stick at," Josey expounded, "evidence in the form of witnesses; witnesses that are ready to burn bridges to have their say. I'm guessing the longer we hold off informing the prosecution the better."

Morris warned, "You've got that right but, be careful who you decide to withhold evidence from, and for how long."

"The, *who and the how* – that's your responsibility, Fin. No one needs to know I'm involved."

"Touché you cunning bugger – but listen, have you thought about the risk to you, coming out in public? You do know the place will be teeming with cameras."

"Not a problem, Inspector."

"Of course there isn't," the cop responded cynically, "why would I even think to doubt it?"

"See you there, Inspector—"

Morris pictured the cheeky investigator smiling on the other end of the line, he had one he couldn't wipe away himself, yet was left nervously wondering about the PIs comment, *there's more than one way to influence which way this goes,* not to mention his ambiguous promise, *I'll see you there—*

CHAPTER SEVENTEEN
Judgement Day

With all the courtroom participants present, it was a matter of waiting for the Presiding Judge to make his appearance. The jury, everyday citizens randomly selected by the sheriff from election rolls, had a myriad of expressions that barely gave an inkling of their attitudes to the accused. Gathered to hear the opposing evidence about to be presented, they mostly appeared bemused by their present unfamiliar environs.

In the front row sat the small group of witnesses expecting to be called to the stand, among them the bearded farmer, a prime site from which Josey could scan the faces of the jury.

Carl the middle aged woman sat in the back row watching for people that may appear agitated, or that might be paying too much attention to the aged farmer.

"All rise," a commanding voice echoed from the timber walls as the Judge breezed into view in his bellowing black gown.

The attendees remained standing until the judge had taken his seat. A single pounding of his gavel raised the usual shuffle and rumble as all re-seated.

At his lawyer's side, immediately in front of the row of witnesses, Mitchell Bryant appeared nervous as expected. Josey noticed he was taking repeated glances at the men and women of the Jury as though more worried about them than the judge; the man with the scary power of dishing out the sentence for those found guilty.

A lot had happened prior to this meeting of the minds, both sides of the fence had honed their plans to impress the court; equally to that of sporting teams scrutinising tactics to be adopted on the day of the battle.

Josey knew how diligently the prosecutors would be working toward finding convincing arguments that may sway the jury to their way of thinking. He had applied quite a bit of preparation himself, being neither a witness nor defender as had been established, including by the prosecution, mandated the essential inclusion of the witnesses now seated with him. It was satisfying to know the people who had helped in preventing him from participating in the trial, had no idea he was sitting in the courtroom right behind the accused.

Those aware of Josey's presence were Mitchell and his Barrister Grant Parnell, Inspector Vin Morris, who was sticking his neck out more than anyone else in the room, and of course Carl. None of the witnesses that Josey had mustered during his investigation needed to know the detective was present; it would only have served to make them nervous, and perhaps somewhat of a hindrance to a favourable outcome.

In the week leading up to the trial, with Morris's help Josey walked the witnesses through the minefield of what to say and what not to say while in court – and how to phrase their answers, including protocols in speaking to the judge; primarily only if questioned; *Never plea to the judge, it's not illegal but it will annoy.*

Prior to these preliminary meetings with the witnesses, individually they had only been familiar with their own accounts as they recalled them; bringing them together effectively strengthened their convictions. Mitchell was included in the last of the three meetings so that the witnesses could meet him and get a real feel for the person they were being asked to defend.

Josey had one final piece of advice, "When you are on the stand, don't appear to be his friend, or give the impression the Bryant's are nice people – of course don't give the opposite impression either."

One thing had been troubling Josey even before the meeting of the witnesses, Mitchell had been distant and lacking concentration. Perhaps it was just the lead up to the impending court case, but Josey sensed it had everything to do with his dogged hunch,

The car crash and Josey's run-in with the

perpetrator was the moment he noticed Mitchell's demeanour suddenly alter. It wasn't fear that he saw, rather it was *desperation*; sparking this needling feeling Mitchell was holding something back.

He glanced to the police prosecutor Ivor Stanford, known to have clearly disagreed with the witnesses list presented by the defence, admittedly on time yet at the very last minute. He further objected on the basis they were all a result of the investigations of a paid private detective hired by the defence to expressly conclude innocence. The fact Stanford had gained knowledge of the witnesses from Sergeant Dave Jenkins was handily omitted in the lawyer's objection to the court.

Fully expecting the anomaly would come up during questioning; Josey and the Inspector had tutored the witnesses on how to explain their reasons for agreeing to give evidence in defence of the accused.

The defence Lawyer addressed the judge with, "Your Honour, if it pleases the court I would like to bring to the stand, Sonya Westfield."

"You may."

"Thank you, Your Honour. I then call, Mrs Westfield. Would you please approach the stand?"

Sonya left her seat and began her walk to the front, balking at the sudden and loud voice of the opposition. "Objection, Your Honour, it is known that this witness has been piloted to lie by the private detective hired by the accused."

Judge Schmidt gave the prosecutor an irritated

glance, "Do you mind if we are given a chance to establish this for ourselves, Mr Stanford? Objection denied."

Stanford sulked as Mrs Westfield continued her way to the stand and took her seat to be sworn in.

"Mrs Westfield, can you tell the court what evidence you wish to present?"

"Yes I can. I have photographs of the little girl, taken by me, three days after her abduction—"

"Objection!"

"Again a little early, councillor; what is it?"

"The witness's claim that it is Sophie Bryant in her photographs is hearsay."

"Maybe it is," The judge told him dismissively, "but again, do you mind if we let the jury decide once they've viewed the evidence? Do you have these photographs, Mr Parnell?"

"I do, Your Honour." Parnell walked smartly to his desk and picked up the evidence, returning to show the witness prints of the shots. "Are these the photos you took, Mrs Westfield?"

"Yes they are,"

He paced across to the jury and handed the evidence to a young woman selected as head Juror; she was able to compare Mrs Westfield's pictures with the family shot of Sophie when she was aged four, the same one that everyone had already seen on television. Satisfied, she nodded respectfully and passed the prints on.

The prosecutor was decidedly uncomfortable with the positive way the jury was nodding while inspecting the pictures. "Your Honour," he pleaded—

"Yes, yes I know councillor, looks can sometimes be deceiving." He turned to the members of the jury. "These pictures should not be considered absolute proof they are of the missing girl. You are directed to wait and hear further evidence that may be presented today before making any decision."

"Thank you, Your Honour," Stanford grovelled.

Schmidt just looked at him.

Farmer Josey wasn't worried; the *further evidence* the judge mentioned, had fire enough to continue helping the defence's case along.

When Jillian Edison took the stand to offer her special insights, Josey noticed the Margaret River cop squirm in his seat.

Josey recognised the clairvoyant attesting to the little girl being alive could potentially be damaging to either side, but she did have a good track record within the police force for getting it right, and in the end it would come down to the jury's perception. If her clairvoyance had shown the little girl was *dead,* she may well have been giving evidence for the other side.

Regardless, Josey felt her record added credence to the so called hearsay photographs—evidence is evidence. On careful consideration prior to showing up in court, Edison's exceptional track record was considered well worth highlighting in front of the jury.

"Mrs Edison, can you please tell the court what it is you do."

"Yes, I am second-sighted."

"For the benefit of the court can you explain what that means?"

"It means I am *clairvoyant*, one who can see things that have not been witnessed, things that have happened in the past or indeed still happening."

Parnell wasn't expecting to get an objection from the police prosecutor due to the fact the clairvoyant was practically a member of the police force herself, and in that time she had hit the mark fifty times, which she was proud to announce. The defence lawyer paused just long enough to see if Stanford had a question for the witness – he *did*, prompted by the judge eying him with a view to perhaps gaining an overdue response.

"Yes, sorry, Your Honour. *Your Honour* this is pure conjecture."

Driven by his opponent's embarrassment Parnell got cocky in offering an unnecessary Point. "Perhaps you wouldn't think so if our clairvoyant were to have been on the side of prosecution today, Councillor."

"That'll be enough, Mr Parnell. Do you have another argument to offer?"

"No, Your Honour;"

Edison's time on the stand was never going to be long, a person's beliefs are difficult to contest. It wouldn't have mattered if she had claimed the opposite – she had to be right one way or the other.

"That will be all Mrs Westfield," Parnell announced, "you may step down."

An unseen smile raised beneath the beard of the farmer in the front row, the clairvoyant's seed was sewn.

"Not so fast," Stanford protested getting to his feet to approach the stand. The two lawyers gave each other an unreadable glance as they passed each other.

With Edison re-seated Stanford got started. "You say you have over fifty cases in which your Intel has been correct is that right."

"Yes, it is."

"Please tell the court the number of times that you have been wrong."

Jillian wasn't perturbed by this question, she knew it wasn't a perfect science; in fact it wasn't a science at all. "Ten times," she announced unashamedly.

Stanford desperately wanted to label it guesswork but knew he could not, who knew when she would be on his side next. He also knew that he may already be in trouble with the fraternity for questioning her powers at all, so he let it go. He hoped he'd created sufficient doubt though to cause a little damage.

Josey already understood the position Stanford would be in with questioning the clairvoyant and again smiled to himself.

Judge Schmidt was peering down at his notes and without looking up addressed the defence councillor, "Mr Parnell, it says here that the defence actually has a witness that knows the identity of the person alleged to have abducted Mr Bryant's daughter."

"Yes we do, Your Honour."

"Is the witness in the courtroom today?"

"He is, Your Honour."

"We'll call him up in a moment. Let's start with the perpetrator, is he here?"

"No your honour, he was one of the campers on the night Sophie was taken, unfortunately we don't know where he is."

"Your Honour, this whole thing is a farce."

Schmidt turned on the prosecution disapprovingly. "I'm sorry, did I hear an objection?"

"Sorry, Your Honour."

"Mr Parnell, I suggest you get on with telling the court if this mystery man has a name?"

"We have only what he called himself, Reg' Chappell. Mr Chappell was not his real name, Your Honour. We have been unsuccessful in locating him. He is however thought to have been the person to take Sophie Bryant on the night of her disappearance due to the evidence of our witness."

Judge Schmidt zeroed in on the police prosecutor sitting at his desk. "Did you know about this, supposed abductor, Mr Stanford?"

Stanford cleared his throat and glanced down at his notes as if the point had no real importance to put to memory. "Yes I did, Your Honour."

The judge's brow lifted inquisitively, forcing ridges into his forehead. "And?"

"And we believe the claim is irrelevant and unproven, Your Honour."

Schmidt shifted his eyes onto the defence councillor. "Let's hear what your witness has to say, Mr Parnell."

The defence lawyer glanced toward his witness

sitting in the front row and called him to the stand.

Disinterested in watching the witness's ponderous approach to the stand, the judge cast his eyes down to whatever was splayed out on his bench and began writing, all the while listening to the shuffle of feet. When he looked up again he was presented with the realisation the next eyewitness was by all accounts blind, needing to be assisted to the stand by the defence lawyer. He made no attempt to question this, easily able to reason that people can become witnesses by many and varying means.

Once settled and having vowed to tell the truth, the witness waited. He turned to the voice when it came.

"It's Grant Parnell here, Mr Shackleton. Can you explain to the court how you know of Mr Reg Chappell, and how you know it was he that took five year old Sophie Bryant from the holiday camp in the middle of the night?"

"Well, I didn't *see him* if that's what you're asking, but if you call me *Mr Shackleton* again we might not stay friends – the name's Jock"

"Sorry, Jock,"

An appreciative murmur lifted from all the attendees, Josey even detected a slight curl in the corner of the Judge's mouth, a welcomed addition given the court frowns upon untethered statements more often than not.

There was something about Jock that allowed him to get away with it. The rest of his evidence was expressed with a measure of self-control, explaining to everyone in the courtroom how hearing is often fine-tuned when sight is lost. He explained that in this way he was easily able to build a three dimensional image in his mind of where the man had come from, who he was with and in which direction he was going. "The guy was in the cabin next to me, that's where he came from, that's where he was staying. I heard the little girl's voice, and footsteps – his were first. He came down the wooden steps carrying the girl, and then they headed on up to the northern end of the beach . . ."

Parnell realised Jock considered he had completed answering the question. "Is there anything else you can tell us about; any other things you may have sensed?"

"Oh, sure, the guy reeked of musk, I told—"

Josey's heart skipped a beat; Jock had come close to mentioning the private detective just as he managed to stop himself.

Parnell turned to the judge as he began rounding the stand to help his witness down. "I have no further questions, Your Honour."

The judge swung in on the prosecutor. "Do you wish to cross examine, Councillor?"

"Just one question, Your Honour," he responded as though glued to the seat. "Mr Parnell, can you ask your witness to affirm that he has not made this story up."

Cheap shot the defence lawyer thought as he was assisting Jock down the three steps that led down from the hot seat. "Did you hear the question—?"

The judge jumped in sounding incredulous, "Are you happy for defence to do your job for you Mr Stanford?"

"Sorry, Your Honour. He got to his feet and addressed the witness from where he stood. "*Did,* you hear the question – *Jock?*"

"I *heard,* and I'm not impressed. You can cuff me when you figure out I made up my story, but you needn't waste your time, I'm not a liar and I'm not wrong about what I *hear – ever.*"

His answer was the reason Stanford initially had no interest in cross examining him. He felt the jury had been served with a voluminous amount of doubt, enough to predict the verdict was going to be *innocent;* there was just one provision left, Sergeant Jenkins—the biggest believer in Mitchell Bryant's guilt—could swing that around. Stanford decided to give him a shot.

From the stand, Jenkins mentioned the two known facts, the blood around the car, and the blood on the knife that was proven to be Sophie's, both items having been deliberately hidden from police. He then made the mistake of offering his opinion that Mitchell Bryant was expressionless when questioned, appearing to exhibit no remorse whatsoever over the loss, or indeed the death of his little girl.

Parnell picked up on this. "Perhaps he had no remorse because he was aware he hadn't harmed her; and that multiple sightings, not permitted in today's proceedings were—"

"I'll stop you there, Mr Parnell – I suggest you quit while you're ahead."

He did, because the judge was right, it was an opinion which amounted to leading the witness even though it wasn't the witness he was speaking to. It was a point that the prosecution missed out on mentioning.

The Jury deliberated for no more than a half hour before filling back into the courtroom, presumably with their verdict.

The judge swivelled his chair to face them. "Members of the Jury, how do you find the defendant?"

The thirty year old chosen head juror stood to make her announcement without facing the accused. "We the jury find the defendant, *innocent,* Your Honour."

Pleased reactions resonated throughout the courtroom, drowning out the sound of the Judge's gavel.

Josey's eyes were on Mitchell, the apprehension that had been prevalent in Sophie's father since the car crash was still with him. And yet, having been found innocent of abduction and the crime of murdering his little girl, there was no hint of celebration. Josey acquired the ominous sense that had hung over him since the crash, the feeling one gets when it's feared something has been missed.

And then it came – bursting into the joyous room like a clap of thunder. Drenched in sudden tears, Mitchel Bryant, the man found innocent by twelve jurymen, screamed out, directly facing the Judge, the man with the power to apply sentence. "Your Honour – The jury has made a mistake — I am Guilty!"

The prosecution lawyer, although shocked,

morphed from 'Glum to Glee'.

Some of the revellers in the room who hadn't quite heard what was said had to ask. In the fading sound of success, Mitchell repeated his confessional. "The Jury has it wrong . . . I am *guilty* . . . I killed my daughter."

Judge Schmidt suddenly took on the persona of a character from the famous *Madam Tussauds*, solidly subdued to immobility, as are those cold-wax human replicas. His eyes stared incredulously at the accused – in fifty years on the bench, for him this was an absolute first. He wasn't even certain the verdict could be withdrawn.

The courtroom fell completely silent. The incredible confession was being absorbed. Someone, perhaps from the press, ran from the court presumably bent on revealing the result, as if infected by the stillness of the judge. The Jury; confused by their own reasoning that Mitchell Bryant's innocence seemed certain to them, couldn't help wondering how they got this so wrong?

Refusing to be intimidated by the flurry of complacent glares coming from those on the prosecution bench, the clairvoyant clung to her belief Sophie was still alive, and voiced it to a companion she had entered the court with. She would have expressed her belief to Josey if she'd known he was in the courtroom.

The grey bearded farmer couldn't help noticing the unbroken resolve in the clairvoyant's body language, and wanted to assure her of his own understanding of the truth. Josey would do that as soon as he wasn't playing *Farmer Joe*.

As big a bombshell as this confession was, it hadn't dented his hunch, in fact it had strengthened it.

What he had to do next was clear.

Carl saw him leave his seat and make an exit without engaging, which he emulated while avoiding any sense of a connection between the farmer and the woman he was playing.

CHAPTER EIGHTEEN
Josey Confronts the Accused

Josey had a meeting back at the Silo to inform his people that Mitchell's confession was not the end of his own involvement in the case; that there was more than met the eye.

Beverly Bryant was unable to shed any light on why her husband would suddenly claim to be guilty after weeks of claiming otherwise. "How could he have," she reasoned, "I was with him the whole time, you know that as well as anybody."

Josey couldn't doubt her, but he also silently rejected the notion she didn't understand why he'd taken the blame.

With the media running wild, Josey needed to remain out of the limelight more than ever in order that he may continue on with the case. He decided it was time to bring Mitchell into the picture to gain his reaction; to see if his retort supports the hunch.

Along with Carl he went to visit Mitchell at the place where he had been confined, the authorities had no idea what to do with him, because in the eyes of the law he had been found innocent.

Mitchell didn't need to know about the disguises being employed by Josey and Carl, so Josey asked for Inspector Morris's help in getting in to see Mitch without being seen in public. Morris organised an unmarked vehicle to take them from the silo and right into the grounds of the locality.

Although told he would be receiving visitors, Mitch wasn't given information about who they were, and so upon their arrival they were sharply unwelcomed.

Carl was warned by Josey that the reception might not be warm; he didn't give a reason because what was going on was still a hunch.

Mitchell's less than amiable mood prevented the visitors from even opening their mouth to explain their presence.

"I don't know what you two are hoping to achieve by coming here."

Dismissing the reprimand they took up their seats opposite him at a small table; both of them bolt upright in the uncomfortable wooden chairs provided. "Maybe we're just after the truth," Josey proposed.

Carl remained straight faced, offering nothing more than his keen ability to listen.

"How'd you two get in here anyway?" he carped. The question was reasonable, even his wife Beverley hadn't been allowed a visit.

"This was Morris's doing, he doesn't believe you're capable of harming your little daughter either, Face it Mitch, *what possible motive do you have?"*

Mitchell became a little restless in the face of the ensuing silence from his guests. "One of you had better speak up because I've got nothing to say."

"No? Josey queried, "your wife does, she as much as gave you an alibi. Bev claimed you wouldn't have had a chance of killing Sophie, *you and she never left each other's side the whole time were her exact words.*"

Mitchell's eyes blinked briskly, darting around the room nervously. "All right, Detective, clearly you think you know what's going on. Tell me why that is."

"I'll repeat the evidence given in court if you like."

"Why don't you start with the blind-guy's evidence; what he says he heard is as weak as water."

"So is your point of view on that."

Josey reminded him Jock was in a location allowing verification the man lived right next door, and not to forget the park owner backed him up, adding the fellow had a fictitious name. "It seems incredible you wouldn't have laid eyes on your immediate neighbour at least once."

Josey privately conceded it was quite reasonable to imagine the next door neighbour might have chosen not to ever show his face, and he guessed it wouldn't have been hard for Mitch to simply miss seeing him exit his cabin, but in any event, whether or not Mitchell saw him wasn't the main argument. He reiterated. "You say Jock's evidence is weak. No one else in the courtroom saw it that way. When Jock says he heard where the abductor came from, which happens to be right next door to you, and also hears that the guy has Sophie with him, there's no reason to doubt him. Like he said, he has *heightened hearing*."

Mitch either found no defence, or was reluctant to express any.

"Which means, your daughter was carried from the camp that night, in the arms of a man staying right next door to you?"

He rejected a second offer for a response with further silence.

"Mitchell," Josey pushed, at which point in time are we expected to believe you killed your daughter . . . Was it after your neighbouring camper, and without complaint from Sophie, left with this man – alive and well?"

Clarity and facts were simply serving to annoy him. "What the hell do you want me to say to this?"

Josey glanced at Carl for perhaps some input.

Which he gave, "Look, I haven't been on the case with the detective from the beginning but it's clear to me, the detective just wants to understand why you're lying about killing your daughter when clearly you haven't. The irrefutable evidence says you are innocent; nothing else makes sense. Just tell the truth, we can't help you if you don't"

Mitch held on Josey. "The truth can be a dangerous thing, Detective; I'm guessing you know that better than most . . ."

"In this case, the same can be said of holding back."

This rattled him. "I made a confession, how in hell is that *holding back*?"

"Give me a break, Mitch, everyone knows your innocent, so you need to give this bullshit up. You're treating everyone you know like they're out-and-out idiots, including your wife."

His ensuing silence suggested he might be about to clamp up.

Josey had one more important point to make. "You've never once disputed that on the morning of the next day, following her disappearance; your daughter was witnessed standing side by side with her abductor."

"It's a sighting, how many of those turned out to be false?"

"It was more than just a sighting; one has to be consider why she was heard calling him *'father'*. Since you're her father, who do expect she was talking to?"

"I don't expect anyone was; I don't even believe the story is true."

"I think you do, and I think you know exactly who this man called *father* is." Josey then conceded, "I have to admit, I can't be sure if you also know who attacked me."

The accusation appeared to render Mitchell somewhat unhinged, his eyes again darting about rapidly . . .

Josey's deadpan expression remained void of any

sort of judgement, yet laced with a warning, "Consider this, your misconceived *reasons for the lies* have already been acted upon; resulting in violence."

Given the general consensus that his confession was absurd, and the unavoidable fact his plan was rapidly unravelling, even to the point of putting others at risk, Mitchell began to realise that there was no further point in trying to convince people he was a murderer, but he wasn't ready to come clean about what he knew. In relation to the attack on Josey, he felt holding back his true thoughts and troubled concerns were no longer tenable. "Believe me – I have no idea who attacked you; I do however believe it is connected to your investigating my daughter's disappearance."

He could see Josey knew more than he was letting on, and that he was simply fishing; he had a desperate plea though, "I have to say, Detective, you're interference in searching for Sophie is also contributing to possible violence, and in no uncertain terms threatens to endanger my family."

Josey smiled inwardly, this embattled man's plea was as truthful as he was prepared to be at the moment. "I hear you, Mitch," he expressed earnestly.

Expressing relief that his position was beginning to be understood, all that was left was to place trust in the detective's sense of morality. "You have to promise me one thing; please don't do anything further that places my wife and daughter in any sort of harm's way." He lowered his gaze to the table and tears dripped to its surface like the first sign of rain, and perhaps the storm that was yet to follow.

Josey turned to Carl and gently advised, "We're done here."

CHAPTER NINETEEN
Conscience

The pleading advice openly handed out by a man torn between truth and saving his family, tore at Detective Josey's heart. He was well aware that the plea to keep the Bryant family safe was not to be considered lightly. He need only think back to his own family's terrifying experience at the hands of a crazed killer.

He reiterated this feeling of responsibility to Maxine and Carl, who he'd chosen to meet well away from the location of the Silo. They sat at a secluded coffee shop with a view to figuring out what to say to those holded up in the Silo. In particular Josey didn't want the whole context of the discussion with Mitchell to be spoken about in front of Beverley. He felt certain the both of them were harbouring a secret, and he wasn't ready to let her know they were aware of it. Given the restriction now applied to all phone calls from the silo, Bev wasn't about to find out by accident. So far she didn't even know that Carl and Josey had paid her husband a visit. She would eventually be spoken to about it, but only when more was known.

In the meantime, the discussion had with Mitchell was not to be broadcast, as it served no end.

Being hundreds of kilometres out of Margaret River annulled the need for Josey to be the farmer, or *Carl his wife*. When referring to Carl like that, it would bring about faltering mirth, because it was intended as armour against further violence while they searched for Sophie, a fact that never left their minds.

The most solid assurance Josey could offer, in relation to Sophie being alive, was founded on the evidence. Yet her exact location was yet to be proven.

Josey's assertion surpassed that of the clairvoyant. Max wondered though, why not open up to Beverley. "It might not be such a bad idea, hearing you say Sophie is safe would put her mind at ease wouldn't you say?"

Josey edged. "I think she already knows, Max"

Maxine knew right then that she wasn't being told the full story either, which wasn't a problem because Josey always had a good reason for holding back information; his hunches weren't always right, at least not at first. "What about Vanessa, do you think she knows Sophie's safe?"

"She hired me remember, it's unlikely. Right now

she doesn't need to know either."

Maxine nodded in understanding and gave Carl a glance. "So, what do you want us to do?"

"Max, I want *you* to stay at the Silo, Carl comes with me."

"And what do I do at the Silo?"

"Relax and be my sounding board, take care of communication and make certain they don't kill each other."

They grinned in recognition of his point.

"Max I'll call you with our developments and vice versa."

"You do have a clue where Sophie is, right?"

"A clue yes, once we confirm her location you'll be first to know."

"Sure."

"We're also hoping to gain more about Mitchell; a bit of his history will go a long way to understanding him."

Josey noticed Maxine's hesitancy, "Max?"

"Look, I'm not sure if it's important," she told him reflectively, "but Vanessa and I got talking back at the silo and she let out that her brother had a bit of a temper back in the day."

"Interesting, in what sense?"

"She didn't elaborate when I asked, but it apparently came to a head while he was working as a lay teacher, at the Catholic school in Margaret River."

Josey showed greater interest in this information than would have been expected from either one of them.

Max queried the reason with a knowing frown.

He was grinning now; a reaction they were familiar with.

Carl took a punt. "Care to enlighten?"

They weren't to know this was a piece of information that fitted his hunch like a glove. It was time to fill them in on a few things, starting with the stalker, the guy who ended up running into the Catholic Church as though he knew the place.

Carl thought he knew what Josey was driving at. "You're saying this joker is connected to the church."

"There's no doubt, he's also the one who took her from the holiday camp."

"Why in heavens would the church have anything to do with this?"

The penny dropped on Maxine. "The convent; there's a convent right next door to that church." Her face had irradiated. "The Nuns, are you thinking the nuns have Sophie?"

"Since you've brilliantly guessed my hunch," Josey confided, "Yes I trust they're protecting Sophie at the request of her parents. I believe the man is a priest, which explains why Sophie called him *father*."

"This is starting to make sense," Maxine decided.

Carl needed more information. "Hang on a minute, what are they protecting her from?"

"From the same guy that attacked *you*," Max offered Josey.

"Yes, but it seems certain he is not the abductor; the abductor is a priest; tasked with taking Sophie to a safe place."

Carl raised a point. "But he should have known you were ostensibly hired by the Bryants, why not just tell you she was safe with the nuns."

"Because the Bryants believed it would have put her life in danger, the location is meant to be a secret, and it needs to be *kept* that way. Mitchell in a roundabout way was begging me to make sure I do the same, so we need to handle this carefully and not make things worse than they already are. Mitchell was extremely guarded at our meeting, and although he didn't come right out with it, I guarantee he's aware of a dangerous person who must never find where Sophie is – *why?* I don't exactly know, but I intend to find out."

Maxine was absorbing all this, her sleuthing powers hard at work. "The guy who tried to take you out is *not* with the church then."

"Correct; and now we need to find out who this guy is, and stop him without his finding out our connection to the case, which if we're not careful could lead him to the convent."

Carl looked worried. "How can we be sure he hasn't found his way there already?"

Maxine scowled at him. "Carl, don't even think it."

"He's right, Max; we need to work fast on this." Josey summarised. "At least we know why Sophie called the priest *Father*."

Having already worked out the meaning of the word *father*, and the inclusion of the church's involvement in what was really going on, Josey was happy everyone was finally on the same page. "Now we need to work out a safe way for our alter-egos to obtain an invitation to the convent, and to the attached school to learn more about Mitchell's history there."

As ordained, following their meeting, and disguised as their alter-egos, Josey and Carl pulled into the driveway of the local Nunnery, located right next door to the Church and school in question. While Carl remained in the vehicle to keep watch, Josey, again in his farmer disguise, which had marginally been altered to make him appear a little more corporate, with leather jacket annexed by a smart computer case, headed off to enter the building to where he was to meet with Mother Superior, the mandatory person elected to answer his questions.

The way Josey had got around the real reason for his visit was to claim the company he worked for was producing a nationwide television documentary about Nondenominational Teachers in Australian Catholic Schools.

If he had not been believed, Josey would never have made it beyond the peaked archway that gaped open in the front wall of the building, final entry made only at the discretion of the Nuns via a massive timber door. What had clinched his success in achieving an audience with the Mother Superior was an initial meeting with the director of the churches' own film studio. Once the manuscripts, which Josey had borrowed from a close friend in

Sydney, were shown to the Catholic Film Studio director, he was in the door.

The place where Carl had parked the car allowed him to see anyone on foot or otherwise that might decide to enter the Nunnery. The long driveway that led through the garden back to the roadway was the only way in, unless someone was agile enough to manage scaling a twenty foot brick wall draped in spiked Bougainvillea vine.

A Nun responding to the bell resounding at the other side of the door, young judging by the sound of her, asked politely, "Who is there please?"

"It's Mr Thomson. I am expected by the Mother Superior."

"Yes, I know; wait one moment please."

After appearing in a letterbox sized window she'd slid open in the huge timber door that filled the entire archway—and following an extensive verification as to who he was—she allowed Josey access to a large shining tiled area that was graced with pristine white oversized icons of the faith. The marble figures weren't alone, real live plain clothes sentinels stood equally as still, bar their watchful eyes constantly observing and assessing.

Josey sensed this was the right place, the place where he believed Sophie was being held. He felt this level of security was decidedly unusual. Another clue Sophie was here. The guards weren't from the police; had they been, he would have known about it from Morris.

From there he was ushered through a labyrinth of halls that eventually led to the solid and secured door of Mother superior's office. Josey thought highly of the security level, *but was it the perfect haven for little Sophie? - or perhaps only reasonable at best?*

Mother Superior was a middle aged woman of small stature with a kind face. Josey knew her to be someone of high rank. When he saw her sitting at her teak desk, head down and presumably hard at work, she instantly projected authority, even before she looked up and stood to face her expected guest being chaperoned in by the young nun, whom she then dismissed amiably.

"Mr Thomson I'm told," she smiled gesturing to the seat opposite her. "Please sit, I'm Sister Joseph." She beamed welcomingly. "So, I understand you are our Hollywood man come to film our good nuns."

"Not quite film and not quite Hollywood, Sister. I'm just one of the producers at a small tightknit company."

"Oh well, someone has to be the producer I suppose."

Josey valued the light comment as a typical *nun-joke*, likening it to a *dad-joke*, an ascription attributed to his own casual sense of humour when it fit. He lifted a grin enough to see beneath his bushy beard. Unrecognisable to anyone who knew him, Josey was now the typical film industry type.

"Tell me what I can do for you," she offered.

"To be perfectly honest, Sister it's pretty simple; we're looking to interview some of the kindergarten nondenominational teachers at your school here. The questions we ask are non-invasive; it's more to do with the choices they made in becoming teachers to our younger members of society. We're calling our documentary, *Leading Our Children*."

Josey continued with this ruse for a few minutes and quickly realised Sister Joseph was more interested in getting on with the rest of *her* day rather than *his*.

He was pulling out a laptop from his bag when the sister voiced her intentions. "I think that I will leave you with someone else who can offer you more time, Mr Thomson. My apologies, I'm very sorry but I need to be somewhere in five minutes."

"I was hoping to leave you with a treatment to—"

She raised her hand to silence his speal. "I'll introduce you to my secretary; she will take care of whatever you wish to leave with us. If you would like to meet our teachers next door she will be able to organise that for you too."

"Do you mean *now*," he responded happily hurrying the laptop back into its carry bag.

She smiled at his child like excitement. "Well, that is up to her. If you would like to wait here Mr Thomson I will have her come to see you." The sister stood and rounded the desk to say her goodbyes. "Her name is Sister Ann, I am sure she will not keep you waiting."

Josey accepted her outstretched hand taking hold of only her fingers in a light goodbye gesture.

"Good luck to you, Mr Thomson, perhaps we will meet again."

He watched her sweep away then sat to wait . . .

. . . When Josey exited the Nunnery two minutes later his smile told his cross-dressing chauffeur they were in business. Before he was fully into the passenger seat Carl risked asking the obvious. "I don't suppose you saw her?"

"No I'd have been disappointed if I had. Thankfully the place is locked tight, the way we like it."

"Good, so you've got a list then?"

He patted the computer bag on his lap. "I have."

The *list* as Carl had called it contained half dozen names of people who worked at the school a decade ago, at the same time that Mitchell was there.

Carl gestured to the list. "When do we do this?"

"Right now; we've got a guy still works here."

Carl was impressed.

"Park the car away from the entrance it's a short walk to the pre-school."

They left the car at a designated parking spot and took a brisk walk, no more than a hundred yards from the Nunnery. Minutes later they were sitting in the office of Jonathon Burns.

"Yeah I knew Mitch; he's in a lot of hot water I see. Is that what this is about, Detective?"

Josey and Carl had switched from film makers to private detectives; it was unlikely John Burns would be talking to Sister Joseph anytime soon. "Sort of, we've been hired by police to do some of the leg work."

"I haven't seen the guy since he left, he wasn't well liked I'd have to say."

"How do you mean."

"How do I put it – he had a bit of a problem with his temper our Mitchell."

"Really; what was he like with the kids?"

"Not good, that's the reason he was asked to leave the school. The Nun's weren't going to stand for it."

"Was he violent at all – with the kids?"

"The day they fired him he was. He ended up taking a ruler to one of the little girls – smacked her over the back. He claimed he meant to slap her bottom, but he knew like the rest of us that smacking of any type is not allowed. Personally I'd like to believe it was just an accident. But, as I said he did have a temper."

Josey and Carl couldn't deny they were disappointed by the man's claim. The temper problem wasn't news to them though, it was the reason they were here having already gleaned the incriminating information from Mitch's sister Vanessa. It was looking more and more like there was some truth in Mitch's lack of control. The circumstances driving Mitch's temper were the key to finding out how much truth there was; Josey would make sure to find that out the next time he paid Mitch a visit, which would be real soon.

"Are there any other incidents you can recall?"

John chortled inoffensively. "I didn't see it but I heard a penknife was discovered stabbed into the top of his desk one day. Rumour also has it the stabbing followed some sort of rage following a class."

"Did he have any of his own kids at the school when he worked here?"

"He only had the one, you know *Sophie*. She was here. I never saw him hurt her to be honest. I wouldn't believe everything you see on TV."

"When did he finish up at the school?"

"About a year ago, Sophie left when he did."

Two things were gleaned from talking with Jonathon Burns, Sophie had attended the convent school at the same time as her father, and also that Mitchell Bryant wasn't the placid gentleman he was hitherto portrayed to be. For some, this might have served to suggest he could be a killer, except for the almost-certainty Sophie was alive, which a lot of people didn't believe.

Josey was convinced the five-year old was safe in the protective custody of the Nuns and no one else need know, especially not Jonathon Burns. There were a few other things to be kept under wraps at the moment, such as Mitchell's vague reversal on his proclaimed guilt. There's also the unestablished perpetrator, it was best he remain a nebulous character so as not to build the hearsay even further.

If any of these things were revealed publicly at this point, those who doubted Bryant was innocent would begin flooding the airwaves with harmful questions. For instance, who was she being protected *from*, if not from her bad tempered father?

Was that person the one who was behind the wheel of the other car on the day of the orchestrated smash in which the detective helping the Bryants was supposedly the victim?

These were all good questions for others, but not for Josey. One question did remain though; was the person in Josey's *hunch* one and the same as the man who tried to kill him? *And if so, what exactly is his beef; not only with me but also with the Bryants and their little girl?*

He began to wonder if this guy meant no harm to the girl, perhaps his only problem was with Mitchell and Beverley. The orchestrated car crash and the phone call minutes before, both amounted to being based on the same motivation, to stifle the investigation.

The abductor, thought to be a priest, was most likely the person behind the call, and possibly had been sanctioned by the church. It was necessary to figure out why the hypodermic man would want the same thing as the church. The church's reason made the most sense; they had good reason not to have anyone find out where Sophie was. Hypodermic man having that same reason was, indeed, hard to figure.

Which of the two men would most want him to cease the investigation?

Then – it dawned on him.

The perpetrator did have the same goal, but for a very different reason. That reason being, he already *knew* where she was; and that he wanted to make his move before the detective unravelled the plan – not just the plan, but who was behind the whole thing.

This changed everything, now Josey had to figure out how the perpetrator had beaten him to the punch. Perhaps he'd used the same logical application as he; that is, gaining the first clue that the Bryants daughter Sophie had attended preschool there with the Saint Joseph Nuns, along with her father.

Wait! Maybe this wasn't the first clue, perhaps he already knew that too?

This regurgitated the hunch Josey had days ago; that the perpetrator *is known to the Bryants,* feasibly enough to then believe Sophie might be being held somewhere within the umbrella of the church.

This was all beginning to make sense, which meant, for Josey, alerting the convent about the perpetrator was more urgent than ever, it was well and truly understood this guy was capable of killing.

Keeping Sophie safe remained the driving force in the case, and time the one thing he didn't have a lot of.

It seemed almost too extraordinary to be real, but the events that occurred early on, when Josey first arrived in Margaret River, were pulling him firmly towards the hangman's noose, he'd been a target from day one and it was beginning to feel altogether very uncomfortable.

It was becoming apparent that all the answers were in one place, and *that place was right here.*

"I think it's time I paid another visit to the church," he told Carl at his side.

Carl lifted his head from the headrest and opened his eyes groggily. "Aren't we already here?"

"You're reading my mind," he pointed to the structure with the stain glass windows, "*Right here* is where it all comes together, buddy."

Just like the short walk from the convent to the preschool the church was only a quarter of a block away with no dividing fence. The walk gave time for Josey to fill Carl in on what had been running through his mind.

Carl was completely confused about the connections that Josey seemed to be plucking out of thin air. They reached the broad stairs leading to the church entrance. "Are you thinking you'll find the priest in here?"

"Not necessarily, but it'd be motivating if he was. We have to keep in mind that the Bryant's know who the perpetrator is, not just who he *is*—that they actually do *know* him; and it has to be connected to the reason Mitchell is trying to convince everyone he killed his daughter. Either way, it's just as certain Mitchell and his wife both know the famous priest – *personally*, and well enough to ask for his help in hiding Sophie."

"All right, let's do it," Carl pressed enthusiastically.

They ascended the wide staircase and freely entered the welcoming entrance, Josey finding that this time it was void of worshipers. The confessional had a light on above one of the three cubicles, which probably meant someone was inside confessing their sins the the attending priest.

That priest could well be the driver of the black Mazda, the stalker—*the abductor*.

The two dubious worshipers sat in one of the pews at the back of the church, a rare sight for anyone who knew them, and yet at the moment they appeared an innocuous couple spending a little quite time, heads bowed as though in prayer.

A few minutes passed before the red light above the confessional blinked out, the forgiven parishioner came out and slid into a nearby pew, presumably to carry out his penance. He'd paid no attention to the bearded man sitting at the back of the church in prayer.

Josey had his head bent forward with eyes tilted up in the direction of the confessional; he had a perfect view of what happened next.

The vicar came out of the centre door as the absolved man was making his way to the exit.

The appearance of the priest was a perfect match for both the so called stalker *and the abductor*. Although recognised, Josey knew this everyday priest was neither – *in spite of his having acted like he was at least one of them.*

Without pause he quietly followed at a safe distance so as not to be heard. The clergyman negotiated three small steps to reach the platform on which the Altar sat; genuflected respectfully before heading off through a side door that took him from view.

Cautiously continuing; quickstepping now to close up the gap that had formed between them, Josey came to a stop one side of the doorway and listened. He could hear muffled tones just a short way into the room.

He peered around the edge of the jam and saw the priest and a young man dressed in dark trousers and white open neck shirt, in fact it was the deacon he'd run up against on his first visit. The two men whispered in casual conversation, so low that it couldn't be clearly heard.

The priest reached for a bottle of wine in which they both partook. This was an unexpected development; Josey had to think very carefully about what he was doing. It was impossible to imagine what might happen if he were to barge in and make accusations.

He would have formulated a new plan and proceeded more prudently except that time was of the essence. He didn't want to do anything that jeopardise his chance of convincing the clergy of the danger Sophie was in.

The reverend picked up reflected movement in his dark glass of wine and spun his head to check, catching a glimpse of Josey moving clear of the doorway. It was as if the shy intruder had been standing there listening.

The spooked priest suddenly bolted from the room, leaving the deacon to deal with the situation. The young man made no immediate attempt to move. Although surprised, both by the priest's sudden departure and the reappearance of the intruder in the doorway, the deacon calmly placed his wine down on a little table next him before straightening up to quiz the uninvited guest. "I'll be calling the police right now unless you can explain why I shouldn't."

Josey had no idea if the lightly built deacon might be a wolf in sheep's clothing, about to pounce at a moment's notice. He glanced beyond where the deacon held his ground; toward the doorway where the runaway priest had gone through.

Pulling out his identification was a stall, not for the

purpose of springing into action, but rather because he wasn't at all comfortable about making a fuss. Flipping open his leather pouch he reiterated the information that was printed on the ID, "Private Detective Cameron Josey. I'm here only to seek the priest's help, are you in a position to ask the reverend to come back? I promise you I am not a threat to you or anybody."

The deacon took a cell phone from his pocket and started to dial. "You could have been more diplomatic about it.

Josey dismissed the coment while asking, "Where's that doorway lead to?"

"Somewhere you can't go, now I suggest you leave, I'm calling the police."

Josey ignored the dubious warning because police arriving might be timely and a best course of action.

Unhindered and indeed unperturbed by the deacon's suggestion of diplomacy he took chase, entering the mystery door while hoping the priest wasn't just inside with something in his hands to clock him with.

His immediate reaction after entering was confusion, the man wasn't waiting with a heavy object to defend himself; he wasn't even in the room. He must have entered the narrow corridor that begun on the opposing wall. A glance over his shoulder confirmed the deacon had not followed.

Braving his way into the dimly lit windowless hall he eventually found himself in a maze of finely finished tunnels with ever diminishing light. Permanently sealed doors led out of it left and right—all locked bar one.

He took a moment to take it in; thinking *what the hell is this place?*

A noise coming from the open doorway takes him in that direction in time to see the man leaping from a tight stain glass window that he'd opened to escape.

When Josey reached the opening he looked out and saw it was a fair jump to the ground outside.

A real leap of faith from a Church Window he thought as he followed, landing on soft earth at the rim of the church's private graveyard, about ten feet below, the slowly decaying field of tombstones the only reminder of parishioners long gone.

Following a quick recovery from the decent jump he saw the man entering a crypt with the use of a key. He bolted toward it to head off the priests intention to prevent him from following.

While fumbling to lock the metal door the priest realised that he was out of time. The man chasing him was already upon the entrance to the crypt pushing from the other side, so he abandoned his efforts and ran between the four shelved coffins that graced the concrete walls, and then descended a flight of stairs into pitch darkness.

When Josey entered the crypt, he could only see what light from the open doorway allowed. It was enough to get a glimpse of where the priest must have gone, an opening that permitted an exit from the back of the crypt; the only other way out. On reaching it he saw there were stairs leading down to a tunnel that ended god knows where.

Suspecting it wouldn't be a dead end he entered using the torch on his cell, yet if the priest was still in the tunnel he wasn't within sight.

In the hope the passage wasn't a labyrinth he pushed on, pursuing the subtle sound of footsteps proceeding heedfully in complete darkness, and yet at a superior pace. Relying only on the dim penetration from his phone, it was a precaution Josey decided to emulate. The fellow was progressing well in territory familiar to him, his sound receding as he drew away – eventually, falling into weak sounds of a door opening then closing, and what appeared to be another door doing the same thing – then silence.

Not expecting any sort of ambush but ready if it happened, Josey advanced through the tunnel at a slow pace, the fading glow of his cell not helping. Eventually he came to a door, presumably the one he heard the man pass through, closed as expected but not locked. It opened toward him revealing a tiny room.

Left and right of him were small opaque windows that appeared capable of being slid open.

There was a collapsible seat that hinged from the middle of the doorway he'd passed through, and another closed door adjacent; dim light bleeding in around the rim of the jam. It wasn't that Josey didn't know what this room was at this point; it was just that he had never been inside a *confessional* before, and particularly not the cubical intended for the priest.

Did every confessor's room have a tunnel at its

back?

He switched off what was left of the glow from his cell and opened the door inwardly, revealing the inside of the church with its rows of timber pews; still empty except for the calm and collected priest. Beside him sat Carl with an expectant grin. Further back, standing in the aisle was the uncertain deacon. No sign of police meant no call had been made, and seeing Carl sitting happily with his new friends meant he had managed to appease all fears that Josey and he were there to inflict any sort of harm.

Josey left the dubious confessional and approached the relaxed group.

"We've been waiting for you," the out of breath priest advised. "Your partner here has explained what this is about, Detective. I'm sorry I took you on a wild goose chase. Forgive me but you didn't look much like the detective I saw on TV if you don't mind me saying."

Josey didn't mind, although he wasn't particularly in the mood for banter; it was picked up, particularly by Carl. He was well aware Josey didn't normally lack a sense of humour; Sophie's safety really had him worried; not enough to avoid getting something off his chest.

"Do all your churches have secret tunnels?"

The priest changed his demeanour, recognising it was a serious question. "These were built during the Second World War, somewhat closed off now thankfully. If they weren't you might well still be in there. My name's Father Madden, the man you've been looking for. Apologies for the way I behaved in that. You can call me *Robert* if you're uncomfortable with Father."

"*Father's* fine, we know you as *that* anyway."

"Yes, so Carl here tells me."

"And apology accepted; we know your heart's in the right place." Josey needed to get straight to the point. "I think you know we're not *your* enemy either."

"Nor we yours, when you didn't pull that pistol from under your jacket I kind of figured. Thankfully my deacon came to the same conclusion. Knowing where the tunnel leads to he came here and waited. That's when he was approached by your man."

Josey glanced toward the deacon standing in the aisle keeping his silence. "Are you okay," he asked out of respect for the ordeal he'd put him through.

"I'm fine, Detective, the young man volunteered, "no harm done."

The Deep concern on Madden's face shed doubt on this being precisely true. "Detective, I won't enter into how you found out Sophie is with us, and it concerns me that you did, but I sense there's something we can help you with."

"Your disquiet is well founded, father, and yes there is something you can do, to help Sophie; more than you already have.

Madden's stress intensified. "My God, you're scaring me?"

"It should, there's someone else who knows she's here, and he's extremely dangerous. I know the convent already has heavy security over there but they'll need more."

Madden was beyond alarmed. "I expect you mean to involve the police?"

"I do, but we need to be careful how we go about it, it could draw the wrong kind of attention."

"How do you mean?" Madden glanced at the deacon. "Terry, call Mother Superior—"

"By all means," Josey agreed, "Although it's best you leave this to me, let's just say I have a very trustworthy ally in the police force."

"Should we have doubts about the police in this?"

"Not to the point of avoiding their involvement."

Madden gave Josey an assurance. "You should know the deacon and I are capable of protecting *ourselves* if the guy should come here."

Josey didn't let the doubt he felt be seen. He also didn't make further mention of the power of persuasion that he had with Inspector Morris. He settled on saying, "Bolstering Sophie's safety is all that matters."

That importance came sooner than he ever expected; they were about to discover that the real danger lurked elsewhere at that very moment—

Josey's burn cell trilled in his pocket; it was Rebecca – "*Bec*, everything all right?"

Her breathless reply warned *things* were not. "I think he's *here*!" Her terror had speared from the phone like a living beast.

"*Who—?*"

"He's t'trying to get to us, he, he's already inside the Silo – where are you – please you need to come quick, we're all terrified! Call Morris, we need police."

Madden saw the terror in Josey's face and the concern written on his partner's. "Detective—?"

"Be on the alert here, father, right now my family are in immense danger—we have to go!"

He and Carl entered into a sprint toward the exit. "The good news is he's not *here*," Josey called back, "but he *will be* – warn everyone! *Robert* - do it now . . .!"

CHAPTER TWENTY
Silo Revisited

Carl – *Drive!*" he urgently begged while shakily fumbling to clip his seat belt, the beard and the wig had already been torn free and discarded

Josey's urgent appeal transcended that of Rebecca's, his panic encouraging Carl to plant the throttle—

The *closed* gate ahead zoomed toward them at a rate that bore a terrifying life of its own, placidly indifferent to the impending need to move from the path of the rapid vehicle, and as yet receiving no instruction to allow passage, something that could only occur in an agonisingly slow manner and only when a vehicle's presence is sensed waiting—

Way too close for comfort, locked wheels gouged into loose gravel, momentum scarcely providing the ability to stop in time, the nose of the bonnet ending within a hand of the languid barricade before halting.

They could still hear Rebecca screaming her desperate message of *haste*, yet powerless to obey.

A rich clunk-and-whir began the gate's annoyingly patient movement along its track, frustratingly sluggish in any event.

"We're on the move, sweetie," Josey lied into the phone.

Rebecca's frantic voice was drowning *his-own*.

"Rebecca listen to me, sweetheart, find out if Pat has a gun."

Carl considered the gap in the gate was now as wide as it needed to be; he wasn't waiting a second longer. Although the released thoroughfare was tight he hit the throttle in hope. Both sides of the bodywork dispatched sparks and paint, the mechanical gate shaking and shuddering noisily in protest at the offence.

Josey's mind was racing as fast as the abandonment of Carl's usually safe driving. It wasn't an issue; he was putting trust in his sidekick's skill. Nothing mattered more than getting to the Silo as quickly as humanly possible. Yet the hour-long drive ahead of them at this breakneck speed was never going to achieve a prompt arrival—

He connected with the police hotline and spat out the urgency with succinct clarity; then managed to bring Inspector Morris on-board without ado.

Morris was in fact totally mortified; his immediate concern was departmental red tape. Aware of the time it would take them to reach the Silo, something needed to be made happen – *and bloody fast*. "I'll get this done," his buoyant voice aired from the phone's P.A, but killing yourselves or someone else isn't going to help."

He was being a bit of a copper, though his warnings made them think hard about his point. Everyone staying alive was the ultimate goal and reckless driving didn't comfortably contribute to this scenario—

One hundred kilometres away at the embattled silo, the perpetrator was where he needed to be for the moment, not where it would have suited *him*, but rather where the terrified occupants at the top of the Silo wanted him. He wasn't going to let the unexpected challenge spoil his plan. It was a delay he didn't need though. From the base of the elevator shaft he stood staring up at the cables and metal rails for any sign of a means to climb. He'd already tried the button that commands the lifts descent for pickup, prevention clearly orchestrated by someone at the top, or perhaps designed to stop undesirables from operating it. *An Undesirable is not how he saw himself.*

Being unable to just shimmy up the greasy cables was infuriating; and there appeared to be no available alternatives. So he thought he'd give them all a decent scare. Perhaps with a bit of luck the floor on which his targets stood was incapable of stopping bullets.

Wouldn't that be fun?

He fantasized, visualising those in a western movie

being forced to dance, driven by the gunfighter stirring the dust at their feet.

From a small leather bag he'd placed on the floor he removed various metal components, deftly fashioning the perilous parts into his firearm of choice, finalising the fit by screwing on the silencer; all as calmly as a *tradie* might load an innocent nail gun.

He smiled to himself, enjoying the feel of the weapon in his hand. With muzzle aimed at the underside of the towering floor, he imagined *that firing a normal weapon inside a Silo would probably blow your goddamned eardrums out.* The silencer would take care of that—

He squeezed the trigger in rapid succession—

WHUMP! WHUMP! WHUMP!

As bland as these rapid departures sounded, the trio of terror hit the target with sharp deafening **blows**, resounding echoes forcing him to cover his ears and seek shelter from the ricocheting shells. Contrary to his wishes the bullets behaviour suggested the firm floor of the weird-arse accommodation must be solid concrete.

He thought about what to do next, he'd heard someone make the desperate call less than ten minutes ago; the distraught female voice had reverberated in the tubular structure like the inside of an empty barrel. So his fun-time was limited.

At least they must be shitting themselves up there, he thought.

He was right about that.

All conversation inside the recluse was now limited to whispering. Patrick knew the acoustics of the Silo was as effective as an audio-dish and figured it best not to broadcast their fear. He'd made this rule following Rebecca's desperate call for help.

From the very first moment they realised they had an intruder they'd remained huddled on the top floor; the area Patrick advised was the best place if the arsehole ever managed to find a way up, which he doubted was possible.

They weren't just facing the uncertainty of the crazed man below with the gun; they were living with the mystery of how he managed to find them.

It didn't take Einstein to figure out that this guy was connected to the attack on Detective Josey and maybe to the Bryant's missing daughter by association.

Beverley found herself exposed to questioning about Mitchell, in the sense that if anyone had answers it would be her.

Vanessa bluntly asked the question no one else wanted to, "Did my brother kill his own kid like he says?"

Beverley began trembling and shaking her head in protest, vehemently rejecting Van's suggestion. "No – why would you even say that to me. Do you not know your own brother?"

"Then why say he did – in a bloody courtroom."

Unable to string a sentence together in defence of her husband she buried her head in her hands.

"Bev sweetheart," her brusque questionnaire

instantly mellowed, "if you and Mitch know something the rest of us don't, you need to let on before someone gets killed, including the man I hired to help you guys."

The guilt trip Vanessa was moderately applying began to have a much more poignant effect, especially when she concluded sharply with, *"think about it, Bev."*

Mitchell's wife was taken aback by the unreasonable gruff command. Tears flowed and her voice shook as she resigned herself to having to break a desperate vow. "We *have* thought about it, Van. We haven't stopped thinking about it since all this started. You have to believe me, we saw no other way. We were forced to protect our Sophie, no matter what it took—"

Vanessa wondered what she'd meant by *we saw no other way.* "I can't work it out, but there's something you are not telling us, Beverley."

"What is it that you can't work out, Vanessa? I've practically spelt it out for you."

This revealing comment landed on Vanessa as briskly as a winter chill, albeit welcomed. "Oh my-god, she's alive isn't she?"

Maxine had kept silent, waiting to see if Vanessa's prodding amounted to anything. Now that it had, she spoke up. "She is, Van. Josey told Carl and me about it just this morning."

Surprised, Beverley had no idea the detective had figured it out. The tears that flowed then were a mix of relief and grief, her gentle nod confirming the news that ought to be celebrated, but something told her listeners a celebration was not to be. "Mitch and I made a promise to each other, not to ever *reveal that our Sophie is alive.* Doing so would inevitably lead to her secret location, something we went to great lengths to prevent. Where we had her taken to, it was the safest place on Earth – Now, she's no longer as safe as Mitch and I believed she'd be."

Maxine revealed a little more of what she knew, and some of what she didn't. "She's with the nun's in Margaret River," she explained for the benefit of Beck, Molly and Pat, then to Bev, "And the last I heard she's still safe there, do you know differently?"

Beverley continued to tremble terribly, ostensibly on the verge of a breakdown. "My Sophie is no safer than *we* are." Her voice shook. "You can thank your bloody meddling detective for that," she blurted with instant distaste over her own accusation.

Rebecca and Molly felt suddenly torn.

"He's the one who's allowed that arsehole down there to find us, and Sophie—," she sobbed, unable to finish the sentence.

Shocked by Beverley's bad opinion of Josey, not to mention her unfinished sentence in regard to Sophie's safety, Vanessa moved to console her distressed sister-in-law, now reduced to shivering feverishly in the foetal position—

Whump-Whump-Whump-Whump—!

The dull disturbing noise of bullets *pounding* against the bottom floor had abruptly recommenced. The noise and vibration reaching into their very bones raised real fear that the attacking shards may somehow penetrate all the way to the top floor, perhaps even weaken the concrete enough to send them all plummeting to the base of the Silo. They had no idea the power of the weapon the assailant was using, or what other more powerful armaments he night have.

Thankfully they were not able to witness the gunman enjoying the spectacle. The blitz had raised a shower of concrete dust, and he stood out in it as though it were Christmas Snow, catching the flakes excitedly.

But the clock was ticking, the call for help was out and the closest town with cops was no more than twenty minutes away. He thought to fire off a few more shots before leaving but something caught his eye.

The elevator car had a trapdoor centred in its floor. Below this was what looked like a coil of rope. It took him a while to decipher why it was there. Then it hit him, it was an emergency ladder, fastened into a parcel ready to be unravelled.

He chortled with consummation while depositing a couple of shots, confident the penetrating bullets would set it tumbling–*too easy*—but then, he sent *another volley* when this first attempt failed; still no joy. In his mind's eye he was hard at work figuring out the detail of what was holding it back. He thought he saw the answer; there was a broad leather strap that could well be what was keeping the ensemble intact, a fastener meant only for use from the top, and only once in a crisis.

This is a crisis alright he imagined, *but not the*

*kind that would send them reaching for an escape –
not right now with a crazed gunman waiting at the
bottom.*

He giggled over his twisted fantasy.

Again aiming, this time with both hands, he fired
three shots that hit the mark; he couldn't have been
happier with his accuracy; this was what he'd been
trained for during his three years in the British Army
as a sniper.

The weight of the coiled rope spun down like an
unravelling hall mat.

He thought, *these suckers won't stand a chance
once I get up there.*

The bottom rung came to rest and whipped before
settling exactly where he stood, inviting him to *step
aboard.*

He hesitated, checked his watch, he'd been at the
silo for fifteen minutes. Did he have enough time to
climb, *do his worst* and then climb back down to
escape?

Deciding he should be able to use the lift to make a
speedy escape, especially with no one left to stop
him, he started the climb in the belief he would be
gone by the time help arrived.

The first few rungs of the rope ladder revealed it
was not going to be easy-peasy, but the expected fun
was far too enticing to give up now. He tucked the
weapon inside his belt to free his hands—

Since the last shots heard, those trapped above
racked their brains to work out if they were in any
danger. Earlier it had been decided the gunman had
no way of getting up to where they were; that

comforting thought was about to change.

"Oh shit," Patrick breathed with alarm.

"*Oh shit* what?" Vanessa nervously volunteered on everyone's behalf.

Patrick was heading for the elevator shaft, *why they had no clue?*

Maxine followed briskly. "Stay put everyone." She warned the others. On reaching the lift doors in time to see Patrick was pressing the button to open them she asked in a panic, "Pat, what's wrong?"

"He's on the ladder," he answered as the doors slid apart and he entered.

Vanessa came to a dead stop, afraid to follow. *There's a fucking ladder* she was thinking in disbelief?

Patrick went onto his knees at the centre of the car. "Keep back, Van – I don't know how far up he is."

It was then that she noticed he was holding a solid glass vase that rested on the floor next to him; with his other hand he was sinking his fingers into slots positioned within a square section of the floor, which suggested it may be a trapdoor. Her guess was confirmed when Pat began tugging at it, swinging it open against some resistance to reach the vertical; continuing its rotation until it lay flat against the floor at his knees.

Vanessa dare not enter the lift for fear of being shot; she similarly feared for Patrick, she could only assume the gunman may now be able to see him, reasoning the ladder must be in line with the trapdoor opening. Her voice shook when she asked,

"Can you see anyone?"

With sudden abandonment he relinquished the heavy vase via the gap, graphically answering her question.

On the ladder the assailant saw it coming and swung to the side in avoidance, instinct drawing his eyes to witness the explosion of glass upon the vase's impact, just like his *head* if he were to fall. He turned back to the man peering down from the trapdoor, now clinging to a bucket while yelling an instruction to someone.

"Get me boiling water," Patrick was bellowing in the hope it would be clearly heard, enough to freak the bastard out.

It worked!

Clearly having second thoughts about getting scolded he glanced down the thirty feet of rope that was his only tenuous means of retreating, swaying indecisively.

When he looked back up the bucket had been taken, momentarily reappearing in the hands of a woman who plainly was struggling with the weight of its cargo – *the requisitioned boiling water*. The bucket hit the floor heavily as Maxine unburdened herself of its weight, spilling an amount over the rim of the trapdoor.

Any doubt the water was steaming hot vanished when the small cascade hit the intruder on the hand.

Max saw him flinch, pleased it had hurt.

She thought if Josey had been present he would have been able to tell them who this guy is, and that he was in fact the established perpetrator. It wasn't hard to imagine the climber was therefore the one who tried to kill Josey on the day of the accident.

From his point of view on the ladder, the sight of the steam lifting from the bucket was freaking him out, its contents not something he wanted hitting him at thirty feet from the ground, especially on such an unhinged platform.

When the blistering cascade hit him like the stinging bite of a thousand mosquitos, he'd already hinged his arms around the rungs so that he might cower beneath his hands and forearms. It burnt but wasn't as hot as it might have been closer to the source.

Completing his goal was still achievable, but he'd need his gun. He tugged at the weapon until it came free from his belt, and again began to climb, always looking up to make sure boiling-water-man wasn't there with some other plan to stop him, he had gone from view the moment after dropping the water. Four rungs later, the man reappeared in the frame of the trapdoor.

The climber struggled to take aim, hampered because the rope had a goddamned mind of its own. He pulled the trigger in the hope he'd get a lucky shot, instead heard the tell-tale stray bullet ricocheting somewhere well off the mark.

He had been so busy trying to master the ladder that he didn't at first notice what's happening above.

The man in the gap seemed busy, *what the hell's he doing,* the bastard wondered?

Then he began yelling as if answering the unheard question. "How are you at defying gravity, arsehole?" Patrick was cutting the rope.

"Fuck." This put paid to the assignment.

The now failed assassin began retreating as fast as he dare on the wavering emergency-escape staircase. He let the gun go in the hope it would land on the bag. It didn't.

He wasn't having a good day and still twenty feet left to be off the damn ladder.

As if things couldn't get worse he heard the sound of rotors. If this was the coppers he was close to being *toast.*

With little choice he exchanged the dangerously slow climb for a fast free-fall, controlling the speed with gloved hands grasped around the side ropes – spiriting him double time to the base of the ladder where his bag and dropped gun awaited collection.

With no time to applaud the skilful stunt he gathered his belongings and scurried from the Silo, exiting from beneath the breast of the massive magpie and out into the open. The chopper was closing as fast as his own departure, yet fortunately still out of sight.

He ran for the tree line behind which he had a waiting vehicle hidden from view. It felt like a lucky break, chiefly because he was finally melting into the cover of the forest.

In a too-close-for-comfort moment he was able to lay still and observe the police chopper skimming the treetops directly above his head. It set down on the open expanse in front of the Silo, flattening the long grass into a smooth silky green landing pad. The occupants ran beneath the blades before they'd ceased their dying spin; running with urgency to the entrance at the base of the silo, entering the open door that led to the initial empty space experienced by all first time visitors.

The bastard imagined the reunion that would follow the sickly hugging; their relief made him feel nauseous with anger. He checked for any damage to his gun from the fall and appeared genuinely upset at noticing the hardened paint had been scratched. He was bent on cussing but his preferred profanity was despairingly inadequate to describe his wild rage, instead he ground his teeth together until his jaw ached, accompanied by an elongated primeval growl—

He was dangerously pissed.

He slammed the weapon back into his bag and zipped it shut, not wishing to spend a moment longer looking at the disappointing damage.

Over at the silo, Josey had been first to enter, followed by Inspector Morris and then Carl. They all reacted to the desperate alert coming from above, and saw Patrick peering down from the open trapdoor. "He's only just left," he announced urgently, "you might catch him."

"Is everyone all right, Pat?"

"Everyone is fine for now but you'll need to be quick if you want this guy - *we heard a car!"*

News of his close proximity was enough of a trigger to send Josey back out to see if there was any sign of him. There were no tyre tracks.

The Inspector was on Josey's heels. They heard a car rev in the bush and then power away as though milling on a gravel track.

"Josey," Morris called, "we'll take the chopper."

The pilot saw them returning in a hurry and began winding up for take-off. The roaring machine jumped off the ground the moment they were seated. In less than ten seconds they were away from the open field and hovering over the canopy of trees that spread as far as the eye could see.

What they couldn't see was the car, or hear it above their own noise – the track too was mostly obliterated.

"You might not see dust," the pilot shouted above the roar, "We've had rain."

He was right; this gave the bastard the perfect cover. He could have been going in any direction.

"I'm not familiar with the area," he was forced to admit. "But there's a clearing ahead where he could come out, usually the fire trails do that for safety."

"Would it help to get ahead and check that out?" the inspector suggested.

"Not a good idea, Sir; he might hear us and double back."

"Would there be tracks that don't go to the clearing?" Josey asked.

"It's possible."

"Right," Morris responded, "let's go ahead and *make* him double back."

Josey didn't like it. "Forget that, Vin - I don't want him going anywhere near that Silo, my people are freaked out enough. Let's just stick to the plan, if we lose him we lose him."

Morris offered no argument; he was well aware

that Josey was under the pump given his family's previous trauma.

The pilot needed official confirmation though, "Sir?"

"Do as he says, Terry."

There was some truth in what Morris assumed Josey was concerned about. In essence, it was something else though. In a way the case was over, Josey had only ever been hired to find Sophie, and that was done with. Could he walk away knowing the menace is still out there? He knew what Rebecca would say, his daughter too. Both of them had come close to death at the grubby hands of a madman, which was enough.

The hour long search from the air ultimately failed, as predicted the perpetrator couldn't be located; he had essentially vanished.

Not satisfied with this disappointing outcome, upon return to the Silo Morris insisted on heading into the bush via the same road as the assailant. He had the help of the local police, four officers that had shown up in an off-road vehicle. Morris completely understood when Josey decided to stay and check on his family.

Standing in the open doorway leading into the silo, Josey was watching the descending elevator. Looking outside he caught a glimpse of Morris and the band of pursuers entering onto the forest track.

Hearing the lift reach the ground and the doors open he focused back on reuniting with his distressed family and friends.

Taking the slow ride to the top was nerve racking

in more ways than one, he knew he'd be greeted with fear and dismay, but was yet to discover they all had learnt that Sophie was alive.

The doors slid apart and he saw that everyone was present and accounted for. It was a *relief* to know they were all unharmed. Before he had a chance to exit and express his feelings to each and every one, his anxious girls rushed in to monopolise him with a gratifying hug.

"Thank-god," Rebecca exhaled with her face pressed against his chest, her voice trembling with liberation.

Finally permitted to leave the arms of his family to embrace the others, he saw the residual trauma that hung on their faces. Relief and freedom mixed with knife edge emotions were on the way to driving Josey's case into a volley of distain.

Vanessa took him aside when she had the chance. "You were right; Beverley let it out that little Sophie is alive."

Josey knew she might. "It was a matter of time."

"Everyone's aware *you* already know?"

"Let's join the others so I can explain."

With the group gathered he opened up about the Nuns taking Sophie into hiding to protect her. "The church was getting very concerned I might work out where she was. They didn't know me from Adam, other than what they'd seen on TV, so they took the extraordinary step of having one of their own follow me wherever I went."

Vanessa was puzzled. "The question remains, what were they protecting her from?" She gently focused in on Beverley, careful not to sound as though she was yet again laying blame. "Bev, is there anything you want to tell the detective?"

"She doesn't need to, I already know."

Everyone in the room had the same incredulous look on their face.

"To be more precise, I know the church didn't abduct Sophie, she willingly went with the priest who took her. That's why she was heard calling him *Father*, Father Madden."

Carl had a question. "Why the charade at the holiday camp, why not just take Sophie to the convent themselves, and why in the middle of the night?

Vanessa was first to speculate. "They knew they were being watched."

"From the start, but not by the church."

"By our mystery visitor," she again speculated. "Is he the one who attacked *you*, Cam?"

"He is, but before you ask, I haven't yet been able identify him," he lied.

Maxine knew Josey was revealing as much as he dare at this point.

Vanessa wasn't done. "But you do have an idea?"

He appeared to hedge, taking a few steps to the perimeter of the room before facing his enquirers. He had one answer for Vanessa and an entirely different answer for Beverley. For his wife Beck he didn't want to answer her at all and she recognised it. "You're finished with this," she snapped at her husband. "If you think I'm standing around while you get yourself killed you've got another bloody thing coming."

Josey stayed on her without the words to challenge. He could see she was exceedingly upset.

Mitchell's wife remained totally silent, but Vanessa was stewing, "Do I get a say in this, Detective?"

Rebecca's rage was far from quenched and she turned her rage on both Beverley and Vanessa, "You really don't, and as you can see, my husband has *all* the say, he always does. He'll do what he dam well pleases."

Van couldn't believe what was happening and she made her feelings clear. "Rebecca, you said you were okay with this. What's changed?"

"My mind," with this she sobbed while adding, "is that okay with you?" Her sarcasm failed to disguise her deep stress.

Molly understood more than anyone what her mother had gone through, and still was going through, they both had witnessed hell. "I know you, Dad; Mum's right; you can never walk away from an unfinished case. But this time Mum and I need you to make us a promise you'll leave this to the police. You've done enough." She had set pleading eyes on Vanessa in the desperate hope Josey's client wouldn't add further encouragement.

Josey really had no right to argue with his wife's resolve, or his daughter's point that he never walks away from a case, or leave things hanging in the air. And yet, he needed to find a compromise. "I have one more thing that cannot be left undone"

Rebecca scoffed, displaying her attitude.

"It's imperative that I talk with Mitchell, just one more time, and then I'm done."

Maxine felt she knew why her boss needed to talk with Mitchell; and that so too did Mitch's frazzled wife.

Patrick walked over to a cabinet and took out a bottle of vermouth, spinning round to present it to the others. "I think we could all do with a stiff drink."

No one argued. It wasn't exactly a party that followed but it was a well-deserved sedative.

With anxious nerves somewhat relaxed by the intake of vermouth and at the right moment, Josey began making a quite move to leave for the restroom, locking eyes with Carl as he went. After a covert scan of the busy attendees Carl followed, presumably to be away from observant eyes. As expected, when he entered the bathroom Josey was waiting.

Both men knew if Josey's girls saw them talking in private, it would be realised something untoward was brewing.

"This is between you and me," he told Carl in a low voice. "I did some checking on the Bryants history in the UK and unearthed some disturbing facts."

"Really, like what?"

"I might be clutching at straws but they left the UK in a big hurry."

"Do you see a clue in that?"

"I think they were running away."

"From what?"

"I'm not sure yet but this is where *you* come in. There's a flight out of Perth tonight and I need you on it; you're on your way to their home town to do a little digging."

"Have you already joined the dots on this?"

"Maybe; I'll know that when you come back with answers."

Carl was waiting for more – "That's it?"

Josey handed him an envelope taken from his coat pocket. "I've got a guy over there that'll help you navigate the location and what I need, part of which is finding Mitchell Bryant's parents; everything's in that envelope – keep it in your pocket. He glanced at the closed door to the bathroom and lowered his voice. I'm under the microscope here so you'll be on your own with this – sorry, mate."

"On that score, I thought you *had Beck* on side there for a while," Carl pointed out, "she's certainly changed her mind now though."

"Carl, I prefer not to put it that way, I want you to understand I respect how she feels."

"Sorry, Cam I—"

"Hey, I think you and I have been friends long enough not to bullshit each other. I'd be off the case for real if not for a certain little five-year-old in grave danger. Beck will come round when the time comes."

"Of course she will, she's a very strong lady that one of yours."

"No argument."

"What will you say about my leaving?"

"That you've gone back to Sydney on another

matter. The flight's via Sydney, so no lie. We better get back. Hang here so we're not seen together." Josey made it to the door before turning to make a final point. "Carl, as Vanessa alluded to, this is about our unwanted visitor. He's even more dangerous than what we saw here today, so you need to be very careful over there."

"Always . . . Am I being *me* on this?"

Josey clarified. "You'll be yourself; now with what to say to my girls, the *other matter* that's taking you to Sydney has nothing to do with me or the case, it's something *personal* that you need to do in your own time."

Carl had all he needed to execute his role but had one last question. "Are the girls likely to be concerned with you on your own – enough to start asking questions?"

"I'm off the case, *remember*." Josey swung the door open and left.

Turning to the small mirror on the wall behind him, Carl rubbed his five o'clock shadow, wondering if he would find the time to clean up before his scheduled departure. He wasn't altogether sure Rebecca's concern wouldn't amount to her insisting on knowing if everything was all right with him. Josey hadn't quite understood that was his point in relation to Beck's concerns.

CHAPTER TWENTY-ONE
DNA doesn't lie

When Inspector Morris returned from the search for the perpetrator he was forced to concede defeat. He ended up joining the others at the top of Patrick's Silo for a little *sedation* of his own.

Josey took him aside and told him what he'd missed while he was away, telling him only what he needed to know and nothing more. This powwow ended in Morris agreeing to involve the police at the convent; including the staking out of the Silo for Patrick's protection after the others were relocated. The convent would need protecting in such a way that none of the officers involved would be privy to the detail of the assignment.

This guy was on the loose and presented a certain amount of skill at finding people. The reason for that was yet to be unearthed. Josey thought that perhaps he would find the answer once he spoke to

Mitchell. He didn't try getting the answer from Beverly because of her state of mind and to avoid giving the inspector ideas of grilling Mitch himself, which he figured may end up destroying any chance of getting a positive result.

Those still in danger at the silo, Beverley, Molly, Maxine, Rebecca, Josey and Vanessa inclusive, were transported to a new safe-house on the outskirts of the business district with constant police surveillance; Patrick was offered the opportunity to join them but declined; not lightly mind you; no stranger to firearms, he had bid for a rifle and a licence to use it, the delivery immediately fast tracked by Inspector Morris. Josey's offer to cover the costs was flatly refused by their temporary landlord; he was happy to go *Solo at the Silo* – as he expressly put it.

To make sure the transport vehicle carrying the silo's exiting occupants wasn't followed; the police chopper tracked it from the air until they were safely tucked away in the new location; Beverley Bryant would later be relocated to the so-called lockup with her husband Mitch.

Josey respectfully capitalised on Inspector Morris's generosity, convincing him that Mitchell needed as much protection as anyone, feeling certain that whoever this assailant was, had just three main targets, Sophie, her mother and Mitch.

Protecting Mitch in a place riddled with well-armed police officers worked in well with his wife Beverley being allowed to stay there with him. It was already shown the gathering of everyone in the same place didn't assure the best outcome, at least now the silo evacuees would be placed at two different sites, three if you counted Patrick at the silo.

Morris was on Josey's side in relation to his 'must-do' meeting with Mitchell Bryant, and the detective too was given police protection, offering official transport for all of his travel. These arrangements were presented to Josey's worried wife so that she could feel more relaxed about her husband's overly responsible driven roll. In spite of everyone's belief the wanted man would be laying low in the light of heightened police presence, it was expected he would be lurking somewhere.

Prior to the meeting that was to be held seven days after the Silo incident, Josey and Rebecca spent that time in near isolation, giving them time to wind down the stress levels. They had their own room, as did the others that had been relocated from the silo with them. The detective and his wife made sensible use of their time, making love as many times as energy allowed.

Josey was able to leave Morris to organise the meeting with Mitchell; and for transportation to the facility where they were holding him. Bryant would have been freed immediately after what transpired at Patrick's place, if not for paperwork that needed to skirt the *get-out-of-gaol-card following* his confession. Now at least the Bryants were together under police guard.

On the day of the meeting with Mitch and his wife, Josey made a call to Morris requesting he be picked up an hour earlier than planned in order to make an excursion. The officer who drove him was none the wiser when Josey asked to visit the Australian DNA Testing Laboratory on their way to the lockup. He had been instructed not to ask questions, but couldn't help wondering why his special passenger was getting such preferential treatment from the police force. They entered the underground car park as planned and the armed officer accompanied Josey up to the offices.

The police officer stood in a hallway where he was able to keep eyes on the detective via a glass enclosed office, where he had met up with the contact that had been expecting him. He was seen handing what looked like a drinking cup to the man, who carefully took the object in a cloth as if its contents were sensitive in some way. He then left the office via a second door with the wrapped object and was gone for only a minute before returning empty handed.

They spoke, shook hands and Josey exited to where the officer stood waiting.

They left the DNA Lab and went straight to the location where Mitch and his wife were being held under Police guard.

The discovery that Mitchell had been the one who organised for his daughter to be held by the nuns at the convent in order to protect her, sat well with everyone who knew about it. For the Bryants it was liberating, and a massive load off their troubled minds. They were beginning to feel relatively safe for the first time since arriving in Margaret River;

especially now that they weren't exclusively holding onto their secret. But there was still a secret to be discovered, one that would sink the whole affair into a pit of horrors.

Mitch had been warned that the detective wouldn't be alone. The other guests were already in the room when Josey arrived. Apart from Mr and Mrs Bryant, those in attendance at Josey's request were Inspector Morris, Judge Schmidt, Vanessa Walters, and Carl Norris back from his secret mission to the UK, all having arrived aboard separate police vehicles.

Once all attendees were sat comfortably in a roughly arranged circle of chairs, Josey began to reveal what he had unearthed. He could have started by asking the Bryants if *there was anything they wanted to mention before he began*. He didn't do that because the last thing he wanted was to put Mitch and Beverley any further into the spotlight than they already were.

Josey checked his watch, raising queries about the importance of the time? He glanced at Mitch and Beverly nestled on chairs that had been wilfully set together, they appeared relaxed and ready to have their story aired, although he couldn't be certain how they would react to further disclosures soon to be exposed, in some ways the method by which the information was gained by Carl could be considered invasive. Most of those present were oblivious to what had been unearthed and Josey was aware this was the reason for their tranquil demeanours. As far as they knew this meeting was all about bringing Judge Schmidt up to speed with a view to fast-tracking Mitch's release. His release *was* part of it though.

With one thing and another of a trivial nature done and dusted, Josey got down to the real bones of the meeting.

"Judge, as you've been informed, Mr Bryant had a very good reason to claim under oath that he had killed his own daughter."

The Judge shuffled in his seat with a mite discomfort, "Yes I do understand, although it might have been more prudent to confide in the police before it even got to court. A lot of time and effort by a lot of eminent men and women has been wasted." He swept his hand to the side as though brushing away what he'd just said, and directed his next comment to Mr Bryant. "On the other hand, I think any parent in your shoes might have done the same thing."

Mitch and Beverly nodded their appreciation of his considerate understanding.

Schmidt shifted his gaze to Josey. "I commend you, Detective, for your efforts in working all this out. I have to say though; perhaps you too would have done well to consider involving the police earlier. Off the record, can you explain why you didn't?"

"Yes, Sir I can. You'll be aware that the clairvoyant Jillian Edison had promised us that Sophie was still alive. My investigation at Josephine Jackson's Holiday Park proved without a shadow of a doubt that Ms Edison was right.

"Father Madden, the man who took Sophie from

the park was in fact someone her parents had introduced her to a day or two earlier in Sydney. The witness who overheard Sophie calling her abductor 'Father' was my first clue that she was alive. I didn't connect the term to a priest at first." Josey took a breather to see if there were any questions.

The judge had one. "And how did you?"

Josey unnerved everyone by checking his watch again. He ignored their puzzled expressions and went on. "Once I knew that Sophie was alive and well, meaning Mitchell's confession was a bogus attempt to throw us off the scent, I had to rethink the whole thing. I decided he was protecting someone. That someone was his daughter as we now know; and to make sure she was safe he placed her with the nuns of Saint Joseph. As a Catholic his connection with the church made a whole lot of sense."

Being very familiar with listening to stories relayed by councillors who are often operating on hunches, the judge showed his appreciation of the detective with a profound lift of his grey bushy eyebrows. "Look I'm impressed. So, with what I already know, and what you have explained today," He locked eyes with Mitchell, "I don't see why Mr Bryant can't be released as soon as possible. Of course this is not a court room situation. That said; I am not without a good level of persuasion."

Not a single person in the room doubted that.

The Judge looked ready to leave as he shifted to the edge of his chair; stopped by the muffled *trill* of Josey's pocketed phone. Subtly surprised, the judge wondered why the detective's phone wasn't on silent, interested now to see what he did with it.

What he did was unashamedly take the call, holding up his hand to beseech that everyone stay put. "We all need to hear this," he stated dramatically while closing the call.

Heads turned from one to the other, questioning the untimely request. Even Josey's client Vanessa Walters was confused; no less the Judge, still perched on the edge of his seat. As expected, Josey noticed Mitchell and Beverley were no longer as relaxed as a moment ago; in fact this meeting was set to become the beginning of their understanding their vindication was just the tip of the iceberg.

The judge, no longer on the verge of making a move as earlier decided, warned, "This had better be good, Detective."

Josey met his gaze fearlessly. "*Good or bad* is how you look at it, Judge—"

Mitch cut Josey off angrily. "I need this to stop. What you're about to get into is no business of anyone's but ours. Give it up, Detective."

Judge Schmidt suddenly had a greater interest. "I think I'd like to hear what the detective has to say."

Vanessa had a crisp eye on Josey. "Is this something you haven't even told me?"

Josey paused on her face, she wasn't going to like the position this would put her in. He decided just to get on with what Carl had discovered in the UK, and what his own recent investigation had uncovered.

"I need to tell this from the beginning"

"This is not right!" Mitchell pleaded on top of his

voice. "Please stop"

"Mr Bryant," the judge interrupted with equal fury, "We are going to hear what the detective has to say whether you like it or not. To repeat, I know you're not in court right now, but I'm not someone you need to get offside."

"Shut up all of you!" Beverley cried out in protest.

Even Josey was taken aback by her untethered tone.

Her resigned gaze met her husband's pleadingly, wet by tears that could find no resistance. Her pale voice then shivered out her message. "Let's end this whole thing, sweetheart. I can't take another damned moment of it."

This was exactly what Josey was hoping for, it was about to make the story easier to tell, and perhaps from the horse's mouth rather than his own.

"Tell them," Bev expressly requested of her distraught husband.

His eyes went straight to his sister, carrying a message of painful truth. It frightened her to the core.

The words he spoke were full of sadness, not just for her, but also for him. "I'm really sorry, Sis. I should have told you."

She forced out a response. "Tell me *what*? – Is Sophie still all right?"

He knew to take command of his emotion quickly. "Oh no, it's not Sophie; your—"

His hesitation frightened her all the more. "Mitch, please just tell me."

He attempted to speak but was forced to cry into

his hands, uncontrollable grief. He tried again to deliver the words from a throat that had tightened against the passage of breath. The words that were finally spoken were unintelligible.

Beverly put her arms around him and drew him in as close as the sandwiched seats would allow, trying to calm his convulsions. Her beaten face turned gently to Josey and spoke softly without malice. "It's all right, Detective. Go ahead and tell your story."

Josey felt the restraint of emotion; he hesitated, giving himself the strength to form the words Mitchell Bryant could not.

Josey needed to get this story done with. He cleared his throat, yet still delivered the unavoidable huskiness of sentiment. "When I asked my associate Carl here, to conduct an investigation into Mitchell's family history in the UK, I had no more than a hunch to offer him, and the address of Mrs Carol Howes, Beverley's widowed mother. I'm going to let him tell you what she said."

Mitchell and Beverley squirmed uncomfortably in their seats, and yet at last resigned to the disclosure they had fought so hard to keep a secret.

Carl lifted from his chair to face his audience. His eyes fixed on the two subjects of the horrendous story, his expression full of apology. "Mitch and Bev, I know this must hurt to relive, please forgive me."

Beverley reinforced her declaration of disclosure with a tearful nod.

Carl took in the already stunned faces and began.

"As you've just heard, Detective Josey asked me to meet with Beverley's mother in the UK, to see what we could learn. If it wasn't for her Nephew, who became my chaperone over there, I may never have gotten past her front door.

"But I did, and gradually, she opened up about what happened. She began with the night police came to her door to say Beverley was in the hospital." . . .

CHAPTER TWENTY-TWO
The United Kingdom

Mrs Howes was more nervous than she'd ever been in her entire life; she was being ushered to her daughter's room by a uniformed police woman.

"Beverley is just up ahead," the officer advised the sobbing mother referring to the large closed door being guarded by an armed Policeman.

"This is Mrs Jean Howes," she advised the guard softly, "Sophie Bryant's mother." Upon which he opened the door to allow entry, choosing not to speak.

Jean hesitated; as yet she couldn't see the bed where Beverley lay badly injured following a callous beating.

The officer who had brought her this far gently touched her elbow to coax her forward.

A couple of pensive steps brought her daughter

into view; she was seemingly entwined in tubes that came from every part of her damaged body. Trembling, Jean remained at the doorway, afraid to look closer at the contemptible sight.

"Jean, it may help you both to talk, I'm told she comes in and out of sleep"

Beverley's mother gave the compassionate officer an appreciative glance ahead of braving further steps into the room. At the foot of the bed she could now see her daughter presently had her eyes closed. The rise and fall of her chest gave a measure of comfort, and a reminder that this could have been worse.

She edged quietly around the bed until she was within reaching distance of her daughter, and stood looking down at her black and blue face. A stitched fracture ran along the edge of the hairline, above which sat a bloodied bandage covering her entire skull. It looked as though all her hair may have been removed, possibly to clear the way for even more unseen sutures. Tracking across her blanketed body from neck to toe, Jean could only imagine what other horrific injuries lay beneath the sheets and blankets.

"Mrs Howes, will you be all right if I leave you?"

The voice was a reminder that the young officer was still in the room. She turned to meet her eyes, a pretty girl, possibly the same age as her Beverley. "I'll be fine, thank you for looking after me."

The girl gave her an empathetic smile and a light touch on the shoulder. Absolutely no problem, I hope Beverley gets well real soon."

Jean turned to her stricken daughter and wondered

if that was ever going to be possible. Then considering the lovely officer she reached to gently rest a palm against her arm. "Thank you so much."

The young woman's smile was sad this time; with a polite nod she left.

When Jean came back onto her daughter her eyes were open and startled.

"Mum?" she whispered sleepily.

Jean was quick to answer. "I'm here, sweetheart." Although her mother hadn't asked how she was feeling, Beverley recognised the agonising question behind her mother's eyes.

"I'll be all right, Mum," she slurred, "I don't want you worrying about me."

Both mother and daughter fell silent; taking each other in with a million silent enquiries. Jean finally broke the silence in a quiver, "Do the police know who did this?"

Beverley's eyes gently closed; perhaps it was to shut out the memory.

Her mother inhaled sharply; a moment later, unaware she had been holding her breath, she spoke with little air. "Darling, are you sleeping?"

Getting no response answered the question.

Jean stayed by her bedside for another hour before realising she needed to leave. She gave her daughter a gentle kiss on the forehead, the taste that settled on her lips made her suddenly cry. With a trembling palm she smoothed the thin film of perspiration that had gathered like soft dew on her daughter's forehead; clearly there were deeper issues to deal with. At the door she looked back and studied her motionless daughter, helplessly lying in a hospital bed all by herself.

She returned to her home by taxi, silently crying the whole way there. Usually her son-in-law was the go-to when in need of a lift somewhere, but right now he was working out of town, impossibly bad timing. He already had the bad news about the attack on his lovely wife Beverley while far away and unable to protect her. He instantly put the blame on himself when Jean rang him, just after receiving the news herself from the police.

In a way it was a blessing that Beverley was out of it, perhaps she might stay that way until Mitchell was back. That wouldn't be for another two hours. He had an hour quarter to drive on the freeway and another fifteen to reach the hospital, during which time they kept in touch over the phone to keep up to date on Beverley's condition, eventually meeting him at the hospital when he arrived. They stayed at Beverly's bedside for over two hours while she slept, but before leaving the hospital Mitchell relentlessly prowled the corridors searching for answers on his wife's prognosis; he found that the original doctors that treated her upon arrival were no longer on duty. He eventually managed to contact one of the doctors at home and got to talk with him.

"You don't need to worry too much, Mr Bryant, your wife's injuries are not life threatening."

Perhaps life changing he thought, then said, "Why is she sleeping so much?"

"Anyone would sleep with the drugs she's been given. Sleeping is a good thing - *believe me*. Look I suggest you go home and get some rest. You should have your wife back home in a couple of days."

And that's exactly what happened. Beverly left the hospital two days later as predicted. She was taken to her mother's place because she and Mitch's home was still a crime scene. Mitch though was given permission to enter to pick up clothing and toiletries.

With Bev mostly sleeping, Mitch incessantly quizzed her mother about what the police had said to her about the attacker.

"They were completely convinced it was random," Jean explained. "She was just in the wrong place at the wrong time they said."

"Being at home can hardly be called the *wrong place*."

"I hadn't thought of it like that, but your right. Anyway, she swears the attacker couldn't have seen her from the street because the windows and doors were all closed up. But in contrast the police claimed the front door must have been left unlocked because there was no forced entry."

"She never does that."

"We don't always do the things we tell ourselves we should."

"Does she remember leaving the door unlocked?"

"She's vague on it – understandable I guess."

Mitchell couldn't argue with that, given the injuries she'd suffered to her head.

Jean shrank away into her own thoughts for a moment before regaining her presence of mind. "Will you be able to stay until she recovers?"

"Yes I've taken leave for a couple of months."

"Good, I'll set up the spare room for you – unless you'd prefer to stay in her room."

"The spare room is fine; I just need to be here with her in every waking moment."

That's how the next two months were, it was like clockwork. Although Mitch was right there with her every time she was up and about, he refrained from asking her how much she remembered about the attack. Once or twice she had awoken out of a bad dream, which was uncommon for her. When she'd have one of these dreams he would just hold her until she calmed down.

Mitchell decided to have their GP come around to conduct a few tests on her each fortnight; it wasn't until towards the end of the two months that the doctor gave Mitchell a bit of a scare. Usually they would have a chat after the doctor had seen her, always in the living room in hushed tones. Jean was mandatorily included in those talks.

This particular day, the doctor had some sort of urgency that drove him to abandon the session and leave in a hurry. He had exited Beverley's bedroom after only five minutes with her; his sessions normally took at least half hour. "Sorry, Mitch this is urgent."

"Bev's all right though?" Mitch insisted on knowing.

The doctor patted his arm. "She's fine – *she's fine*," and then left before Mitchell could protest.

Jean was equally concerned with the doctor's sudden departure. Neither of them felt comfortable about it.

"Mitch, I think you should go in and talk to her." Jean advised.

He was hesitant to go into her room at first; he didn't quite know why he felt so nervous about it. He entered after a moment, feeling ready to talk, but was surprised to find she was already sleeping. For several minutes he stood by her bed watching her breathing. Her breaths were uneven, and although desperate to learn what the doctor had said, opted to leave-her-be.

As he walked from the room, he couldn't have known that behind his back, Beverley had cautiously opened her eyes, dampened by tears brought on by her evasion to talk with him.

On returning to the living room he was unable to disguise his depression, forcing Jean to cover her mouth in shock, never before having seen Mitchell so pale and pasty. "There's something really wrong with her isn't there."

He nodded weakly, but then dismissed the query with, "I have no idea *what's troubling her, Mum.* She's sleeping now, so . . ."

Over the next fortnight, Beverley chose to stay in her room most of the time, and occasionally in bed under the covers. Mitchell tried getting her to open up about how she was feeling, yet his efforts failed.

Her moods got so bad that he decided to place a call to her GP, convinced the doctor knew something. Aware the medico's hesitancy needed to be nipped in the bud, he laid it out straight for him,

"If you have something to tell me, tell me now. I know you're being tight-lipped about something."

The pause on the line and the answer that followed was absolute validation, "Talk to your wife, Mitch. I'm sorry but she made me promise I'd leave it to her to explain. She clearly didn't want you hearing it from someone else."

Completely dumbstruck, Mitch remained on the phone listening to the doctor's silence, only hanging up when he heard the line disconnect.

Jean had been standing back making her own sense of her son-in-law's expressions; it was clear to her that the news wasn't good, and on turning to notice Beverley now standing in the doorway to her bedroom, likely having witnessed Mitchell's call, looking completely terrified about it, things were about to get a whole lot more damning.

Mitch was unaware of Bev's presence until Jean drew his attention with, "Mitchell?"

He responded more to the alarm in her voice than the call of his name; the alarm on her face and the flick of her eyes prompted him to follow her gaze onto his wife; frozen in the doorway.

He was shocked by her appearance, his worst fear was materialising, indeed something was very badly wrong with her. When he spoke, his voice sounded weak, void of energy, "Sweetheart, what is it?"

She couldn't move let alone answer him; the fear in her husband's saddened eyes was far worse than what had brought her to this state of worry.

What would this do to him she thought; *and to her mother,* now trembling yet immobilised.

Mitchell walked slowly to his distraught wife, afraid of the answer *she* so far could not find the strength to utter.

It wasn't until Mitchell wrapped her in his arms that she was able to bury her face from sight, a place to release unwarranted guilt.

The muffled words she spoke vibrated into his soul, the outcome devastating – *for him, for her, and for her terrorised mother—*

"I'm pregnant," she sobbed against his heaving chest.

These frightful words would resinate for the rest of their lives. . . . For now, all she could do is imagine his breaking heart, pounding its frantic beat against her ear. She dare not look upon his tormented face, mercifully still hidden from her view.

Realising the child could not be his; Mitchell's mind spiralled down into the world of the only probable person that could be the father—

The *unplanned–unexpected–unwanted foetus*, growing each minute-by-minute in complete innocence, and yet an invader in his wife's reluctant body none the less, was at the cruel hand of *a vile and brutal rapist.*

For him, there was one very obvious redeeming factor;

Beverley had fought like hell.

CHAPTER TWENTY-THREE
A new life

The wailing cry of a new born is a Godsend. Little Sophie let herself be known spectacularly for a good ten minutes. The nurses and doctors in attendance didn't flinch. Her tired and torn mother was laden with many mixed emotions. She now had a wonderful baby girl. She already had a wonderful husband. A husband that had overcome his grief to stick by her; to continue loving her as he always had.

In spite of the horrific circumstances, Mitchell fought his demons throughout the pregnancy, managing to overcome hate and the desire for revenge.

The rapist hadn't been found. Beverley was unable to help. The frenzied attack was a blur. With her grace, the authorities had her hypnotised prior to giving birth, without success. It was thought she was blocking it out. She remembered the pain, even without the hypnotism. The man could have been anybody. The simple act of passing a man in the street raised an alarm in her, *what if this was him?* Beverley lived with this fear for many months, yet the introduction of Sophie into her life began to shift to the forefront of her mind. And the constant support of her wonderful husband, who seemed never to falter in his love and devotion for her, and the wonderful new life, a life that he had no part in creating. He gave dear innocent little Sophie, the same love he might his own flesh and blood.

The Bryant family never returned to the house where the attack took place, opting to live with Jean at her more than amply sized home.

Bliss is probably too strong a word to describe the life they were living over the next difficult three months, but whatever it was, it was about to come to a crushing end.

The night this new trauma raised its ugly head was like any other. Beverly and Mitchell would carry their sleeping baby to her cot, nestled in a small room dimly lit by the purple glow of a Donald Duck lamp. She was a wonderful sleeper, never once waking throughout the night. This circumstance had developed a confidence in her parents to do the same.

Jean's house had been transformed into a veritable fortress, fitted with deadlocks, security cameras and an alarm front and back. But glass is glass, and at three in the morning a darkly clad figure approached one of the rear windows and paused there to inspect the pros and cons of gaining entrance to the home.

From a small bag was drawn a rolled up sheet of adhesive plastic, the type intended to filter the sun. The sheet was adhered to the glass on the left and pressed firmly in place until it had rolled all the way to the right. A small sharp knife was used to trim off the excess left on the cardboard core, which went back into the bag.

One swift punch to the centre of the window frame dissected the glass barrier into multiple triangles of varying sizes, none of which fell to the floor inside. None of which made a sound. The only sound had been the dull thud from the intruder's gloved fist.

With deft hands the bonded glass was carefully pushed in at the top, clearing that edge of its wooden frame. The bottom edge remained where it was, allowing the architect of this procedure to gently fold the ensemble inwards to form a sandwich. Now able to hold the broken glass in one hand, the final task of entering was easy – and more importantly, deathly quiet.

The unwanted mosaic was left leaning against the wall, followed by a moment of adjustment to the lack of illumination in the room. The uninvited guest advanced in shoes that made no squeak, shuffle or clonk on the hard floor of the second room. The only room of any interest was marked by a soft purple glow that was bleeding into the hallway that ran past it.

The cause of the glow and its purpose could be seen from the open doorway. Black sandshoes trod a path to the perimeter of the cot where the baby slept blissfully unaware of the masked presence looming above her.

She slept on as gentle hands weightlessly raised her above the warmth of her mattress, and she floated through the open doorway into the hall, across the polished timber of a living room, to reach the carpeted floor that adjoins the now windowless wall; a getaway gap allowing escape.

Sophie Bryant saw none of this.

CHAPTER TWENTY-FOUR
A damning Confession

A Woman's bloodcurdling scream seeped like poison into Mitchell's rested mind, drawing him reluctantly to the disturbing sound. Pillow and bedding framed what he could see in the dark of the room, along with the void beside him.

From another room, the horrific screaming persisted with what sounded like a call for help – *from his wife?*

Sudden awareness of its meaning drove him to throw his coverings to the floor, ahead of lifting from the bed with the energy it takes to leap from the tracks of an approaching train.

The screams dragged him to the purple glow, to the open door of Sophie's room and the screams of her mother, now at decibel levels that were intolerable.

The room told an immediate and tragic story, his

wife's guttural message confirming the very worst of every possible outcome he could conjure.

Her expression when she turned to the sound of his arrival was at first shock, and then relief it wasn't the intruder returning. If it were, she would have wrenched her baby from the invader with the strength of a lion—

Her husband was suddenly there to hold her; to turn her away from the abandoned cot.

An urgent thought befell Mitchell, prompting him to lean and touch the bedding. The warmth of their baby girl lingered tantalisingly within the sheet, demanding there was still time and chance to rescue her. With her husband running from the room, Beverley quickly reached into the cot and felt the latent warmth that he had felt and understood.

Mitchell was near the front door grabbing hold of his car keys when she arrived at his heels, both of them eying the infiltrated window as they passed the sitting room.

In the shadowy gloom a car engine sparked into life just as they made it onto the front porch, its urgent departure painting an instant picture of their fragile child speeding away in the thieving vehicle, receding into the black cloak of night at the command of a complete stranger.

"I'm coming with you!" Beverly decreed when she realised Mitchell was bent on taking chase.

He didn't argue.

Their Beamer sat dispassionately in the driveway nose first, needing only the key in Mitchell's hand to leap into pursuit. From behind the wheel he made no endeavour to caution his wife to take hold, flinging her against the seat when the rubbers gained grip, squealing the length of the driveway to exit the open gate. Hitting the dip of the gutter and the bottoming of exerted suspensions raised a growling display of fireworks that lit up the street.

They didn't witness what was aroused in their wake, neighbours waking up to the outrageous noise and the wide open door to Jean's house. The rubber trace lines that went some way to explaining what had just taken place did nothing to explain the reason.

In four seconds and a block later they had reached a speed they thought unachievable on their usually quiet suburban street, yet made no gain on the abductor. Its red lights swung wildly in the dark fumes that shrouded all clarity. Mitchell's tears were as silent as his fear, driven to new depths by the wailing sounds coming from his terrified passenger, mother-and-wife in that order, oddly at the mercy of her husband's driving skills.

The distorted red lights blinked from view; taken into the cover of a new street the vehicle had chosen at the last minute to evade capture.

Mitchel reached and entered the same corner seconds later displaying far more recklessness than reliability, although luck and adrenalin had preserved their pursuit without losing traction or time.

The Beamer howled appreciatively as the warmth of its engine climbed to happier temperatures. The tyres too seemed happier to be gaining traction.

The lights again speared from view.

Still close to home and familiar with the streets, a Google image sprung into Mitchell's mind, an aerial view that showed the escaping driver's mistake.

Beverley scarcely had time to scream when her husband inexplicably jammed on the brakes to bring the Beamer adjacent to a street on their left, immediately powering into it.

"What're you doing?" Beverly forced herself to shout.

Mitchell's voice shook from stress and the vibration transmitted from the unevenness of the bitumen beneath the pounding wheels. "This crosses the road he's on!"

His matter of fact answer didn't excite Beverly in the least. "Mitchell slow down you'll kill us–*or Sophie if we cause a crash!*"

Red traffic lights ahead agreed with her logic because unseen the abductor's car with their daughter aboard was approaching the intersection at ridiculous speed.

The Beamer sensed the hidden danger and set off a collision alarm.

So too Mitchell's terrified wife.

"Bev, relax, Mitchell yelled, I've got this."

Almost at the light he proved his point, leaning on the skid-less brakes.

A margin of error brought the nose of the Beamer part way across the intersection, in line with the abductor's catapulting vehicle now set swaying and swerving in a dubious attempt to avoid an imminent collision. The challenge then became a desperate attempt to correct the out of control fishtail that threatened to go either way; to regain and stabilise the line of travel, or fail and flip into a deadly roll.

Mitch felt his wife's nails dig into his bare arm as she clamped onto him, hearts were in their mouths watching the troubled vehicle fighting desperately with the forces of nature, acutely aware that they may be about to unwittingly bring about Bev's dire warning; *causing the death of their precious innocent little girl.*

Relief overshadowed their fears when it became clear the abductor had managed to bring the car back in line, now speeding away from view.

"Don't even think about following," Beverley told him *chillingly.*

She soon learnt her words were falling on deaf ears. Again she was thrown back against the seat as Mitch brought their vehicle back up to speed while squealing left to continue the pursuit. Whatever risk he was taking before, now paled into insignificance with his new even risker driving taking hold of him. Beverley was fiercely yelling at him with no avail.

His new and empowered driving actually managed to close the gap on the receding vehicle, the driver now aware his pursuer wasn't to be underestimated.

Mitch's reinforced confidence evaporated instantly when handed an untimely joker in the deck, an exigent police patrol car with grander handling capabilities suddenly speared into the intersection, wheels in a smoky spin as if just beginning to speed up, unaware there was a second car involved till Mitchell's Beamer came out of nowhere, heavily on the brakes yet unable to avert T-boning them.

Fortunately the impact occurred well within the dying moments of the Beamer's momentum, preventing all outcomes other than a reshaping of the police car's pillion side door, and the indignant expression on the officer sitting just the other side of it.

This copper wasn't in the least bit impressed with the two startled faces staring at him from the offending vehicle. Without turning to the cop driving he offered up a theory. "These two idiots were racing, Sergeant."

Sergeant Myers secured his vehicle with the intention of getting out for a fact finding one-to-one with the offenders, saying as he alighted. "Let's hear their bollix excuses before banging heads shall we."

He rounded the scarred police vehicle pausing to note the damaged door that had been sandwiched. The front tyre was flat to the rim having been stabbed by the torn wheel arch, rendering the patrol car un-drivable. He let that be and stepped over to confront the occupants.

Unable to see the driver clearly through the tinted side window he wrapped on the glass.

The door clipped open smartly and he took a step back cautiously placing a hand on his holstered revolver.

The cop was taken aback when Mitch appeared with tears streaming down his face, a reaction considered way beyond reasonable.

Through the open door Meyers noticed the female passenger was similarly stressed out. Instinct told him that something out of the norm was going on. "Is everything all right with you folks?" He didn't mean due to the accident.

"We're actually not, *no*." Mitch's quick and quietly spoken blubbering-answer rang loud alarm bells.

"We're wasting time here," Beverly blurted.

The officer urgently drew attention to the street where the first car had gone at speed, "If there's a good reason you're in pursuit tell me now!"

"Our daughter is *in that car—she's been abducted!*"

Myers clutched at his radio to call it in, thinking, *a man in his late thirties suggests his daughter would be quite young*, "How old is she?" he asked the father and got the panicked answer from the woman, "She's a three month old baby," Beverley cried.

"Oh my-god," Meyers responded ahead of barking all the detail into his handset including their inability to take pursuit and the need for assistance.

Following a positive response Myers asked Mitchell, "Do you know who has your baby?"

"No! Mitch was becoming agitated; He broke into our house while we were sleeping and took her from the cot."

"Did you see this person or happen to get a licence plate?"

Beverley was heard saying something under her breath from within the Beamer, her words unintelligible.

Officer Meyers looked in at her and saw she was still bawling her eyes out. "Sorry, love, what was that?" he enquired without a hint of indifference.

"I said; you don't need to worry yourselves—"

It sounded to Officer Myers like she had more to say but had choked on whatever it was.

Vince had made his way out from the patrol car via the driver's door and reported, "The chopper's on the vehicle, Sir"

Myers held up his palm to still his partner, keeping his eyes on the driver with puzzled curiosity, noting that he also appeared confused over the obscure comment from his wife.

The terror Mitchell saw on his wife's face was laden with deep troubling unreadable thoughts – *was it guilt that he saw?* "Bev, you're scaring me?"

With cavernous regret she accepted that he had good reason to be scared. And now, on the verge of telling him the truth she felt convinced his heart would be torn in two.

Her morose gaze remained sad and transfixed on her bedraggled husband.

She knew in her soul, that this was about to destroy him; *if what he knew already hadn't done so.*

She thought, *knowing already that your wife's baby is the product of a rapist, would be enough to destroy any loving man.* Now, she was forced to tell her husband just who that rapist is.

Realising the baby couldn't have been his, easily apparent given he was away on an extended trip at the time it happened, would have been taken by many men with far less acceptance.

He never once chose to express *suspicion of an*

affair.

When police suggested they conduct a DNA test he was against it, telling them it was Beverley's choice. Had she taken that DNA test, what she now had to admit to, would have been done with already. As it was, *abduction* and a *car smash* had brought the disclosure to a severe head.

She hoped he wouldn't protest that the disclosure was far too late.

"I - know who has her," she stammered fearfully.

Every fear that she had conjured if he were to have learnt the truth, appeared on his face now. She couldn't tell if his trust in her fidelity would be shattered, or if he actually would accept or believe who the rapist is; *who the real father to Sophie is.*

"Sweetheart, Sophie is with her *Uncle Barry*."

The tears that came from her faithful husband at that moment were more than she could bear. Held captive in his staggered gaze, she sensed that surely her hidden heart must be splitting in two.

Meyers suddenly felt like a *fish out of water*, he was beginning to recognise that these people definitely had some serious issues they were dealing with.

His discomfort prompted him to take a couple of steps back to give the couple space; winking at his partner to do the same.

The two traffic control cops settled a few paces away, pensively watching the couple deal with whatever their grief was.

Officer Shields had no reason to expect his senior partner had an answer to what these people's problem was but asked anyway. "What's this about?"

Meyers scoffed, "Nothing to do with road rage I'll tell you that much."

The attending officers updated the call, labelling it *an unfortunate accident and possibly a questionable abduction*; in which no one was harmed, at least *not physically*. They concluded the abduction was a family issue that would eventually sort itself out.

Neither of them had ever before been faced with what happened next.

The driver's wife Beverley Bryant requested that *no mention of Uncle Barry* be put in their report. She seemed to be the only one of the two who understood what was really going on. The upset husband actually ended up walking several paces from the scene to be on his own. Again, it was realised that his state of mind had nothing to do with crashing into a police car. Or the damning evidence that speed was involved.

The wife, although suffering some sort of emotional disorder herself, was able to coherently convince the police that publically identifying the driver of the other car would not be helpful to anyone, particularly her husband and her baby girl.

Cops being cops, they had natural suspicions that the woman could be protecting the other driver out of duress. She managed to appease them by offering to *call* Barry her brother-in law, *the established abductor*; so that he could then speak with them. She omitted going into why he had taken their baby, or that he had raped her.

She kept the phone pressed to her ear to mask Barry's response, afraid he would nail the lid on his own coffin with his known rampant attitude. The officers could only standby and watch on, reading her expressions for signs of coercion. Neither of them felt completely comfortable with the arrangement so it was Myers that then asked Beverley to put the call on loudspeaker.

It was a desperate call in which her strength under the circumstances was being tested. "*Barry*, listen to me; I'm here with the police, all right."

Barry was unfazed when he responded, "Funny that, so am I."

"Yes I Know." She glanced at Meyers who hadn't quite heard Barry, but had certainly heard her repeat his answer.

Understanding that the so called abductor had been stopped in his tracks already, he presented her with a *good news* thumbs up.

Knowing that Sophie was now safely in the hands of police bolstered her to say, "The police want to talk to you, Barry. Don't say anything stupid. They just need to know you're not a man who would even think of harming his niece." Her evasiveness was essential in preventing the officers asking questions she had no intention of answering.

Meyers wanted to hurry this up, insisting he speak to the man right away. She handed over the phone to him, which he held behind his back to avoid the recipient hearing, speaking in a low voice to Beverley. "Can you at least tell me why your daughter's uncle took her by breaking into your house? Is it somehow the reason your husband is so upset?"

Her expression was a plea. "Officer Myers, it will destroy our family if I tell you. I beg that you trust me. Just talk to him, scare him if you must. If you decide you need to take it further I'll understand."

He flicked off the loudspeaker, freed an uncertain breath whilst considering the woman's unorthodox conditions, before then putting the phone to his ear and shifting into a seriously unyielding voice. "Barry, this is Sergeant Myers – like your sister-in-law says, convince me you mean your niece no harm, and make it sound as though it's not just because you're currently in police custody." He listened keenly in the hope the guy would say all the right things. It became apparent after a moment that whatever Barry said in his defence, had satisfied the copper, for now at least, but this English cop wasn't about to permit this questionable character to walk away Scott free. "You should know, Barry, we will be getting your personal details from Mrs Bryant, information that we may require in the future must be forthcoming upon requisition, and understand that you will be held accountable if you fail to do so in a manner that is completely truthful.

"Also understand that your very forgiving sister-in-law has asked for certain concessions, which are yet to be agreed to. These concessions are not in any way for *your* benefit. They are for the benefit of Mr and Mrs Bryant, and for the continued safety of their little girl.

"Although your family quarrel is not our concern

at the moment; that will change in an instant if you step out of line. You face extremely serious offences if we decide to prosecute, which is still on the cards. . . Are you getting me, Barry?"

The answer must have been affirmation because Meyers sharply handed the phone back to the sister-in-law with not so much as a goodbye to Uncle Barry.

"Thank you," she sniffled.

With some firm coaxing from the police, Mitchell was eventually encouraged to re-join them at the site of the altercation so that things could be finalised. They could hardly believe that the driver was still silently crying, and seemingly unable to speak when spoken to.

Officer Myers decided it was best talking to his wife. "My partner's been on the blower and has been told your baby will be held overnight at the Mercy for medical examinations. You can go there to see her if you'd like, but the advice is for you to go home for now; tomorrow you can go to the hospital and pick her up if all is well – how's that sound, love?"

"That sounds good," she confirmed softly.

Their attention then was taken by Mitchell rounding the Beamer to take up the passenger seat, indicating he had no interest in driving.

The police felt more than happy with this decision, albeit completely confused about everything else in relation to this very strange event.

His wife now the designated driver, Meyers asked her to start the engine to make sure it was still capable of running. It kicked over just fine.

Beverley and her husband were then allowed to leave following the taking of pictures of the vehicular contact and written details of the family.

Meyers didn't mention penalties for the damage to the immobile police car, but he knew a cost of some sort was inevitable. He figured whatever was going down inside this family circle was already more troublesome than the cost of a minor prang.

If he'd been a fly on the wall of the Beamer as Beverly and Mitchel took the short drive back to their home, his belief would have been proven.

They'd driven in complete silence the whole way, not mentioning the elephant in the room until they had slid into their driveway and turned off the engine.

In the dull peace of the cabin, Beverley's voice was anything but steady when she spoke. "Mitchell, talk to me."

Mitchell hadn't turned his head to look at his wife during the short trip. Now that he had, it was clear she carried a massive burden, as did he; it would take time and patience to get past this trauma, *if that was even possible* he thought.

Her blouse was sodden with tears, clearly brought on by regret – and, immense yet undeserving guilt.

Her only riposte to offer her husband was to lean across and burry her face against him. She felt the rock hard rebellion in his stance, a demeanour preventing him right now from consoling her with any sort of truthful warmth – he was incapable of embracing her as had been so easy for him.

They sat outside their empty house like this until the creeping dawn came to paint away the shadows, and to abolish the fear to face the secret. It was hard for them to see that there was a glimmer of hope in the new life that had been created; their biggest challenge would be to accept Sophie's innocence, to accept that she would need *love*.

CHAPTER TWENTY-FIVE
The Shooter

Vanessa looked absolutely livid over having been left out of the family loop; she couldn't move her eyes from her reticent brother. In addition to sticking her neck out hiring a detective when all along Mitch hadn't wanted Sophie found, now she had to live with not being told her niece was the product of her uncle, a rapist no less. Eventually, in hindsight she would believe that maybe he did try to discourage her from using the detective.

Now that the secret was out, Mitchell and Beverley appeared relieved, they had less to deal with.

Emotionally distanced from the Bryant family ordeal, Judge Schmidt made an educated assumption about the rapist. He needed to be super careful about how he put it in front of Mr and Mrs Bryant. He kept his eyes on Carl as he asked the question. "Are you saying this offender in the UK, is in fact the same man that is right now terrorising the family here in Australia?"

Aware the answer was multifaceted, Carl handed the task back to Josey, "Cam?"

Josey was dreading what he must now divulge. The depth of Barry Bryant's evil tendencies bent to depths of depravity that defied imagination. Yes, he had raped his brother's wife and given her innocent little Sophie. In itself this was a despicable crime. That this was a deliberate act to produce a child, using his sister-in-law as a surrogate, is so devious that not many people would ever consider it a process of human thought. But this was no fantasy. Barry Bryant had done this many times before, although before taking Beverley it had only been strangers. Seduction was never part of his plan. He selected women to rape based on their beauty, which together with his own handsome features was guaranteed to produce attractive children.

A chill ran down Josey's spine when he thought about it. The way that this all came to him was largely chance, although if he hadn't decided to do the research on 'rape in the United Kingdom' he would never have come across the appalling articles that he found on the dark web.

Several victims of rape gave accounts of the gorgeous looking man that had forced himself on them when in fact he needed only to ask – he was that stunning to the eye. The description these women gave was a mirror image of Barry Bryant. One woman even claimed the rapist had given her is first name, *Barry*.

Another talented lady sketched him from memory, another mirror image.

These rather deliberately planned trysts only provided a foundation for what was really going on – it was still happening – right now, right here in Australia.

Most of what Josey had learnt about Barry Bryant would stay locked inside his head forever. But the bottom line needed to be said, purely because it was a warning, not just to all those in the room, but to those women yet to fall in the path of Barry Bryant.

"Mitchell, Beverley," Josey hedged, "I wish I didn't have to tell you this; my apologies in advance. What Barry did to you guys is brutal and immoral. But it gets worse. When he took Sophie, you, and perhaps all of us, could be forgiven for thinking he wanted her because she is his daughter. We were wrong, Barry had other ideas," Sadly, he settled on Beverley. "Barry is not only a rapist of the worst kind, Bev; if you hadn't stopped him when you did, Sophie would never have been seen again. He was planning to leave the UK that very day and to take her with him.

"The worst part is; he wasn't taking her for himself; there were people in South Africa waiting for her arrival. These people had paid handsome amounts of money to possess their own little girl.

"For Barry, this was all about money. He'd already abducted a dozen other babies, three of which are his."

As if the horrific experience of being raped wasn't soul destroying enough for the Bryant's, this chilling news was beyond their capability to wrap their heads around. The connotations alone were gut-wrenching.

Mitchell found the words to tag his brother for what he really is. "A fucking Trafficker – Jesus, I hope he rots in hell."

Beverley in particular felt sick about the whole affair. She despaired over what could have happened if Barry had managed to get Sophie out of the UK. A usually protective mother, her mind cast back to the night he cruelly snatched their sleeping baby from the cot in the middle of the night; and then the way in which she had involuntarily contributed; forced to aid his disgusting plan.

Josey glanced over at Judge Schmidt and wondered what he might be thinking.

Schmidt caught his eye and answered as if he'd read his mind. "I think I'd be right in saying Barry Bryant is a clear and ongoing threat to his niece?"

"You don't know the half of it, Judge. He's a bigger threat than anyone would guess." He looked over at Mitchell. "You'd be aware Barry has spent time in the army, right?"

"He did, I'm not sure what he did though."

"He was a sniper."

Everyone felt the cold chill of terror.

Vanessa raised an obvious point. "Oh my God, is Sophie safe at the convent?"

Josey glanced at Inspector Morris.

Morris explained. "Extra precautions have been put in place; we've got a hundred extra personnel over from Adelaide and another fifty from neighbouring towns to bolster our available forces. The Convent and church are locked down as tight as a drum."

Beverley showed her anger. "Does anybody know where my goddamned brother-in-law is right now?"

Josey took the question. "We have a few ideas but that doesn't mean we can relax. Which means," He looked at Mitch, "You and Bev can't stay here. And none of us go anywhere without police protection."

"I second that, Morris added. "It's been arranged.

Josey wrapped up the meeting with, "The police vehicle's that brought you here are waiting to transport all of us to a new location. Don't get tempted to travel any other way." He scanned the faces. "All good?"

Good probably wasn't the right word but it set in motion a shuffle into action, seats scrapping noisily as the gathering stood to place chairs back against the walls. There wasn't the usual chatter one expects at the end of a meeting, only the soft patter of exiting feet.

The Vanguard building where Mitchell and Beverley had been harboured by police for the past several weeks had a small courtyard surrounded by a high stone wall. Three police transport vehicles were parked randomly, waiting for the designated guests. Their arrival prompted the drivers who had been milling about in the cold to move away from the huddles they'd instigated, dutifully approaching their unmarked sedans.

It was around four on an afternoon that had the

chill of a lingering winter. A dark grey shield of cloud banned any chance of warmth from an invisible sun. The ladies wore their long coats high around their scarfed necks in order to trap the warmth gained within the walls of the room they had just vacated, anxious to step into the vehicular shell where they would again be protected from an uninvited freshly introduced icy breeze. And yet with their concerns about the weather, what they *really* needed shelter from lay ominously hidden from sight nearby.

Beverly had her arm laced around Mitchell's elbow as they approached their readied transport.

"Wait," she requested of her husband.

He paused and noted she had eyes on her sister-in-law.

"I just want a word with Van," she indicated.

Still arm in arm they took the few steps that brought them to her side, pausing her at the open door to her intended transport.

Beverly lightly placed a hand on Van's arm. "I'm so sorry we couldn't tell you about Barry, we didn't believe he would find us here—"

The persisting chill gusted suddenly, pushing Vanessa to one side, her movement synchronising with the peculiar punctuality and unexpected sight of blood jetting from her cheek to splatter onto the faces of those closest—

—At first, Van's Brother and sister-in-law thought *she had been hit by some projectile blown in the wind?*

Vanessa lifted her hand to the sting, bringing it

away to see the blood on her fingers.

Josey and Morris instinctively abandoned their planed entry to their police vehicle, already aware this may be the fearful work of Barry Bryant, the trained sniper.

They were just steps away from Vanessa when she jerked backward as if pushed by another gust.

Mitchel caught her fall and was easing her to the cold black pavement of the courtyard as Josey arrived, his eyes distractedly fixed on the only location from where the sniper could have fired, the top floor of a five story building that sat on the opposite side of the road to the stone arch of the courtyard.

A puff of smoke from one of the windows actioned Josey to tackle everyone off their feet, thereby avoiding the bullet that sank into the metal body of the police car above their heads.

Josey was lifting from the disarray of those that had collapsed under his weight when he heard Morris calling his troops to order, those heavily armed officers presently already on the street just outside the courtyard ingress. His directive being to forcefully storm the apartment block where the shooter was.

Some armed officers who had been stationed within the courtyard began to respond to the order to mobilise but were stopped by Morris, "You lot stay put we need you here."

Josey had forced his fingers into the penetration hole made in Vanessa's coat to prize the material apart, to inspect the extent of the wound. He could hear Morris concluding his urgent call for an ambulance, and then to Josey, "How is she?"

Ripping through the underclothing Josey reached the bra strap. The bullet had almost severed it. Below the strap blood was pumping. "You'd better tell them to be quick," he told Morris, and then to Mitchell, "Press down as hard as you can, mate, it'll keep her alive."

"Wait? Mitch shouted when the detective stood and spirited away. His plea had fallen on deaf ears.

Morris caught Josey out the corner of his eye running onto the street with revolver in hand.

Terrified for his own family Josey was ready to kill this guy if he had to.

Mitchell—more concerned with his seriously injured sister—couldn't have cared less about the safety of his brother at that moment, a sentiment that was about to be bolstered by his wife.

"This was meant for *me*," Beverley sobbed to her husband.

Mitchell didn't verbally agree, yet he knew from what Josey had learnt about *mad Barry*, the bastard was now out to remove the only other ownership of his ill earned offspring.

Across the road police were entering the apartment block with guns drawn. Tucked amongst the throng Josey was able to use them as cover against being sighted and blocked from gaining access to the *police only* site. The first thing he noted in the foyer was the group of officers trying to summon the elevator. Others were striding up the stairs.

Would Barry consider trapping himself on the top

floor like this, seven floors up with no way out?

Josey went outside onto a balcony that adjoined a small set of stairs that led to a narrow laneway. From there he was able to see just how close the Apartments were to each other. The distance across to the old warehouse next-door was about a metre and a half. From the street he'd noticed the old building appeared to have been abandoned. A leap from one to the other looked possible, although not one Josey would consider unless there was absolutely no other way of escaping. *Would Barry?*

It was perfect timing that allowed him to spot a solid plank drop into view and bridge the void between the top floors of the buildings. Seconds later he witnessed Barry with sniper rifle and whatever else he had in a bag slung over his shoulder, gingerly negotiating the plank to reach the roof of the warehouse, the cop-free abandoned building.

Sure that he hadn't been seen by Barry making his daring escape, Josey was compelled to thwart the arsehole's plan. He exited to the street and jogged to the front of the adjacent building. Getting in to the alternate escape route proved to be not so easy, the entrance was chained and padlocked. Unnoticed by the gaggle of officers milling about, Josey moved in to inspect the locks. It would have needed bolt cutters except for the fact the chains had already been severed, a task that Barry must have carried out in the dark of night.

The chains slid from the padlocks easily and Josey was able to gain entry, careful not to be seen doing it. He didn't want hapless cops attempting to stop him or attempting to take over. This was a matter of surprising Barry.

The lobby had one set of stairs and one elevator which possibly wasn't working. Even if it were operational it wouldn't be possible to come down while someone was going up, at present neither was happening. the brass hand of a half-circle clock, intended to indicate the location of the elevator car, sat motionless.

Summoning the car would alert Barry to someone having found their way into the abandoned building, so Josey's best option was the stairs. At each floor he would check if the little hand on each of the clocks was static. If it wasn't he would continue upward on the stairs. If the hand on the clock indicated the elevator *was* descending, there was only one place it would be taking Barry – the ground floor, by which time he would have bagged his rifle and been able to exit.

On reaching the third floor Josey kept his eye on the level indicator until it wiped from view as he ascended. When he caught site of the clock on level four he saw the elevator hadn't moved from the top floor. The next two levels showed the elevator had not moved.

Josey hesitated when reaching the top of the stairs on level six, *has Barry already discovered the elevator is out of commission? Or perhaps he knows I'm here, perhaps he saw me in the laneway, or even after that on the street as I entered.*

The burning question of why was Barry not taking

advantage of the lift hung over the operation like a stifling blanket.

This raised another question; *there might be a way to reach a third building?*

No, the only way off this roof was to reach one of two streets. Where could he be lying in wait then, each flight of stairs came into its own lobby without any doors. There was nowhere to hide.

As he pondered this, the sixth floor clock began to descend from the seventh. He thought to quickly dart to the elevator and summon it to stop but he opted for a safer solution, following via the stairs until the elevator came to a stop on the ground floor. The elevator was slow and easy to keep up with, *what could possibly go wrong?*

The elevator reached the ground floor at the same time as Josey reached the final staircase. He paced across with arms and pistol fully extended and ready to shoot, expecting the shooter's assault rifle would be bagged and that all he'd have is a pistol, *at best—*

The door slid aside revealing *the lift was empty.*

He had sent the lift to the ground floor on its own. Perhaps by jumping free after pressing the ground floor button.

One thing was doubtless, the perpetrator was either on the top floor or still on the roof.

Again Josey took the stairs and kept his eyes on the level indicator to make sure the lift never left the ground floor. If it did begin to ascend he had a head start on it. But it also meant that Barry may have used the wasted time to descend the stairs. He paused on the fourth floor and considered that all the areas near the elevator were identical. Each had a corridor laden with closed doors stretching to one of the external walls of the block.

Already supposing Barry couldn't have made it to the ground without being seen, his best option now was to return there and wait for Barry to exit via the only way out, the entrance.

He started out when one of the doors in the corridor momentarily parted then quickly closed. It was the fifth door of about a dozen. Josey stepped quickly and silently across the torn and battered carpet-run to reach the room and give the door a powerful kick, sending it into an unceremonious arch till it hit the inside wall and rebounded. Without entering Josey palmed the door back against the wall to check it sat flush. The room was small with nowhere to hide.

Empty rooms don't open and close on their lonesome, which meant Barry had to be in one of two rooms that branched off the area; one was closed and had a *gent's symbol* on display, the other was wide open.

To reach the gents bathroom he had to pass the open doorway. Traversing the dimly lit space he was able to make out some sort of oily and discarded machinery, none of which were high or solid enough to crouch behind. Whatever else might be in the room was not visible.

He set eyes on the gent's toilet, the only place left where Barry could be. He crouched beside the closed door with his back to the wall, reached up and gently tried the handle. It turned freely allowing the ingress to push forward an inch or two.

This having invited no gunshots from inside, he spun on his knees in one swift movement and flung the door open, lunging forward to land face down with forearms propped on elbows, ready to shoot from the floor.

He could see the whole of the *empty cubical-less bathroom now*, which amounted to only one other possibility – *he'd somehow missed seeing his adversary in this grubby old machine room that had nowhere to hide?*

Feeling tricked, and fully intending to spin and deal with his mistake before it was too late, he was halted from doing so by Barry's miraculous arrival, and the pressure of a pistol barrel against the back of his skull.

He thought, *having a gun in line with your brain is always a clincher.*

He was right; this was a *dead-set game changer*, annexed with a dire warning. "Get up on your knees, shithead, don't turn round. Leave the gun where it is and back away real slow."

Josey faltered, but considering he would have been dead already if Barry had nothing further to say, the delay in responding was no more than a second.

At a good couple of metres from the discarded pistol, having walked backward on his knees, he stopped and waited for the next instruction.

"Well done, Detective, you've done this before. You'll do it again if you behave yourself."

Reflecting the callousness exhibited so far, Josey

had no reason to believe Barry wouldn't kill him if angered.

"Turn around and get a good look at me."

This could readily be death's door waiting to suddenly swing open, reliant on the captor's wishes once his rival turned.

For Josey, with his wife and daughter waiting for his safe return, and now finding himself in imminent danger, meant there was no time like the present to think about the business of dying, *would life simply cease to exist* he wondered, *totally without explanation or reprieve – and with no concern for those left to grieve?*

This was not the time to find out.

He did as he was told and turned on his knees, knowing full well who he was about to face. "Nice to see you again, *Barry*, at least now I've got a name."

"I could have given it to you the last time we met, all you had to do was ask."

"Remiss of me I know, but I was sort of busy trying to free myself from a mangled car."

Barry laughed, heartily amused.

The laugh and the delay in pulling the trigger told Josey Barry was playing with him.

"Is this *pluck* of yours suggesting you've no fear of dying, or is it perhaps, that you already understand I have no interest in killing you right now?

"And why would that be, Baz?"

Barry's smile reeked of complacency. "The answer to that can wait." He waved the pistol toward the ceiling with a mite of impatience. "Stand up real slow with hands behind your head."

Josey was done tempting fate; there was no way in the circumstance of stopping Barry from playing this his way, but had to admit he had no idea what was to happen next.

"I can see you're wondering how I managed to hide in here. You're about to find out; turn round and take a few paces toward the back wall, get moving I haven't got all day!"

Josey then saw a thick metal ring that lay flat within an indent in the timber floor, he was obviously being directed to some sort of storage area beneath, *Barry's hiding place.*

"I think you get the gist, you know what to do so do it."

Josey had to accept that Barry's plan to effectively confine him seemed impossible to prevent. He took the few steps needed to reach the rim of the dubious hatch.

"Stand back, dumb-arse; I don't want you kicking me in the face."

With Josey set at a safe distance the bastard slung the ingress open. "You can take a nap or something while you're stuck down there. Don't worry; I'll let someone know you're here. Like I said, you and I still have stuff to deal with."

Josey approached the rim of the opening in the floor and peered down into what was a dense black hole, into which a crude timber ladder melted from view.

"Down you go then."

Josey backed onto the ladder. Taking the first

cautious steps seemed wrong on so many levels; in spite of assurances, it felt as though he was being forced to enter his own grave.

"One thing, *ol' chum*, leave your cell, I don't want you buzzing the cops before I've a chance to get away."

Josey abided, somehow the dank room seemed better than waiting for Barry to change his mind and shoot.

"Go on then – off you go."

Barry watched him fade from view as he descended, then lent and grabbed the top of the ladder, giving it a solid pull. It didn't budge.

"You off the ladder there, arsehole?"

"No I thought I'd ride up with it," he hollowly joked.

"That's funny." He pointed his pistol into the gaping hole. "Get off the fucking ladder, I've got places to be, people to kill." He pulled at the ladder and this time it came free.

With Josey safely secured in the high-rise dungeon, Barry slammed the lid closed and made a hasty retreat. Below, his sick laugh permeated the black space where Josey was to remain confined – *or was he?*

As it turned out, it took only three minutes for Josey to find a possible means of escape. An old metal cabinet had swum into view in the glow of his lighter, a trinket he always carried for moments like this. He guessed Barry hadn't come all the way down to see the cabinet, satisfied to wait in hiding at the top of the ladder.

The room was less than seven feet from floor to ceiling and the grease laden cupboard was a good six feet in height. Climbing its shelves brought him to the base of the trapdoor which when pushed managed to open with little resistance.

Another thirty seconds saw him retrieve his cell phone, clearly deliberately left behind, and then his pistol from the bathroom. At the elevator he saw the lift had already reached the ground floor. He bolted to the stairs and leapfrogged down the four flights to the exit, stabbing onto the pavement busied by uniformed police running around with their heads off.

No sign of Barry was no surprise.

"Josey!"

He turned to the summoning voice of the Inspector. Morris had seen him exit the vacant warehouse. "Was he in there?"

"He *was*," he answered breathlessly.

"Are you okay?"

"I will be when we get this guy."

He'd no sooner said it when an officer ran up with news for Morris. "Inspector, we've got him."

"Where?"

"Around the corner, Sir."

They ran to where the officer had indicated.

Rounding into the adjacent street they saw him lying in a pool of blood; to their silent discontent still alive. He was conscious and pissed off. He'd taken a coppers bullet to his thigh after refusing to halt when told to and for returning fire on the officer.

Another copper nearby had the black bag that housed the sniper rifle over his shoulder and the *perp's* pistol in his hand.

Barry snapped out of feeling sorry-for-himself and grinned - *cheesy like*. Eying the detective he promised, "Don't get excited, Detective, this doesn't mean you and I are done."

"You look done to me," Josey quipped before striding away without interest in his reaction. Back to Morris he warned. "Watch him inspector, this guy is slipperier than a slug. I'll come back after I check on Mitch's sister."

Morris looked at bloodied Barry with distain and barked an order to the officers. "Get this garbage off the street."

When Josey made it to the Vanguard to check on his family and friends the ambulance had arrived. They already had Vanessa on a stretcher; Mitchell walking alongside clasping her hand. He saw Josey and asked,

"Did they get him?"

"They did, he's in custody as we speak."

Vanessa released an instinctive tear, "So my brother's not dead?"

Josey had to instantly weigh up her feelings about it; was she upset or perhaps pleased? He knew better than anyone that death is such a final judgement, and after all Barry is her flesh and blood, so he settled for, "I can tell you he won't be shooting anyone else today."

What she actually felt was her own

disappointment, distress over her own shortcomings in scolding Mitchell and Beverley for keeping things from her. She couldn't help the release of a tear in remembering she'd missed the point they had been protecting her from the horrific depth of the secret they were keeping. "I'm really sorry, Mitch. Please forgive me."

"Hey, it's over, Sis," he breathed with relief.

She shared a saddened smile with family and the detective as she slipped away into the protection of the ambulance. The ambos shut the doors and one of them focussed a moment on Mitchell, "She'll be fine," he told him with warm assuredness.

As the wailing siren receded, Mitch had words to say about his brother. "I actually thought you guys would have killed him."

Josey explained, "Mitch, *no offence*, but between us, he can thank his lucky stars it was the cops that got him and not *me*."

"Or me; given the chance." He glanced at the gritty detective favourably, "And, *no offence taken*."

CHAPTER TWENTY-SIX
A Nightmare Revisited

Barry Bryant was very disappointed on hearing the arrival of the ambulance siren, perhaps celebrating the saving of his first victim, albeit not the one he was aiming at, thanks to an untimely gust of wind. If his sister was still alive, *she could wait for now* he thought. His plans for the future would also have to wait until the furrow in his thigh was healed; he vowed that wouldn't be happening in any goddamned gaol house hospital.

First he needed to escape from the idiots prancing about like heroes. Not one of these champions appeared to recognise any sort of threat right now, but he would have to work fast if he was to change their minds. The pigs weren't exactly completely stupid though; six of them already had their weapons trained.

He needed a distraction and it was already

arriving, two ambulance officers making their way across from their cool little hospital on wheels to attend to his pissy wound.

With multiple police semi circled around him, he could tell the medicos were feeling perfectly safe to approach. Macho-man went onto his knees while the princess kept her distance. With scissors from his little black bag he got straight to cutting through the trouser leg.

A flesh wound he decided at a quick glance, figuring it was best dealt with in the ambulance. "Are you able to stand?" he asked with an unimpassioned tone.

Barry flinched when he tried. "Might need some help here, boss,"

The ambo waved his partner in. "Grab his other arm, Trace."

As soon as they moved him he bellowed and let his weight fall against Tracey and she stumbled, "Wait, wait," she grumbled. "John, you'll need the stretcher."

Making an executive decision one of the Sergeants stepped forward to take over from the woman, housing his pistol, "Let's get this done, forget stretchers."

Barry again favoured his weight to one side, against the cop this time, while young Tracey was delegated to carrying the medical bag picked up from the pavement.

The unclipped holster on the cop and his gun begging to be snatched was Barry's ticket to freedom. In a swift movement he had it in his hand, a glance verifying it was ready to fire he coiled round with firm grips on collars, spinning the two helpers so they now faced the armed pack on the pavement. "Drop the bag, doll-face," he yelled at terrified Tracey, "keep moving forward."

With the two men shoulder to shoulder and Tracey following, Barry now had a firewall between him and the cops.

"Hold your fire!" a senior officer in the group warned in recognition the line of fire presented problems for the innocents.

Itching to find a gap in the fragile obstacle, the cops kept their weapons aimed, accepting they may in fact remain helpless to intervene.

The Samaritan cop now faced the embarrassment of having his own pistol pressed against his neck, tilted upward and resting beneath the jaw, the bullet was addressed to the brain.

Once past the driver's window Barry stopped and his entourage followed suit, "Listen up Trace, get your sweet little arse up and start the engine. Don't even think about driving off or you know what happens to your boyfriends here."

Aware the gunman's plan was to hijack the ambulance she did as instructed, anxious to see the last of him, if for no other reason than to save her partner being shot.

Barry needn't have worried about her, the beefy engine sparked and rumbled into life.

"Trace, get out and stand at my side and be quick about it."

She again abided, "Please don't hurt anyone," she

pleaded as she moved into position.

He grabbed her long blond ponytail, unavoidably pulling at the roots as he and spun up into the driver's seat before releasing her. The door slammed shut in response to the sudden acceleration of the ambulance's unorthodox departure.

Without knowing how prepared the police were to take chase Barry needed to dump the vehicle as soon as possible. Knowing ambulances are mandatorily tracked made this a priority, and he knew the perfect place.

This wasn't his first Rodeo, he knew quite a lot about what to expect from the coppers, he had no intension of going straight back to his motel on the outskirts of the city. He was aware street cameras were able to build a continuous picture of his rout.

He entered the perfect place inside two minutes, the place he had found to ditch his intended getaway car acquired several hours earlier, now left abandoned in the street near the empty warehouse.

He wasn't to get very far in the ambulance, not that it mattered, the over-height vehicle began modifying the low ceiling of the car park the moment he entered, becoming completely stuck near the ticket gate.

Startled drivers saw him alight and pace away from the carnage, which he did so without being approached.

Barry couldn't help lamenting over the loss of his bag, now in the hands of police, but he knew it amounted to a distinct advantage. His bag of weapons would have made him stand out, and anyway, for what he had to do he only needed a knife. The eight inch blade intended for the job was housed in a scabbard, nestled in a car he'd *purchased* this time, acquiring it with cash from a yard that sells *very second-hand vehicles*.

Busy shopping centres are the perfect place to cover your tracks, even with the multitude of mounted cameras they had. It wouldn't matter; the cops wouldn't be studying Barry's path through the centre til around lunch; it would then take them til after dinner to track him through the burbs. By then he would be at the designated location, which if he played his cards right they would not suspect where that was.

When he exited from the shopping centre onto the street he was just another loaner who had purchased a few items. His few items consisted of some fresh new clothes, anything but leather; that's what he always wore. For now the bag was the best place for them, otherwise the cops would know what his new attire looked like. Of course they would know he'd purchased different clothes but that didn't matter either.

He hoofed it for another three kilometres before reaching an unfinished housing estate, guaranteed not to have any cameras installed, and plenty of bushland surrounding the property. The construction crews that were busily moving about were effectively precluding him from being noticed. No one took any notice when he entered the *portable latrine* and then reappear decked out in a check flannelette shirt, blue Jeans and sneakers.

With shirt sleeves rolled up above the elbows and tools that he'd absconded from a distracted worker, he reached the tree line at the edge of the site. Of course someone with a keen eye might have notice him place the tools down before entering the bush, but then probably presume he was just relieving his bladder.

He trekked on about another kilometre and a half staying just within the tree line, always within sight of civilisation. His endeavour was not aimless; he knew exactly where he was, and where he could safely exit back onto a street in his new outfit.

The mini he'd purchased lay waiting at a gas station. He'd left it there after telling the attendant he needed to walk home to get his wallet as his car was right on empty. The attendant didn't appear to notice Barry's fresh new change of clothes; after all it had been two hours since he first drove into the garage.

Minutes later, Barry wasn't worried about the weird noises the mini was making as it motored along like a lame worn out old horse; his only concern was where it was taking him.

He arrived at his destination and went in through the Iron Gate that gaped open in welcome. The building was decently set back from the road with a gently winding driveway that led to the front entrance. He saw the expected camera perched high atop the stone wall of the historic convent, dutifully recording his passage. Down on the ground there were three coppers standing guard at the front door.

He knew not to baulk or stop. Instead he continued

on the route that looked as though it might go all way round to the back, and possibly beyond.

The rear of the two story building was a whole lot less ornate, yet somewhat crowded with workmen milling about. That didn't worry him either – the four cops dotted along the wall did, their beady eyes on everyone and anything that moved, including the black Mini that had just arrived.

Had the police worked out where he was heading?

He decided they wouldn't have, otherwise he wouldn't have even gotten past the main gate, or the three cops stationed at the front door

At the back, he noted there was only one door on the ground level, quite ordinary and small, apparently the singular way in and out to well-kept gardens. He parked off to the side and sat with the motor running. From behind the wheel it was difficult to ascertain where the cameras might be so he stepped out and lifted the bonnet as if to check some problem or other, his decrepit ride suggesting that might be the case for anyone observing him.

There were three cameras in all; one above the door, and one each corner of the back wall. A few tradesmen where coming and going from the small door. He was beginning to wish he'd kept the box of tools from the construction site, so that he could have blended in. It crossed his mind to abandon the operation, but time was of the essence, especially now.

He stood studying the guy on a lawnmower that was trimming the extensive green mounds in amongst the autumn colours of Japanese Maples, basically killing time while he thought about his next move.

Finished with his observation he closed up the bonnet, swung in behind the wheel and drove on past all the workers and cops like he belonged there. At the far end of the wall he turned to the left and drove a short distance down the south wall till he reached a grassy mound that had been freshly cut. There'd likely be no gardeners wanting him to move his car, although there was a rake left lying on the grass, perhaps out of sight out of mind. Just up ahead, the driveway had come to an abrupt stop, dead-ended by the building itself jutting across it.

This tight little piece of roadway explained why it had been left to just one cop, a circumstance that would later play into his plans nicely.

With the Mini parked on the grass beneath a maple, he picked up the rake and walked with it back round to the west wall.

Approaching the door where all the activity seemed to be, he noted that gardeners entering were carrying tools, indicating they were keeping their paraphernalia at the convent overnight.

He entered with his acquired rake.

The cops paid no more attention to him than they did the other workers.

The gardener carrying a whipper snipper that had just entered the convent ahead of him, walked only a short distance to where the tools were stored. Barry took his rake into the storeroom as the guy who had unloaded the snipper came out. They acknowledged each other and Barry watched him until he'd gone back outside. With no one else approaching he then took a moment to have a good look around the inside of the lockup. The room was small and square with shelves that carried more than just gardening tools. He spotted some items that would prove useful when the time came. Until then he needed to keep a low profile.

Close to the lockup a gents' toilet marked one of two other doors that led out of the broad hallway, the one at the end a much larger door with 'Staff Only' printed above it, and no doubt strongly locked.

Back at the exit to outside a camera hung, annoyingly spying on everyone who came and went.

Deciding he would deal with that when the time was right – and also survey the tools he might need later – he made his way to the latrine. He stayed in there for the time it would normally take to use the trough, checking for cameras. As expected there were none. The camera outside in the hall would know that he went in so it would need to know he'd come out, not just from the gents but to also see him leave the building. He did so minus his rake, replaced by a small toolbox, and so far knowing everything he was doing would appear perfectly legitimate.

At the car he pretended to check something under the bonnet, his intension being to reach the presumed end of day for the workers. The length of time he spent with his nose in the motor bay was bound to attract the attention of the cop, which was exactly what he wanted.

As expected, the single cop standing next to the south wall eventually left his post and casually strolled over to investigate the antics of the tradesman with the beat-up Mini. "Tough times?" he asked sounding impressed with the oddly phrased comment.

Barry played along; he liked this copper more and more with every passing moment. "You should see the *Lam* I've got parked at home."

The cop laughed, "That's what they all say," but then made a sensible point, "Maybe you should do *this baby up,* there's not many around these days."

Barry thought; *keep talking chatter box.*

And that's exactly what he did; the talkative cop providing him with a perfect reason to arrive back too late to return the tools to the lockup.

On returning to his little Mini carrying the toolbox, and still under the intrigued scrutiny of his uniformed friend, he secured it in the boot. He knew the car would be sitting there on the grass until well into the wee hours of the morning, and a good alibi would be needed in the event an enquirer approached, other than his buddy the south wall cop. Again for his benefit he scratched his head as if he was pondering what to do.

Is there a problem, mate, he heard him ask without leaving his post.

"Yeah, I'm locked out; I can't get these tools back."

"Just take them with you," the amiable cop suggested assuming authority, "who'll know?"

"Yep, that's the plan." With the ruse in place he

got back in behind the wheel, seemingly intending to leave. The starter motor whined for a good thirty seconds without creating a spark. He tried again, pumping the pedal until he'd successfully flooded the engine.

The cop appeared at the open window and spoke empathetically, "That don't sound too good."

"I thought I fixed the fucking thing," Barry grumbled.

"You might have a bigger problem; they shut the front gate here at five." He looked at his watch, not noticing the smirk on Barry's face. "That was two minutes ago."

Barry shrugged. "I guess I'm sleeping' in the car for the night then."

The sentry looked worried for the first time.

"What choice do I have – I doubt the *nuns'll* invite me in," Barry expressed light-heartedly.

The guy was clearly worried about getting into trouble with his superiors, so Barry bantered with the copper for several minutes about not having road service, about the locked gate and the absence of a solution. The sentry's concern was the fact a locked in maintenance worker has so far been unprecedented.

Barry suggested, "Call them; and see what they say."

"Stuff that," he mandated, "So long as you stay in the car I'll just say I didn't see you if I'm asked."

"Good man – what's your name?"

"Trevor."

"Thanks, mate, I owe you one."

"Just so you know; I don't sleep on the job."

And that was that. Prepared for the long wait ahead Barry made sure he didn't catch a moment's sleep either, his mission was far too important.

At three in the morning his buddy Trevor was replace at a shift change. Pretending to sleep he listened to their exchange, picking up enough to know they were talking about him, *who's the guy asleep in the car,* that sort of thing? The new guy didn't sound too happy with the situation either.

After the replaced copper left to go home, the 'new-guy' wandered over and tapped on the window, too curious to leave well enough alone.

Barry jumped convincingly as if shocked from sleep. He shielded his eyes; the cop was blinding him with his torch. The guy helped himself to opening the car door and asked the occupant to step out.

Barry obliged sleepily, again so convincingly that the hapless cop didn't see the screw driver coming at his throat. Racked with excruciating agony he attempted verbalising, producing nothing more coherent than a churning warble. *That was the point of course.*

When Barry nonchalantly appeared from around the south wall moments later wearing the uniform that *new-cop* no longer needed, the west-wall copper, assumed to also be on the new shift, saw him stepping into the light, spill from the garden lamps, enough to see the south-wall guy was not familiar, but not unusual on special operations like this one. Though leaving your station *was definitely unusual*.

"Hey, what're you doing here, buddy. You do know we're on camera."

"I just need a light, no big deal."

"Well make it snappy and get back to your post."

Barry had a fat juicy cigar rolling between his fingers and a spare he placed in the top pocket of his mate's leather jacket.

"If I get in strife I'll be coming for you," the recipient of the smoke joked wearing an appreciative grin.

Barry was waving over the other two coppers.

At three in the morning one could be forgiven if tempted with the chance of a little break to pass the time. As they approached Barry and his first very satisfied beneficiary of a fat cigar, it became apparent the walk might well be worth the trouble.

Just a little closer Barry thought, this needs to be quick and neat, and with no shooting. But he still had the police pistol in his pocket in the event of an emergency, not to mention the eight inch blade now tucked in one of his long socks.

Strike one was copper one, then two and three. They all took the unexpected shaft of the screwdriver in rapid succession; a string of hits that took no more than three seconds. Clutching at their bloody throats, one-by-one they buckled silently to the pavement.

He now had to work fast. Who knew who might be watching the cameras?

From the pocket of his acquired jacket he removed

the miniature cordless drill he'd borrowed from the storeroom. The tiny tool was almost soundless when he drilled into the lock on the door. With the screwdriver shoved into the newly drilled hole he prised to the left, drawing the plunger free of the jam.

The door swung in a little and he stopped it before it drifted into shot. The camera mounted above the door that pointed the length of the hall allowed for a blind spot of about thirty centimetres. Enough not to be seen drilling into its fragile electronics from underneath. Without the assistance of a monitor he had to be able to trust the device was no longer transmitting anything but black.

He entered the hallway and fast stepped down to where the greater challenge waited; *to gain entry to the Staff Only area.* It proved to be easier than he thought; the little drill whispered its way into the substantial deadlock as though it were Swiss cheese; it had a resemblance by the time he'd finished – *he grinned.*

The area that he now stood in wasn't large, yet was uncluttered, and practically pitch-dark, the only light being provided came from the red blink of a camera and some manner of alert system. No alarm sounded, meaning it was either letting itself be heard somewhere else in the building or simply a motion alert to let occupants know they are not alone. Whatever it was, now that he was inside the main part of the nunnery, it didn't matter. His plan had nothing to do with not being identified, which would come later when he was well away on the next phase.

He came into a larger space that appeared to only have one purpose, to house a staircase. His black sneakers silently carried him to the bottom rungs of the plain timber stairs, where his stopped and listened for any hint of movement. The deadly quiet amplified the buzz ringing in his ears.

He gripped the dead copper's torch ready to blind the first luckless character that might jump him from the shadows. He daren't use the pistol. He still lamented the loss of the silenced weapon that he'd lost to the cops, but he had the screwdriver, the better way to shut someone up undetected anyway.

At the top of the stairs he was presented with a hallway that was as generous in width as the one he'd entered through downstairs. It was long though. At a rough guess there appeared to be around fifteen doors, all closed. With precise care he tried the handle of the closest, a sphere shaped metal nob that turned a full circle before stopping. Lightly pushing inward offered no resistance. Holding for moment while listening, he again heard no sound, now he had to hope the hinges were well oiled.

He lucked out.

With continued care he opened the door enough to enter the room. It was darker than the hallway; he smartly closed the door on the dim exterior to avoid being silhouetted, then while standing at the door to let his eyes adjust, the gentle snore of a single sleeper told him that she was genuinely asleep. *Being a nunnery it had to be a female*, he thought.

He slowly approached the sound and stood there

with the torch pointed at the ceiling, gaining enough glow to observe the woman in the bed.

She was hardly a woman; her angelic face was that of a teenager. Minus her Habit, she was close to hairless.

Barry took the pistol from his jacket, the pistol he knew he couldn't use, but she was soon to be so fearful for her life a water pistol would be just as effective. He put his hand around her throat and lightly squeezed against her windpipe in preparation to wake her.

The first thing she saw when her eyes opened was the pistol. Then becoming aware of the man leaning over her and the hand increasing pressure on her throat, her instinct was to scream – *she couldn't.*

Barry lent in close and whispered as unthreateningly as he was capable. "I am not here to hurt you, I need your help."

The young novice nun trembled at the thought of what this intruder might do to her, and why?

"There is a young girl here who is being held against her will. Her name is Sophie. I'm her uncle, and I'm here to take her home. If you don't believe me we can ask her; we can ask her if she knows her Uncle Barry. She'll know me as soon as she sees me I promise." His whole sweet persona wasn't working, so he pleaded. "Please, tell me where she is being kept."

The young woman didn't believe a word of what he was saying.

In *his* mind she had no reason not to, she was being unreasonable. He stood and aimed the pistol at her face. "Get up and take me to where she is right now or you can kiss your goddamned holy-arse goodbye."

"All right," she hastened nervously swinging her long nightgown covered legs from the bed.

"Good girl," he grinned.

Following her from the room Barry couldn't believe how easy this was becoming. The fresh young nun was nervous, yet at the same time strong somehow.

He thought, *Perhaps her religious beliefs are stealing her from fear of death.*

He knew how that was, he was raised a Catholic himself and he had become convinced there was a better life beyond the grave. Now he craved a better life above the grave. While at school with the nuns, he'd felt they had *developed* a lack of respect for man's free will, the promise made within the indelible words of the bible. They needed to understand that he was here now exercising his God-given right, especially now, because they were keeping his daughter from him.

Even if he did possess some latent esteem for their religious order, it wouldn't change a thing, he needed his daughter and that's all there was to it.

Keeping real close to the novice while they traversed the dark hallway; practically walking in her footsteps, the pistol was ready to shoot if anyone got in his way. At the end of the hall the anxious nun tapped lightly on the last door.

No one stirred so she knocked a little louder.

"Yes, what is it?" the sleepy voice of a middle

aged woman filtered into the hall from inside.

"Reverend Mother, its Mary."

There was a pause before she complained, "Do you know what time it is young lady?"

"Forgive me, Reverend Mother."

Barry poked her in the back with the gun. "Tell her that your dead if the door doesn't open in ten seconds."

"There is a man here holding a gun on me." Her voice had shaken convincingly.

The so called Reverend Mother suddenly appeared ashen faced at the open door, alert but not terrified. "You don't need to kill anyone this night. Tell me what it is you want."

Barry could scarcely conceal his amazement. These bloody women had nerves of steel he thought, which he'd fix real soon if they tried any tricks. "Back up, *Mother* so we can come in and chat."

The steely nun did as she was told without turning her back as he pushed Mary in ahead of him.

Just inside the door he stopped and scanned the room, which was reasonably lit by a bedside lamp. There was one other single bed against the wall to his right with someone in it, someone small judging by the lump in the bedcovers.

Excitedly, he thought, *it's her!*

Waving his gun at the ruffled bed the mother-nun had left in a flurry, he demanded, "Stand over there and don't move or make a sound." He crabbed across to the bed where his child lay peacefully sleeping, he could hear the calming rhythm of her gentle breaths.

"I'm taking this sweet child now," he smooched.

His soothing tone had something phoney laced in it; and the nun's weren't buying his cuddly smokescreen for a second.

"Sophie, *pet* - it's your uncle, Uncle Barry - Wake up, sweetheart; I'm here to take you home." Getting no answer he moved closer to the bedside and shook the covers. It was then that he noticed the bed wasn't quite entirely against the wall, which alarmed him a little. The gun that pressed against the back of his head then, was more than an unexpected alarm; it was a sudden dose of reality. He'd been tricked.

"Real easy like, Barry," Josey's voice commanded, "Throw the pistol on the bed and step back."

He could feel himself hesitating, *Why not swing around now and blow the detective's head off.*

That idea quickly changed when Inspector Morris appeared out of the gap noticed earlier at the back of the bed. The fissure like slit didn't seem big enough for such a solid man to fit through.

What the hell is going on here he wondered?

Barry heard heavy shuffling behind him, it sounded like more cops were on the hoof, an army of them.

"They're Police, Baz; you could say you're somewhat outnumbered. Lose the gun."

Without turning around to face his nemesis he kept his voice even and unafraid. "Well hello again, Detective Josey; couldn't you have handled this by yourself?"

"If I had you'd be dead right now."

Barry pointed the gun at the helpless girl. "All of you need to back away right now or precious little Sophie here will be the one who's dead."

From the impossible fissure where the inspector had wormed his way into view, with a dramatic flurry he now threw back the covers to show Barry that Sophie's little body was no more than a *horseshoe-pillow*.

Barry released a sickly laugh.

The two nuns had been watching all this in complete horror, it appeared to them that this brutally insane man hovering over helpless Sophie, a child in their care, was about to be murdered in her sleep.

The Reverend Mother could only think to beg, "Please don't hurt her; she's just an innocent little baby."

Barry turned on the nun with a confused frown, their obvious fear a mystery to him. "Why would I hurt her, I'm here to take her home."

The sisters couldn't have possibly understood the fantasy that the gunman had been secretly conjuring in his mind.

Who had he been talking to just now?

They didn't much care to know, so long as his promise not to harm the child wasn't an empty assurance—

A phone rang – somewhere far away . . .

Josey cell was blaring from his bedside table, bringing him out of a light sleep. Blindly reaching across he deftly accepted the call with his hand, putting it on loud speaker. He glanced at the time, *3.30*. "Speak to me; I gather this must be urgent."

"So urgent it's too fucking late."

Josey sprung upright from the pillow already alarmed by the tone of the caller. "Fin, what's happened?"

"He's got her, mate."

He knew instantly who he meant. "Shit, how?"

"Can you meet me at the convent?"

Keen to abide Josey hurled the covers to the floor and got to his feet to gather yesterday's jeans from a heap of clothes on the floor. "I'll be there in ten – Is anyone hurt?"

"*Weirdly* no, just one copper found unconscious."

The word *weird* was about to become the word on everyone's lips.

CHAPTER TWENTY-SEVEN
Weird Barry

Josey and Inspector Morris were set to meet with the officers that had been on duty at the convent when the drama played out less than an hour ago. Upon their arrival and subsequent entry to the spacious foyer, they met with the two nuns who had been witnesses to the abduction ordeal.

It was quickly learnt that the sisters had commitments preventing an immediate discussion with the Inspector and the Detective. Although their brief apology, and half hour request for postponement, took just five minutes, it was adequate time to recognise the stress they were under.

The usually stoic Reverend Mother was particularly distraught throughout this momentary dialogue, feeling responsible for having suffered the loss of the Bryant's daughter *on her watch*. Sister

Mary was unable to talk about it at first, she just cried when spoken to.

Josey had seen enough crazed criminals in his time to understand this was not the fault of the custodial nuns. If anything, Sophie should have been relocated by police in case Barry were to work out where she was. Josey himself may have to accept some responsibility for missing that point. This guy had the nose of a bloodhound, he'd found Josey easily enough. Although it was reasonable to believe the media spotlight on him would have contributed, the means by which Barry found the safe house at the silo was also still unknown.

With a half hour to spare while the nuns were busy, Josey accompanied Inspector Morris to meet with the four officers that were on duty at the time. How Barry got past four policemen without being seen required an explanation.

At the rear of the nunnery, the officers responsible for preventing any possibility of a breach in security, stood shamefacedly when Inspector Morris approached.

No one would ever suspect that they were supposed to be dead - Clearly they weren't.

The group were vague about whether or not they had witnessed the intruder among the workers earlier in the afternoon, but had to confess to allowing him in to urgently visit the bathroom. His first five minutes in there equated to *what the urgency was*, and was assumed to be correct based on the pungent aroma present on re-entry.

"It didn't seem unusual at first," the officer that

had been on watch at the door explained to the Inspector. "The time he was in there, you know. I went in looking for him after about ten minutes, to see if he was okay like, and, he was nowhere to be seen."

"The vent cover on the floor didn't give you a clue about where he was?" Morris asked dubiously.

"It wasn't on the floor, Sir."

Morris thought about that for a moment, "It is now, constable, which means he was already in the vent when you went in looking for him. He was probably holding it in place. If you'd have looked up you may have seen his fingers poking through the cover."

The officer's embarrassment landed like a weight. "*Oh shit.*"

"Next time if you're not sure about something, don't ignore it until you're able to make sense of it."

"I will Sir. Sir, can I just say, I decided not to worry about where he'd gone in the end because I figured he must have come back out of the building while I was outside taking a leak—" he pulled himself up when the nuns suddenly exited from the convent and approached,

"All right let's leave it there shall we." Morris had also noticed the arrival of the nuns and decided to cut the coppers loose. "You officers can head home," he instructed.

Wallace pushed out an apology but was met with affirmation of his dismissal, "*Tomorrow,* Constable."

Mother Superior ignored the young officers but

Mary managed a shy glance as they left.

Neither the detectives nor the nuns felt that this talk was in any way a time to lay blame, this would require unity; the only way ahead if they were to try and save Sophie.

What hadn't been made clear in the brief encounter with the nuns earlier was the reason for Barry's strange behaviour, as explained by the Reverend Mother. Now with the sisters return Josey was keen to dig a little deeper, Sophie's life could depend on it.

Upon request the Reverend Mother enlarged on her story. "The gunman, he was aiming the weapon at Sophie while she slept, and then inexplicably began muttering, I'm not sure but it seemed to be about things that weren't really happening – like it was all in his head."

There was a slight clue in this for Josey. "Are you able to recall any of what he actually said?"

"I can't remember the exact words, although at one point he mentioned your name – *Detective Josey!*"

Sister Mary remembered something to add, "He said, *nice to see you again,* and then something like, *you should or could have done this on your own.*"

"Yes, Sister Mary is *right*," Mother Superior realised.

"When he mentioned my name, do you think it sounded like he thought I was in the room?"

"Yes, " the two nuns answered in perfect unison.

The Sisters' combined experiences were tremendously helpful, because without their eyewitness testimonies the fact that Barry was having hallucinations might never have been realised until it was too late.

This was definitely fuel for Josey.

The fantasies about killing the duty police, and the detail of what Barry saw in his head while looming over his daughter asleep, would of course never be realised by anyone other than Barry; or perhaps not even by *him* if he failed to remember it. The destruction of the lock mechanism on the secured door at the end of the corridor, if retained, would also remain a figment of Barry's imagination, along with the obtaining of a police uniform and the generous handing out of cigars.

The *known facts*, indicated entry into the restricted area was via the air-conditioning duct in the gents' toilet, and the damage applied to the camera over the outside door was designed to avoid early detection.

His method of reaching the area containing the staircase to the upstairs bedrooms was clear; each and every vent cover had been left lying where he'd discarded them. It was surmised that Barry would have likely considered replacing the covers an unnecessary effort; his identity was never intended to be a secret.

In confidence, the Mother Superior was discretely advised of Barry's rape of Sophie's mother, resulting in him becoming her father, lurid details omitted.

The rape confused the head nun because as she told Josey and the inspector, Barry had called himself Sophie's *Uncle*, not *Dad* or *Father*.

Of course without all the other details of Barry's evil deeds, she was secretly forgiven for the confusion.

Barry referring to himself as her *uncle* and not her *father* was further fuel for Josey; it suggested he was protecting the five year old from his true crime.

The question remained; did Barry want possession of Sophie as his biological daughter, or for some other entirely different reason?

Morris needed to talk to Josey alone about his take on what they were learning. He first turned his attention to the nuns. "Reverend Mother there's little more we can do tonight, so if you ladies would like to go back to bed we understand. And please do not blame yourselves for this; we are all dealing with an extremely duplicitous character."

She nodded sadly. "We will pray that Sophie remains safe and free from harm; and that you and your officers are successful in finding her."

"Thank you sister, we can use all the help we can get."

She gestured to the door. "Would you gentlemen like to come back through the convent?"

"That's alright, Sister, we have our vehicles around the side here."

The kindly nun subtly bowed her head and piloted Sister Mary away with her.

"And now for the difficult part," Josey released on a heavy breath after the nuns had entered the convent and closed the door, "informing Mitchell and Beverley."

"Right," he looked at his watch – dawn hadn't

poked its head up yet. "Let's give them a few hours shall we. I'd like to talk things over with you first"

"That's fine." Josey appreciated being invited to join in on releasing the bad news to Sophie's parents, but he wasn't all that sure he'd be in their good books.

Morris thought the detective was uncharacteristically flat. "You don't need to blame yourself for this *either*, Detective."

"Could I have worked this guy out earlier? I'm not sure. Like you say, he's cunning."

"And, from what we've just heard, psychotic."

"Agreed; having said that I don't believe Sophie is in any immediate danger."

"Based on what – keep in mind he's tried killing her mother?"

"Even so I still don't think he intends killing Sophie; calling himself Uncle in front of her suggests he cares what she thinks."

Morris baulked. "Bloody hell, I can't imagine he cares about anybody or anything. He certainly doesn't seem to care about exposing his intentions."

Josey made a cautious point. "I think the reason for that is he doesn't know how much we know."

Morris also exhibited a hint of caution when he asked, "Detective, please tell me you don't have any updates on where he might be taking her? If you do we need to work together on this, no more holding onto hunches."

Josey fully understood that the normally ideal days of withholding information on this one was over, but he still was concerned about drawing volumes of media attention. Media reports would be as clear has a roadmap for Barry, allowing him to watch every move the police made. Of course Morris couldn't be more onside with Josey if he tried, and basically Josey *did* want the police involved because Sophie's safety was paramount. "Vin, I promise there is nothing beyond what Carl unearthed in the UK, and what you and I have already discussed."

"I have to say I'm truly fearful about Sophie being with this guy."

"I'd be lying if I said I wasn't."

"Cam, this is actually not your responsibility anymore, you were hired to find Sophie – and you've already done that."

"I appreciate you putting it that way but Inspector I need to stay on this case until that little girl is back at home with her family."

"I'm hearing you." Morris breathed away some of the built-up tension he was harbouring and offered his hand in staunch support. "I know you're as anxious as we are to get started. Stay in touch and we'll work through this together."

Josey knew that any plan would be potentially risky; his only litmus was not to endanger young Sophie in the process. From what the nuns had said about Barry's demeanour, it did appear to confirm his goal was not to kill her, which could conceivably change in a heartbeat if he were to be threatened in some way, or if his plans were to go askew.

The trick was, *not to corner him.*

The challenge – *to locate him without doing so.*

James William Davis

CHAPTER TWENTY-EIGHT
On the run

By morning, Father and Daughter were on a train ride aboard the famous Ghan, a rail journey from Adelaide to Darwin. It provided Barry with the time to work on his relationship with his little girl. He didn't have to work hard; she was apparently having a ball, especially being able to believe that this was just another part of her Australian holiday, sanctioned by her parents. Barry made sure they kept to themselves and during their isolation he convinced Sophie that the especially short haircut he was giving her was to prepare for the warm place they were going to. She had asked him why it was warm and he told her because the sun shone every day. Barry had bought her a pair of blue shorts and some blue sneakers. With the haircut, shorts and sneakers she could easily be taken for a sweet little boy.

If an unavoidable approach were made he would

introduce himself as her uncle, just as she believed he was.

He had a complete scenario worked out if questions were unavoidably asked; *like what's his name?* Barry's answer was, I'm sorry, it's a secret; I've encouraged him not to say his name – you know, it's his parents idea, their overly careful.

Most people would agree with the parent on this score.

If he thought there was risks of Sophie hearing someone refer to him as a boy, he would pre-empt or talk over the enquirer with, "*It's* very excited about seeing the crocodiles." This was a comment that would likely send chills through the veins of enquirers if Barry's psychotic history were known to them.

Any questions about where her mum and dad were, he would explain that they stayed behind to save on the outrageously overpriced cost of travelling on the Ghan, which people other than the wealthy would heartily agree with. Margaret River was never mentioned. No one was suspicious of Uncle Barry because his little nephew was as he'd said, *having a great time of it.*

His $5,000 ticket gave him beds that converted into lounges during the day, the cabin boasting a table with deluxe seating along with two ottomans. Sophie loved staring out the window at the passing scenery, usually becoming heavy eyed and finally falling asleep. He would carry her then to one of the lounges to continue her nap.

Sometimes during her naps Barry would pour

himself a drink and get on his cell phone. He'd speak in hushed tones so as not to disturb his daughter, part of which was more about her little ears hearing things she shouldn't. In theory she wouldn't understand what was being said but he wasn't taking any chances.

"It's Barry," he'd say when he rang the usual number. He never once put the person on the other end of the line on speaker. "Yes, no problems, everything is going well." Then he would listen for minutes at a time to what was being said.

"We're arriving at Alice Springs today and Katherine tomorrow, Darwin the day after . . ."

He grabbed the notebook and pen that he kept with him; sat at the small table to write down instructions, voicing as he wrote, "Batchelor . . . yes of course . . . right . . . see you there, Bye."

As promised, they arrived in Darwin on time and as expected, welcomed by the January torrential rain of a tropical summer.

Sophie giggled with delight when they had to run from the terminal to a big four wheel drive car that Barry had waiting to be picked up.

She let out a joyful shriek as Uncle swept her up into the passenger seat on her knees, from where she was able to watch his undulating figure cross behind the wall of water smashing against the impenetrable glass, for her, *it felt like being inside a waterfall.*

"This is fun," she affirmed excitedly while he climbed in dripping water everywhere. He playfully flicked his drenched hand depositing raindrops across her face to give her a laugh.

"All right now," he announced leaning across her to uncoil the restraining strap, "we need to get you in your seatbelt young lady. You'll need to sit down properly."

"I won't be able to see," she protested straining taller to see through the windows.

"Oh okay then, let's get you fixed up." He twisted to the back seat and grabbed her soft backpack. "Lift up, tulip, you can sit on top of this."

She did as he asked, grinning her head off now that she could look out the windows. He clipped her in firmly and sedately drove away from the airport.

Sealed roads carried them south to an oasis called Batchelor, a distance of ninety kilometres, in which he'd stopped ten minutes out of Darwin to fix Sophie up a little higher using his carry bag, so that she could get an even better view of what lay ahead.

Giant ant hills and distinctively sparse trees dotted the dead flat ground without obliterating distant horizons. The monotony managed to put her to sleep in fifteen minutes, only awakening sometime later when the vehicle made a sudden stop.

"Look out the front, Sophie," She heard her uncle say.

She lazily stretched up to see over the dashboard. The sight of a big mean looking Buffalo standing in the middle of the road staring defiantly at them; was not something that excited her, *she wasn't at all sure about the beast.* "Is he going to hurt us, Uncle Barry?"

"No, he's afraid of us; watch this." He gave a long

blast on the horn causing the animal to baulk a little.

Sophie covered her ears and shut her eyes, not opening them again until a loud shuddering crash violently rocked the vehicle. Crying in fear this time, she covered her eyes with her hands.

"What're you crying about," he chuckled, "I thought you said you were having fun."

She didn't appreciate her uncle laughing at her. "I'm scared, I want to go home."

He just kept laughing while pushing his foot on and off the throttle in an attempt to tease the wild Buffalo.

Sophie screamed above all the frightening sounds, unable to look at what was happening.

"If you think this is scary just wait till you see the crocodiles."

To her, Uncle Barry sounded very mean.

It wasn't her imagination; clearly he was completely uncaring of the little girl's desperate fear.

"I don't want to see a crocodile – I want Mummy and Daddy," she whimpered sadly.

Barry looked at her as though she was suddenly a pest; his expression was harsh and frightening. The tears that then streamed across her cheeks sent him a message he understood. He'd gone too far. He needed to be careful. His little daughter was a very valuable commodity and must not be harmed, physically or mentally. "I'm sorry, sweetheart," he promised as he rummaged for a used handkerchief in a shirt pocket, reaching across with it to gently wipe her face dry.

The Buffalo's evolving disinterest was unnoticed until it snorted in disgust and ran from the roadway to safer ground amongst the anthills, destroying one of the tall mounds in careless retreat.

"He's gone now, look."

She reluctantly opened her eyes to make sure he was telling the truth, some of the trust she had bequeathed on her uncle was gone. The memory of the anger on his face could not subside, sniffles preventing her from further protests or wishes.

"All right then," Barry breathed, giving the retreating animal one last glance as he drove on.

When they came to a place called Cahills Crossing, he began to regret having scared her because he wanted her to see the crocodiles. This was a well-known place to see the reptiles. When the water level was raised high enough above the weir to stop traffic, the crocs would cross down river and wait in gangs, patiently waiting for fool drivers who would take the risk of driving into the swollen waters. Scores of people had died here, having been swept into the mouths of these hungry monsters. Their strong jaws could hold a victim beneath the water until drowned, ahead of a needy feast.

In spite of the heavy rain, the river had not yet risen to the point of stopping the occasional vehicle wishing to cross, but the crocodiles large bulbous eyes and armour like scales were clearly visible for any one courageous or dumb enough to dispel fear.

When her uncle encouraged her to look out at them, it was clear little Sophie was not one of the brave, nor one of the dumb. "No I don't want to look at monsters," she insisted emphatically with her bottom lip quivering.

Uncle Barry didn't like her obstinate attitude. "Look out the damn window now or I'll stop the car and throw you in the water." He saw that Sophie was frozen solid by his threat. She knew about crocodiles he figured, mostly in cartoons he bet, what kid didn't. Yeah she knew that they could eat a person; that is exactly what happened to Captain Hook in Peter Pan—

He stopped the car half way across the weir, stepped out into the soft flow of the traversing water and rounded the back of the vehicle to reach her door.

The look on her face was priceless when the door swung open, the only thing separating her from the monsters, was him.

He clipped her free of the seatbelt, pulled her from the car and in one clear sweep threw her in among the waiting reptiles.

These hungry beasts didn't see a terrified frightened little girl; this was merely food for them. Watching from the edge of the weir as she was taken beneath the water to drown, Barry was feeling absolutely no remorse, he was revelling in it—

—"Uncle Barry!" she screamed.

Getting no response she forced herself to repeat the plea. "Uncle Barry – I'm scared."

Since she had not dared to look out the window,

and sensing the car was stationary in the middle of the weir, she reached across to where her uncle sat with hands gripped on the steering wheel and prodded him gently to gain his attention, *it did*.

He shook his head, clearing his mind; he'd again been off with the hallucinatory fairies – not that Sophie knew or would have understood anything about that.

The bubbling spill crossing the weir, and the gentle prodding from his daughter, had brought his mind back, away from the self-induced horror. *He knew this.*

It wasn't possible just by looking at him to tell what might have been going on in his head, and therefore to appreciate whether or not he was recalling whatever took him away in the first place, *yet remembering he always did*, this was his fantasy, every single detail of it – recalled without guilt or shame. He would then move on effortlessly, managing to put his conjuring routine aside as though it were perfectly normal.

He slipped the vehicle into gear and continued across the weir, still thinking about this latest episode, and some other recent experiences. Differentiating between what was real and what wasn't was never a problem for him. He knew that raping his sister-in-law was real, evidence by the little lady sitting at his side. He admits to himself that trying to shoot Sophie's mother was preceded by the fantasy of doing it, the only difference being that in the fantasy he had succeeded.

His attempt at killing her at the silo-safe-house had

also been preceded by the fantasy of doing so, again successfully; but that didn't cause him to feel the rehearsals in his mind were to blame for the subsequent failures.

Kids are so forgiving; they don't retain scary things that happen to them so long as it is followed up with a little love. During the journey to their final destination Barry had been the model uncle. By the time they reached *Cooinda Lodge* where they had a room waiting, Sophie was back on side. She wouldn't even be alive if Uncle Barry had gone through with his fantasy for real.

Thank the *preservation of common decency* she knew nothing of it – or that the reason her uncle hadn't carried *out* his fantasy was because of her immense importance to him.

The lodge was nothing short of a pacifier. Sophie thought this was better than any place she had ever been to, especially since it had a pool, a cinema and a kid's playground.

Barry let her play at this outdoor adventure park under the feminine eye of a security officer, while he checked in before settling into their comfortably furnished air-conditioned room, a welcome retreat from the summer heat.

He went straight onto the in-house phone and made a room to room call. "It's me, is everything in order?" He put the phone on speaker and placed it down beside him on the bed, settling in against the generously pillowed bedhead.

"All good here, we're advised the subjects will be arriving in a couple of hours, time for a shower and a bite to eat. How's the little girl going?"

"Good as gold."

The man released a satisfied sigh, "Shall we say half hour in the restaurant."

"Sounds good to me, see you then."

When he returned to pick up Sophie at the playground, he found a woman talking to her from across the iron fence that kept the kids in and the adults out.

He didn't miss noticing the young woman was a little bit attractive, but he had no time to imagine an intimate scenario with her. He summoned the security officer with a wave and told her when she came over that he was taking Sophie to the room.

With eyes fixed on the lush talking with Sophie, a pang of concern tightened his entrails. *She seems okay though* he thought and settled to wait for his daughter to be brought to the gate by security.

Showered and with a whisky under his belt, Barry arrived at the restaurant with Sophie in tow. She suddenly went shy when presented with an unexpected stranger, who was already sitting at a table waiting. The man stood respectfully as one might do for royalty, offering his hand to both uncle and niece. The white bearded man had been warned not to refer to her as Barry's daughter, or to make mention of her cropped hair.

Sophie thought he looked like the man on the posters at the chicken shop, where she goes with her parents. When he introduced himself as *Ronnie Pendent,* she made no sense of who he was, or why Uncle Barry was meeting him.

Ronnie held her tiny hand lightly with the tips of his fingers and gave a respectful dip of his head. "It's a real pleasure to meet you, young lady."

Shyly and silently she continued staring at his snow white whiskers.

A well-presented lady in her prime arrived at the table and bent to kiss Pendent; receiving a polite welcome, a distraction for Sophie until the woman's focus came back on her. "My, what a beautiful girl you are," she expressed sounding like she was gloating – then to Barry. "You did say that your Sophie was special; I have to say you have not disappointed."

"I aim to please," he responded with a wry grin.

Everyone in the know had been primed not to say anything about her looking more like a boy than a girl.

The meal arrived and lasted a half hour before Pendent received a call that brought it to an abrupt end. He closed the call and pocketed his phone. "They're here." He told the others.

Ronnie Pendent and the woman were first to leave the table, followed by Barry with Sophie in his arms. When he reached their private room, the others continued on down the hallway. Although mystified, Sophie was pleased to see them go. Inside with the door closed Barry sat his daughter on the edge of the bed and went to his carry bag that sat atop the three seater couch. He took what looked like a folded piece of blood red cloth from it and came back to lift Sophie into his arms once more.

Outside in the hallway, Ronnie and the woman

reacted as Barry and his daughter came out from their room.

Pendent then led the way to an apartment door at the end of the hall, retrieving a cell phone from his coat pocket to dial out. "Tristan, honey – it's us," he said when the call connected.

The door opened immediately and a pleasant looking young woman appeared; enthusiastically waving them in with her eyes fixed on the beautiful five-year-old.

Sophie's discomfort quickly surfaced when her father handed her across to this woman as he smooched past her on entering. Sophie's outstretched arms beckoned to be taken back by her father, but he was already on his way into the room with his back turned.

"You're all right, sweetheart," Tristan assured Sophie; "I am one of your uncle's very close friends."

The woman's gentle voice had little effect, because even more frightening than the stranger holding her, were the ten or so people standing about the room hidden beneath deep red tunics. The part that covered their heads was pointy on the top; she thought *they looked like upside down ice-cream cones.*

"This is a fancy dress party, darling," Tristan avowed. "Doesn't it look like fun?"

Terrified tears and a dropped lip indicated she wasn't sold, "No, I want to go home." A sniffling sob morphed into a distressed hiccup. Her bearer, realising there was no calming her, turned pleadingly to the group of party goers for help. One of them stepped forward; the shoes protruding from below the hem of the red garment indicated it was a man.

Once he came close, his upside-down ice-cream-cone looked even more frightening to the five-year-old. He quickly removed the hood; its absence revelling that the person beneath was Uncle Barry. She squirmed from Tristan's hold to welcome the familiar arms of her uncle.

"We need to get you dressed now, sweet," he told her gently. "Then you can join in on the party."

Barry carried her across to a long cloth covered table that was laden with used glasses and many half drained bottles. To Sophie the cluttered array meant nothing, for the party goers the spent bottles explained in part the merriment that had already beset the attendees. Clearly the drinking had preceded the donning of their hooded costumes by a good amount of time.

It was then that Barry abruptly appeared rattled. He looked around the gathering as if searching and then announced, "We're two people short; who's missing?"

Most in the room, having paired up prior to donning their tunics, were quickly able to ascertain who the absent couple were. "It's the recipients," a fresh young female voice revealed.

Someone else called, "We thought the Hortons were coming with you, Brother Barry."

This was putting Barry on edge because these were the key players, and although they were initially running late, they had arrived a good half hour ago.

The Hortons had promised they would be here on time, so where the hell are they?

Not having met them due to their delayed arrival, he was at a disadvantage. "Somebody go and get them," he snapped in annoyance, "They're staying in room ninety five." Barry's gruff tone had not sounded in the least bit party-like.

"I'll go," the first woman who spoke volunteered, her haste suggesting when Barry says to do something he expects you to do it quick.

No sooner in the hallway and she ran into the late arrivals approaching, already fully clad in their party outfits, including their complete head coverings.

"You're not supposed to dress up outside the room," they were cautioned by the woman on errand duty, "You should have been told?"

"Sorry," a woman's voice responded.

"Leave them off until you get in, Barry will want to see your faces – a warning, he's not in a good mood."

When the trio entered the party room they got head turns and a clap of sorts for being late, along with a few disapproving murmurs.

The husband and wife team were around middle age, well groomed from what they could see. The woman still had a nice face, and might have been stunning when younger, her Cleopatra hair style sat high above the collar at the back and she hadn't yet developed any wrinkles. Her husband looked like a business executive, hansom with a neatly knotted tie protruding and inch or two above the rim of his blazing-red costume. The round spectacles that he wore were small rimmed and thin on the lens. They both wore grins that told only one story, they were very happy to be there.

Barry nipped the unorthodox discontent in the bud. "All right people, let us welcome our guests with a little well deserved decorum . . . Everyone, this is Nickolas and Simone Horton, with us today all the way from South Africa. His voice rose to accentuate, "Give them a show of appreciation for choosing to become a part of *Life is Precious!"*

His voice got even louder. ". . . Dear friends of life; is a brand new life not *Precious?"*

This inciting question required a mandatory answer.

The responding ovation became disturbingly rhythmic, as would the blunt stamp of many marching feet, continuing until Brother Barry raised his arms to ebb the noise. "Believers of *life is for all,* let us begin this journey of hope, for a new life for this little family, Nickolas, Simone and gorgeous Sophie."

The Horton's attention was drawn to Sophie standing side by side with Brother Barry, his renowned presence momentarily without head-covering so that he may easily be recognised by the *recipients*.

Regular attendees were very familiar with the reason for this, recipients were only ever given a description of the leader; photos were never permitted publication.

The Hortons, unfamiliar with the ritual about to be

undertaken, followed the lead of all the other couples. They donned their Hoods, and shoulder to shoulder with the others they shuffled into position; joining hands until they'd formed an open circle. At the centre of this human chain stood a small oblong table, covered in a thick red cloth that hung all the way to the floor.

On the bench where Barry and Sophie stood among the disarray of bottles, there was an item brought from their room. He placed her down to stand, bringing her little face level with the bench top. "This is for you, Sophie," he told her warmly as he held it up for her to see.

Her eyes followed the bright red garment unravelling from beneath his grip, revealing a tiny version of the party outfits, made to measure.

A woman with a kindly aged voice arrived at the table with some sort of orange coloured lolly water. "Her *sedative*," she whispered to Barry.

He took the drink and pretended to take a sip. "Oh yummy," he promised Sophie after licking his lips, "This is really tasty. Have some, sweetheart."

She shook her head. "No I don't want to."

The woman gave Barry a knowing look and took the drinking glass from him without any fuss.

He nodded with equal calm, "Thank you, Rose," and then lifted Sophie to sit her on the edge of the bench. "Let's get you dressed so that we can start the party. Hold your arms up, sweetie, there's a good girl."

Sophie shook her head and defiantly folded her arms, prompting the woman to return, prepared to assist.

Sophie didn't see the hypodermic that emerged from beneath her loose fitting sleave, and only barely felt the light prick it provided when sunk into her arm.

The people linked in the human chain could see no more than the backs of those attending to Sophie, yet they watched on in complete trust.

Finally the cute red costume lifted into view, and then lowered from sight as it was fitted over Sophie's head.

Barry turned with Sophie in his arms; she looked so sweet, like *Little Red Riding Hood*, although now there was a noticeable somnolence about her.

With her head now resting sleepily on her father's shoulder, she appeared impressively calm as they approached to pass through the gap in the human chain to reach the makeshift altar at the centre, whereupon Barry laid her on her back. For all intense and purposes she could have been sleeping.

The linked attendees began to sidestep, their chainmail circle rotating with increasing momentum, their voices rising in unison in a monotonous chant.

Barry reached back to his hood and pulled it forward to finally cover his head, then entering into an overpowering Gregorian chant. His melodic pious yet monotone voice elevated beyond the droning choir of faithfuls, delivering an unintelligible message.

Sophie was blessed with being unable to register this strange and disturbing sound, the secretly administered sedative had now rendered her completely anesthetized.

Barry broke from the chant to deliver an invitation. "Nicholas and Simone Horton, are you present?"

From the secrecy of their hoods they responded with deep enthusiasm. "Yes Brother Barry we are here."

"Then the Dark Lord calls you to the altar. Will you step forward now and accept your daughter?"

The ordained couple broke free from the chain, their hands still clasped while taking the few steps requested. "We accept the Dark Lord's gift with open hearts," they promised.

Brother Barry swept aside from their path with the flair and creativity of a Shakespearian actor, allowing the receivers to approach the tiny altar. Once there they separated to take positions opposite each other on either side of the platform. Simone was first to bend and kiss Little Sophie gently on her forehead, albeit her touch hindered by the mandatory Hood. She straightened to permit her husband to offer his kiss. Having done so, and although fully aware Sophie was insentient from an administered drug, he whispered, "We are here to take you home, sweet girl,"

He covertly raised his head to face his wife. It was a signal. A subtle nod from her was enough to set their plan in action, a plan that appeared to be shaping into abduction.

Barry sensed no warning ahead of Nicolas' sharp turn with Sophie in his arms. And then Simone revealing the gun she'd been hiding beneath the long sleave of her tunic. "Don't try stopping my husband," she warned.

Barry's accustomed rage raised blood-impacted veins, not without a tinge of dismay that he may have been outsmarted, *about to be ripped off.*

Simone tore away her hood to expand peripheral vision, eyes set on the almighty leader. "You may have guessed we're not the Hortons, your so called recipients are still in their room, surrounded by police as it happens."

A concerning murmur from all the attendees filled the room.

"Don't listen to them," Barry bellowed above their disquiet, "these imposters are just attempting to scare you. I guarantee you there are no police or they would have been in here already." Without shifting his gaze from whoever this woman was, he maintained his persuasive instruction. "Do not allow the Lord's baby to be taken from us! Secure them and I will call the police myself."

Barry's promise seemed to settle the group, enough to perhaps dismiss the worry of being arrested.

Although having successfully taken hold of Sophie, now firmly in his arms, Nicolas found the encirclement by the brethren was threatening to prevent him from reaching the outside of the human chain. He daren't make a move for fear the threat to Sophie may be too high a risk. With no further need of his hood he threw it to the floor, it was time to let Bryant believe his game was up.

Even before Barry faced this curbed *villain,* who

had chosen to conduct this daring act, he'd began to suspect that he and his cohort may well be working with the police. As impossible as this subterfuge appeared, if these two were themselves not actual police, it left just one other possibility, one that he daren't mention in front of his faithful brethren. "I have to hand it to you people," he admitted to Josey through clenched teeth, "I can't fathom how you found this place without my being aware."

Barry was being careful not to expose the possibility they were all in *deep-shit*, or that the intrepid detective was anyone other than Nickolas Horton the recipient; here to abduct the girl to avoid the exorbitant fee. Right now he needed his brethren believing there was something spiritual worth fighting for.

In light of this standoff situation, Josey decided his only defence was to expose Bryant's true agenda. And to let the brethren see that he was not Nicolas Horton, some of whom knew what the Hortons look like.

Barry being held at bay by Carl gave Josey the time he needed to remove the prosthetics, providing them all with the unbelievable transformation.

It brought a few gasps of dismay, even a trickle of admiration from some.

Barry was silently seething now, and as a result becoming more dangerous by the minute, just as Josey had predicted he'd be if cornered; a situation hoped to be avoided by making a clean rescue.

"Listen to me, all of you,' he commanded with the dictatorial tone of an authoritarian, "your Messiah is not whoever you think he is; nor is this innocent little girl available for sale. I warn you again, we *are* working with the police. If anyone hurts Sophie the officers will be in here before any of you can blink." Josey reached beneath his gown and retrieved a Wi-Fi that he held high above his head for all to see. "The police are listening to this conversation right now. What you do next will determine just how much trouble each and every one of you are in.

"If this man has convinced you that Sophie is available to the highest bidder, than you all need either a reality check or you're as corrupt as he is—"

"Shut the fuck up," Barry screamed at the proliferating detective with no further interest in hiding his mood.

"Or what?" Josey snapped ahead of again facing the faithful. "Barry here is a *serial rapist*. He raped his brother's wife; producing this sweet child as a result."

A male voice interrupted. "Don't listen to him this is a fabrication, ask him what he's done with Simone and Nicolas Horton – perhaps they are in their room as he says, lying dead on the floor."

"They are safe in police custody. You can check, go to their room, you'll see I'm telling the truth – Go," he sharply barked to encourage the halfwit to get moving.

Barry offered neither encouragement nor distain, which confused the man a little, but he hastily left to carry out the errand anyway.

Following Josey's lead Carl joined him in

removing the prosthetics that had turned them into Mr and Mrs Horton.

From what the nuns had said about Barry, it was difficult to understand if his present quietness right now was space for one of his delusional fantasies, and if it was, one could only imagine what dastardly events must be playing out within its dark walls.

Josey decided to test the theory. "This is not in your head you crazy bastard, this is real, Barry."

A woman now offered objection to Josey's affront, "How do we know what you're telling us is true?"

Josey thought about how to answer a person who believes her Devil is involved in giving the unsolicited sale of children a tick of approval. "I don't pretend to understand what you people believe, but is it worth hurting this little girl to figure out the truth here; either way you *will* learn the truth I can assure you – not just from me. If you decide to prevent us from leaving here to take Sophie home to her parents, you can lament your decision from behind bars. You need only to wait and learn the Hortons are safe, *and in custody*. Have you yet wondered why your friend has not returned from checking on them?"

The man sent on the errand to check on Mr and Mrs Horton had already learnt the truth.

After knocking and entering the Hortons' room, he saw that they had indeed been placed in custody. Two uniform coppers and a plain clothes guy stood around as though they had been expecting a visitor.

The plain clothes guy presented himself as Inspector Morris, followed by a serious suggestion he stay and join the two detainees. The weapon hanging straight-armed at Morris' side cemented the sentiment—

At the decidedly sombre party, a resounding crash drew the attention to the altar; Barry had hurled the ensemble toward Carl causing him to stumble and fall, effectively neutralising the threat he'd originally offered.

This triggered a collective effort from a few of the most faithful brethren, those nearest to the abductee, to pounce and tussle with Josey in an attempt to release his hold on the girl. The seconds it took to regain his footing and his bearings, it presented Barry with the chance to reach the outnumbered detective and snatch Sophie from his arms. The line of escape Barry then took traced a path through the gathering to reach the door and exit into the hallway on the run.

A few diehards did all they could to prevent Carl and Josey taking pursuit, giving Barry enough leeway to exit the lodge unobstructed, other than by a couple of unaware people blocking his way.

Beyond the main ingress and with maximum luck of a rabbit pursued by an army of gunmen that were unable to fire amongst innocents, Barry was able to reach his waiting four-wheel drive. He flung the door wide; recklessly jumping in behind the wheel with Sophie on his lap; still unconscious. With no time to clip in he stabbed the ignition and slammed his foot on the throttle—

—*Spinning wheels* eddying gravel into the air was the heart stopping scene facing Josey and Carl as they came out from the lodge, the receding four by four speeding away, again with Sophie on-board.

Visitors swivelled their heads, bedazzled by the chaos that was seemingly created by the man carrying the child. They witnessed it all from where they'd broken step, and now three guys were running to their vehicle ahead of a couple of uniformed and plainclothes police hot on their heels heading toward a parked police car.

The three men in the lead reached their car as the police coupled with the one parked behind them, the envoy immediately leaping into pursuit, the wailing police car screaming intention to move people out of the way.

There were more police coming out of the Lodge to join in on the pursuit in a third vehicle, it too appearing to be likeminded in following the one that had left ahead of them, all in a big hurry to catch up to the car with the little girl.

Inspector Morris had mandatorily taken the wheel of the first police car, with Josey at his side and Carl in the back; travelling nor-east on the Arnhem Highway toward the Crocodile infested Cahill Crossing.

If the situation wasn't bad enough already, undesired rain was beginning to intensify.

With the commencement of the tropical wet season this kind of torrential downpour was to be expected, and it was understood the weir would already be beginning to reach impassable levels.

The Alligator River would be rising rapidly.

If the weir were to prevent Barry from crossing, it

presented two scenarios. One he would be forced to turn back, or worse he may consider taking the risk of crossing. Even in four-by-fours it was not safe to cross in fast flowing waters deeper than half a metre.

Both men knew the statistics after having done their research in advance of beginning their pursuit, a pursuit instigated way back in Margaret River.

Maxine had used the same dark web address that aided Josey in working out Barry's doings in the UK, and discovered he wasn't working alone; in fact he had many followers who understood their little group of deviants were more than just *Dark Lord Cult members*, these people were also very interested in money – money from the sale of stolen children, *no surprise*.

It turned out to be a worldwide network, because of this Max suggested they take a close look at people coming into Australia not just leaving. It raised the question about how do you make a list of the best candidates among thousands of travellers. Her answer was to make a worldwide list of names for people with birthing problems, meaning they can't have kids. Then check those names against new and recent arrivals in Australia. People would likely use their real names for travel, but when it came to joining the brethren of the Dark Lord Cult, it was okay to use no name at all.

This time-consuming research, employing the burning of candles at-both-ends, Max and a small band of backroom coppers were able to narrow it down to the South African couple Nickolas and

Simone Horton – arriving in the Northern Territory at the beginning of the tropical wet season.

Inspector Morris, with the sanction of New South Wales police, marshalled the gathering of a Northern Territory *special-opps* group to survey the areas noted in the traveller's itinerary – hence the *Cooinda Lodge.*

Even with all this success, their plans to save Sophie had now taken some very dangerous steps backward.

"You don't think this arsehole is crazy enough to cross the river do you?" Morris asked nervously.

Josey scoffed. "Actually I do!"

"We need to pick up the pace," Carl offered.

Morris squinted through the rain impacted windscreen. "Not so easy," he promised keeping his eyes on what little he could see of the road.

Josey offered, "We're close enough, so long as we can keep him in sight we're in good shape. If he's even half way coherent he should be aware of the crossing.

"And if he's *not* coherent?" Morris asked.

"He seemed on top of it when he turned the tables on us."

Morris accepted the logic and offered no argument. He needed to keep close enough so that Bryant could see that he was still being tailed. This would ensure he didn't choose to stop and make a run for it on foot. It wouldn't be an easy task if he did; given it was a forty one kilometre stretch from the Hotel to the crossing.

Their hearts were in their mouths knowing the

massive risk to Sophie, not just the breakneck speed they were doing on a rain drenched road with nearly nil visibility, but also what the unstable man at the wheel might choose to do when he reached the weir. They could only hope that the sedative they gave the Sophie was still working.

When they reached the forty kilometre mark tension rose in anticipation of what was about to go down – nothing really mattered other than Sophie's safety.

In Barry's mirror, the bedazzling backlight from the second police vehicle, trailing tightly on the first, established they were closing fast. He reasoned their plan amounted to bringing all three vehicles bumper to bumper just as the swollen crossing mandated they must stop.

He played it out in his mind; *Josey would leap from the vehicle on the passenger's side, his copper mate from the left. Josey would then appear at the window to do his worst while the cop snatched Sophie to safety.*

That's the way it would have happened if he'd let it.

He brought his vehicle to a stop and waited until his pursuers had pulled in behind him.

With all his adversaries out of their cars and on the hoof, Barry planted his foot, surging his four by four onto the raging torrent covered weir.

Hidden in the fast flowing river's exploding surface, downstream of the weir, expectant eyes raised for a better view, several beasts vying for an advantage over their hungry counterparts. They had seen this before; they knew it often ended in a decent meal.

Those desperate to rescue Sophie from unimaginable horrors looked upon this devastating scene with sinking hearts. Although they couldn't see the crocs, they knew they'd be there, lurking, waiting.

The big vehicle, now stuck a third of the way onto the crossing, had lurched dangerously close to the barrier of boulders that lined the downriver side of the weir, having aquaplaned as soon as it hit the swollen river, wedged there with no chance of reversing back. The rocks were the only thing preventing the vehicle from being swept away by the river.

The torrent relentlessly pushed against the pillion wall of the newly introduced blockade, lifting over the roof to continue the compulsory flow, cascading onto the hidden welcoming party that had gathered beneath its fall.

From inside the seriously tilted cabin Barry was faced with the task of escaping. The driver's door was hard up against the rocks. Sophie had been thrown down into the well at his feet, hard up against the throttle and brake pedal. She stirred.

Barry thought, *being awake could either make dealing with her easier, or harder.*

That aside, the trick was for him to stand and reach the opposite window that now faced skyward; presently being closed was the only thing stopping the river from spilling in to fill the cabin.

First he needed to lift his daughter from where she

was lodged. She was still under the influence of the drug he noted as he lifted her up and onto the passenger seat, where he had to hold her in place while he rummaged in the glove box. Locating a substantial metal torch that could serve as a tool, with which to break through the glass, he began pounding against their only avenue of escape.

All of this could have been one of his self-induced fantasies except for the fact these events were being witness by those at the rim of the weir.

This was all very real.

In the afflicted vehicle, Sophie was coming around. "I'm scared," she whimpered to her uncle.

"You're safe with Uncle Barry — do you know how to hold your breath?" he asked without pause.

"I don't know," she cried.

The least said the better he decided as he took blows at the window again. The window suddenly opened with no warning, *probably a short in the electronics*, he thought. There was no time to ponder it, water exploded in and pushed them back against the driver's door. The cabin filled quickly. Having gripped Sophie's arm at the instant the water invaded he was able to lift her toward the open window. With a bent elbow pressed back against the outside wall he prevented himself from being washed back into the vehicle. Sophie coughed up water ahead of attempting to scream. Instead she began to gag. She didn't see the crocodiles waiting at the base of the rocks, but Barry did.

Those on the bank now saw them too.

Short of staying with the decommissioned vehicle

and waiting it out, there was no recognisable escape albeit from the crocodiles or from the police.

Carl tore his eyes from the wearisome events taking place and turned to gauge Josey's take on what was happening, not doubting for a second that his boss would be blaming himself for Sophie's demise.

Carl didn't like what he then saw, yet the thought had also crossed *his* mind; but venturing into the torrent that powerfully traversed the rocks, was absolute suicide. "Don't even think about it," he warned. You'll only kill yourself.

"He's right, Detective, Morris attested, "their safe so long as they stay put."

Josey didn't look too sure. "I know I said don't corner him and that's the only reason I'm still standing here. Right now he is *definitely* feeling trapped."

"We put out a call for help," the inspector contributed. "Apparently the locals are known to have rescued quite a few people here. I'm not sure if it was as bad as *this* though."

One of the coppers interrupted, "Inspector, we've got company, not sure if he's the guy come to help."

The group checked back up the road and saw the aboriginal man being referred to.

"Better not walk on rock," this local man warned on his approach. "Slippery out there, boss, plenty of your-mob die."

Your-mob' is an inoffensive aboriginal phrase for *'you white fella's'*.

One of the young local constables added, "Plenty

of *their-mob* die here too don't worry about that – saving *us* usually. This is Skipper, everyone"

With an impressive grin Skipper exhibited a row of perfectly preserved off-white teeth—

A *shrill scream* portended the sudden and sickening sound of the wedged vehicle breaking free of the rocks that had fastened it, gravity taking it and the hapless passengers to the province of milling crocodiles.

From the hopelessly out of reach sanctuary of the bank they bore witness to the beasts writhing in expectation, swimming with the flow of the river and the metal-box, like those that had previously plummeted in with gifts which were usually unachievable to snatch without falling foul to the will of the once a year torrent.   From past experience the beasts knew the foreign body would submerge and give up its cargo. This time they were even luckier, the cargo was already in the water.

"We can follow the river," Skipper yelled. "Come, bring car, I'll show." He was pointing to an unsealed track that branched off the road into the bush.

Everyone began hurriedly boarding the four wheel drive police vehicle – *almost everyone.*

"Where's Josey?" Carl cried out to the others as he was about to join them.

They then caught a glimpse of him as he dove into the river from the public viewing platform, swept away in the foaming torrent and gone from view in seconds.

Skipper was all business now as he invited himself to go with the police. "We can be quick – there a spot where everything come to *stop* – I take you now!"

Riding a wild torrent infested with hungry crocs was somewhat above Josey's pay-grade; especially at water level; the crocodiles favoured hunting ground. Josey was several metres behind and he could see the four-by four with Barry and Sophie abreast having fallen from it, but there was no sign of a single reptile. It brought to mind something he had been told, *for every crocodile that you can see, there's another ten that you can't.*

It was a daunting thought but not half as formidable as would be having to announce to Mitchell and Beverley that she had been taken by one. What he was doing was pure instinct; driven as he was by adrenalin and a fear of failure to protect. Each moment of not being attacked and taken underwater to drown before being eaten was a moment cherished. Preservation prompted the idea that crocodiles may possibly be most efficient when in still waters, where they could slowly and deliberately weigh up their chances of a successful hit.

An instant chill ran through his veins when a dark shape surfaced nearby. It was just a piece of floating timber. It was a short reprieve; movement on the bank caught his eye. At the same time he became aware the conditions were changing. The river was slowing. The calming surface was allowing him to realise what he'd seen a moment ago was a gang of crocs that had been perched on the muddy bank. He dared to look back and saw some of them slipping into the water. It was at this point that he wondered if they moved with the same agility and speed as sharks. The time it took to think about this, *was yet another moment to cherish*.

Josey knew enough about guns to realise that they will most likely still fire if wet, *but how wet?* He knew they would fire after having been exposed to heavy rain, or immersed in water. They'll even work underwater if they haven't been submerged for too long. He wanted to be sure. He pulled his pistol from the holster, held it in the air and pulled the trigger. *It worked*.

The gunshot attracted Bryant's attention away from the task of getting Sophie back aboard their unlikely amphibious motor car. The good news in this for Josey was that Barry still had reason to protect her.

The instability and movement of the burbling river made it difficult for Barry to spot anything in the water that might be swimming, but he managed. The arm in the air and the gun that he'd heard made it easier, yet desperately disappointing. Seeing the detective in hot pursuit seemed close to *impossibly gallant*, but there he was. The selflessness made him feel sick with hate.

A little less vulnerable knowing his gun works, Josey began to paddle with his legs in the hope he might gain on the vehicle. At its present distance he was unable to use the weapon for fear of hitting Sophie, yet with the flow of the river still slowing he was in hope of being offered a chance.

Of course no doubt the crocodiles were likely

making the same assessment to gain *their* goals.

Ahead of the ensemble the water appeared to be glass smooth, judging by reflections from overhanging trees. It crossed his mind to reach the bank, leave the water and run faster than the slowing current of the river. At that very moment the car hit something beneath the water and flipped on its side, the upside being it was now stationary in relation to the path of the river.

Reaching the bank became mandatory for Josey, not *just a logistical idea*. He hadn't seen Sophie and her father hit the water but it was a definite possibility in light of the jolt of the impact. He rather hoped Barry might have managed to keep a hold of the vehicle and in turn Sophie. He wondered if Bryant's motives might be changing considering the possibility of death for him was still high on the list of outcomes. Or was he callous enough to be still considering the financial forfeiture if she were to slip away from him and be taken.

The calmer water assisted Josey in reaching the bank, but once there found the mud was as obstructive as syrup. *He managed.* Once on his feet he slogged through the slop until he was level with the obstruction, part of which could now be seen above water; a thick brow of a submerged tree. The snagged vehicle was a good seventy metres out and, although he could see those stranded aboard, they hadn't as yet seen him due to having positioned themselves with their backs turned.

The tenuous way in which it held the four-by-four from advancing downstream, produced the hope there was plenty more branches below the surface, and with a bit of luck stuck firmly in a muddy foundation.

From the perspective of the three foot high bank, Josey could see the dubious life raft was encircled by the company Barry and Sophie had been sharing while in the water. He counted five reptiles, and did the sums on the popular saying. However many there were, they were totally as interested in the entrapped people as him, but for a very different reason.

Those down river had to swim upstream against the slowing current so as to maintain their position in the circle. The meal for all was becoming more and more assured the longer their targets remained marooned. Their unwavering persistence in negotiating smaller branches clouding the route amplified their chances of success even further.

The beast's marathon swim was taking place just this side of the submerged tree; there was no chance of Josey helping them without becoming the meal himself. The situation needed to change and fast, the desperate couple were dangerously low in the water and sooner or later at least one of the hungry reptiles might suddenly make a lunge, they were known to have reached in and taken people from stationary boats.

Josey looked down river and noticed there were other trees that had yielded to the eroding banks. But that wasn't all that he saw, there was a broad patch of white-water suggesting rapids, or perhaps a drop-off of some sort. Not a waterfall he expected, this part of the world was known to be mostly flat. It occurred to him the crocs would not want to go anywhere near it. At the very least what he was seeing had to be rapids, meaning it would most likely be laced with rocks and boulders. He held his breath to listen above the roar of the river, feeling sure there were indeed rapids, and possibly not something to look forward to if you wanted to survive them.

As feared, one of the more aggressive crocs advanced toward the target, secrecy no longer its consideration.

Josey was tempted to abandon caution and leap into the river, an act that would see him encircled by the monsters.

When one decides to make a dangerous move like this it's common to seek a better way before committing. His delay in acting promised to pay off when he noticed a chance that might decommission the risk of diving in with hungry crocs. First he needed to draw Barry's attention.

He pulled his gun; he'd thought about using it earlier but figured blood in the water might set off an eating frenzy. It was too late to second guess that now. He fired. Not wishing to waste a bullet, he'd aimed at the croc that seemed the most brazen, a forerunner anxious to gain a meal before the others.

It took out the beast's eye, and blood or no blood the crocs went wild, raising a blanket of white-water that cloaked father and daughter within the fray.

Bryant reasoned the shot had come from the riverbank behind him, unaware the detective had made it out of the water. The churning veil raised by the fray was preventing him from verifying it was Josey who fired the shot.

Beyond the visually impenetrable spray he then heard a desperate shout permeating through—

"Barry listen, you need to get the hell *out of* there while you still can, there's too many of these buggers to shoot.

"More will come.

"You're not safe where you are.

"There's an overhanging tree downriver that's in line with this one, close to the bank, take a look you'll see, the flow will take you right to it."

It crossed Josey's mind that Bryant might not be prepared to escape the crocs only to end up behind bars. An even more worrying thought was that Sophie wasn't making a sound.

Is she too terrified the scream?

Or is she perhaps still delirious from the drug?

Josey continued to plea with Bryant to do as he says.

"It's in your path I can catch you as you pass beneath the bough, but let me get ahead.

"Stay where you are until I'm in position

He got no immediate response.

"Are you with me, Barry?"

Still nothing.

"For *god sake man* this's your one and only chance!"

As if to cement the dire warning, Sophie's piercing scream resounded above the roar of the river, suddenly awake and terrified now. Her desperation encouraged Barry to take the detective's unarguable advice, something he wasn't at all comfortable with.

"All right," he screamed in annoyance, "fuck off to the other tree."

Josey ignored the less than amiable response.

In the porridge like consistency of the muddy bank, Josey scarcely managed to pull his feet free of the mud, but once he did he moved quickly, arriving at the fallen tree in time to see Barry was readying himself to comply with the plan.

Clambering onto the thin trunk that arched over the river like an archer's bow, he precariously grappled along it, reaching the point where with any sort of luck they would pass beneath.

He dangled his arms in the hope of pulling Sophie free of Bryant's hold with one hand and steadying himself on the trunk with the other.

That was the plan, and he hoped Barry realised there was no way he could take his weight at the same time as lifting Sophie from his arms.

It didn't play out exactly like that. Josey did manage to grab hold of Sophie's outstretched arm on their way beneath, leaving his other arm dangling for Barry to take hold.

"Barry this won't work, I need both arms for Sophie."

"So how the *fuck're* you going to help me?"

"For a start, grab hold of her legs once I get her part way onto the branch; we'll figure out what to do after that." He looked up to see what the crocs were up to and saw they had settled down, and were regrouping. "We need to be real quick about this."

Josey warned.

This was a powerful incentive for Barry to comply.

Sophie had clung to the detective, wrapping her arms around his neck.

Barry held fast to Sophie's legs, feeling somewhat terrified about still being in the water.

"All right, sweetheart, I want you to hold onto me real hard while I lift. I'll need both arms to hold onto Uncle, will you be able to hold on?"

She buried her face against him and made no answer.

Josey was the only one who could see the danger they were in.

The gang of reptiles; done fighting, they'd regrouped and were coming in faster than the flow, which was still slow but increasing now that they were closer to the drop-off – either way, the calmer waters were aiding the beasts hunting skills.

They were only thirty metres from reaching the bough, which equated to thirty seconds before they'd have their way.

This was a deadly stalemate, something had to give or they would all be taken.

Josey locked eyes with Barry in the hope of reasoning with him. "Do the right thing for once in your life, let her go, mate – she doesn't deserve to die like this." He checked the crocs with about ten seconds left by his reckoning, but they were nowhere to be seen, the river flow had taken them wide, toward the rapids; the monstrous gang had been swept beyond their targets – *momentarily*.

They knew better than to be taken to the drop-off.

Turning against the tide, their mighty tails drove them upstream, once again toward their goal.

Josey had to twist to face the crocs that were now advancing from behind. He had the pistol in his left hand, which wasn't ideal for him, but he fired two wild shots to inject some discouragement.

On Barry again, now with the pistol aimed at the rogue's face, he laid the situation on the line. "I can't save you both, let Sophie go; you'll reach the drop off before our friends can get to you. Take your chances on the rapids – chances are the crocs won't follow – you need to hurry; otherwise we can end this right now; your choice." The gun was his only trump card right now, with the crocodiles no more than five metres away, if he was ever to lift Sophie from their hungry mouths, he needed to shoot, not at *them*, but rather the man who calls himself a father. He didn't cherish the thought of killing her father right in front of her, or anyone else for that matter. Something like this would stay with her for the rest of her life, not that the memory of the crocodiles wouldn't.

But, with Bryant remaining defiant to the point where it seemed he'd take his daughter with him rather than give her up, Josey made his choice and fired.

The bullet never reached its mark; Bryant was swept clear of the detective's bullet, having been snatched away by powerful jaws, both now in the grip of the river.

The beast that *had* taken hold of his leg had likely been distracted by its success in obtaining a meal, enough not to realise the rapids were too close to escape.

Barry saw his daughter boosted from the water as he went, lifted to safety by the meddling detective.

Then in his mind he saw the branch that his daughter and Josey felt safe on, snap under their weight, depositing both of them in amongst the expectant reptiles. He saw their blood spill, thinned by the torrent as their life's force followed him to the falls.

Thankfully, this was his final fantasy before realising he was looking into the eyes of what he perceived to be a mercilessly-hungry-killer – for real.

Freefalling together now, the hunter and the hunted, doomed to ride the rapids among a new infestation – *rocks and boulders* – to end amongst whatever lay beyond.

This was no fantasy.

CHAPTER TWENTY-NINE
Saving Sophie

Atop the precarious branch, Josey drew her in tightly, holding her close to avert her witnessing her father's calamitous end.

Yet, the two of them were by no means out of trouble.

The milling beasts swam over each other in an attempt to be first to reach their prize.

Although presently out of range of the threat, Josey knew the situation might quickly change. He needed to back away to the safety of the bank, as dubious as that was.

How many shots did he have left?

He had plenty of bullets in a plastic box in his pocket but trying to reload while holding Sophie was not an option. "Sophie, I want you to close your eyes," he told her keeping her face hidden. "Listen to what I say now, will you do that for me?" He felt her nod against his chest. "I'm going to fire my gun again, are you ready?" She didn't answer so he knew she was as ready as she'd ever be.

She didn't see Josey shoot but she heard it. She also heard the tell tail thrashing of the crocodiles beneath.

While the agitated animals were busy assessing what they were now dealing with, Josey began the scary process of instructing Sophie on what comes next. "I want you to keep hold of my hands and lay flat. Keep your eyes closed. I will not let you go I promise. Do you understand?

"I'm scared," she admitted with the utmost conviction.

"I know, sweetheart. I'll keep you safe if you do just like I tell you. Lay flat now with your legs out straight behind you. Do that now Sophie, I promise I won't let go of your hands."

She bravely did as asked while he crabbed backward until they were both flat on the log facing each other.

"Now Sophie, I want you to start crawling toward me as I slowly move back. Try your hardest not to let yourself slide sideways; – Are you okay to try?"

Her answer was to sob, her eyes firmly closed. She sensed the detective was beginning to draw away, just the way he told her he would, and as promised never letting go of her hands, it gave her confidence and the strength to do as he had instructed; though the wild thrashing of the beasts, the roar of the river and rumble of thunder all built a terrifying image in her head – she saw herself in this wicked picture, *desperately wishing she wasn't.*

"We're almost there, sweetie."

Josey felt his shoes slip on the slimy solidity of the mud that lined the riverbank; his eyes still firmly on the whereabouts of the beasts. Knowing they were able to walk and run, and fast at doing so, certainly faster than a man in mud, meant they were not home free just yet.

With this risk in mind he thought to reload the pistol before one of the crocs worked out their best option to gain dinner was to attack on land.

"Sophie we're safe now, he fibbed, "so I'm letting go of one hand. Keep your eyes closed, sweetie, we'll be away from here real soon."

He needn't have worried about her opening her eyes; she had no intention of seeing what was going on around her.

Josey used his free hand to pull the box of bullets out from his jacket and balance it between the log and his chin. With his head the only thing shielding the open container from the pouring rain he nimbly reloaded, opting to close the box in spite of the ammunition left being a little dampened.

"All right, I want you to open your eyes and keep them on *me*. Don't look anywhere other than at my face, do you understand Sophie?"

She nodded nervously and hesitantly did as asked.

"Here we go."

From her point of view with eyes firmly fixed on the detective, she saw nothing other than his extended arms holding her hands, his shoulders mounted on elbows, and a determined face that wore an encouraging smile.

She felt her clothing strain against the rough bark of the broad bough, and saw the detective's struggle as he wriggled backward, toward the edge of the river.

"We're nearly there, sweetie." His shoes reached the mud as he spoke and with toes dug in he began clawing at it. "We need to be very quick now, so soon as I'm standing I want you to stand too. Don't worry I'll help you. As soon as you're on your feet I'll pick you up and carry you away from here – get ready."

His actions then matched his plan to the 'T', even to his secret prediction that his feet would sink deeper into the mud, driven by the extra weight; not a great feeling when you see the curious crocs beginning to approach the riverbank. "Cover your ears, sweet," he advised grabbing his pistol from a jacket pocket; and without delay firing at one of forerunners that were advancing toward them. The bullet met its mark somewhere near the bulbous eyes, changing the brazen beast's tiny mind. Its blood mixed with rain and the croc retorted in pain, sanctioning the fact pistol bullets could penetrate their thick skins at close range.

Josey whisked Sophie into his arms and ran, creating the effect of moving in slow motion. Slow as it was, it was fast enough. The black mud petered out a few yards up ahead, quickening his pace. The river too was moving faster as it got closer to the rapids.

At a stone's throw from the drop-off, Josey felt

certain there was nil chance of encountering more crocodiles. He elected to take to the bush with a view to making his way to lower ground, where he hoped he'd find a way across to the eastern side of the river. In his mind's eye he tried to imagine where the aboriginal track was, the one taken by police. He knew it had to be somewhere at the very top of the steep rise on the eastern side, and accepted that he'd have to make the climb to find them.

It was a climb that would not be easy, storm produced cascades had developed between massive boulders that dotted the face of the substantial hill.

The river too was laced with similarly sized boulders, obstructing and broadening the flow, shallowed but still with an amount of pace. Smaller rocks marked a maze of possible paths to the other side; just how slippery could not be determined until stepped upon.

Without choice he ventured onto the maze, treading gingerly in the knowledge losing a footing could also amount to losing Sophie.

As noted, the waters still moved at a substantial speed yet lacked the depth to apply substantial force, *that*, and the stepping stones; the only thing making passage possible – if taken with care.

To his right lay the base of the fall, where the river bubbled; randomly endeavouring to find its level. If Barry was beneath it there was no way of telling.

But Josey ached to see he was actually dead, hoping he might get close enough to the base of the rapids to check for any sign of him. He wanted to be sure that part of her life was done with for good. He would only make this observation if Sophie could be prevented from seeing it. He had protected her from watching her father fall into the rocks and so long as he could continue guarding her from grizzly details like this, in time memories of the horrendous event would hopefully fade.

The hope of locating Bryant's body came to pass at the half way point in the crossing.

Although the body of her father was far enough away that recognition could be considered doubtful, it was easily recognisable as a human body just the same.

Josey asked Sophie to once again close her eyes; a ruse to again prevent her from seeing the corpse, not just Bryant's but the doomed crocodile as well. The beast was thrashing in the throes of death, creating a sound accompanied by the animal's guttural complaint.

With eyes closed, Sophie's heightened sense of sound applied a picture in her mind. She'd heard the calamity of the hungry crocodiles and seen what they looked like when she first crossed the river with her uncle, but the picture in her head now outweighed all she'd seen or imagined. "I want Mummy," she whimpered.

Her fear broke his heart. "I'm taking you to see her, sweetheart; don't cry, you're safe now." Josey wasn't as sure about that as he sounded.

Once passed the boulders and onto the eastern bank they were faced with a steep climb, which he hoped would lead to the Aboriginal track and a waiting police vehicle. Although there were no certainties there either, he felt it was his best option. In spite of the typically disruptive storm rebuilding, which had subsided for the last ten minutes, he pushed on.

Carrying Sophie was hard enough without the growing cascades of runoff that threatened to keep challenging. He took each step with great care, perishing the thought of slipping. Fifteen minutes of this torturous uphill trek made it impossible to continue. The risk of being swept away with Sophie in his arms was too great. He needed to find cover. Taking refuge beneath the downside of a sizable boulder he took a spell, placing Sophie down with his legs wrapped around her to prevent her sliding away.

While resting, he used the time to look round for any sign of more substantial shelter. Through the sleet, a dark shape interrupted the grey of the storm, just a few yards away. It could be a cave or grotto. To get to it meant cutting diagonally across a couple of thankfully smaller cascades than the ones he had already crossed.

Sophie opened her eyes for the first time since leaving the river.

The dramatic spectacle that raged around them filled her with a little wonder, and fear. She considered the river below and realised the great distance the man carrying her had come. She recognised that he must have had to make his way through giant boulders and waterfalls.

Looking up the incline she also feared how far

there was to go. Her little arms suddenly wrapped around his neck and squeezed him firmly in a gesture of appreciation, a thank you for just being there.

What then came from her mind blew Josey away. "I don't know your name."

The words swam across him in a wave of emotional wonder, and a blunder that hadn't even entered his head. "Oh, I'm sorry, pet; my name is Cameron."

If Josey had shed a tear at that moment it wouldn't have been possible to notice. "Hang on tight; I see a place to get us out of the rain. You ready?"

She nodded her approval and Josey set out on the task at hand. Knowing the protection of the cave would also offer rest, recuperation, and an escape from the chill of living in wet clothes; it would also protect them against the very real danger of hyperthermia. This part of the world at this time of the year wasn't particularly cold, around twenty degrees Celsius, but lengthy exposure in wet clothes, along with trauma, is still a dangerous combination.

He slipped more than once atop loose rocks and rain drenched mud, fearful of failing to protect the little girl in his care. Battling against the odds of living or dying they finally reached and entered the yawning mouth of the grotto, a sanctuary guarded against the wind blown deluge.

Inside, the weather was rapidly beaten into a magical lull, the cave; pitch dark.

Looking back, the rim of the grotto framed just

what they had escaped from; the storm, relentlessly speeding by unabated, so very fast that scarcely a drop of rain wavered from its destructive course to enter.

Although Sophie felt warmer out of the wind, it didn't prevent her shaking off a shiver. With eyes adjusting to the dark, she began to nervously study the dim walls and ceiling. The shadows that suddenly danced to the savage rhythm of blinding lightning strikes, along with conjoined eruptions, put together, did nothing to help quell her chill; nor did the sheer mystery of the place they were in, a place that had no door. This prompted her to recall the vile river monsters. Their ability to walk on land raised the hope they couldn't climb the hill, as had the detective.

"Don't be scared," Josey told her soothingly, pulling her close for warmth as they sat against the cavern's back wall. He removed his wet jacket and placed it around her shoulders. He was under no illusions; they were still in deep trouble given the chance of being stricken by hypothermia, especially if they were unable to start a fire, and soon.

Josey knew of a few survival methods, most of which would need some essential props. Before he could do anything he'd need light. He removed his cell and checked to see if it still worked. There was a chance it might, having been zipped up in a pocket of his wet weather gear. In near darkness he felt for the on button and pressed it in sincere hope. The dark interface immediately lit up, weakly illuminating the inside of the cave.

For Sophie, seeing detail in the craggy surfaces looked more frightening than the light from the storm. When Cameron turned his light off, the former returned. Now she couldn't make her mind up which one she hated the most. It made her mind drift away to the memory of being wrapped up warmly in bed with her mummy reading to her from a story book. *Oh how she wished she was there now*.

Josey heard her whimper and he knew he needed to work fast to get their temporary house in order. "Hey, do you know what I'm about to do?"

"No?" she whimpered with a quiver.

"I'm lighting us a nice warm fire, would you like that?"

He felt her nod against him, accompanied by a shuddering shiver she had no control over.

The phone's battery was on fifty per cent, which was something at least, while in use though it would need to be quick. The dull glow from the interface turned into a harsh floodlight, clearly providing a tapestry of what lay about on the ground. A small discarded campfire, which he had noticed on the way in, showed they were not the first visitors. He wondered if these people had been lucky enough to have matches, and had they dropped or left some?

Not too far from the untidy circle of ash there was a small mound of dry grass, presumably left for the next visitor, or perhaps they just hadn't used it. But bless them; they had provided a healthy amount of tinder for at least a short stay or a quick warm meal, sadly the latter would not be possible.

"I want you to block your ears again because I

need to shoot my gun." He eased away from her and got to his feet. Her puzzled eyes followed him as he stepped toward the mouth of the cave. "Where are you going?" her little voice shook in a mix of fear and cold.

He paused and turned to face her. "I need you to put your hands over your ears while I shoot out into the rain, *do like before* okay?"

She already knew that Cameron had used his gun to shoot at the crocodiles, and logic told her that the monsters might now be right outside the cave, having climbed up from the river. *But she could see no connection between that and lighting a fire.*

Josey suddenly realised his unintentional mistake from her expression. "Hey, the monsters can't get up here, sweetie."

"Then what are you shooting?"

He thought her annunciation and attitude sounded more like that of an eight year old, commanding a proper answer. "I'm starting a fire, you'll see – block you're ears now."

He raised the pistol toward the sky and she quickly clamped her hands against her ears, defusing the sharp sound of the six shots he fired and the delayed echoes that bounced back from the craggy walls. Josey had an additional and ulterior motive for the display, the sound would let their friends know they are still alive and in the general vicinity. They might be conflicted over who fired the shots, but that was a chance he had to take.

"I don't see a fire." Sophie shivered while he turned back in with the gun still smoking in his hand.

"No?" he quizzed playing along, "Watch." He bent to the mound of dry grass and picked up a single culm and poked it into the hot barrel of his pistol. A light flame took hold, which he carried over to the tinder. He brought a good fistful of the sticks to where Sophie was now watching on with growing interest, enthralled by the detective's antics, and his eventual success.

The tinder had accepted the tiny flame offered, gently growing in warmth and light.

Sophie unravelled her folded arms and presented the palms of her hands to the flickering warmth. She wriggled closer to the increasing heat while Josey was busy collecting some more substantial dry brush and firewood that was lying around, enough to keep the flames alive until it was time to leave their temporary abode. From this first fire he made two more, creating a semi-circle that faced the rock wall.

She smiled into the fire appreciatively. "I think you are a magician?" she offered without lifting her eyes, again sounding older than her years.

"Do you know what?"

"What?"

"I think you are a very smart girl, and a brave one."

She shrugged, happy to just soak up the warmth from the growing ring of fire.

"We have to take off a few of our wet clothes, pet," he told her while discarding his Jacket, "they'll only make us feel colder." He removed his shirt, shoes and socks ahead of helping her. "Now we can dry them next to the fire."

She grasped his logic when he slipped his waterproof jacket across her bare shoulders. "Here, this will help keep you warm – leave the front open to the fire."

With knees folded back against her, the jacket went all the way to the ground upon where she sat, capturing the warmth.

He nestled against her to share his body warmth; it wasn't long before she was sound asleep. This little girl had survived an ordeal that she'd never totally get over, certainly never forget.

He too gave way to exhaustion – his mind ebbing from the mesmerising flicker of the campfire's dying glow; its dimming dance against the oppressive black walls struggling to continue . . .

Josey finally drifted uneasily into the oblivion of sleep, so ending a gruelling day . . .

. . . Or was it?

At first, in the restless dream that followed, he didn't sense her slipping from his side.

Nor did he sense the reason.

Then, as senseless as it was – Barry Bryant stood towering over him, with Sophie in his arms. He was smiling; Sophie too; painting the picture of a very happy father and daughter.

Josey syphoned his thoughts in search of any sense in this abhorrent image—?

Did I not see this Lazarus-like creep lying dead at the base of the falls—?

"You look confused, Detective," Lazarus' sarcastic

voice suggested.

It not for Sophie's shrill and sudden objections to being held against her will, Josey might still have been inside this nightmare, believing that he'd somehow got the whole thing wrong.

He hadn't.

Her cry was the sickening sound of terror. She had neither the energy nor the gumption to plea for her *mother* – or for her *father*, whoever she believed him to be right then.

Has Barry told her the truth about himself?

Perhaps in the cosy confines of the train he had filled her head with conflicting stories? Perhaps he made her doubt the intentions of the people who she believed were her parents? After all, they had locked her away with the nuns without explanation.

The possibility he coaxed her would have been feasible, given Josey and Carl had never lost sight of Sophie since Barry took her on the Ghan. It had been noticed she went with him everywhere willingly, remaining calm the whole time.

During the long journey, the perfection of Carl's alto egos had allowed for openly milling amongst the passengers, to the extent they had even made some friends. Never once did their presence raise any suspicion.

Now, all this seamless work had come completely undone.

Still weak with exhaustion, Josey had no cards to play, groggily aware that the gun was in the jacket Sophie was wearing.

Barry smiled at the irony. "Never mind, detective,

I'll take good care of your pistol, and your jacket, and little Sophie here. She's safe with me, you know that."

Sophie squirmed.

"Don't worry, cherub," Barry sang like he really cared how scared she was. "I mean every word I say." He had two weapons now, the gun, and the knife he'd had on display the whole time, held in the hand of the same arm that nursed his daughter. The long blade, if faced specifically, may well have allowed Sophie to see her own reflection in it.

As it was she could not bring herself to even look.

"You're being very quiet, Detective – nothing to say?"

"Well, I will say this; you're not getting very far carrying her in this storm."

Noticing Josey eyeing the wound above where the crocodile had taken its bite, he glanced down at blood oozing profusely onto his trouser leg. "Don't let this fool you into thinking I can't manage, I've already climbed from the river and I've plenty left in me. So here's what you'll do if you don't want anyone getting hurt." He put the knife to Sophie's throat.

She recoiled to the cold touch of the blade pressing against her skin; gaining a small nick, enough to draw blood.

It stung and she wept in terror.

Sick with anger Josey struggled to his feet even as Barry was drawing the pistol on him.

"Don't do anything rash now – I know your gun is empty in case you're wondering, but that's what we're about to remedy – Sit!"

Josey quickly weighed up the options –

There weren't any.

He conceded defeat and sat as instructed.

"Good boy. Now, how 'bout you grab the box of ammo I know you got there and toss it out in front; careful not to fall short . . . Do it, Detective. Your part in this is done."

Beaten, he fumbled in the leather pouch that looped around his belt and extracted the backup ammunition, while doing so recognising the slimmest chance of turning the tables.

He anticipated the throw and flung the container of bullets while unclipping the lid. The contents cascaded from their container and scattered across the ground, far enough away from Barry to force him to take a step forward to gain his prise.

He recognised Josey's ploy but took the steps anyway; cautiously choosing to only come to those slugs furthest from the detective's reach, confident the hero wouldn't risk Sophie's safety.

He really only needed a single bullet to end Josey's annoying persistence, yet was able to grab three.

From where he sat with bended knees Josey applied a sharp kick at the spent campfire, lifting dying embers into Barry's face, following with a lunge that allowed him to take a firm hold on Sophie.

Barry's combat skills kicked in as the detective's brazen extraction set up a spin - switching the knife from hand to hand to come from behind and sink the long blade deep into Josey's back.

The pistol spiralled and lodged somewhere out of sight.

Sophie screamed and drew her mind from the violence with her eyes clamped shut. The darkness encouraged images of what she had already witnessed. In her mind she saw her father doing hurtful things to the detective. She was sure she would be next.

His rough touch and hateful voice, attempting to convey kindness toward her, was doomed to failure.

She reluctantly opened her eyes and saw that her only hope of rescue lay in agony on the ground – and *helpless.*

Her reprieve had been fleeting, now again in the arms of her deranged father, left brushing at his eyes and ash-powdered-face, he looked ready to kill. "Goddamn you, you fucker - she is *my daughter.*"

No reaction to Barry calling her his daughter raised suspicion. "You told her didn't you?"

"So what if I did. I don't mean her any harm; she belongs with me . . . All *you* need to do is *back off.*"

He then noted she had her face turned away so as not to look at him.

"I don't think she wants to go with you, *Daddy.*"

Rage infiltrated Barry's troubled mind, raising blood routs of trace lines across his temples. "You forced my hand, arsehole – this is on you."

"If you can't see what all this is doing to your daughter, think about where it ends, do you really think she'll love you after what you've done?

Sophie is way smarter than that—"

"Josey, this is Carl—If you're hearing this, fire your pistol if you're able—!"

This impossibly loud windswept voice emerging from out of the storm suddenly promised a game change. Not that Barry's doings were a game; far from it.

– we're already on our way down to find you—"

Barry's injury was no longer his only problem. Given the amount of cops he'd seen at the lodge, he knew the amplified voice had to be from them. He figured it was only a matter of time before they had eyes in the sky. They'd be in the air already if not for the conditions.

Gun Shots rang out yet again – followed by—

"If you can hear me – stay where you are and sit tight – we are on our way—"

It was hard to know where the voice was originating, but it had to be coming from higher up.

More Gun Shots! – This time sounding closer, but that might just be a trick of the wind. Barry wasn't taking chances. As he needn't worry about Josey following he made a hasty retreat with Sophie in his arms; stepping out into the storm.

All his helpless daughter could do was close her eyes and scream, out into the torrential rain, again to where the crocodiles live.

Josey's mind commanded that he take chase but his draining energy had other ideas. The fact he could still reason told him he hadn't sustained a fatal injury, this assurance was circumvented by the amount of blood he was losing. The shock of being stabbed was taking time to come to grips with

A deeper assessment of his state told him his stabbing injury wasn't life threatening; well not in an immediate sense. He was bleeding yes, and in a heap of pain, but the knife had passed through what is commonly known as the love handles – *through and through*—

He feebly searched for where the empty pistol had landed, disgusted with himself, it would have taken just one remaining bullet to change the regretful outcome. It wasn't just this that was bugging him, it included the fact Bryant had slipped through his fingers so many times, and the count was climbing.

Immensely annoyed by the failure, he fought against pain to scrape around for the pistol and found it had slid in amongst some remaining kindling. He then fisted handfuls of the scattered bullets and roughly lodged them in a jacket pocket for easy reach, filling the chamber then while unsteadily getting to his feet.

His blood pumped alarmingly, driven by the sheer exertion, applying a sense of undue pressure to his upper arms – the stuff of heart attacks.

He reached the torrential curtain at the mouth of the cave and realised the enormous obstacle of even seeing through it, let alone following. As hopeless as it seemed he had to try. Once in the midst of the storm he was faced with the added problem of not being able to hear anything beyond rain.

He thought he heard a scream down toward the river. Was it a scream or the call of a bird—?

Another sound crashed above the storm—

Three more shots, their echoes washed away by the gale.

The source was from atop the hill as before. He knew it was his friends, still up on the track, or perhaps they had advanced downhill by now. He responded with *three shots* of his own.

The voice that bounced back from above definitely sounded as if it was getting closer—

"Josey, fire once if you're low on bullets — let us know you're okay?"

Josey sent off the requested shot.

With no chance of his voice matching the decibels of the loud speaker, he followed up at the top of his voice with, "I'm here – *I'm here* – Sophie desperately needs our help!"

With no response he realised being heard above the squall was futile, *as expected*. He also realised the sound of gunshots would have reached the ears of Sophie's Captor. And Sophie too, yet it was doubtful she would understand it to mean that help was on its way, *or was it?*

He was feeling weaker by the minute.

He had no choice though; he needed to push on toward the river, toward where he could still hear sporadic screams; at the same time hoping to be followed by police. But then being followed wasn't going to be exactly easy, or maybe not even possible, there was no telling if conditions might be even tougher further up.

His first attempt to proceed down the water washed incline amounted to losing his footing, slithering into one of the muddy streams that raced down the mountain in search of the river. The ride wasn't the smooth slippery-slide he recalled bravely descending at *Water-World,* and far less deliberate. With each rock and stump that hindered his passage, pain mercilessly reminded him he was keenly injured. Usually, *newly acquired pain* admonishes *existing - not this time.*

On the upside, it was giving him a speedy advantage in reaching the river in time to spoil Bryant's plan to escape yet again.

He certainly succeeded in arriving in time, but wasn't then faced with the scenario that would have finally seen Sophie freed from her father.

Not easily at any rate, not even close.

What he saw upon approach to the riverbank clamped icy chills around the base of his spine. With thirty feet left to slide into the mud, to his horror he saw the dreadful predicament Barry had placed his daughter in.

With his daughter in his arms, he was stuck fast, effectively surrounded by a posse of crocodiles.

Josey had kept the gun in his hand throughout the unorthodox downhill slide, and now couldn't shoot with any certainty of hitting the intended target. Reaching the mud cushioned his speed as effectively as a brake.

The beasts either ignored him or hadn't heard the stifled sound of his arrival, lingering intently on their very certain kill as they drew closer.

On his feet, Josey fired a shot in the air, causing the crocs to baulk for a moment, but then with no recognisable risk they regrouped.

With the pistol then aimed and gripped in both hands he fired with intent to kill. He would explain later to the authorities for his reckless action.

The shot met its mark, passing through the jelly-like eye of one of the beast's single-minded brains. Again the writhing encouraged an angry response from the others, resulting in the distraction Josey needed.

This didn't mean his next move would be easy, yet hesitation would be fatal.

In five sludgy steps he was right in amongst the fracas. The sound of snapping jaws rose above the growl of their anger, yet unable to compete with the screams of a five year old child.

Sophie felt she was being lowered onto her feet, into the mud, aware only of the grip that enveloped her arm, the grip from her mad-as-an-axe father.

Both father and daughter were at this point oblivious to the detective's presence.

If not for the hold on her arm, Sophie would have had every chance of negotiating an exit from the mud, her light steps less likely to sink and restrict her movement.

But Mad Barry's mind presented no evidence of this logic.

Josey trudged closer to be heard, to be able to reach for the girl, and to gain the accuracy he would need to gain attention "Barry!" he yelled in the hope he'd turn and face him.

Bryant spun to face the new and unexpected threat—

Josey *fired*, extracting a chunk of cartilage from the ratbags ear without time or the inclination to deal with Barry's insanity.

Sophie then felt herself being pulled away from her father's grip, this way and that, not at all certain if it could be the work of the crocodiles.

To her immense relief, she then saw it was Cameron, her saviour, once again pulling her to safety.

One of the crocodiles took the opportune moment to drag the bigger meal from the mud, clamping onto its leg, pulling it free, and dragging it toward the water.

Barry Bryant didn't deserve the death he was then finally awarded by the detective.

Covering Sophie's eyes, he aimed and *fired*.

Barry was dead before being left to the mercy of the hungry mob, mercy being the one thing they don't possess, not when they are hungry—

Josey held Sophie's face against his chest while quickening his stride in the glue-like mud to reach the edge of the muddy bank, eventually able to step up onto solid ground. Short of breath he told her, "You're safe now, sweetheart."

If only that were true!

Instead, the powerful wrenching haul that took her from his grasp at that moment was hard to comprehend or accept.

What evil force of nature allows such a cold and callous conclusion he thought in horror as Sophie was being dragged across the mud, the insidious intentions of the reptile unravelling as the beast backed into the river, back into the murky safe depths of its feeding dominion, back to join her father in one awful, final twist.

Driven by the unquestionable need to not give up on little Sophie, Josey clung on, by choice he entered the murky turbulence of the river without a thought for his own life . . .

Within this dark swirling world, where visibility stood no chance of existence; rescue was *impossible.*

CHAPTER THIRTY
The Repercussions

Carl stood beside the four by four that was mandatorily paused at the conclusion of the track.

The media had swarmed like bush-bugs, vying for a nibble.

The police, well *they were being police*. A constable down from Darwin was dutifully preventing anyone from venturing down the treacherous slope to reach the river.

Carl had other ideas. "If you think I'm sitting here on my thumbs you can think again."

The Queensland cop remained on his opponent before saying in annoyance, "Do you suppose I'm offering you people a choice?"

"Ease up, Constable Scott," Morris directed.

Scott didn't appreciate being reprimanded by an *off-stater* from New South Wales. "I'm just saying, that terrane is more dangerous than it looks."

Morris moved as close as he dare to the drop-off. "He's got a point, Carl—"

"We don't know if he's down there," the redeemed cop added, "the river goes right the way to the coast."

Skipper chipped in, "Rapids down there - no way past, boss."

Carl fired his pistol in the air without warning.

The two shots that bounced back strengthened his resolve. "He's down there."

Morris stepped back from the edge and took a couple of paces toward Constable Scott with his arm stretch out. "Give me that thing." He then helped himself to the microphone clipped to Scott's utility belt. "Detective Josey, this is the police – is that you down there?" The amplified message stabbed from the PA perched atop the vehicle and cut into the storm.

The indignant constable looked mildly aggravated.

A disciplinary glare from the inspector pulled his horns in; Morris then getting on with his message. "I repeat; this is the police – if you are safe, fire your pistol twice."

Three shots rang back. This was a message. "Are you in trouble? One shot for yes."

One shot came back.

"Is Sophie with you?

No response.

"Repeat – is Sophie with you?"

Still no response.

"Detective, in the hope you are still able to hear

this – we will be getting help to you real soon – we are at a standstill up here - stuck on the aboriginal track – there is no way down for us – stay were you are if possible – we have organised a search party – west side of the river . . . respond with one shot if you are receiving – I repeat, respond with one shot now.

There was no response.

The earlier gunshots had been enough incentive for Carl to face whatever dangers might be presented in negotiating the climb down.

Skipper noticed Carl's anxiety and approached him, "We can go, boss - *keep-you-safe* - if that okay."

"*More than okay*, Skipper," Carl agreed gratefully.

When Morris turned and looked for the detective's friend Carl to talk with him, he was gone – so too the aboriginal man. In disbelief, his expression had become a profound blend of worry and irritability—.

"You have got to be kidding me," the inspector breathed uneasily.

Skipper and Carl made it to the river with scratches and knocks that would later need attention. Close to the muddy bank they witnessed a chilling sight, dozens of crocodiles were milling about close to the rapids. There was no way of knowing what took place here, more than an hour ago now. Skipper was right, anyone being swept along by the river could not have gone beyond this point, unless having gone over the rocky staircase, in which case the boulder ridden rapids would have maimed or killed them. The sheer number of crocodiles was disturbing in that it suggested something must have brought them there. The depths of his stomach did acidic summersaults; he didn't want to think about the possibilities. But think about it he did – this was turning into the worst day of his life. If any of the *potentials* had already come true, it wouldn't only be *his* bad day.

He felt quite sick, yet they needed to get beyond the rapids to make sure there wasn't anyone lying injured. It wasn't a good idea to wait around thinking about it either; they were drawing more attention from the crocs than was comfortable.

Skipper took a few steps down river toward the beginning of the rapids. "Come, Baru not follow."

Clearly *Baru* meant crocodile and Carl was happy to stay on the same page as a man who would know more about protocols in the area than he ever would.

They came across the croc, lying dead in amongst the boulders, but no sign of Josey or the girl.

While negotiating the scattered rocks and boulders that stood firm against the river, Carl thought to call out in case Josey and the others were close by somewhere, perhaps in the surrounding bush.

The only response he got was the echo of his own voice.

It crossed his mind the reptiles might decide to leave the river and follow them on foot, particularly if the beasts were hungry enough, *they certainly seemed to be*. In spite of assurances from Skipper they wouldn't, he couldn't ignore the urge to keep a watch over his shoulder while searching for any more grim results.

These were people he deeply cared about – all bar one Barry Bryant.

Again his stomach rolled disturbingly.

Back on the track, Inspector Morris was getting very nervous about having received no signals and began to worry if Carl was okay.

An hour past before he and Skipper finally made a return to the track, delivering the news.

The first thing learned was their people hadn't been located.

Carl was surprised at what was going on; even the numbers of press had increased; amounting to more media than coppers. The incessant questioning of police outnumbered all measure of patience among officers that were too slow to avoid the railroading. Carl was particularly being pressurised.

Morris stepped in to end it. "All right that's enough you lot. We need to get this man some attention."

He was right; the climb down and back from the river had inflicted its toll on Carl.

The press were ignoring the injured man's demise, and even Morris's advice to back off, raising their voices in a babbling whinge fest.

Morris's gunshot got their attention. "Do I need to shoot someone?"

Although not believed, his threat was enough to put their tales between their legs before making a disgruntle retreat.

Within minutes, nationwide news broadcasters

were showing pictures of crocodiles that populate the infamous Cahill's Crossing, making no apology for the clear connection to Sophie Bryant. Speculation was running wild.

Morris walked Carl away from the madness to get his wounds checked by the Ambulance officers; earlier notified by police. "Don't beat yourself up about this, what you did going down there was admirable."

A chopper drummed loud and low overhead, they wouldn't have been allowed in the air if the weather hadn't let up a little. "That's us by the way. If Sophie and your boss are down there we'll find them."

Carl had his doubts, an hour later so too did everyone else. While being treated in the back of the ambulance he was able to hear one of the speculative broadcasts guessing this-and-that about what had happened to the people who fell into the crocodile infested river. They were even going to the point of reminding people of the *killer crossing*.

Hearing it prompted Carl to say to the ambulance officer. "I need to make a call."

She was completing the bandage on his right arm as she let him loose. "All done here; go for it."

"Thanks." He'd stepped a few paces away when his call connected. "Bec' it's me."

"Oh my god, Carl; I knew this would happen," she openly cried

"Don't listen to the news, love. Josey's been in tighter spots than this."

Morris stood watching from over near the grouped

police. He was thinking it might be advisable to quiz him on who he was calling. With all the slingshot news circling around it would be worth working with him in contacting relatives over the difficult few hours ahead.

On being approached by the friendly cop, Carl had absolutely no problem with the suggestion they join forces in dealing with it.

If it had been a *difficult few hours* as Morris had termed it, it would have been an absolute blessing; particularly if things had turned out positively. Not only did things not go positively, it all went horribly wrong Carl was forced to admit to those who asked; the choppers and a land search failed to find anyone or anything. There wasn't a scintilla of evidence the trio had survived the experience.

The press began to show their teeth in ways that were upsetting for those personally involved in what was looking more and more like an imminent loss. Mitchell and Beverly Bryant locked themselves away from the limelight in a motel that they acquired close to the search area, answering phone calls to just a few select people. They'd had calls every day from Vanessa, calling in support and needing some of her own.

Rebecca and Molly tried to add their support but were quickly rebuffed, which was somewhat unfair in that Josey's family were pining over the disappearances as much as anybody.

Inspector Morris also rang on that very first day their daughter was deemed missing. His call was to assure them the police were doing everything they could to locate Sophie and the others. He was more than a little surprised to learn Beverley was applying blame on the detective for placing their daughter at risk; using her to bait and catch Barry.

Morris shifted responsibility onto himself without hesitation. "That was my doing as much as his. Please remember that Josey's family are suffering too . . . Anyway, don't give up; finding nothing so far could be a good sign." The moment it came out of his mouth he knew his wording of the sentiment was as bad as it could be.

His call was cut-off—

Jillian Edison didn't escape scrutiny either, as she was about to find out on day two. She saw who was knocking on her door through the blinds.

The reporter almost lost his footing when he stumbled back a little when the door opened sharply, he didn't really expect it would open at all.

She immediately let fly. "Don't speak you grub, I know who you are and I've seen the garbage you've been feeding to people that I know and respect; so bugger off."

"*Whoa*," he protested, "I was hoping you could tell me if Sophie Bryant is still alive – *can you?*"

"That's cute; if I told you she *is* –would you even believe me?"

"That's not up to me; my readers make up their own minds."

"Well, I suggest you make your own mind up about this! She reached around the door and came out with a walking stick supporting an ornamental brass knob that looked lethal enough to break open a skull. "Walk away now or leave on a gurney – your choice."

He held up his hands and retreated to the front gate before giving her the finger.

"Nice," she whispered in disgust.

Two more days went by with no sign of the missing people. Then, on day four, news came through that Josey had been found, lost wandering through the bush by an aboriginal man.

The media went completely crazy; speculation grew to unprecedented new heights. Morris and Carl flew back to Darwin to see Josey in the hospital where he had been admitted. After four days of having partaken nothing but water he looked as you'd expect. He was on a drip to build up nutrients and had so many bandaged injuries he looked like a patch quilt.

The Queensland police had already spoken to him as expected. The media throng that encircled the entrances to the hospital had tried to do the same but without success.

On their visit to Josey in the hospital, the conversation *had with Carl and Morris* was kept short by order of the doctors. It wasn't until the end of the week when he was sitting up in bed and off the drip that they were able to find out more about what happened.

For Morris, the somewhat sketchy explanation was disappointingly inadequate in Josey's blow by blow description of what went down, beyond what might be imagined or expected already. But having been there when Josey jumped into the river to rescue

Sophie and perhaps even her father, anything other than being taken by the current – accompanied by crocodiles - was clear enough.

The exact details following that, as told by Josey, were expressed as tactfully as possible, understandably; even so they were harrowing. At the time, the close calls with death occasionally produced hopes of escape, but then stealing all hope of survival for either father or daughter.

By now Sophie's paternal heritage was well known in the press, even the disgusting disconnection with his flesh and blood was beginning to surface.

The saddest thing of all for people to accept was the cruelty of fate itself. The thought of what happened to Sophie; too difficult to contemplate, could not be easily put into words.

Josey's *unreadable* tears were spent by the time he opened up to the Inspector. "There was nothing I could do – I swear to God I tried."

Morris wasn't having him blame himself. "Forget that stuff, Detective. I saw the way you jumped in that river with no concern for your own safety. You don't need to apologise for anything."

Josey's cell trilled quietly from the small table beside his bed; he checked to see who was calling and quickly decided it wasn't about to interrupt the meeting.

"You can take that if you want," Morris offered.

"No that's fine, I'll call them back."

"Look I need to get out of your hair anyway. Get some rest. I'm sticking around the area for a few more days, I'll pop in again."

"Appreciate you coming in, Fin."

"No problem," They shook hands ready to leave.

Josey's offsider made a move to leave as well. "I'll be on my way too."

"Carl, can you give me five minutes? I need to talk to you about a couple of things."

Morris understood and recommenced his exit. "Right, I'll catch you guys later."

The moment the inspector left the room Carl asked, "I gather you're about to tell me who that was on the phone."

Josey grinned, almost with a sparkle in his eye. "Very perceptive, you gather correctly. Do you think Morris noticed?"

"That the person who called was none of his business?

"*Yes.*"

The person on the other end of that call was definitely not someone for Morris to be concerned about. "Well, whatever he thinks he saw makes no difference. Pull up a pew, Carl."

Even the detective and his partner couldn't be absolutely certain that Morris *had* indeed noticed the subterfuge, in which they got him to leave the room before Josey took the call, and in fact the detective's highly suspicious request for a private chat had set the coppers overactive brain into complete overdrive.

Josey's wife and daughter came in to see him several times during his recuperation, each time having to break through the army of reporters.

The press knew the story by now, or thought they did. The yarns being fed to them weren't anywhere close to enough.

The so called facts of the case had first surfaced following a statement given by the Queensland police, a reiteration of what Josey divulged. Following questions asked of the detective, and people who were also on scene at the time, the police had no reason to doubt he was telling the truth.

Mitchell and Beverley Bryant came to Darwin too, which might have been surprising if it was known Beverley mistrusted the PI. After receiving the same hustle and bustle of ploughing through the dissatisfied-reporters, the quiet of the hospital ward was like an oasis in contrast, nurses and staff respectful of what they all were going through.

Rebecca wanted to say to her husband *I told you so*, but seemed to refrain out of consideration for Sophie's mum. The Bryant's seemed to have made an about face too, deciding not to place any further weight on Josey's shoulders than he already had.

The press continued to feel robbed, hounding Mr and Mrs Bryant, and anyone who knew them, for months on end.

Josey never again agreed to speak publically and they eventually gave up on him.

He did give in to a chat with Inspector Morris though, having been feeling guilty about leaving him out of the loop. Of course Morris's insistence *there was more to the story* helped Josey in his decision to open up. From the inspector's point of view the detective seemed ready to tell the story from head to toe anyway, clearly able to quite rightly shift his focus back onto Sophie's deranged father; and the entire blame on him for little Sophie's demise.

Josey figured it was only right to enlarge on what he saw on that horrible day without holding anything out – he had developed complete trust in the head cop over the last few months and it was high time to tell him everything—

In particular, the telling of how Barry died needed to be told honestly. Yes, Morris already knew Sophie's father had been taken by a crocodile; what he didn't know was – Barry had a bullet in him before the croc had his way.

Morris had a surprise of his own, reaching into his pocket to remove something and place it on the bedside dinner table.

Josey stared at the bullet, recognising what it meant.

"Your slug I believe."

The mildly mortified look on Josey's face prompted Morris to say, "So far, only you and I know about this. And that's the way it stays . . . Now tell me the rest."

Josey did just that, *with no stones unturned.*

The Bryant stories continued in the media, growing from fact to fiction; such things as the mother being completely implicit in the circumstances surrounding the pregnancy. Other sensational yarns emerged, even suggesting the detective who witnessed the crocodile attack was lying about what he saw—not that their made-up story didn't have an element of truth to it.

It hearsay circus got so bad that Josey closed his Sydney office and his family took an extended break.

The Bryants had taken all they could stomach from the *loose cannons* as well, laughingly referred to as the honoured members of the press; moving from place to place so often that the persistent hounds eventually gave up the hunt. In the end, the muckrakers had no idea where everyone had disappeared to …

… At least a year after Sophie's death, Josey reopened his office believing it was safe to do so. He received one or two phone calls seeking an interview but that was it. Life went on. A further year after that, now that family holidays were becoming safe enough not to be detected and pursued, Josey and his girls decided to leave the city for the relative quiet of a country estate.

They boarded a twin engine Cessna at Bathurst, a town they'd driven to west of Sydney, the other side of the Great Divide. They set down on a property on the outskirts of Alice Springs and were greeted by a grey-haired gentleman who introduced himself as Robert Josephs, a man they'd been told had owned and lived there alone for over fifty years. A small understated crucifix pinned to his short sleeved open neck shirt indicated he was a priest, who preferred not to make any great fuss about it. Everyone had been warned not to refer to him as *Father*.

He met them on the tarmac as they exited the small plane; the tarmac being the front paddock in front of his large ranch style house, surrounded on four sides by generous shady verandas.

"Everyone else is here, they're all anxious to see you," he offered as he strode toward them with such haste it appeared he might not manage to stop; arm extended to take their hands in turn. With pleasantries done, he ushered them out of the heat and onto the verandah adjacent to the house's main entrance.

While still negotiating the timber steps, the wire screen door swung open with a solid push from the inside, allowing the promised flood of waiting guests to stream out and welcome Josey and his family.

Hugs, kisses, and barely discernible chatter said it all, this was a joyous occasion, a time to celebrate. They embraced the person closest before circulating to greet each and every other of the attendees. Among the guests already at the house was Mitchell with his wife and sister, Maxine and Carl, and of course, not to ever be forgotten, Inspector Morris, who *unofficially* made a call from Margaret River to offer his best wishes.

The last person to hug Josey was his client Vanessa. "There's someone inside anxious to see you, she's so excited I think she is about to explode. Come on let's put her out of her Misery."

Josey allowed Mitchell's wife and sister to lead

him inside by the hand, like a new schoolboy entering class for the first time, promptly followed by the entourage keen to watch the reunion, the whole reason they had travelled all the way to *The Alice*.

His heart skipped a beat when he saw her standing at the other side of the large room; her weight leaning against a walking stick, smiling at the man who saved her life. Written on her face was how she thought of him. Detective Josey was her silent hero, a man who gifted her with the rest of her life, a life of solitude, away from the endless scrutiny that would have been impossible to escape if she'd remained in the outside world.

Sophie, now seven years of age, was for Josey a magnificent sight, alive and well.

He took a step and paused, preparing to cross the room and take her in his arms.

She countered with a step of her own and gestured with her palm fully extended. "Wait, I want to come to you, Uncle Cam."

Josey's heart swelled with such pride he thought he may never again be able to loosen the tightness that gripped his throat. He watched her walk toward him with the aid of her stick, with the same determination he'd seen when faced with death.

Satisfied that Sophie was alive, no one had tried to push Josey to tell his full story. Only the people inside this room knew where Sophie was being harboured; including a few of the Mercy Nuns in Margaret River – only a very small group of others knew she was even alive. This is the way everyone wanted it.

Josey felt that his role in saving Sophie was of little account, but Sophie had other ideas. On reaching where Josey stood waiting, she held onto him for ever so long. Gently easing away she led her uncle to the couch, where they sat facing each other.

She then spoke ever so softly, "Mum tells me that you don't want to talk about how you saved my life."

Light murmurs of doubt filled the room. The adult like confidence of this young girl was enthralling in one sense, but presented clear concern that that she should not dwell on such horrors.

Mum and Dad shared a little tear the moment they set eyes on her. They couldn't have felt prouder of their little girl, but she had a message for them.

"I want everyone to hear my story," she told family and friends stoically – "*the real story.*"

The *real story,* as Sophie had called it; was both terrifying and *miraculous* at the same time, and even more chilling coming from the lips of the brave little seven year old – *forced to re-live it.*

"I thought I was safe – we both did. But we were terribly wrong . . ."

. . . The powerful wrenching haul that took her from his grasp at that moment was hard to comprehend - *or accept.*

The insidious intentions of the reptile unravelled as the beast backed into the river, back into the murky depths of its feeding dominion, back to join her father in one awful and final twist.

Driven by the unquestionable need to not give up on this terrified little girl, Josey clung onto dear life – entering the murky turbulence of the river, without any thought for his own life.

Within this dark swirling world where visibility stood no chance of existence; and rescue *impossible,* with eyes broadly open, yet completely blinded, he could rely only on his senses, cruelly defying information for what seemed a hopeless amount of time, yet not enough to succeed in his task.

Discarding the *fear and panic* of dying, he put himself in her shoes, imagining that she would not be able to dispel *either*, only to believe in the blessed hope of being rescued by him, as he had done so before.

This was different, this time he had no card to play, and could only guess at what might be running through her mind – *he knew it wouldn't be anything good.*

Though, through the opaqueness of her present world, fate handed her a vague and thin expectation, a dim form, silhouetted against a background that seemed to *sparkle busily?*

Was it the rain dancing on the river—?

Perhaps trauma was creating insights beyond the normal capability of a five year old, but whatever it was, it was allowing her to realise she was looking *upward*, up to where the sky gave way to the distant sky.

In front of it all, the shadowy silhouette of a man, the man she had decided to call her uncle – her *real uncle*, not the hateful father who was ready to give her up to the crocodiles. She realised then that the detective had been holding onto her hand from the time she was being mercilessly drawn into the water. With desperate determination Sophie reached for his other hand, the one drifting like loosened seagrass.

Josey felt the gentle touch sweep across his palm. His immediate response was to recoil from it but then registered it was *her*. He also understood there was a reptile that wasn't about to give up a meal, still firmly attached to her leg.

He paddled deeper, one armed, past her to where he knew to find her hungry anchor.

In his mind's eye he imagined the great toothy clamp that had a brutal hold of her; and the eye that resides within its massive head. With his fingers he envisaged the rim of the eye and positioned the pistol at its centre and fired.

All hell broke loose as the beast responded to the sudden and foreign invasion, *thrashing,* dangerously threatening to place Sophie and he in the path of its writhing tail.

She felt her leg free from its grip, and then the strong pull that then lifted her skyward. She and her uncle broke the surface of the dark river to merge into the grey gloom of the torrential downpour; exploding like a cleansing shower around them.

There was no time to dwell – this was a bonus chance of escape. Josey worked quickly, Sophie was gulping in a panic, trying to find air among the strings of rain that could have been strands of harsh wool as far as it felt.

And where were the other beasts he thought as he sensed the touch of mud – *the bank*?

With syrupy strides he ploughed through it until it gave way to the firmness of higher ground.

Remembering Skipper's assurance about *the Baru*, without flailing he climbed to where the beasts would choose not to follow.

Safe, he placed Sophie on her back, too exhausted to avoid being a little rough. He realised then that she had stopped breathing, without knowing for how long. He was about to resuscitate her but she regurgitated some of the muddy water. Experience taught him there may be more in her lungs – he was right, she threw up a dozen more times – eventually able to breathe; lapsing into a frightened whimper . .

.

. . . "Over the deafening storm, we thought we heard someone calling – we froze to the faint sound – holding our breath – waiting and hoping it wasn't our imagination.

"Then, suddenly they were here; helping us, Carl and his friend Skipper –

"We were all taken to the family's Aboriginal home in the bush. It was a little bit scary, but I felt safe, just so long as I never-ever had to see another crocodile."

Josey expanded, "Long story short, finding us alive, the plan just sort of grew. Part of which was the plan for Skipper and Carl to return to the track, where Carl cooked up their fabricated story. With the help of the nuns in Margaret River, Sophie was picked up from Skipper's place on day three; and by land and air brought up here to the property—"

Heads turned in unison to the sound of the wire door, opening to a young boy entering as though inviting himself to join the gathering. His teeth and black face shone in splendid contrast as he took in all the new faces, a somewhat brighter light shining when his eyes met Sophie's.

"This is Tommy, Father Josephs explained. "He and Sophie have become great mates since coming here."

Clearly basking in the glorious wonders of *puppy love,* this was the happiest his girl had ever been in her life, and it showed in ways that promised celebration.

In an attempt to glean Josey's reaction to Sophie's newfound inner strength, his wife was momentarily drawn from the revelry.

What she saw was completely unexpected.

Her husband was *crying? – and trembling?*

Quietly moving to his side, she supportively hooked to his elbow. "Josey, what's wrong?"

Having lived with this man, in near recluse since the terrifying risk to Sophie's life, Rebecca knew where this was going. This sudden reaction was pure anguish, a man still paralysed by the past two years. In all that time he hadn't had the stomach to take on a single case; this was a man still blaming himself.

Carl saw what was happening and stepped up to check on him. "Hey, what's all this then?"

His friend began to convulse.

Concerned, he reached for a nearby chair and sat him down. "Mate, what's happening?"

This was nothing short of a meltdown.

Sophie caught the disturbance out the corner of her eye and broke away from her friend, wiping away the smile no one thought the young boy would ever lose.

The others gravitated to where she was going, to where Josey sat in the chair in the company of his wife and Carl. From behind, Rebecca's arms draped across her husband's shoulders, her face resting against his head.

Crouched beside the chair, Carl was attempting to console him.

Sophie sat atop her haunches, directly in front, looking into his troubled face, her hands rested on his knees. "Uncle, why are you crying?"

Josey opened his drenched eyes and saw her worried face swim beneath his tears.

The nightmare sank into his soul, his spirit threatening an unadorned breakdown.

She rose quickly to her knees and reached for him, her gentle fingers sweeping away pent up emotions.

Tommy wasn't sure what to make of it; left standing on his own while the others gathered around the man crying in the chair.

Eventually, partly driven by the embarrassment of the attention he was drawing, Josey's convulsions began to ease. He was spoiling the reunion, the last thing on earth he wanted. The sight of little Sophie, *not so little anymore*, and finally smiling, slowly bought him round, mustering his energy for a weak grin in return.

"That's better, Uncle," she pledged.

His chuckle broke free as would a knot of air that had been trapped in his chest, raising nervous relief from all the others.

Tommy broke through the throng holding a glass of water. "This is for you," he told the detective.

Sophie looked at her friend with admiration, took the glass and helped Josey drink.

"Just so you know, Uncle, I'm planning to tell my story, in a book, so you better be okay with that."

Josey glanced around at the gathering uncertainly. "Well - *I guess –*"

Light murmurs of doubt filled the room. The adult like confidence of this young girl was enthralling, but there was clear concern that writing a book might not be a good idea.

Josey appeared to agree. "How were you thinking of telling your story?" he asked a little nervously.

Sophie understood why everyone was on edge about it. "Don't worry; I won't use my real name, or anyone else's."

"I think people will know who you are anyway," he strongly suggested.

"I don't think so, it'll be a novel – I'll change a few things, you know, add a bit of *drama*."

Josey's laugh was the release he needed, inviting the others to join in. "I could be forgiven for believing there is more than enough drama already," he chortled.

An amused murmur flooded the room this time.

Facing her audience she said with the biggest of

smiles, "I'm pulling your leg, Uncle. In *my* story, it's all about a new take on *Peter Pan* – and definitely *without the crocodiles this time.*"

Sophie Bryant had finally found an uncle she could truly believe in

. . . and a Mother and father to love forever.

9 781764 195805